UNDERMARCH

DEREK GORDANIER

Undermarch
Copyright © 2021 by Derek Gordanier

All rights reserved. No part of this publication may be reproduced, distributed, or transmitted in any form or by any means, including photocopying, recording, or other electronic or mechanical methods, without the prior written permission of the author, except in the case of brief quotations embodied in critical reviews and certain other non-commercial uses permitted by copyright law.

tellwell

Tellwell Talent
www.tellwell.ca

ISBN
978-0-2288-6263-5 (Hardcover)
978-0-2288-6262-8 (Paperback)
978-0-2288-6264-2 (eBook)

DEDICATION

For Carrie and our children: Drake, Veronica, Victoria, and Calvin.

And for Troy, Don, and Lance, my friends who supported me in this, as in all things.

THE AERIE COAST
Far
Caliss
River Dancer
The March
River Vinefruit
Khendyl
The Alasian Forest
Speakwater
Salt Fens
Marsh Ruins
Eliard
ALASIA

TABLE OF CONTENTS

Introduction vii

Chapter One 1
Chapter Two.. 20
Chapter Three... 31
Chapter Four 38
Chapter Five 50
Chapter Six 55
Chapter Seven 69
Chapter Eight... 79
Chapter Nine.. 86
Chapter Ten.. 96
Chapter Eleven 103
Chapter Twelve.. 129
Chapter Thirteen 146
Chapter Fourteen 152
Chapter Fifteen.. 163
Chapter Sixteen 177
Chapter Seventeen 196
Chapter Eighteen 198
Chapter Nineteen.. 222
Chapter Twenty... 242
Chapter Twenty-One... 263
Chapter Twenty-Two... 285

Chapter Twenty-Three	305
Chapter Twenty-Four	324
Chapter Twenty-Five	337
Chapter Twenty-Six	351
Chapter Twenty-Seven	365
Chapter Twenty-Eight	373
Chapter Twenty-Nine	386
Chapter Thirty	392
Chapter Thirty-One	409
Chapter Thirty-Two	423
Chapter Thirty-Three	435
Chapter Thirty-Four	446
Chapter Thirty-Five	457
Chapter Thirty-Six	469
Chapter Thirty-Seven	479
Chapter Thirty-Eight	492
Chapter Thirty-Nine	499
Chapter Forty	509
Chapter Forty-One	516
Chapter Forty-Two	521
Chapter Forty-Three	530
Chapter Forty-Four	538
Chapter Forty-Five	543
Chapter Forty-Six	548
Epilogue	561
About The Author	563

INTRODUCTION

(An excerpt translated from the Codex of the Legends, Library of His Imperial Majesty at Zistah)

―⚏―

Man beheld the world in the newness of time and uttered at the wonders therein. These utterances he etched on the Stone.

Thus, the name became the thing, and the thing its name, and man rejoiced when Creation answered his call.

And man held dominion and raised great works upon the face of the world.

Then came an age of discord when man spake the names of Creation, not to fashion wonders, but to destroy his enemy with fire and water, earth, and wind.

And man contended one with the other to win lordship, for the things of Creation respected not who spake, only that their names were spoken.

A tumult went through the world. Mountains crumbled. Oceans heaved. Flames devoured the land, and the winds scattered its ashes. Soon the works of man lay in ruin, and the world resembled not what had been.

Man beheld the chaos and repented his folly. He sought to destroy the Stone, lest his striving consumed the world.

Always the Stone prevailed, for the things of Creation suffer not the destruction of their names, lest they also cease to be.

Despairing, man buried the Stone in a secret and terrible place to set the names of Creation forever beyond his reach.

Time passed, and the generations of men forgot the Stone.

Man called things in the world by new names, but Creation respected them not, nor hearkened to their call.

Yet some walked the world who remembered the names carved on the Stone.

And these guarded the names in tradition and shared the knowledge with their brethren.

They came in time to be called the Magi, or those who spake Words of Power.

And the Magi moved throughout the world, seeking the Stone that was lost, that their power might be made whole. And they were feared and shunned by all.

CHAPTER ONE

The tang of salt air, a sudden gust of sea breeze, the bang of a door thrown wide on its hinges—in all that followed, scents, sensations, and sounds such as these reminded Vergal of Sh'ynryan, the man who walked into his life, unannounced and unwelcomed, in the Aerie Coast city of Caliss.

At that time, in that place—the sprawling island kingdom of Aerie's lone toehold on the mainland—Vergal lived alongside his sister Alonna in a room above the Wayfarer Inn, the largest lodgings house of the city's burgeoning port district. Alonna worked in service to Carek, a burly man whose severe hawk-like nose betrayed a rapacious temper to match. Carek owned the sprawling inn that stood a stone's throw above the bustling harbor and—so far as Vergal knew—all those who toiled within it.

On the day Sh'ynryan arrived, Vergal was a boy nearing twelve years of age. A shock of unruly raven hair framed an open, honest face upon which the boy's every passing emotion fleetingly appeared. Slight of build, though fleet of foot, Vergal's lean body seemed perpetually coiled against an energy he struggled constantly to contain. Life had taught Vergal hard lessons young, and the trauma of his trials manifested still in a tense and anxious demeanor. Vergal kept a constant internal vigil against the distressing jolts that the sudden clamors, raised voices, and boisterous behaviors so common to his everyday surroundings could provoke in him.

Outside, a bright mid-summer sun only weakly penetrated the inn's grimy windows. The taproom's interior was a gloomy place of deep shadows. Vergal sat cross-legged in one such dim pool, his back pressed to the cold fieldstone wall, distant from the flickering light thrown by the blazing hearth. His eyes roamed restlessly over a frayed and faded map spread on the floor in front of him.

Vergal spent many hours of his day in such a manner, poring over musty maps that Carek—in perhaps his sole act of generosity toward the boy—had allowed him to keep rather than discarding in a larger heap of kitchen trash destined to be dumped in the harbor.

The words printed in elegant script on the parchment baffled him. He could not read them because he had never been taught to read, but he delighted in the maps all the same. His fingers traced the outlines of the ocean's rugged coastlines, and he imagined the roar of the mighty rivers as they wound in serpent-like fashion out of the mountains.

Sometimes Vergal dared pilfer a chunk of coal from the kitchen's fire pits and used it to draft maps of his own design. These maps he drew on swathes of linen taken from the inn's stores. Though rough and messy, these maps thrilled him as he sketched by the flickering half-light of the candles in his room, helping him pass the long hours Alonna spent at work downstairs in the tavern.

Vergal imagined himself king and lord over the domains that emerged from under his lumps of coal. He pondered where best to raise great fortresses in defense of the marches of his realm. He thought long on where to build the port cities and mining towns that would funnel the riches of his kingdom into awesome capital cities that straddled broad rivers draining to the sea.

And when he finished one great realm or another, Vergal carefully folded his map and secreted it in a drawer in his room. He then filched new supplies and began the process anew.

Through his study of maps, Vergal learned to understand scales of size, properly equating the pinprick that represented Caliss, for example, with his own smaller existence within that same spot of ink. He easily perceived himself as a minuscule part of a larger, grander world surrounding him.

Political boundaries he also discerned. This river or that forest divided one empire from the next, though the land rolled on, uninterrupted by man's arbitrary constraints. For instance, Vergal knew he was subject to the pirate king at Far, an island city leagues out into the Western Sea, rather than the Imperial governor in the Arasynian city of Speakwater, which shared the Alasian continent. And all because of a line drawn on a map! The concept fascinated the boy.

Vergal's heart raced when he envisioned the breadth of the world hinted at in his maps, even as he resigned himself to the likelihood he would never see any portion of it beyond the flotsam-choked bay below the Wayfarer's grounds.

Poverty, after all, forged as steely a shackle as chains. Vergal and Alonna were bound to the Wayfarer by the food and lodging that his sister's service purchased for them both. It was an always tenuous and stressful arrangement endangered constantly by the innkeeper's ill-temper. Carek menaced, bullied, and bellowed, and, when seized by particularly foul humor, he accused Alonna and Vergal of ungratefulness toward him and threatened to turn them out into the rough streets.

All this badly frightened Alonna, who fretted about their futures. Vergal always commiserated with his sister so as not to seem unsympathetic or unappreciative of her work, but in truth, Carek's bluster concerned him less. Alonna's brooding, blue-eyed beauty was the talk of the port district and drew many admirers, however unsavory at times, who spent extra coins in the taproom to linger in her presence over their cups.

Vergal, with wry insight beyond his years, understood Alonna's value to Carek. The boy knew that Carek, despite his dark moods, felt protective toward Alonna—and Vergal by extension—though perhaps in the way a man defends a prized asset.

On that day, the taproom of the Wayfarer presented as the dim, comfortless place it always did—a place where shadows shrouded the low-beamed ceiling and collected in the corners of the stone walls. The hearth that dominated the eastern wall radiated only meager warmth since Carek fueled it sparingly, but it spewed copious smoke that added significantly to the oppressive atmosphere.

The door banged loudly open, aided by a vagrant ocean breeze rising from the bay. The sudden shaft of late afternoon sunlight flooding the room disintegrated the gloom. The brilliant flood from the doorway dazzled Vergal, where he sat against a wall.

The wind rippled his maps, causing them to curl against Vergal's palm, and ruffled the boy's black hair. The blended scents of saltwater and decaying things that bespoke the ocean filled his nose. Squinting against the glare, Vergal saw silhouetted in the doorframe the figure of a cowled man, as perfectly black against the sunshine as if cut from a starless night in the Watergate Mountains.

The figure stood motionless. It might have been sculpted from stone, save for a slight swivel of its head. The few patrons seated at the bar raised a ruckus in protest, lifting their hands to shield their eyes against the glare.

The man in the doorway seemed deaf to their howls. The sunlight filling in around the figure revealed a tall, thin man. The black cowl cladding him paled in the filtering light to a vestment of rich red satin, stitched everywhere with silvery, embroidered symbols. A medallion clasped a cloak at his throat, where a trim grey beard disappeared beneath a high collar. A thick and knotted walking stick, previously concealed against the backdrop of his flaring cape, appeared in the man's right hand.

If the stranger's apparel attracted the eye, then his face captured it completely. Short-cropped dark hair salted with grey framed a gaunt face composed of sharp planes and angles. His green eyes blazed as they swept the room; his thin lips were unsmiling.

At last, the door closed shut behind him, and shadows reclaimed the room. The grumbling patrons at the bar turned back to their cups. The tall man at the door tucked his walking stick beneath his arm and began pulling off thin gloves. A slight sneer lifted his lip as he scanned the room.

Something in that grimace sent an inexplicable stab of fear through Vergal, who sat hunched in his corner. Licking his dry lips, the boy called weakly, "Alonna..."

The babble of conversation in the room should have drowned his call, but the stranger heard him immediately. The wan face snapped in Vergal's direction; the flinty green eyes pinioned him as they took his measure.

Then a thing happened that set Vergal's heart tripping in his breast: The medallion at the man's throat erupted with color.

The fierce eyes scrutinizing Vergal widened slowly. The stranger looked down his thin nose at the glowing metal in open-mouthed astonishment. His eyes drifted slowly back to Vergal, his lips forming slow, silent words.

Vergal stared, entranced by the colors shifting over the surface of the disc and washing the man's pale features in the muted light.

The man tapped the medallion quickly with his forefinger and the display faded. When he lifted his eyes again at Vergal, his gaze was speculative. The cunning in his expression made the stranger appear vaguely hungry.

"Alonna!" Vergal called again, now with greater urgency. He pushed backward on his rump to wedge deeper into the corner.

"Vergal! What?" came Alonna's cross reply as she stepped quickly through the arch dividing the taproom from the kitchen.

Her long powder-blue dress, cross-tied at her breasts, caught in her feet and tripped her, nearly sending flying the tray she held. Alonna steadied herself against the bar and set down the tray. A thick tendril of jet hair tumbled in front of her eyes. She brushed it irritably behind one ear.

Alonna stooped in front of her brother. She hooked her finger under his chin and lifted his gaze to meet her narrowed eyes—rich blue mirrors of his own.

"I told you, sit out of the way and keep quiet," Alonna said firmly. "Be still, or you can go this minute back to the room." Her voice fell to a husky whisper, "If you bother Carek ..."

A gruff voice interjected, freezing Alonna mid-sentence. "Wine," it demanded.

Alonna turned to find a tall, gaunt man in rich attire easing into a chair directly behind her. His long legs stretched beneath the table and crossed at the ankles. The man loomed close enough for Alonna to scent his exotic, spicy cologne.

"Wine," the man repeated curtly, "the best bottle in your cellar if you please." He unfastened the clasp at his neck and swirled his cloak over the arm of his chair. His walking stick lay in easy reach across the table.

Alonna appraised the newcomer in a single glance. His tone was perfunctory and invited no discussion, the voice of a man accustomed to being served. She took stock of his fine garb and especially the plump leather purse cinched to his belt.

She smiled and straightened, smoothing the lap of her dress, her decorum restored. "Your pardon, sir," she said. "Of course, wine, straightaway. Allow me to move this boy out of your path …"

"Leave him," the man said. He spared a disinterested glance at Vergal where he sat on the floor, surrounded by his maps. The expression of amazement that had crossed his face when the medallion strobed to life had given way to a mask of indifference.

Vergal blanched. He lifted his head imploringly to Alonna, too afraid to speak. Alonna bit her lower lip, returning her brother's worried stare.

"The boy will surely be underfoot," she said hurriedly, bending to haul Vergal to his feet. "It's the work of a moment to move him…."

"I said leave him!" The acid in the tone froze Alonna in mid-crouch.

"It's the work of less than a moment to bring a patron his wine," the red-robed man said evenly. He jingled his purse meaningfully. "And it could carry a greater reward."

The clinking coins decided Alonna. The weak smile she offered Vergal did not touch her eyes as she moved briskly away. Vergal stared, horrified, at his sister's retreating shoulders.

Vergal found himself in a predicament. He wanted to gather his maps and dart up the stairs, but the stranger had as much as insisted he remain in place. Alonna's acquiescence had inferred he should obey. Uncertain what to do, Vergal busied himself, fumbling with his maps. He dared not meet that bleak face nor look at the strange medallion that had sparked when Vergal laid eyes upon it.

He kept low to his maps and pondered his options for what seemed a long time.

Finally, his skin crawling under the man's silent scrutiny, he braved a glance. However, the man was not watching him. His eyes followed the drama behind the bar where Carek gestured wildly while arguing with Alonna.

Alonna returned sheepishly to the table. "I beg your pardon, sir," she said with a curtsey. "He will not break the seal on his best wine until ..." she faltered "...until he sees you can pay."

Vergal held his breath, uncertain how the stranger would react.

"I told him you were able!" Alonna added hurriedly. "You are a man of means; I knew straight away. But ... oh, sir, surely you see the situation," she ended miserably.

The man smiled, ruefully and without mirth. He unclipped the purse from his belt and fished a coin from its depths. Vergal and Alonna gasped in unison at the flash of gold.

"Take this," he said, unperturbed. "Bring me wine and food. If I find those and the service to my satisfaction, I will give you a silver noble of your own."

Alonna nodded mutely. Her fingers clenching the coin trembled. The gold piece was more than a working man on the docks earned in weeks. Vergal wondered if his sister had ever held such a sum in her life.

"One more thing," the stranger said. He reclined in his chair and jerked a thumb at Vergal. "Bring something for the boy to eat; he can join me at my table."

"The boy ..." Alonna said, puzzled. "That is kind, sir, but there is no need."

The man's frown swiftly reappeared.

"I offer a boon, and you refuse?" the man said, indignant, his voice rising. "Presently, I shall grow irritated and retrieve my coin and leave, but not before I inform your temperamental master of the profit his servant has cost his establishment. What do you suppose his response?"

Alonna's jaw clenched, but she said nothing.

"In any event," the man continued, "this boy could use a meal. I hear his stomach rumbling from here."

It was true. Vergal's mouth watered at the mere mention of food. His stomach had sent up a mournful growling, as it did nearly every afternoon when the scent of roasting meat rose from the kitchen. However, Vergal had learned long ago not to seek food after the mid-day meal. Alonna could scarcely afford to feed them daily on her wage, and Carek had a penchant for applying a wooden spoon to the posterior of any young boy who issued complaints within earshot of patrons.

As if reading Vergal's thoughts, the man added, "And if your innkeeper has an objection to the boy joining me, he can inform me directly." His mouth stretched in an unpleasant smile, exposing rows of prominent, straight white teeth—another rarity among the Wayfarer's dock-district clientele.

"As you say, sir," Alonna said in a resigned voice. She dipped her knee, casting a meaningful glance at Vergal as she did. *Behave*, her look implored.

In an instant, Vergal found himself alone in the company of his strange benefactor.

The man's splayed hands rested on the table, one finger absently drumming the knuckle of the other hand. "I don't dine with strangers, boy," he said, "tell me your name."

"Vergal, sir." It came out as a croak.

"And mine is Sh'ynryan. Very well, we are properly acquainted. You may join me at the table."

Vergal hesitated, but he remembered Alonna's soundless plea. He began slowly gathering his maps.

"A strange hobby for one so young," remarked the man who called himself Sh'ynryan. He jutted his chin to indicate Vergal's maps. "You have the appearance of an unlearned peasant boy, yet you sit in dark corners poring over maps like a Zistinian scholar." Sh'ynryan chortled at his own jest, a harsh barking sound.

Vergal set the rolled maps on a chair and climbed carefully into a seat of his own. "Yes, good sir," he agreed meekly.

Sh'ynryan scowled. "I told you my name, and I will thank you to use it. I need no honorifics nor am I particularly 'good.'"

Vergal gaped, aghast at the departure from propriety. Sh'ynryan chuckled at the boy's expression, and this time, Vergal detected genuine mirth buried in the sound.

"Very well," Sh'ynryan said, "I see we must ease into this."

The wine arrived, delivered by Carek, who grinned widely and nodded ingratiatingly. He presented a full glass with a flourish. It was the cleanest glass Vergal had ever seen used in the taproom. Carek placed the bottle on the table.

"Welcome to my inn, sir," Carek said. He went on, "Your coin marks you as a distinguished man, a man of means and—begging your pardon—I pray you will forgive the earlier difficulty. Ports the world over deliver customers long on thirst and short on coin, so I thought it prudent ..."

Sh'ynryan's disgusted snort stopped Carek short.

"Yes, well, you will find all you desire here," Carek continued smoothly. "My serving girl is at your disposal, as is this boy."

Sh'ynryan arched an eyebrow. "Oh, this boy is yours to dispose of then?" he asked.

The toothy—though, in places, toothless—smile pasted to Carek's face never faltered. "Begging your pardon, sir?"

"You pay this boy a wage that gives you leave to place him at the disposal of others?" Sh'ynryan clarified.

"He is the brother of my serving girl, and I care for them both," Carek replied. "They live here in my inn."

"Ah, you care for them. I see." Sh'ynryan lifted his glass and swirled the glass twice delicately, sniffing its contents. His eyebrows lifted. "Well, well," he muttered. He sounded surprised.

The line of questioning baffled Carek. He shifted his weight between his legs, eager to leave but unsure if he'd been dismissed. His smile faded.

Sh'ynryan went on, "So their accommodation is an act of charity upon your part? The woman provides no service in return for her keep?"

"No... yes... That is to say, she serves my customers."

"Ah!" Sh'ynryan exclaimed, lifting a long finger to punctuate his remark as if acknowledging a salient point that had been raised. "So, a service is rendered, and a wage fairly earned. The woman, in turn, purchases her keep and that of her brother, thereby returning a portion of her wage to you as profit. Now we arrive at the heart of the matter."

Carek seemed perplexed. Vergal, seated at the axis of the volley, squirmed in his chair.

"Since you so obviously fail to grasp it, man, my point is this: The boy, I discern, lives with his sister in accommodation purchased through her labor. She is therefore not indebted to you. By what right, then, do you command her brother's time?"

Carek's expression grew pained. Sh'ynryan had placed his purse on the table in plain sight of the innkeeper, whose eyes seldom strayed from it.

"Bah, I tire of this," Sh'ynryan grunted. He waved his long fingers dismissively in Carek's face. "Bring us food and milk for the lad. Do it now."

Carek needed no further prompting. He scurried away, and Vergal released a pent-up breath. A nagging internal voice suggested Carek would likely hold Vergal responsible for this humiliation if for no other reason than the boy had witnessed it.

Sh'ynryan watched the man's retreat. "There is a lesson for you, boy," he said, easing back in his chair and lacing his fingers across his stomach. "The laborer is worthy of his hire. Or her hire, in this case. It is an old saying, but true. Such men build their fortunes upon the ignorance of those who recognize neither their self-worth nor the value of the work of their hands."

The meaning of many of the stranger's words eluded Vergal, who was a young and uneducated boy, but he intuited their deeper intent and nodded sagely. Sh'ynryan nodded in response.

The food arrived, served by Alonna. Her clear eyes were wide, her smile forced as she set down steaming plates. She stabbed an anxious look at Vergal but offered only a pleasantry before departing.

The two began to eat in silence.

Vergal's self-consciousness about dining with a stranger did not show. The aromatic food distracted him. He devoured the roasted meat—succulent, lightly-spiced venison—and fell ravenously on the serving of potatoes. He purged his plate of the last boiled carrot. At last, he pushed away from the table. His contented sigh drew a level gaze from Sh'ynryan.

Vergal remembered at the last moment the manners his sister always worked to instill in him. "Thank you, sir," he said uncertainly.

Sh'ynryan allowed the formality to pass. He leaned forward in his high-backed chair, studying Vergal intently and playing absently with the stem of his empty glass. The faint heat from the smoky hearth wafted over them, carrying the soothing drone of taproom conversation. Vergal, who was growing drowsy, stared at the ruins of his plate, unsure what to do or say next.

Sh'ynryan broke the silence. "Where did you acquire these maps?" he asked agreeably.

Vergal's hand moved protectively to the beaten scroll cases on the chair beside him.

"Carek ... the innkeeper ... he gave them to me," he answered. "Alonna brought them up one day after cleaning the cellar, and I saw them in the trash pile."

Sh'ynryan interrupted. "You likely saw many interesting things in the trash. What drew you to these?"

Vergal considered the question. He had never contemplated his reasons for rescuing the maps. Passing through the kitchen, Vergal had spotted them nearly covered by the heap: Several tightly rolled tubes of parchment fraying at their edges and spattered with filth. The scrolls had seemed wholly out of place, lumped with the rubbish. The delicate ink drawings shone up at him like the finest lace. Vergal had begged Alonna to ask Carek for the maps.

It marked the first time he had made a request of the innkeeper, even if he lacked the courage to do so directly.

Carek, with the briefest of glances at the trash pile, had laughed and said Vergal could have not only the maps but the potato peelings and old soup bones if he fancied them too and had walked away unconcerned.

Vergal retrieved the maps and brushed them clean. He felt as if he was handling a clutch of rubies. He counted the dirty, worn maps among his most prized possessions.

Vergal realized he had left Sh'ynryan's question unanswered and began to stammer a reply. The man held a hand aloft to stop him.

"Easy, boy!" Sh'ynryan grinned in his distressing manner. Vergal supposed the smile was intended to convey levity, but it somehow expressed annoyance instead. "I want the right answer, not a hasty one."

"It was only that they looked so ... wrong, lying there with the garbage," Vergal replied after a pause. "Words and pictures are for learning, not for the trash heap." He trailed off, shrugging.

Sh'ynryan nodded. "I understand," he said, and Vergal sensed he did indeed.

"Let me see what you have here then," the man said. He held out his thin hand for a scroll case. Vergal surrendered one wordlessly.

Sh'ynryan pushed away his plate and set aside his wine bottle. After a moment of rustling papers, several maps lay spread across the table.

Vergal felt ashamed of the stains and tears that marred his maps. The strange man with the elegant garb and extravagant jewelry likely was accustomed to only fine things, and Vergal's garbage-spattered maps hardly qualified as luxury items. Yet the fine-boned hands smoothing the maps did so gently, using as much care as Vergal might have taken. Sh'ynryan's half-lidded eyes lost their flinty sheen as they roamed the images. An appreciative whistle escaped his lips.

"You have a treasure here, Vergal," Sh'ynryan said.

It was the first time the man had addressed Vergal by name, and a shudder rolled down his spine at the sound of it.

"A treasure? How so, sir?"

Sh'ynryan ignored the question. He stabbed a spindly finger at an expanse of curly-waved ocean, in which cavorted a fanciful, snarling sea monster.

"You see here?" He passed his hand slowly over the gulf of ocean separating the landmasses. "I have traveled a long way over these waters. The distance is only the span of my hand on your map, but a journey of many months. Do you understand?"

Vergal nodded, then blurted, "But why have you come?" before realizing the answer was surely none of his affair.

A predatory gleam rekindled in the depths of Sh'ynryan's hard green eyes.

"I have come searching for something," he replied slowly. "I have searched for a long time, and I thought I had a long time yet to look."

"You've found this thing then?" Vergal dared ask.

"I think so." His eyes searched Vergal's face intently. "I am not yet certain. Perhaps, though, I am close."

The obvious question bubbled behind Vergal's lips: What was it Sh'ynryan sought? However, the man had turned his attention back to the scrolls and did not appear disposed to offer the information.

"I have made a long journey," he said, his expression distant. "My home is a vast realm of deserts and jungles far to the south, where cities of domes and spires cut from the wilderness rise along the banks of mighty rivers." Longing softened the man's harsh features as he spoke.

"You are far from home then," Vergal offered. "I have not seen any such lands on my maps."

Sh'ynryan shook his head softly. "Indeed, I am, young man. And I have a long journey yet across this abominable northern rock." He pointed again at the map. "Here! This is where I travel next."

Vergal followed his finger to a break in the great fin of the Watergate Mountains, where they reached down from the north. A depiction of a brooding fortress bridged the gap between the mountains. Vergal recognized it instantly.

"The March," Vergal said.

"You know this place?" Sh'ynryan asked with interest.

"I have never seen it, except on my map. But I have heard men in the inn speak of it many times. The

March is the great fortress beyond the Danea River on the border between Aerie and Arasynian Alasia."

Sh'ynryan smiled, looking pleased. "Well said. You continue to surprise me. But go on. What else do these men say?"

Vergal frowned, considering. "They hate it, sir. They say it guards the only overland route East, and the lord there takes tolls and tithes from the merchants and travelers as they pass. From the way they speak, I imagine the fortress walls stretching across the pass like a curtain of stone, as if the mountains broke not at all in that place."

Sh'ynryan laughed aloud at the imagery. He slapped the table merrily. "You are a delightful boy," he said. "And you have a turn of speech. I dare say you would make a fine bard, painting pictures with words the way you do."

Vergal returned the smile, unable to help himself.

A comfortable silence settled between them as their attention turned again to the maps. The background bustle of the taproom intensified with the early evening crowd. Vergal detected a faint rumble of thunder beneath the clamor. Rain speckled the darkening windows of the inn.

Sh'ynryan nodded at the window. "I noticed those thunderclouds on the horizon today when my ship entered port. We are due for a storm, mark me."

A hand fell on his shoulder, and Vergal turned to see Alonna studying them sitting together. She wore the same agitated expression.

"I beg your pardon, sir," she said. Her voice was firm and carried a hint of steel, though she smoothed her dress nervously. "It is past time the boy prepares for bed, and I really must insist ..."

"Of course!" Sh'ynryan said expansively. "Pour me another glass of this unaccountably good wine from my bottle, and he is free to go." He turned to Vergal and said, "It has been a pleasure speaking with you, Vergal," his eyes boring into the boy's. "We will speak again."

To Vergal, Sh'ynryan's dismissal seemed to carry the weight of a threat.

CHAPTER TWO

"What did he say to you? What did he want?" Alonna demanded.

She crisscrossed the cramped quarters of their room like a caged mountain cat. Her thick hair bounced in time with her pacing. The flickering candle on Vergal's bedstand stretched her shadow into a monstrous thing that capered on the bare stone wall.

Vergal struggled to stay awake. His face and teeth freshly scrubbed, his belly full of an unexpected late meal, and now wrapped in a cocoon of blankets to ward the chill air, Vergal was drifting steadily down toward sleep.

The soothing cadence of the rain drumming his window invited his eyes to close. "I told you, Alonna," he said, stifling a yawn. "We talked about my maps and such. He wanted to see my maps."

Alonna snorted. "To see your maps! Indeed! A grown man dressed in such finery, interested in a boy's stupid, grubby maps." She snorted again, an ugly, incredulous sound. "Not likely!"

Vergal shrugged and shifted beneath his blankets. He drew his knees nearly to his chest and wrapped his arms around them. If a warmer, more comfortable spot in the world existed at that moment, Vergal struggled to imagine it. If only Alonna would keep quiet!

"He took rooms here; did you know that?" Alonna snapped. "The big suite of rooms; the ones Carek uses. The rooms we all ..."

Her voice trailed off. She shook her mane of dark hair angrily.

"He will be here tomorrow, and the next day, and the days after, and perhaps next month if that big purse of his accounts for anything," she spat. "And he gave me this." She opened her clenched fist to reveal a piece of silver. "What does he hope this to buy?" she sneered.

"What do you mean?" This time, Vergal could not smother a yawn.

"There are men in this world, Vergal," Alonna whispered ominously. "Evil men ..."

She paused, scowling at Vergal from across the darkened room. Then suddenly sobbing, she rushed to his bedside and dropped to her knees, clenching his blanketed shoulder in her hands.

"Oh, but I'll not burden you with this, little brother," she said tearfully. She scrubbed the heels of her hands across her damp eyes, then laid a cool hand across Vergal's brow and brushed back his tangled hair. The gentle sensation nudged Vergal closer to sleep.

"I'll not let him harm you, Vergal. I promise." Alonna wept openly now.

Vergal's eyes were closed, but he frowned, confused. "I'm not hurt, Alonna ... I'm not ..."

He drifted between sleep and wakefulness. The candle's flame lightened the darkness behind his eyelids.

The soothing hand on his brow lifted.

Vergal heard his sister moving about the room. She snuffed his bedside candle. Then her silky hands returned to smooth his hair and lightly caress his cheeks.

As Vergal descended into sleep, he distantly heard her solemn promise: "I'll not fail you, little brother. Not as they failed us."

The door opened, and the blackness beyond his clamped eyelids lightened briefly. The distant bustle of the far away taproom swept into the room then disappeared when Alonna closed the door behind her.

Her key turned in the lock; darkness descended.

Alonna's footsteps faded in the hall.

Then only the sounds of tapping rain and far-off rolling thunder.

Then, nothing at all.

—⚏—

He had been dreaming of his parents again.

Running across a storm-torn landscape, he chased their departing souls from the bloodied bed where their bodies lay, butchered. A sluggish, ankle-deep mist swirled around his feet. A foreboding cavern loomed ahead. Behind him, Alonna wailed over their parents' corpses, screaming for Vergal to return.

"You cannot follow!" Alonna cried.

Vergal pressed on. They were there, just ahead: two flitting figures sweeping through the gloom.

His legs pumped furiously in pursuit, exploding plumes of mist with every brisk footfall.

The cavern twisted, dipped, then rose again as Vergal gave desperate chase. His parents stayed just ahead of him, the toes of their bare and bloodied feet drifting above the eddying mist. They glided smoothly as if carried on a current above the uneven rock floor. Ahead, they turned a corner ... and disappeared.

Vergal moved his legs faster than he thought possible. Since he could walk, Vergal could run. His wiry frame moved at startling speed when he forced it. However, this surge of momentum was something entirely new. His heart hammered in his chest; his breath blew out in bursts. The mist erupted beneath his churning feet. Yet still they outdistanced him. He screamed for them as he pursued them around a sharp corner ... only to find the cavern floor gone, opened now to a fiery pit.

Vergal barely stopped in time. His arms windmilled for balance at the lip of a massive precipice.

Flames and smoke belched upward on columns of blasting heat. Far below, the nearly insubstantial shades of his parents plummeted into the vast expanse.

They turned, falling, stretching their arms to him.

Their open mouths howled pleas lost beneath the roar of the rising flames. He watched in horror as the curling flames swallowed them from view.

Then Alonna was there, younger, pale, weeping. She cradled a babe in her arms.

"You could never catch them," she sobbed. She held forth the bawling child in her arms. Vergal recognized the babe's black hair as his own. "You are just a baby!" she screamed.

Defeated, Vergal sunk to his knees. The clammy mist swallowed him to his chest.

"We'll speak of this again!" Alonna cried. Her voice faded down some unimaginably long corridor.

"I told you, we would speak again!"

Thunder crashed. A flash of lightning washed the chamber in stark white light. Vergal emerged, confused and gasping, from the depths of tortured sleep. It took a blurry instant to comprehend the cold, thin hand clamped across his mouth. Sh'ynryan's grim face loomed menacingly above it. The medallion at his throat swirled riotous color. The eerie light melded with lightning streaks outside his open window to scintillate in the silvery strands of his beard.

Sh'ynryan smiled coldly.

"I told you we would speak again."

Times of leisure were few for Alonna in Carek's employ, but on some summer days, between preparations for the mid-day and evening meals, Alonna found reason to slowly tend to work on the Wayfarer's grounds. Vergal always accompanied his sister on these errands. Drawing water from the well or collecting firewood from the pile behind the inn allowed them to linger over the task and gain a few free, precious moments to talk and reminisce and to savor the warm sunshine on their skin together.

On one such occasion, as they chatted pleasantly and picked from the woodpile, Vergal lifted a log to reveal a large snake.

The sight of the serpent froze him in place. The primal revulsion of such a hazardous encounter overwhelmed him. The serpent rose slowly off its coils, hissing. Every raw instinct in Vergal's body urged flight, but he could only stare in a torpid state of shock, too terrified to move. The snake's jaw unhinged to reveal wickedly curving fangs, and its dead eyes locked his from above its gaping maw, its tongue flailing inside.

Alonna yelped. A quick thrust of the log in her hand shoved the serpent, hissing, back into the pile and abruptly ended the drama.

The same helpless horror he felt at that long-ago encounter revisited Vergal with utter clarity now.

Sh'ynryan's cold eyes transfixed him from above the icy hand laced across his mouth. Vergal felt the same loathing and menace as when the snake had slithered suddenly near his hand. Sh'ynryan's voice, when at length he spoke, sounded sibilant as the serpent's hiss.

"You are the one," Sh'ynryan whispered, awed.

The medallion's light strobed slowly in his unblinking eyes.

"Now there can be no doubt," he said, speaking as if to himself. "I was a fool to have missed it before."

Thunder smashed outside. Lightning painted the room in dazzling light. Sheer sheets of rain washed the windows. The cacophony seemed to affect Sh'ynryan, drawing him from his quiet contemplation. His voice hardened. His eyes narrowed.

"Get up, boy," he snarled. He drew back and seized Vergal's arms with fingers that dug deep as talons. "You are coming with me."

The threat released Vergal from his shock. He screamed. He thrashed his body. His hands clutched Sh'ynryan's wrist, twisting and pulling to release his grasp, but the man's fingers remained locked to his biceps, hurting them. In his writhing, Vergal's forehead knocked Sh'ynryan solidly in his mouth, drawing a sharp curse of pain, but the man's grip stayed fastened. Vergal flailed his head in desperate negation, wild with fright. He drew a deep breath and screamed again, "Alonna! Alonna! Help me!"

One hand released Vergal's arm, but the relief from Sh'ynryan's cruel fingers proved short-lived when the same hand slapped painfully again over his mouth. The hard hand pressed the boy's head back into his pillow. Vergal felt the heat radiating from the man's bony palm as Sh'ynryan applied mounting pressure, locking the boy's screams behind his clamped lips, turning them into wet gurgles deep in his throat.

Sh'ynryan's splayed fingers also partially covered his nose. It grew difficult for Vergal to breathe as his head sunk deeper. He flailed and wriggled his body in a battle to draw breath, but Sh'ynryan remained unmoveable. The man's thin frame disguised an iron grip.

"Enough of that!" Sh'ynryan hissed.

The man leaned so firmly into his hand that the pillows threatened to envelop the boy's face on all sides and smother him. Vergal's struggles grew weaker; he needed all his energy now to breathe.

Vergal quieted and was rewarded by a lessening of the blockage across his nose. Breathing became nearly manageable. He grew quieter still, and again came a slight easing of the pressure against his mouth and nose.

Through it all, Sh'ynryan remained still above him, staring directly into his eyes.

The gurgles in Vergal's throat faded to whimpers between gasps for air. The boy's terror mounted, but his fighting instinct drained away. It felt too good just to breathe again.

"This is not how I wished to re-acquaint Vergal," Sh'ynryan said. "Still, I will do what is necessary to fulfill my purpose. Do you understand my resolve?"

Vergal, a young boy, did not fully understand the words Sh'ynryan used, but he gleaned their inherent threat. Wide-eyed with fear, Vergal weakly nodded his head against Sh'ynryan's pressing palm.

"Good, that's good ..." the man whispered. If his tone meant to sound soothing, it fell far short. "Listen closely, Vergal," he went on, "because these next few minutes will make a great deal of difference in how this night unfolds."

The directions came quickly, crisply. Sh'ynryan would forthwith remove his hand, but under no circumstance—no matter what inclination seized him—must Vergal scream, struggle, or do anything that in any way constituted a call for help. Remain completely still and calmly listen, Sh'ynryan instructed. Anything less than absolute obedience would result in unpleasant consequences.

The voice in which Sh'ynryan issued these directives invited no disagreement or debate. One last sharp clench of the pincer-like fingers around Vergal's mouth foreshadowed Sh'ynryan's resolve.

The hand lifted. Vergal pulled in a deep breath. The cool night air flooded his aching throat and chest. No draught of cold water on the hottest day ever tasted so sweet. Relief did not embolden him; however, he feared the clutching hand too much to invite again its awful grasp. He trembled so violently that his teeth set up a quiet chattering—a technical breach of Sh'ynryan's admonition to remain silent, but one Vergal was powerless to stop. He feared a renewed assault, but Sh'ynryan paid no mind and smiled instead. The expression did not reassure; it looked cold and reptilian in the shadows of the room. Vergal thought again of the snake in the woodpile.

"Excellent, that's exactly right. Remain quiet." Sh'ynryan said softly. He was hunched so near that their noses nearly brushed.

Vergal's rapid breathing had turned to whimpering. He struggled to contain the sound, but, again, Sh'ynryan paid no heed.

Now came new directions, delivered in a silky calm voice. Vergal was to dress, quietly and quickly. The clothes he had worn through the day remained bundled on a nearby chair, and those would suffice.

Vergal, trembling still, moved to obey.

"I think you'll find your sister has locked the door to your room quite securely from the outside, which proved damned inconvenient in coming here," Sh'ynryan said conversationally as Vergal shrugged into his clothes. That declaration snapped the boy's gaze to the room's open window. His eyes grew wide. Did this monster somehow enter his room through his upper-story window?

Sh'ynryan threw an open satchel on the bed. He moved about the room, putting himself between Vergal and the door. Clothing snatched from a chest of drawers disappeared into the bag. So too did shoes and his map cases! All the while, Sh'ynryan talked casually about the night outside, the wickedly rising weather, and did Vergal have a coat? Ah! There it was. He hastily rolled this too, and into the satchel, it went.

The unconcerned way the man packed his belongings and what those actions implied overcame Vergal's torpor. The shock of the certainty this stranger intended to take him out of here, away from his sister, broke through the terror compelling his obedience.

Vergal awaited his opportunity. He found it when Sh'ynryan opened a closet door to peer inside.

The boy bolted, screaming, and hammered his fists upon the door.

"Help! Alonna, please! Help me!" Vergal shrieked, pounding the door. "He's got me! He's in here! Alonna...!"

Then Sh'ynryan was upon him as Vergal grabbed the unmoving door latch, tearing him away. The cruel fingers sunk savagely into Vergal's bruised arm; the hand slapped across his mouth, choking off his screams.

The man lifted him off the ground and shook him viciously. His sharp chin jutted into Vergal's shoulder as he growled directly behind Vergal's ear, "Silence, you little fool!"

Vergal had little choice in the manner. His air came only with difficulty again. He writhed in Sh'ynryan's arms, but his struggles proved as futile as his previous attempts. He couldn't breathe! Sh'ynryan's arm came around his neck and squeezed. The lump of hard muscle beneath the satiny cloth of the man's robe cut his air. Black specks swirled in the boy's vision. The last words he registered on his descent down the black tunnel toward unconsciousness would win the boy's blind obedience in all the arduous days ahead:

"If you value your own life so little, boy, perhaps your sister's life matters more!"

CHAPTER THREE

Wind and rain lashed his face. He woke cold and shivering and confused, unsure of what had happened until the sight of the dark-cowled man looming over him restored every detail with terrifying clarity.

Vergal lay curled on his side, his face pressed to cold stone. Rain drove down from a pitch sky. He was outside, but he could not tell his surroundings. The rain fell densely in slanted sheets, obscuring details beyond the dark figure of Sh'ynryan standing over him. The man's cloak was slick with rain and wrapped tightly around him. The satchel packed with clothes rested at his feet.

Vergal groaned and hoisted himself on one arm. His throat ached abominably, and it hurt to swallow. Sh'ynryan remained unmoving, watching him through the veil of driving rain. Vergal sat up unsteadily and pulled his knees to his chest, huddling against the wet and the chill. He suddenly realized he was weeping; the rain soaking his face had obscured the fact until now.

"If you start screaming again," Sh'ynryan said, straining to be heard over the drumming rain, "then your little nap will resume. Not that anyone will hear you up here, in any case."

"Up here?" Vergal looked around him, squinting through the downpour. "Up where?"

"The roof."

"What? How?"

A bolt of forked lightning tore the sky behind Sh'ynryan, illuminating their surroundings. Sh'ynryan had spoken truly; in that brief flash, Vergal spotted the stone cornice bordering the roof and, in the distance, the black expanse of the city's harbor.

The last thing Vergal remembered was hammering at his locked door before Sh'ynryan dragged him away. Surely he had not merely opened the door afterward and carried Vergal openly through the corridors to the roof stair? But if not, then how had he arrived here?

Sh'ynryan interrupted his thoughts. The man bent low beside him and laid a hand on his shoulder. Vergal flinched, but this time, the hand fell gently. The man crouched, the length of his rain-wet cowl pooling around him. The hot slash of color staining his cheekbones had faded, restoring chalky pallor to the man's sharp features.

"I know you are frightened, Vergal," Sh'ynryan offered in a reasonable tone, one that lent Vergal courage enough to meet the man's gaze. "I regret that. However, I told you I intend to fulfill my purpose. Do you still doubt my resolve?"

Vergal said nothing, only trembled in the rain.

Sh'ynryan righted himself, sighing. "What you must think of me ... coming to snatch you from your bed like a ghoul!" he said ruefully. "I promise you, though, my actions are borne of necessity. You will come to understand that soon enough. And if you listen to me, no further harm will befall you. It is not my desire to harm you—certainly not!"

Sh'ynryan's face grew cunning as he leaned back toward the boy.

"But I can harm you, Vergal," he said in that same steady tone. "You believe I have that power, do you not?"

Vergal nodded mutely. Alonna's earlier admonition tumbled through his feverish mind like an omen from another age: "There are men in this world, Vergal ... Evil men ..." How perfectly her words described this demon in its red cape!

"Then believe this also: If you in any way jeopardize my plans, your sister will suffer. This, I vow. Though it will pain me to do so, I will destroy her, and you shall witness her dying breath."

Sh'ynryan had made the same threat in the inn and now again on its roof. Vergal utterly believed him. He would obey this man to assure his sister's safety. Imagining the merciless Sh'ynryan trapping his sister alone in her dark room as he had so effortlessly trapped Vergal was enough to set the boy's heart tripping in his chest. He could not bear to subject Alonna to such a horror. If it took his obedience to this madman to spare her that fate, Vergal intended to comply.

"Do you understand? Good. Then let us dispense with these threats." Rising, Sh'ynryan hauled the boy easily to his feet.

They stood in the rain-drenched darkness, watching each other until Sh'ynryan broke the trance. "Come," he said perfunctorily and turned the boy toward the lip of the roof.

It took all Vergal's willpower to smother the panic rising in his chest. He summoned the image of Alonna at work downstairs in the taproom, oblivious to the drama unfolding above her. He longed to be enveloped in his sister's arms, nestled safely in her warm fragrance as she often comforted him through all his many nightmares and fears and sorrow. She had been his salvation over the years, and Sh'ynryan's awful vow echoed in his thoughts: "Your sister will suffer!" Vergal could not allow that. He resolved then to take the threat of this demon-man far away from her.

"Excellent, Vergal," Sh'ynryan said as Vergal allowed himself to be guided to the roof's edge. He patted the boy's shoulder. "This is an excellent start."

They stood looking over the crumbling cornice at the cobblestone alleyway far below. The Wayfarer stood four storeys above its front common, with alleys on three sides threading between neighboring buildings.

"Who are you?" Vergal dared ask, his voice cracking. He continued in a whisper. "Why have you come? What do you want with me?"

Sh'ynryan slung the satchel he carried over one shoulder. "Who I am and what I want will become clear in time," he said. "For now, you need only know you are leaving with me. Hurry now, be quick; we must be away."

"But what about Alonna?" the boy ventured in a meek voice. "Will she know where I am? Will I see her again? Will she ... be all right?"

Vergal's throat thickened beneath an onslaught of raw emotion. He dissolved into fresh weeping. In his mind's eye, he perfectly saw his sister's panicked reaction upon finding his room dark and empty.

Sh'ynryan watched him sourly.

"I have made provision for your sister, boy; I am not completely without remorse," he said. "When she returns, she will discover a bag of coins on your pillow. It contains wealth enough for her to escape the service of that taproom tyrant.

"She will be rich beyond a peasant's imagining, although I presume the gold will afford cold comfort. Days from now, an agent of mine will deliver her word that you are safe and that no harm has or will befall you."

The dejected boy dropped his chin to his chest. "It will break her heart."

"It may well break her heart, but that is a matter of supreme indifference to me," he replied. "I assure you I have provided for her material needs. If she is wise, your sister will escape this hovel and set up comfortably somewhere she can live out her life. I have directed my agent to make this choice clear."

Sh'ynryan shrugged. "If she is unwise," he went on, "she will wallow in pity and waste herself here. In either case, my dealings with her are finished so long as you continue to obey. Do I make myself clear?"

Vergal's sad image of his sister changed from one of heartbreak to happiness. He imagined Alonna in future years, well-dressed, well-fed, and contented in a neat house of her own. He saw her freed from the simple linen of a serving maid, living securely in a manner she never could in Caliss, safe from the horrible threat of Sh'ynryan. It was the same dream of the future Alonna had held forth for them both. Vergal would not share it, but at least his sister would have it. A leisurely life had been made possible for her, but only if Vergal kept brave at this vital juncture and followed Sh'ynryan down the unknown path that stretched ahead of him.

Sh'ynryan sensed his conflict. Reaching into a purse on his belt, he produced a gold coin. He pinched the coin between his thumb and forefinger and held it in front of Vergal.

"This is an Arasynian gold crown," Sh'ynryan explained. "It bears the likeness of the emperor himself. This coin is the currency in all the known world. I have left these for your sister. It is a small fortune, Vergal, and if she is prudent, she shall never want for anything again."

Vergal stared, transfixed by the gold. He would do this for her, he resolved in that moment. Though terror gnawed his insides at the prospect of a road beside Sh'ynryan, he resolved to free Alonna into a future his sister deserved.

Sh'ynryan dropped the coin in his purse and cinched the drawstring. "Does this complete our agreement then?"

Vergal thought he detected trepidation in his voice. The medallion at the man's throat pulsed again as if too, awaiting the answer.

"Your sister's freedom and safety, for your obedience?" he prompted.

Vergal nodded. The medallion blazed briefly, a triumphant taunt by Vergal's reckoning.

"Then come with me," Sh'ynryan said softly, turning the boy again to the roof's edge.

He instinctively flinched from the precipice. "But how will we get down?"

"You must learn to have faith in me, Vergal. I only put my hand to those things I know I can accomplish. You will learn this. For now, only follow my lead, and I will deliver us safely to the street below."

Sh'ynryan took a knee in front of the boy. "Now brace yourself," he said. "I am going to speak a word to you. It is a powerful word, and it will be unpleasant to hear, but it is necessary."

He leaned his head until the hair of his beard scratched Vergal's ear. Sh'ynryan whispered a word. Vergal frowned. The word sounded meaningless, like gibberish, not in fact like a word at all, and spoken in a strange inflection that rose harmonically, as if bridging the octave of a song. However, the boy's confusion fast turned to consternation when a sudden dull roaring swelled in his ears.

Strange heat flowed through Vergal, invading him, threading a warm tendril through every vein in his body. A sudden gust of wind, divorced from the rainy gale lashing them, lifted Vergal's hair from his brow. This wind collected and eddied around him, roiling like a whirlpool. Vergal felt buoyant as if floating in water. He yelped and grasped Sh'ynryan's mantle in panic when he realized he was floating, his feet lifting—rising—off the roof.

"What is this?" Vergal cried. "Help! Stop!"

"Easy, lad!" Sh'ynryan yelled over the rush of churning wind.

The vortex intensified, swirling around Vergal's legs, creating a column around him and a cushion of air beneath him. His knuckles whitened from the effort of gripping Sh'ynryan, but he nearly lost his grip in shock when he realized the wind had seized the red-robed stranger as well. They were rising together, swiftly, like an arrow shot into the rainy night.

Vergal screamed as the rooftop plummeted away from beneath his feet.

CHAPTER FOUR

"Alonna!"

Alonna froze with one foot poised on a stair.

"Alonna!!" It was Carek. And he sounded angry.

Alonna turned around slowly. Carek stood glowering at her from the doorway to the kitchen.

"You have customers," he grumbled. "Where are you going?"

"To look in on Vergal," Alonna replied meekly. She smoothed the front of her plain apron—now splotched with spilled drink and stained with food as the night wore on—and lowered her head. Her dark hair spilled to veil her face. She demurely swept a stray lock behind her ear.

"I'm worried about him, Carek," she went on. She lifted her eyes but not her chin to meet the innkeeper's disapproving gaze. "I've seen to everyone's needs; it won't take but a moment to look in …"

Carek stormed to the stairs, leaning so close to her face that she recoiled from the sour stench of his breath.

"I have an inn full of thirsty patrons, and here I find you, sneaking away up the back stair?" he yelled. "Your brother is fine. He's safe in the room I provide for you both. Now back to work before your next job is to find a place to sleep in the streets!"

Carek transfixed her with a hard stare to ensure she was suitably cowed. Satisfied, he turned away, mumbling irritably.

Alonna straightened on the stair. She brushed her hair out of her eyes and fought to stave off tears.

The worry gnawing at her since Vergal joined the red-cowled man for dinner had grown to dreadful proportions. Her entire body itched to run upstairs to their room at the end of a drafty back corridor to check on her brother, to watch him at sleep for just a moment, and to ease her mind.

But the fierce storm that lashed Caliss had driven people indoors, and many had sought refuge in the taproom of the Wayfarer, where the huge hearth and chill ale offered respite from the whipping wind and rain. The crowd had steadily grown throughout the evening, and Alonna had been run off her feet. With each turn on its hinges of the inn's door, Alonna despaired of ever finding a chance to check her brother and ease her mounting anxiety.

At last, the storm had steadied, however, and the crowd became manageable. After a quick circuit of the taproom to refresh cups, Alonna darted for the back stair, where Carek had accosted her.

She cast a longing glance up the dim stairwell, wiping her eyes and cursing herself for a thousand kinds of fool. Vergal was safe, she reasoned. She had left him sleeping in a locked room to which she held the key. The red-robed man had unsettled her with his rapt attentiveness toward the boy and further startled her by afterward taking a room, but that was no excuse for her mounting hysteria, Alonna admonished herself. Giving way to her growing sense of unease would only further antagonize Carek.

Soon after the dinner hour, the stranger had walked out into the storm. He had not returned. So why should she fear some undefined harm befalling her brother at the man's hand?

She did not know why she feared. But fear she did. And that disturbed her most of all.

In an agony of indecision, Alonna lingered at the foot of the stairs. Across the hall, Carek stood in the kitchen barking unintelligible orders at the other servants. He turned mid-tirade and spotted her. He frowned and beckoned roughly for her to come near.

She glanced back again at the stairwell. An image assailed her of the red-garbed stranger seated beside Vergal in the taproom, scrutinizing him with eyes that seemed at once soulless and ravenous.

That image decided her.

She bolted up the stairs.

"Alonna!" Carek brayed behind her.

Alonna ignored him; she flew up the stairs under the barrage of an unsettling intuition. Carek gave chase. Alonna heard him pounding up the stairs behind her, cursing a streak. She knew the heavy-set man had no chance of overtaking her fleet pace. Her hand verily skimmed over the rail as she took the steps a pair at a time.

She turned dreary corners on the stairwell until the flights opened on the plain, white-washed hallway leading to her room.

This floor of the inn housed the servants. Here the comparatively comfortable environment of the lower levels gave way to more utilitarian surroundings. Alonna peered once behind her to see if Carek had closed the distance, but the hall behind her remained empty, bathed in switching shadows from a lone lantern on its hook.

She skidded to a stop in front of her chamber door. She had a bad moment when she could not place the key in the pockets of her apron, but her frantic fingers soon closed on the slim piece of metal. She jammed it in the keyhole just as Carek, red-faced and puffing, crested the stairs.

"Alonna!" he bellowed.

Alonna turned the lock, flung open the door, and rushed inside.

Vergal was gone.

She knew it even before her vision adjusted to the darkness.

The blankets were peeled back on the bed, and the window stood open behind a crack in the curtains. They rippled and flared in the eddies of wind and rain from outside. Alonna rushed to the bed, patting it furiously, searching with her hands to refute the evidence of her eyes.

He was gone.

"Vergal!" she cried, hot tears standing in her eyes. "Vergal, no!"

Behind her, Carek slid to a halt in the doorway, gripping the doorjamb and breathing heavily. "Alonna!" he roared between heaving breaths. "Have you gone mad? Did I not just tell you ..."

Alonna whirled on him. "He's gone!" she shrieked. Tears and fire strove in her eyes, and Carek flinched at the spectacle. "I knew it!" she cried. "You would not let me look in, and now he's gone!"

Enraged, Alonna fell upon him with her fists. She hammered his arms and barrel-like chest. Carek fell back several paces to her fury but, regrouping, seized her flailing arms and pushed her away. She stumbled and landed heavily on the floor.

Carek stood uneasily at the door. His head ticked between Alonna on the floor and the rumpled sheets on the empty bed. Confusion twisted his face as the reality of the situation dawned on him.

"You mean ... he's gone?" Carek said uncertainly. He looked about the darkened room, bewildered. "Where did he go?"

Alonna drew her knees to her breasts and rocked slowly in time with her sobs. "He's gone, he's gone," she murmured. "I told you, he took him, just like I knew he would."

"Who? Who took him? You're not making sense."

"That man!" she screamed. "The man in the red cape with the bag of gold. The one who invited Vergal to eat with him. He did it; he took him, I know it."

Carek blinked a few times. He shook his ponderous head in disbelief.

"Surely not, Alonna," he said in a voice that approached gentleness but fell just short. "Why? Who would want to ...?" He shook his head again. "No," he said, his voice firming. "Vergal has run off and hidden somewhere. He's a boy, and boys do stupid things."

Carek's bushy eyebrows knitted. "I'll gather the cooks, and we'll look for him. We'll find him. And I'll thrash him with a ladle to teach him never to frighten his sister so again."

"No," Alonna said, her head bowed. "You'll not find him. He's not here. The man took him. Search the room he rented; you'll see he's gone. He's not coming back." She fell into a fresh bout of weeping.

Carek shook his head stubbornly. "We'll find him, Alonna. Just rest here a moment and calm down. Relax now, but after this, the three of us will have a long talk. I'll not have my livelihood threatened by Vergal's stupidity and your foolishness, do you understand? We'll get this settled tonight. Believe it."

And with a final disbelieving glance into the room, Carek lumbered away.

Alonna stared for a long time at the door through which Carek had departed. At length, she scrubbed the heel of her hand across her eyes to dry them and climbed to her feet.

She closed the door and lit several candles to better survey the cramped quarters by their faltering light. The tangled bed coverings seemed to her mute witnesses to some unspeakable crime. She stared at them a long time as if they might relent and offer an explanation for the horrible scene that had unfolded in the room.

She sat at the edge of the bed for long moments before it dawned on her something was out of the ordinary. Without realizing, she had been studying a round leather bag, half-concealed by the scattered pillows. Curious, she leaned in and scooped the bag. She felt coins packed tightly within.

"What is this?" she asked the empty room.

She opened and emptied the bag. Gold poured out, a small hill of it that spilled across the bed. The round coins absorbed the candlelight and cast it back brighter, purer than before. Alonna struggled to comprehend what she beheld. She spread the coins with the palm of her hand, dumbfounded, transfixed by their color and their cold shape.

Lost in thought, absently stirring the gold, her hand uncovered a scrap of paper buried in the mound. She unfolded the scrap and lifted it closer in the uncertain light to read the words written there, in a spidery, slanted hand:

Your brother will be kept safe. The gold is yours to escape this place and that man. Tell no one of this at the risk of his life and your own. Believe that I can harm him and you if you disobey.

There was no signature. None was needed.

Alonna pitched forward in a faint, scattering her new fortune in gold.

In the days that followed, Alonna lapsed into stony silence. Her heartbreak shared space with a growing, quiet, deadly resolve. Vergal was gone, truly gone. A thorough sweep of the inn and its grounds and the surrounding streets had turned up no trace. A search of the red-caped stranger's room indicated the man had fled, precisely as Alonna had predicted.

Reasoning that her silence endangered Vergal's life more than speaking out, Alonna ignored the abductor's threat and reported the crime to the local magistrate—a fat, sweating man who claimed his cushy station by reason of distant kinship to the pirate king at Far.

The magistrate offered a rousing speech in defense of both the length and the severity of the king's arm in dispensing justice, especially against miscreants who stole children. However, he seemed at a loss to explain how he intended to track and apprehend a perpetrator who had disappeared into thin air. He provided the city watch with descriptions of the culprit and promised to keep Alonna alerted of developments.

Alonna relinquished any hope of finding Vergal through official means before the gates to the magistrate's manor had closed behind her.

Alonna said nothing of the note and the gold. She guessed the written mention of the coins would invite the wrong kind of interest from the authorities, especially from the king's tax collectors who had a reputation for voraciousness in their pursuit of revenues for the royal treasury. And though she wasn't thinking clearly in those initial days after Vergal's disappearance, the germ of an idea—a plan—was forming in her mind that would require money. Likely plenty of it.

Alonna pulled up a board in the floor of her room and hid the bag of gold beneath. She pushed a heavy trunk of her clothes over the spot to conceal her rough handiwork. And she continued to plot.

Carek's reaction surprised Alonna in the foggy first days following Vergal's disappearance. After failing to find Vergal that night, or the following day, Carek's blustering against the boy and Alonna dwindled to be replaced by a grudging concern for both as days without sign of the boy stretched on.

Alonna suspected the innkeeper felt guilty for denying her time to check on her brother when there might still have been time to foil the crime. Or perhaps he simply feared losing Alonna's services to her growing reclusiveness.

Through it all, Alonna remained silent. She worked by day—another of Carek's concessions; he found a new woman to work the hectic evening hours—and she received patrons' condolences without comment.

At night, she ate tasteless dinners in taverns far from the Wayfarer, where none knew her or Vergal and where a coin delivered in payment would not raise eyebrows, despite Alonna's simple mannerisms.

She took the change from her meals in coins of silver or bronze, which she knew could be used to purchase goods without drawing suspicion to herself.

The days passed, and Alonna quietly purchased items of clothing and other things she deemed necessary for a long journey as the petals of her strategy further blossomed. She smuggled these wares to her room at the Wayfarer, where they joined the gold in the space beneath the floor.

Brandy and wine—luxuries she could never afford before—now became staples of her evenings. Late at night, Alonna locked her door and sipped from her assortment of bottles, drowning her growing misery and, temporarily at least, repulsing the inky darkness in her soul by the light of candles.

Sometimes she hauled the bag from its hiding place to count the coins and dwell on her rapidly forming plan. Other times she lay sprawled on her bed simply thinking, drinking from her bottles until the light blurred in her vision and the room began to spin, sinking her into a dreamless sleep.

Those dark days often found her thoughts turning from Vergal to her parents, though she knew her brother's disappearance had provoked the painful memories. Having Vergal wrenched from her left a numbness inside that reminded Alonna sharply of the mind-addling grief she endured after losing her parents.

She had been a child, not much older than Vergal was now, when it started.

An ocean voyage of many months had brought her family to Caliss. They were far from their ancestral home at Zistah, a shining city in distant Arasynia, where gleaming domes and towers soared high above the tangled canopy in a verdant land of jungle and lakes.

The fresh wind sighing out of the mountains stirred the great lake into a glittering mass of jewels beneath the tropical sun. The green mass of the jungle choked the rising slopes beyond the gleaming city walls. Alonna recalled it all perfectly and remembered how happy her young life had been there—until the day of her father's announcement.

The family would move, said her father Teraud, a dignified man whose hair and trim beard was salted with grey even from the days of his youth. The decision was sudden and unalterable, and young Alonna had wept bitterly. Her mother Marillee sat stone-faced nearby, the baby Vergal cooing in her arms, but offered nothing in response. Vague reasons for the decision were provided, but the look that passed between her parents convinced Alonna the true motive would not be forthcoming.

A jumble of activity over the days that followed left little time for conjecture. The governess who cared for the children was dismissed. Men arrived to pack the furnishings and belongings in their palatial home and move them to a warehouse near the harbor. The family members followed, taking rooms in a lakefront inn. In the days before their departure, Alonna accompanied her father to the marble-clad shop of a moneychanger in the temple district. There Teraud withdrew his entire holdings.

A muted conversation between Teraud and the wizened shopkeeper led to an exchange of scrolls. The men pressed their signet rings to wax seals to complete the transaction, and soon after, a sturdy chest was loaded onto their waiting carriage.

Two grim-faced men wielding spears and wearing swords belted at their waist joined them for the return trip. They clung to the outside of the carriage as it twisted through the winding avenues, staring suspiciously at all passers-by. Alonna linked their defensive demeanor to the jingling noise rising from the chest with each bump of the carriage wheels over the uneven flagstones. The men posted a solemn guard outside the family's rooms at the inn, saying nothing, watching everything.

Alonna's final trip into the city came on the morning of their departure. The carriage again dropped them in the heart of the district outside of the Imperial Library, a sprawling construct beneath a soaring gilded dome.

Inside, the scent of dusty tomes and oiled woodwork assailed her. Books and scrolls crammed the space along the ornate vaulting shelves that lined the length of the curving walls, heaped atop massive plank tables and even in places stacked in musty mounds on the cold tile floor. The cavernous interior overwhelmed her, and Alonna stood mute at its center, craning her neck to take in the colorful, cavorting friezes ringing the lofty rotunda.

Meanwhile, Teraud held a heated conversation with the librarian, a thin man with a drooping right eye whose speech escaped him in a lisp. The man's animated gestures set his gauzy mantle swinging and jangled the platinum circlets and amulets on his wrists and neck. It was plain even from a distance that the librarian was incensed. His voice took on a hectoring tone. The conversation rose and fell between the men until Teraud turned abruptly away, his expression crestfallen. Clutching Alonna's hand, Teraud led her briskly toward the door. The librarian followed, his footsteps and shrill voice echoing in the vast hall.

"They will not suffer it to be lost to them, Teraud, you know this!" the librarian cried as they emerged into the harsh light of day.

Teraud, his face a mask, continued in stony silence. He clenched Alonna's hand firmly and led her into the crush of people milling about the central plaza. Her father offered no reply to Alonna's many questions as they walked.

Alone now upon her bed, watching the candlelight paint the stucco of her room's ceiling, Alonna realized years later she still had no answers.

CHAPTER FIVE

As abruptly as it had started, the rain stopped. The effect was as though someone had ceased to pour a bucket.

Vergal mopped his brow and pulled the tangle of rain-slick hair out of his eyes. His drenched tunic and sodden hose clung to his back and legs. The boy trembled violently, though not from the wet and the cold. The shock at his unnatural passage from the wind-lashed loft of the Wayfarer's summit to the cobblestone alley far below had set him to shaking. He leaned uncertainly against the alley's rough wall.

"I feel ill," Vergal moaned.

"No doubt," Sh'ynryan agreed. "But there's no time for that. Stay on your feet!"

The boy's wide eyes sought out Sh'ynryan's impassive face. "What happened? What did you do? How did you do that?"

But Sh'ynryan was no longer listening. Something had caught his attention. He tugged Vergal's collar once sharply. "Silence!" he warned.

Vergal caught the sound—a faint jangling from the depths of the black alley beyond. He glanced back but saw nothing except the light thrown by oil lamps reflected in the puddles. Then the staccato slap of footfalls and tones of muted conversation reached his ears.

"The night watch," Sh'ynryan growled. He stepped into the shadows of a recessed wall, drawing Vergal into the folds of his cloak. "Not a sound from you, Vergal," he warned, "or I'll carry you up and hurl you out over the harbor!"

Vergal, still numb and shaking, nodded mutely. Sh'ynryan paid him no heed; the man had started a low whispering. The dull roaring Vergal experienced on the rooftop returned to fill his ears; the strange heat coiled through him once again. He cried out involuntarily in fear, though Sh'ynryan had already clamped a hand over this mouth in anticipation.

This time the sensation was different. No churning tunnel of wind descended to seize him, as before. Instead, the feeling was of sand flowing, as a handful does smoothly, quickly, through splayed fingers. Except his entire body felt fluid in this way. And what was that sound? Vergal had the strangest impression of hearing rumbling, clattering stones.

The odd sensation mounted. The watchmen approached down the alley, a group of mail-shirted men clad in conical leather helmets atop their heads and who held cruelly-curving pikes. Vergal realized it would be impossible to miss them. Once they emerged from the pool of lamplight, their eyes would adjust to the gloom, and they would spot Sh'ynryan at once, his back to the wall, his hand clamped over a boy's mouth. What might be their reaction then? Vergal didn't know whether to feel fear or relief.

Then a step backward, forced by Sh'ynryan's clasping arms.

Then total darkness.

But not silence.

The rumbling noise of stone grating on stone persisted in Vergal's ears. Beyond that, the noise of the soldiers' footfalls, stamping loudly on the cobblestones accompanied by the thud of their pikes' shafts on the ground.

How do they not see us? Vergal wondered.

And then he knew.

The sounds in his ears. The darkness. The sinking feeling of stepping back into the shadows where no further shadows, only a solid stone wall, should have been.

Sh'ynryan had dragged him not just against the wall but inside it.

In this instance, the guttural intonation that had lifted him into the night sky had melded Vergal to the cold stone of the alley wall. Panic rose. The grating sounds in his ears and the shifting, uncertain feeling that pervaded his body defied logic yet seemed completely reasonable considering his captor's earlier feats. In the span of short hours, Vergal had come to accept the proof his experiences had forced upon him: That the unnatural became natural when Sh'ynryan uttered his words of power.

He held no disbelief at the realization of what otherwise was unbelievable: They stood within the wall, melded to the stone. No other explanation could account for the two of them slamming against the hard brick, only to sink further back into darkness as if into shifting, forgiving sand.

From the darkness, Vergal heard the soldiers talking and laughing. He thought he counted the noise of five men but had no way of knowing. He imagined them peering into shadowy corners. He heard them kicking over garbage bins and discarded crates as if searching— albeit half-heartedly—for something.

Vergal considered making some sound to draw the men's attention but thought better of the idea. The men might hear but see nothing, leaving Vergal at his tormentor's mercy once they moved away.

The chattering guards continued down the alley and out of earshot, oblivious to Vergal's predicament. Not long after, the sensation he previously experienced gripped him once more, this time in reverse. The grumble of grinding stones grew distant in his ears, and the sensation of sinking into sand turned to one of emerging from under it. Dewy night air filled his lungs. The darkness evaporated to be replaced by lamplights as piercing as the midday sun. He fell, gasping, to his stomach on the slick alley floor.

It took a moment to compose himself. The retching sounds rising behind him suggested Sh'ynryan might need even more time. Vergal pushed himself up on trembling arms in time to see Sh'ynryan take a knee. The man was folded over, his staff on the ground, his right arm laid across his stomach. A thick line of spittle swung from his lower lip. The slimy stream caught and reflected the lantern light grotesquely.

"Don't...you...move..." Sh'ynryan warned him between laborious breaths.

It was an unnecessary threat. Movement seemed far beyond the realm of Vergal's capabilities right then. Regulating his breathing was proving challenge enough.

And yet ...

Vergal took note of Sh'ynryan's weakness. The threat the man posed at the time paled to the thundering nightmare that had ripped him out of his room and hurtled him into the night air. His fear of the man had not lessened, but the sight of Sh'ynryan bent double, and heaving like the common drunks Vergal regularly spotted outside the tavern gave him pause, if not hope.

Hope, like men and like fear, takes time and travail to be fully born. It had its conception in Vergal in that moment.

CHAPTER SIX

The sea voyage with her parents passed in a blur of nausea for the young girl Alonna, who confined herself to quarters and battled her churning insides by fixing her gaze on the room's single unmoving fixture: A wardrobe affixed to the cabin wall. She noticed that concentrating on one object helped deflect attention from the various other items that slid about her room of their own accord as the ship climbed then crested high swells on the open sea.

Nighttime was worse. With no fixed reference point, her insides lurched in time with the heaving. She clamped her eyes tightly and willed her stomach to settle as she prayed for sleep. The strategy seldom worked.

She ate little, and her lack of appetite alarmed her parents. However, one whiff of the steaming contents of the dinner plates delivered to her cabin convinced Alonna her stomach would abide nothing more than the thin broth and bread that became her mainstay.

She cried incessantly in those days and raged in the tempestuous tone only the indignant young truly achieve. Her mother held her at these times, offering affection and assurances of her love in response to the explanations Alonna always demanded but never received.

The sickening days at sea wore on. Her misery deepened.

And then, one day, the voyage ended.

Alonna went above deck late one morning to find a clear shaft of sunlight in place of the continuous fins of water and sprays of mist that usually greeted her. A vast blue sky, unmarred by the perpetual shroud, stretched around her. The violent dip and heave of the ship as it rode the high seas had subsided into a barely perceptible sway.

Landfall!

Tearfully, this time for joy, Alonna flew on bare feet in search of her father. She found him assisting sweaty sailors as they prepared the deck to guide the ship into port. Teraud caught Alonna in full flight and held her tightly. She sobbed gratefully into the fine cloth of his tunic. Her father whispered reassuring words into her ear, promising her the long journey had ended. They were home, he told her, in a new land where they could settle and live happily together.

The end of the sea voyage so overjoyed Alonna that she failed to make her usual response to these promises: They had been settled and happy together back at home, so what had changed? Why had Father ever decided to leave?

Alonna found the new land strange and foreboding. The tropical sun that glittered so brilliantly on the azure waters of her homeland gave way to a dull disk that barely lightened the slate-grey waters of the sea.

The gentle sweep of creamy sand that formed the margin between water and land in the country of her birth was here little more than a jumbled rocky strand. The land emerged roughly and abruptly from beneath the churning ocean to start its long climb to fortress-like mountains that loomed on the horizon in nearly every direction.

Her father explained how their new home was a northern land, where the sun traveled more distantly on its path through the sky and where the sea left its warmth far behind on its mad wash to the top of the world.

In truth, Alonna understood little of what he said. The foreign surroundings puzzled and frustrated her, and soon she grew critical of them. The dark pine forests were scraggly and drab compared to the lush, scented trees of home, she observed caustically. The skies constantly brooded, and so too would she, Alonna threatened, until Father took her home! She longed for the sun to fall full and warm upon her face without first struggling through the tattered clouds that raced ceaselessly over the mountains.

The family's wagon train coiled on bumpy roads out of the port city of Eliard into the vast interior, where menacing forests to the west and north pressed tightly all about until even the distant mountains were blotted from view. Along the way, the towns and their hardy inhabitants, so much larger and fair-skinned than the natives of her home, also fell victim to Alonna's caustic observations. Her father laughed at her spitefulness and assured Alonna she would appreciate the beauty surrounding her with time. It was different, perhaps than the splendors of home, but splendid still.

In one sense, he had been right. The ruggedness of the land appealed to Alonna as their rattling wagons moved north. The wagon drivers often stopped to make camp in rolling foothills dressed in wildflowers at that time of the year. Alonna delighted in how the high meadows came alive with riotous color whenever the wind stirred their fragrant heads to nod.

Water roaring down from the mountains ran colder and cleaner than anything in her experience. It roiled everywhere across the wild landscape in awesome spectacles of sight and sound.

The sweet mountain-fed waters became a treat to Alonna. She often leaped from her wagon to run gleefully down grassy banks to a shallow place where the streams rippled over polished stones. There she knelt to drink pure cold water she collected in her cupped hands. The hardy elk and moose that emerged soundlessly from the shadows of the forest startled her with their immensity and majesty. Alonna had to admit the slight gazelle and antelope of her homeland seemed sickly by comparison.

The wilderness eventually opened into a wide plain, and the rough dirt road they followed flattened into a paved stone highway as the wagons approached the city of Speakwater. They entered the city through the soaring arch of the massive main gate. Soldiers in burnished plate mail stood at rapt attention as they passed.

Alonna marveled at the newness of the buildings that rose along the arrow-straight avenues of the Alasian capital. The entire city appeared new and freshly scrubbed, as if a flawless stage setting had been dropped astride the rushing waters of the Vinefruit River that had inspired Speakwater's name. It was so different, she thought, from the decay that marred many of the ancient temples and great houses of commerce in her native land.

Speakwater was a colonial city, Teraud explained. As the capital of a new country, the city was in many ways still under construction by the Arasynian Empire since its founding a century earlier. The passage of time, he told Alonna, had yet to crumble the city's stone monuments or dull the luster of its marble-clad facades, as it had in ancient Zistah.

The Empire had taken care to craft a capital that adequately reflected its glory. Government buildings rose on massive scales. Cultured parklands lined the Vinefruit's twisting course through the city, dotted everywhere by the rambling stone manors and gated mansions of scribes and bureaucrats and moneychangers. Arches and soaring pillars capped by statues and symbols of the Empire—the griffin, the wheatsheaf, the Emperor himself—lined most streets, especially near the heart of the city where libraries and universities jostled the Imperial barracks and armories for proximity to the sprawling palace of the Imperial Governor.

Yet for all its grand aspirations, Speakwater's stunted size betrayed its youth. Alonna noted how the city rose abruptly from the surrounding plains without margin or preamble, appearing uniformly built in a single-minded frenzy of sameness.

While there were no slums in Speakwater, there were also few truly unique neighborhoods. Each city section seemed stamped from the same mold, all shiningly sterile in a contrived setting. It seemed foreign to Alonna, who had grown up in Zistah, where the full spectrum of glorious wealth and crushing poverty could be found around nearly every turn of a narrow city street.

Speakwater was a place without history, she decided, one that mimicked outwardly the older cities after which it patterned itself yet lacked their souls. The blandness of the place began to grate on her nerves, as every turn of a corner yielded up the same monument-lined avenues and more of the same uninspired elegance.

The journey had also begun to take its toll on the money chest that rode in Alonna's wagon.

With each passing day, the noise of jangling coins within grew muted as her father, his face grim, dipped within to pay the waggoners, the guards, and the progression of nameless innkeepers along their way. Alonna did not know their destination, only that they had not yet arrived when the wagon train turned west out of Speakwater and struck out across the Great Western Highway. The ragged pyramids of the distant Watergate Mountains loomed ahead.

Still reflecting on the enigma of Speakwater, Alonna failed to take much note of the western leg of their trip through the omnipresent forest until they arrived at the March.

The sheer size of the fortress overwhelmed Alonna.

It spanned a pass in the Watergates like a massive stone curtain. It shined with the same scrubbed-stone newness that marked the buildings of Speakwater. A huge portcullis stood opened, and the road followed a bare stone tunnel through the bowels of the keep, where torchlight guttered behind barred portals high on the vaulted walls.

Alonna did not catch sight of them, but her father told her of the Imperial archers that manned those wicked apertures, ready to rain death on invaders that dared pass the portal. Alonna shivered and kept a careful eye on every torch-lit opening as they passed.

The land beyond the March turned wilder and more broken than anything the train had previously encountered. The neat farming villages and small towns that dotted the road east of the March disappeared completely on its western side, swallowed by pine-clad mountain flanks. They were truly in the mountains now. It had seemed to Alonna as if the March had marked the boundary of two separate countries. Teraud, though, had assured her that they traveled still in Arasynian Alasia.

The paved highway tapered into an ill-kept dirt road that stitched its way through the overhanging forest. Crude wooden fortresses rose on fire-cleared land beside the road every dozen leagues. The forts were staffed by bored Imperial soldiers who exacted exorbitant prices for barely adequate food and lodging. Alonna's father, grumbling at the soldiers' avarice, chose more often to set up camp away from the safety of the forts as the road wore on and his money chest grew lighter.

Finally, the journey neared its end.

One day the forest parted, and Alonna beheld a broad valley through which a brackish river flowed sluggishly along its bed. For days, the winds soughing through the trees had carried the tang of salt air, overpowering the cloying perfume of the interminable evergreens with the scent of the ocean.

The turgid river emptied at the horizon into a shallow delta of mudflats. Alonna's eye tracked the jellied coastline far beyond the river to where an indistinct smudge stood against the lighter line of the distant mountains. Teraud jumped from his wagon and joined his daughter at the lip of the valley. He kneeled behind her and wrapped his arms tightly around her.

"Do you see it, Alonna?" Teraud asked. His voice sounded relieved behind the girl's ear.

"I see something, Father," she replied, raising her hand to shade her brow and squinting hard against the glare of the midday sun. "But what is it?"

He laughed, and Alonna smiled at the sound. It had been weeks since her father spoke so happily.

"It's home," he explained simply.

"Home?" To Alonna, it appeared only a lump in the distance, the shadow of a foothill descending from the mountains. She turned to face him, her eyes questioning, but he gazed past her across the river. A smile played on his lips that didn't entirely touch his eyes.

"It is called Caliss, Alonna. It's our new home, in a new land."

He stood up and held out his hand to her. "Come, daughter," Teraud said gently, his smile widening. "Back into the wagon until we reach the Danea River bridge. Then we'll walk over it together, you and I, to become the first in our family to set our feet in the Aerie Coast! What say you?"

Caliss fell far short of the romantic images her father's eagerness had raised in Alonna's imagination. From the gruff customs guard who refused to let them dismount on the Aerie Coast side of the bridge, to the wild-eyed ruffians that attacked the wagon train as it approached the city wall—only to be beaten back by her father's guards—Alonna's hopes for a new Zistah on the western shelf of Alasia were severely undermined even before the pitted wood gates swung open to admit them.

Her first glimpse of Caliss toppled her hopes entirely.

Whereas Speakwater had offended Alonna by the uniformity of its grandeur, Caliss did so with unrelieved ugliness.

The town spread like lichen across a rocky headland above a deep harbor. The natural setting above the tossing sea was spectacular enough, but the ramshackle buildings that dipped into every shallow trench and mounted every granite knob went a long way toward obscuring the intrinsic beauty of the place.

As the wagons wound toward the docks, Alonna could see plainly how the town had evolved in a quick but jumbled spill from the harbor to slosh up against the distant city walls.

Tall stone buildings with slanted slate roofs crammed together along twisting streets. The streets turned sporadically from crumbled flagstones to dirt and often terminated in dead ends or narrow alleyways through which the wagons could not pass.

A stable near the gate had filled the air with the overpowering odor of manure as the company entered Caliss, but that had paled in comparison to the stench of the harbor, where the nearby open-air market mingled the exotic scents of its spices and foodstuffs with the smell of rotting fish, stagnant saltwater, and waste that wafted from the bay.

The fleets of vessels crowding the jetties and at anchor in the bay cloaked the harbor in a creaking forest of masts. In the distance, Alonna spied an indistinct shelf of rock that penned the great bay at its southern end, where it opened to spill into the ocean beyond.

The world here seemed composed entirely of sky and water, rock and salt air, all marred by the hideous scents and constructs of the town that crawled up the headland from the ocean to the gated walls and the surrounding forest beyond.

The residents were another matter. While the town repulsed her, Alonna was often struck by the beauty of its inhabitants. Even clothed as they were in simple garb as they went about their business, there was a glint about the eyes, a tilt to their chins, and a roguishness in the smiles of the Calissians that etched a tempestuous loveliness in even the plainest faces.

Their confidence reflected an independent inner spirit that made Alonna think immediately of her homeland. The people of Caliss seemed different from the pale northerners she had encountered beyond the Danea River in vast Alasia.

And so, even as Alonna discovered herself in the most destitute of places, she reveled in the richness of the people that surrounded her. That, in part, eased her homesickness. It gave her hope that the future stretching ahead was not as bleak as her musings had convinced her on the lonely sea voyage that carried her from Zistah.

They had taken rooms in a sprawling stone inn. A painted wood sign above the door in the shape of a cluster of grapes identified it as the Wayfarer.

The inn—a rambling building crowding the summit of the headland—looked down a weedy green common to a sweeping vista of the bay and the leaden sea beyond. As Teraud counted coins from his shrinking supply, the portly, hawk-nosed innkeeper had flattered Alonna outrageously. The perceptive young woman knew his blandishments were based less in sincerity than a desire to curry favor with her father.

Though sparse, their rooms were adjoined by a door as Alonna had grown accustomed to on the journey. Alonna settled into her room while a cradle was hastily assembled for Vergal in her parents' chambers. As the wagon drivers unpacked their belongings, Alonna began to suspect with mounting anxiety that her stay at the Wayfarer might be protracted.

Her parents, their heads bent together on the bed in the middle of the commotion, whispered to each other but set their faces in wide smiles whenever Alonna tried to work her way closer to eavesdrop on their conversation.

They constantly deflected her questions, vexing Alonna greatly. But the flicker of fear the girl noted in their eyes belied their bright smiles, and Alonna, who felt pity for them without precisely knowing why, bit back her angry retorts.

In those days, the questions Alonna did permit herself veered wide of the subjects she learned brought anguish to her father and the haunted expression back into his eyes. She relented in her heated demands to know why the family had left Zistah and instead asked about their future in Caliss. Where would Father work? Where would they live?

Would the tutors she once had be restored to her in Caliss?

This last was of great concern to Alonna, who had enjoyed her education at Zistah. She harbored dreams of one day also teaching.

These speculations on the future delighted Teraud. He smoothed her inky hair and painted pictures with words of a fine house in the city noble's quarter, an army of tutors for herself and her baby brother Vergal, and he spoke proudly of the work he had secured as a scribe in the service of the king at Far.

Alonna smiled at Teraud's exaggeration. She suspected the casket of coins they had nearly depleted on the journey north fell far short of the price of a new home. And she doubted employment in the colony of a northern Pirate King could ever rival the income her father had earned from the Imperial Library at Zistah.

Alonna marveled at how her father had so suddenly uprooted the family and moved them away from their life of splendor in Zistah. She clearly saw the man in the long robes and the drooping eye, yelling at them from the steps of the pillared rotunda of the great library.

"They won't suffer it to be lost to them!" the librarian had yelled across the crowded boulevard after them.

Alonna closely searched her father's face, distracted as he spoke glowingly of their prospects for the future. She recalled how the librarian's shouted warning had bowed Teraud's head in shame. She felt the tightening grip of his hand on hers again. He had pulled Alonna into the concealing crowd, and, remembering that, Alonna realized something else: Her father had been frightened. The expression on his face had been desperate. What had the librarian's warning meant? The puzzle gave Alonna much to consider in the weeks to come.

Teraud began his service to the king's magistrate. He dressed again in finery, as in Zistah, although now his clothing was more suitable for a northern climate.

Outwardly, he must have appeared to the citizens of Caliss as the same wealthy scribe he had once been. But Alonna knew differently.

Teraud no longer spent his days transcribing great books of lore, as he had in Zistah. Alonna overheard him tell her mother how things had changed.

Now Teraud toiled in dim cellars beneath the manor, where the scribes worked busily by failing lantern light, copying tax records for delivery to the palace at Far. The king was a meticulous keeper of tax accounts, Teraud observed sourly, explaining how His Majesty considered even his own bureaucrats' modest incomes as a prolific source of revenues for his treasury. "Pirate King" was not a misnomer for the sovereign of the Aerie Coast, Teraud liked to scoff in private. And, indeed, the coins that her father added once a month to his casket appeared meager to Alonna in comparison to the great jingling purses he had deposited regularly with the moneychangers in Zistah. Alonna watched sadly as her father, the brilliant scribe once in the employ of the Arasynian Emperor, was reduced to a glorified bookkeeper.

Alonna was careful to position herself nearby whenever the cask was opened. Though a novice in economics, Alonna suspected the glittering heap inside the case—more interspersed now with silver and bronze than with gold—meant a home of the family's own remained out of reach. Glumly, Alonna began to despair that she would live in the Wayfarer's drafty rooms for the rest of her life.

The seasons turned, and Alonna grew a year older. Winter blanketed Caliss, and in the north, the season was a howling invader, its shrieking mouth stuffed with snow. The sharp cold was utterly foreign to anything in Alonna's experience.

The severe cold drove the family indoors, where they watched with amusement as Vergal took to clutching furniture and hauling himself up on pudgy, uncertain legs. Alonna, sunk in her own inner turmoil, had not concerned herself much with her younger brother in the past year, but she began to take note of him now.

It was difficult not to notice the boy as he discovered his legs were good for something other than sticking straight out in front of him. Vergal stumbled and bawled and laughed and clutched and dragged himself all about the rooms, making a general nuisance of himself but charming his older sister with his exuberant naughtiness.

With Vergal to entertain her and with happier dreams for the future to sustain her, Alonna passed the days of her first northern winter pleasantly, watching from the inn's windows as concealing snow softened Caliss's ugliness and blissfully ignorant of the horror that would visit her in the spring.

CHAPTER SEVEN

Having composed himself, Sh'ynryan hooked his hand under Vergal's arm and hauled him to his feet. He inspected the boy gravely for signs of injury and, seemingly satisfied, pulled Vergal after him down the dark narrow alley.

Vergal trembled violently but stumbled along obediently. "Where are we going?" he chattered.

"But I've already told you," Sh'ynryan replied. His tone was mocking, but his voice sounded as shaky as Vergal's own. A plunge into a solid stone wall apparently took its toll, even on monsters. "Think!" Sh'ynryan demanded. "Don't you remember our discussion over supper?"

Suddenly Vergal did remember. "The March!" he exclaimed.

Sh'ynryan smiled. "Yes. The March."

"But how will we get there?" Vergal's eyes grew wide as a horrible thought occurred to him.

"We won't ... I mean, it won't be like on the roof, or at the wall..." This time, the man laughed aloud. Sh'ynryan's manner grew more confident, less furtive, with every step that carried them away from the Wayfarer Inn. "You'll see," he said mysteriously, leaving Vergal to the mercy of his own imagination.

As the rain dried up, people began to trickle back into the streets. They emerged from taverns and houses, alleys and shops, careful to avoid the puddles of water that reflected the gibbous yellow moons that had reappeared in the storm-torn sky. Many people were raucous and rowdy, with the boisterous manners of those who had taken shelter from the storm in cups of ale and were now eager to resume their interrupted nocturnal carousing.

The street noise was familiar to Vergal, who had resided all his life in a port town, and it was even strangely comforting. The normalcy of his surroundings made him realize the world at large had remained the same throughout the surreal hour in which his had been irrevocably changed by the appearance of Sh'ynryan.

They walked briskly over the wet stones, through the growing crush of people. Vergal, still panicked and dreaming of escape, sought the faces of passing strangers, fantasizing that someone would recognize his plight and somehow intervene to save him.

However, nobody did. Those who looked at all did so with the briefest of glances. Vergal reminded himself that even if someone took note of his predicament, no resident of Caliss could possibly oppose the will of Sh'ynryan nor stop him from exacting the vengeance against Alonna that he had implacably set as the price of Vergal's disobedience.

Vergal began to whimper again, squeezing his eyes against tears of self-pity. He hung his head and collapsed into abject thoughts as he walked.

"Here we are," Sh'ynryan said at length.

A large stone stable rose in front of them. The building abutted a stretch of the city walls, not far from the city gates. Unlike the tall, red tile-roofed buildings that huddled together on the narrow street, the whitewashed stable occupied a straw-strewn square all its own. The stench of animals and manure that emanated from the yard immediately told Vergal why. He wrinkled his nose as the overwhelming odors bombarded him.

Despite the late hour, people and animals crowded the stable and its wet square. Horses and mules stood together in cramped corrals, grazing on hay forked over the fence to them. The stable hands moved among the animals, shoveling waste, grooming coats, fitting tack and harness. Beyond the corrals, the doors to the stable proper stood open, and a guttering wedge of torchlight spilled onto the flagstones. Sh'ynryan guided Vergal toward these doors.

"I don't suppose you ride?" Sh'ynryan asked without looking at him.

The question caught Vergal unaware. "Horses?" he asked.

Sh'ynryan snorted. "No, fire-breathing griffins. Of course, horses! Use your sense, boy!"

"I've never been on a horse."

Sh'ynryan nodded glumly but offered no reply.

Inside the stable, an overweight man in a burn-spotted leather apron stood plunging red-glowing tongs into a barrel of water. Steam hissed off the seething water with every dip. A door stood open behind him to a simple smithy where metal implements hung from pegs lining bare stone walls. The doorframe mostly concealed a large black anvil in the room. A smoky red light indicated a forge somewhere just out of Vergal's sight.

"Gelbrek?" Sh'ynryan called.

The man at the barrel turned at his name. He fanned his hand to disperse the veil of steam and pulled the tongs from the barrel. Vergal saw a horseshoe clamped there.

The smith approached them, wiping his hands on his apron.

"I am Gelbrek, aye, what of it?" he said brusquely. The man's lids narrowed to slits in the puffy flesh enveloping his eyes. "What business have I with you?"

"I wish to buy fresh horses for a journey."

"Then talk to my men outside," Gelbrek said gruffly, turning away. "They will sell you an animal as easily as I."

"You are the owner here, are you not?" Sh'ynryan pressed. "I think I prefer to deal with you directly."

Gelbrek grunted and continued to the barrel.

"You deal in goods other than horses," Sh'ynryan called after him.

The man paused, his back to the pair.

Sh'ynryan's voice took on a needling tone. "Or have I been misinformed as to the variety of your selection?"

Gelbrek turned back, his face expressionless.

"I deal in horses, livestock, and equipment," he mumbled. "I am a smith. That is all. Whatever else you seek is unavailable here."

Sh'ynryan smiled placidly. *"Falfrayed,"* he said suddenly.

Vergal glanced at Sh'ynryan, puzzled. *Falfrayed.* What sort of gibberish was that? Vergal assumed he misheard, but then his mouth gaped in fear. Was Sh'ynryan speaking another of his powerful words?

Vergal's eyes shot to Gelbrek, who he half-expected to see consumed by a pillar of fire or thrown suddenly across the room to be impaled on the sharp implements hanging on the walls.

The word had a much different effect on Gelbrek. His brow expectantly lifted as he stood across the room from Sh'ynryan.

"Oh, come now, Gelbrek, that's what you need to hear, is it not?" Sh'ynryan said. "Please do not tell me I have spent good coin and precious time chasing down your code word, only to find it worthless. That would leave me with a rather sour view of your network's efficacy, sir."

A sly expression crossed Gelbrek's face. He craned his neck to peer past Sh'ynryan. He tipped them a lopsided smile devoid of several teeth and raised a pudgy hand to beckon the pair forward. He crossed the floor to a horse stall located on the far side of the stable.

Sh'ynryan followed wordlessly, Vergal in tow.

The stall door squeaked open to reveal Gelbrek on his knees, patting the straw on the floor with outstretched hands. Finding something, Gelbrek made a fist and heaved.

A rusty screech reverberated as a trapdoor, concealed in the floor beneath straw and a thin layer of dirt, yawned open. Flickering torchlight stabbed up from the shaft.

"Come," Gelbrek said, beckoning. With a nimbleness that belied his bulk, the smith swung his legs over the lip and disappeared into the hole.

Vergal turned wary eyes to Sh'ynryan. The fiery glare from the open trap door looked to Vergal's fanciful imagination like the mouth of a dragon.

The boy shied at the prospect of jumping into the creature's throat.

"Come, Vergal," Sh'ynryan said, ignoring the boy's stricken expression. He nudged Vergal toward the trapdoor. The two peered inside.

Firelight danced on stone walls that trickled moisture. Wooden steps a short way down the wall descended steeply to a bare earth floor. Vergal placed a cautious foot inside, then started down.

He dismounted in a narrow corridor that ended in darkness just beyond a lone torchlight. Sh'ynryan followed him down the stairs and, pausing briefly to get his bearings, pushed Vergal into the gloom ahead of him.

They turned a sharp corner to find Gelbrek waiting nearby; a hooded lantern held level with his head.

"Here," Gelbrek rumbled. He trained his lamp's thin beam on a bronze-bound oak door. Without another word, he opened the door and walked inside. Light spilled out the half-open portal, cutting a fiery wedge out of the darkness.

"What is this place? What are we doing here?" Vergal whispered.

"Buying horses. Be quiet! Move!"

After the secret trap door and the crooked approach down the foreboding tunnel, Vergal feared to find a musty tomb or, worse, a dungeon behind the large door. He was unprepared for the sight that greeted him.

Braziers burnt merrily in alcoves that ringed a cavernous circular brick room. Thick carpets of various exotic weaves and colors were strewn over a polished stone floor. Tapestries draped the walls between the alcoves, and plush furniture stood everywhere—gleaming wood tables, overstuffed divans and chairs, marble statues, and tall shelves lined with leather-bound books.

The room buzzed with people and conversation. Men sat playing dice at a long oak table or lounged indolently in chairs, reading or dozing. Others sat sharpening weapons and talking amongst themselves, pausing to sip from foaming flagons.

To a man, all were smartly dressed in fine doublets and snug-fitting hose. Many wore rings and amulets that winked in the firelight, and their hair and beards were neatly groomed.

A sharp laugh intermittently punctuated the drone of voices before dissolving into the background hum of conversation. Some men glanced briefly at the new arrivals only to turn back to their original pursuits, seemingly disinterested in the visitors.

Vergal's fears of a smoky dungeon, well-stocked with manacles and chains, racks and thumbscrews, melted away. Sh'ynryan took in the room with a glance and smiled slyly at Gelbrek, who had snuffed his lantern and now stood facing them.

"I see I was not misinformed," Sh'ynryan said.

"For the price you paid, I certainly hope not," Gelbrek answered cordially, all trace of his former gruff manner now disappeared. The man smiled broadly, showcasing straight if somewhat yellowed teeth that shone dully in the braziers' light.

Vergal blinked, astonished. He was sure the man had been missing several teeth moments earlier!

"You'll find I am a man who delivers the service for which I'm paid," Gelbrek said.

"And you'll find money does not present an obstacle to me," Sh'ynryan replied, with a flick of his hand. It reminded Vergal of his mannerisms at the Wayfarer Inn. "I expect to pay for services I demand, so we should get along famously," Sh'ynryan added.

"So you shall, and so we will!" Gelbrek exclaimed, slapping one meaty hand on his thigh.

The smith gestured to a couch. Above it, an exquisite tapestry rendered a knight lancing a fanciful dragon that curled and twisted in a lurid caricature of its death throes.

"Please, rest," Gelbrek bade them. "I'll have drink and food brought to us. Let us conduct our business in comfort, as befits gentlemen who demand the best."

Gelbrek laughed again, a hearty, infectious sound that even coaxed a grin from Vergal. Sh'ynryan, however, was no longer smiling.

"My time is limited," he said. "I would discuss our business and be away."

"You know, then, the services and goods I offer?" Gelbrek said. He lowered his bulk onto the cushy seat, apparently untroubled by Sh'ynryan's demand for haste.

"I do."

"Then tell me, what do you require?"

"As I've said, I require horses. Two of your finest mounts, for much depends on their speed and endurance."

Gelbrek nodded. "These things I can provide easily. You need not have sought out my agent nor risked yourself to attain my code for that. Those wares are available to anyone who visits my humble stable."

"There is more."

"Ah," said Gelbrek, leaning back easily. "I thought perhaps there might be. Please, go on."

"I require passage out of the city with this boy."

"But the city gates are a stone's throw from here, friend, and the passage is free. Why do you come to me for this?" Gelbrek's voice had taken on a bantering tone.

Sh'ynryan smiled thinly in response but said nothing.

"My reputation precedes me," Gelbrek said at length, slapping his thigh again. "I can see the breadth of my services is known to you. Well enough then; I can provide this thing for you as well. And your reason for avoiding the city gate is none of my affair, so long as your coin is the right color."

"Then my coin buys your discretion as well as your wares?" Sh'ynryan asked.

"Friend, my service is built upon discretion," Gelbrek said seriously. "Any other goods I offer are peripheral to that central need of all my clients. They come to me—and they return to me—because my silence is guaranteed. Good commerce, especially in my line, is built upon a satisfied customer."

Sh'ynryan nodded as if he had anticipated this answer.

"But the question remains," Gelbrek drawled, tossing one round arm casually across the back of the couch, "how fare you at keeping secrets?"

"I offer nothing less in return for what I ask," Sh'ynryan replied.

Gelbrek clasped his hands and leaned forward to rest his elbows on his knees. His smile faded. All trace of his previous good humor had flown.

"That's good news indeed, my friend," he said ominously. "Because if ever I learn you breathed one word of me to any authority, in Caliss or elsewhere, I'll have you gutted and your carcass tossed to the dogs before dawn the next day."

Vergal recoiled at the threat. To his amazement, the smirk stayed glued to Sh'ynryan's face throughout the exchange.

"Then we understand each other," Gelbrek said, clapping his hands together and rubbing them briskly. "Splendid! Now that we have dispensed with obligatory caveats, shall we resume our business?"

Sh'ynryan said nothing.

"Your horses can be ready immediately, well-rested and ready for the road," Gelbrek continued. "You can be outside the city walls with your mounts in the space of an hour, with none the wiser. But I sense our business does not conclude there."

"I require supplies and rations, enough for a long journey for three people, traveling lightly and quickly."

"Three people? By my count, you are two." The fat man tipped a sly wink at Sh'ynryan. "Have we arrived, then, at the real reason you sought out old Gelbrek the smith?"

"Indeed," Sh'ynryan replied coolly. He gestured to take in the men lounging around the wide brick room. "In addition, I wish to hire a companion to travel alongside us."

Gelbrek reclined and crossed his ankles comfortably. "And that, my valued customer, is Gelbrek's specialty!"

CHAPTER EIGHT

The gold changed Alonna's life drastically. No matter how many times she dipped into the purse in the weeks following Vergal's abduction, she seemed hardly able to put a dent in it. But spending the money was not always easy.

Nearly every day, she packed a bag with some of her carefully folded new clothing and sneaked into the merchant's quarter. There she found an alley or a dense copse of trees in one of the quarter's many parks and hurriedly changed into garb more befitting the upscale surroundings. To perfect her guise, she had purchased several small, beautiful items of jewelry which she wore on such occasions. She especially favored an ivory cameo she wore on a thin gold chain at her throat, and she was equally fond of an engraved gold circlet she used to bind her flowing black hair.

The rings and ornaments she wore were fripperies, meant only to bolster her disguise. The cameo and circlet, however, she loved. The cameo's creamy silhouette somehow reminded her of her mother. And the circlet arranged her hair in a manner that allowed several curly tendrils to escape and bounce elegantly on her bare neck and shoulders as she walked. Alonna noticed the style was fashionable among the quarter's society women and, regardless, she thought her cascading ringlets made her look fetching.

The men of the quarter appeared to agree. She was quite unprepared for the attention her unattended strolls attracted. Her would-be suitors' blandishments ranged from forward to shy, and though Alonna found some of the more modest men to her liking, she rebuffed them all.

She had no time for distractions. Despite the luxuries her gold afforded, Alonna never forgot how she had obtained it or who had provided it. As she walked the boulevards and streets of the cramped and busy merchants' quarter, her only concern was to quickly procure the goods she needed to begin her hunt for her brother's abductor.

She intended to kill that man when she found him.

Alonna tried to appreciate the humor of her situation—melting discreetly into the bushes as a pauper only to emerge again as something resembling a princess—but her clandestine trips to the quarter were beginning to make her feel ludicrous. Arriving there dressed in the simple linen of a servant, only to spend her time there resplendent in gleaming finery seemed a preposterous thing to do, an affront to her newfound dignity.

Alonna longed to drop the facade altogether, take a room at a posh inn somewhere in the quarter, and stop sneaking about. But she convinced herself the pretense was necessary. She knew well the value of the coins she carried, and a serving girl from the docks in possession of a laden pouch would raise unwanted attention and suspicion in the quarter. Nor could she leave the Wayfarer already dressed in her gowns. That would provoke a barrage of questions for which she had no ready answers and likely lead to a search of her room by Carek or someone more unsavory.

Lodging somewhere in the wealthy districts of the port town would also only beg unwanted attention from the royal tax collectors, whose avarice was renowned.

So Alonna continued her charade.

She worked mornings at the Wayfarer for the pittance she could barely restrain from throwing back in Carek's face. At night, she stole to the merchant's quarter to take her evening meal and haunt the warren of crooked streets and boulevards that housed the expensive shops of the port town, like the woman of means she had secretly become.

The cramped space beneath the floorboards at the Wayfarer was now stuffed with sundries, so she took to secreting her new purchases in a secure room at a warehouse. The owner there was an affable retired soldier who took his commission seriously, and executed it discreetly, and employed a phalanx of guards to reinforce his resolve to protect his customers' goods.

It was there Alonna stored her latest purchases: A pair of slender, curving swords the weapon-smith who sold them called "scimitars." The swords were favored weapons of the desert nomads of faraway Zistah, the smith explained, exotic things rarely seen in the north. Alonna had never seen their like. The gently curving blades entranced her. And when she had scrapped her finger along the edge of one to test its sharpness, it had instantly drawn blood. Smiling grimly, Alonna had smeared her finger along the length of the polished steel, enjoying the way her reflection blurred behind the sheen of blood.

She vividly imagined plunging the blades through the scarlet robes of the man who had abducted Vergal.

Now she need only learn how to use them.

On a moonless night, harbor fog drifting inland to blanket Caliss in a damp mist, Alonna trod a crooked alley hugging the city's eastern wall. She walked furtively, moving through the wells of shadows lacing the walls between lights thrown from upper story windows. She discarded both the frills of the merchant's quarter and the livery of a tavern maid for more utilitarian wear. Her soft leather boots reached nearly to her knee. She wore a murky frock over supple buckskin breeches, all concealed beneath a cowled black cloak that nearly brushed the ground as she walked.

She was dressed precisely according to the instructions of the swarthy little man to whom the weapon-smith had introduced her.

Alonna fidgeted with the new scimitars holstered uncomfortably beneath her cape. She followed the exact route along the wall the little man had described. His veiled threats should she disregard his orders still resonated but did not deter her purpose.

A chill, which had nothing to do with the clammy mist, coursed down Alonna's spine. It seemed surreal to know her martial training would soon begin. Her breath escaped in excited gasps as she prowled the alley.

The alley turned abruptly, opening into the street beyond. Alonna pressed to the wall, taking stock of the busy road from between the buildings that bracketed the entrance to the alley.

Across the street, a whitewashed stable abutted the wall next to the city gates. The road separating the alley from the stable was thick with pedestrians and rumbling carts. Early evening traffic passed quickly through city gates that would soon be closed and bolted for the night.

Her mysterious contact had been clear that nobody should observe her entering the stable. Yet Alonna had no idea how to cross the intervening space without spurning that command.

Alonna stood there for long moments in the darkness, considering. She screamed when a vice-like hand fastened to her shoulder.

"Quiet!" a low voice hissed in her ear.

Pain shot through Alonna's shoulder as the talon-like fingers dug into her cloak and bruised the flesh beneath. She tasted leather as a second gloved hand clamped across her mouth.

Her heart thumping, Alonna fumbled with the scimitar's hilt beneath her cloak, but she was thrown heavily to the ground before she could draw the weapon.

Green eyes flashed in an errant bar of light that stabbed the alley from the street beyond. The rest of her assailant's face was lost in shadow, concealed beneath a cowl, not unlike her own. The man held a cudgel in one gloved fist. He tapped it absently against one thigh.

"I'll have your coins, miss." The voice drifting down to her sounded cold, venomous. "Then what might I take next?"

The cudgel rose in the air.

Spurred by panic, Alonna yanked mightily on the hilt of her scimitar. It rattled noisily from its sheath. Lying prone on the cold stones of the alley, she held the blade above her in a warding gesture.

"Back away!" she screeched at the man, who stepped back a pace at the sight of the sleek curling blade.

Alonna dug the heels of her boots into the alley and pushed herself backward on her bottom. She leveled the blade on the dark figure looming above. Her arms ached from holding the weight of the sword directly in front of her body. Its wicked point began to waver.

"I warn you, I will defend myself," Alonna warned in a voice she tried to make sound threatening, but which warbled with terror. "Move away from me!"

The man responded by swinging his cudgel, expertly slapping the scimitar out of her grasp. It skittered loudly across the paved stones, plowing a wispy furrow in the mist. The mist washed back in on itself, concealing the weapon.

She reached for her second blade, but a booted foot kicked her hand, pitching her arm wide to the side before she could draw it.

The figure advanced a step. Sobbing from fright, Alonna reacted by driving her leg straight out in front of her. The heel of her boot solidly connected with the man's knee, resulting in a satisfying cracking sound.

The man bawled an oath and toppled, clutching his leg.

Alonna scrambled to her feet, pulled out the remaining scimitar, and pointed it toward the fallen man. He writhed on the ground between her and the exit to the street. The tip of the blade shook in front of her. Alonna edged slowly around the man, one eye on her assailant, the other scanning the ground for her lost scimitar. Her heart thumped wildly in her breast. Tears fractured her vision. Her wrist throbbed where the man had kicked her.

The prone man snatched at Alonna's foot as she passed. Frightened and angry, she instinctively sidestepped and retaliated with a sweeping kick that caught him full in the cheek. The man's head rocked from the force of the blow and thudded on the stones. He groaned once, then lay still.

Edging forward, Alonna poked out her boot and nudged back the cowl obscuring the man's face. She swore when she recognized the smarmy features of the agent she had paid to introduce her to a sword trainer.

"You bastard," she breathed. Her adrenalin pumping, she drew back her foot and prepared to deliver another kick to the unconscious man's face.

"Stop!" an urgent voice demanded from the shadows. Alonna spun, nearly dropping her sword.

Nothing there, only mist snaking down the alley.

"I'm afraid I cannot allow that, dear," the unseen watcher said, a tinge of regret, perhaps, in the voice.

Unnerved, Alonna turned and ran. She skidded to a halt when two figures stepped around the corner ahead. The streetlight filling in around them eclipsed their features. The silhouettes did not advance on her. They stood impassively, blocking passage to the street.

"What do you want?" Alonna cried. She turned all about, searching the shadows for the unseen voice. "Let me go! Just leave me alone!"

The voice again, soft, soothing, said, "Leave you alone?" A soft chuckle slid out of the darkness. "My dear, it was you who sought out us."

CHAPTER NINE

It seemed to Vergal, on those rare occasions he cared to revisit it, the nightmare of his abduction had been painted in flickering firelight. From the sooty red glow of the tunnel leading to Gelbrek's underground sanctum to the brazier-lit illumination of the lair itself, Vergal remembered most of the blurred hours since his rude awakening by the half-light of torches.

Nothing changed after Sh'ynryan and Gelbrek concluded their business. Two brawny men led them out of Gelbrek's complex and through yet another damp earth tunnel, holding torches aloft to light the way.

The men had blindfolded Sh'ynryan's newly purchased horses and now walked stealthily ahead of them. Only the spitting of torches, the fall of horses' hooves, and the dripping of water in the distance broke the eerie stillness.

Vergal's terror at being snatched from his room had been replaced by an exasperation at the monotony of his predicament. His lack of sleep and the lateness of the hour combined to make him surly, and, braving much, he turned his annoyance on Sh'ynryan.

"Wherever we're going, is most of the way under the ground?" Vergal asked acidly. He was tired and irritable; his feet ached from constant trudging.

Sh'ynryan looked down and chortled. "So, the cub has teeth," he replied simply and returned his gaze to the torchlight floating above the undulating rumps of the horses ahead of him.

I hope the horse kicks you in the face, Vergal thought sourly, though he kept his internal ruminating private from his captor. The passage stretched onward, and Vergal fell into his silent musings.

After a distance, Vergal noted a slight rise in the tunnel that became pronounced. The blindfolded horses grew restless, whinnying and snorting eagerly for the fresh air ahead even before Vergal detected a lightening in the surrounding darkness.

The ruffians guiding them took turns extinguishing their torches. In the absence of the crackling flames, Vergal heard rise an undercurrent of cricket song. He strained his ears and made out the soughing of the wind in the leaves of trees. A fresh night breeze suddenly caught him in the face, chasing the tunnel's stagnant air out of his nostrils. Relief flooded the weary boy, and his step quickened.

A few steps farther and the tunnel widened and lightened around a rock-hewn mouth. The group emerged beneath a glittering dome of stars arching above the ragged ring of surrounding night-time forest.

Sh'ynryan and Vergal glanced about to get their bearings, but their guides merely slipped the horses' reins into each of their hands and made quickly for the tunnel.

"Wait!" Sh'ynryan called, stepping after them but getting yanked back a step when his horse tossed its head. "There was to be another member of our party awaiting us."

The men's laughter rolled back hollowly from the tunnel. "Oh, that one's about, never you fear," one called, his voice receding with distance. "He'll find you soon enough."

Vergal couldn't tell if that sounded like a reply or a threat.

Sh'ynryan continued to scan the surrounding darkness, but Vergal craned his neck to drink in the star-filled sky. Away from the lights of Caliss, the night sky blazed in a spectacle of heavenly light. Stars glared everywhere to fill the eye—a glorious backdrop for the twin moons that rode above the forest canopy.

Vergal remembered Alonna telling him how some sages believed every star was a sun, shining down on a different world like unto their own. The theory struck him as fanciful, but Vergal experienced an odd shrinking sensation as he gazed into the shining night sky. It invited him to imagine his insignificant existence within that vast cosmic scope, as he once had in relating his maps to the broader world encompassing him. The expanse above dwarfed him; he felt infinitely smaller than a speck of sand, on a desert blanketing a world. His mind reeled at the concept.

A jingling of harness ended his reverie. A man mounted on a roan steed materialized ghost-like from the trees. He reined his horse and sat regarding them from his mount, a lopsided grin stretching his lips.

"Ah, you would be my prospective employer, no doubt," the man called in a booming voice that sounded like a laugh.

Sh'ynryan scowled and waved his hands. "Be silent, man!" he hissed. "You'll have the city guard down on us!"

The man on the horse grinned again. Vergal noticed how his lips couldn't seem to stretch in a straight line. Instead, they lifted at one corner or the other to display white teeth that gleamed in the starlight. He clicked his tongue to still his prancing roan before swinging deftly from the saddle. A faint rattling of chain mail accompanied the man's movements, but his rich surcoat concealed the armor.

Nonplussed, the man continued in the same hearty voice, "Oh, you need not fear the guard, friend. I don't know how far you think you journeyed through Gelbrek's tunnel, but I assure you it is much farther than you imagine. The walls of Caliss are well away from this place."

Sh'ynryan said nothing, only pinioned the man beneath a penetrating stare.

The man shrugged, unconcerned by the scrutiny. He turned to rummage through a saddlebag. Vergal took the opportunity to study the newcomer.

The man stood perhaps a hand's length shorter than Sh'ynryan, though he was not so thin. The distinct curvature of a well-muscled arm lifted the loose sleeve of his surcoat. He wore his medium-length black hair in a mass of curls that spilled over his shoulders and bounced when he moved. A trim black beard framed his crooked smile. He wore calf-length leather boots. His long surcoat, embroidered on the front in silver thread with a dragon figure, was cinched at the waist by a broad belt from which depended a scabbard. The jeweled hilt of a longsword flashed in the moonlight above its sheath.

The man, sensing the scrutiny, tipped Vergal an exaggerated wink. The boy flushed scarlet to realize he had been staring. Vergal lowered his head, embarrassed, and pretended to find something of absorbing interest on his shoes.

"I'll have your name, man," Sh'ynryan said brusquely.

The man in the surcoat laughed, his eyebrows lifting. "Will you, now?" he asked heartily. "Would that be the name my blessed mother gave me those years ago or the name by which my fellow scoundrels have come to know me?"

Vergal caught another quick wink from the dark-haired newcomer during this exchange. The man's sideways grin had not faltered, and even in the dim light, Vergal saw mirth dancing in the depths of his eyes.

Sh'ynryan, caught off balance, scowled, and the man laughed once more—a robust, infectious sound.

Vergal felt a smile stretching his lips. Did this man take anything seriously? A mental image rose of the bearded newcomer stretched out on a rack, his thumbs in screws but laughing all the while in the face of his frustrated torturer. That made Vergal laugh aloud, earning a dark frown from Sh'ynryan.

The man smiled, dragging a gloved thumb to scratch the thin hair under his lip. "Let's discuss the business at hand then, shall we?" he said. "If we will be sharing the road, as Gelbrek informs me, I propose we put forward some names."

He bowed with a flourish, keeping one hand wrapped on his sword hilt as he bent forward. "I am called Guile," he said, straightening. "It's not my given name, you understand, but one I've grown fond of over the years and one, I think, not entirely unsuited to my character."

His gaze moved earnestly between Sh'ynryan and Vergal. "And how may I call my new travel companions?" the man called Guile asked.

Sh'ynryan glared coldly at the man. "Listen to me," he said at length, in the dead tone that so chilled Vergal. "I do not easily suffer fools. I paid Gelbrek for an experienced sword to accompany us. I did not part with good money to coddle a fop with an uncontrolled sense of humor."

The smile never melted from Guile's face, but the man's reply matched Sh'ynryan's for coldness.

"I appreciate your honesty. Now, listen to me," Guile said. His voice dripped venom in a manner incongruous with the merry countenance affecting his face. "The money you paid Gelbrek was for the privilege of this introduction, nothing more. The real fee for the best swordsman in Caliss, I think you'll find, does not come cheaply. I alone decide with whom I travel, and, I warn you now, you appear exactly the sort of a sour, arrogant wretch I absolutely detest."

He gestured at Vergal. "If not for this likely looking lad beside you, I am inclined to believe my sword would already have found your ribs, and I'd be on my way down that tunnel, with your purse for my troubles and some choice words for that fat slob Gelbrek for wasting my time."

Sh'ynryan's mouth gaped. He sputtered to reply.

Guile held up a hand, shaking his head. The merry light remained in his eyes as if he had not, in the span of his last breath, just uttered a deadly threat. "Now, what say we begin these introductions anew, eh? I think now you see the situation in its proper light, and we can discuss business in a forthright manner, without misunderstanding."

Guile slid with a crash to one knee in front of Vergal, gripping the boy's shoulders in a companionable manner.

"So, what say you, lad?" he boomed, "Have you a tongue in your mouth to tell ol' Guile your name?"

"I am Vergal, sir," he replied instantly, compelled by the good manners Alonna had worked hard to instill in him.

Sh'ynryan had found his voice again. "Silence, boy," he growled.

"Still surly, I see," Guile sighed. He stood to face Sh'ynryan but not before rolling his eyes and grinning at Vergal.

"Forgive my abruptness just now, but I believe it best we clear any lingering misconceptions early in our professional association." Guile looked Sh'ynryan evenly in the eyes. "Certainly, I am not prepared to cast you perpetually considering my first impressions, and I am confident by now you realize your mistaken assessment of me as a—what was that you called me? A fop? Eh? What? Ha!"

Sh'ynryan looked speculatively at Vergal, who was in turn regarded the mercenary with undisguised admiration. A grin slowly replaced the man's scowl.

"Very well, then ... Guile, was it?" Sh'ynryan said at length. "You obviously are not the vacuous fool I first assumed. I regret the misunderstanding. In fact, considering things further, I believe you may be exactly the man I need for the trek that the boy and I are planning."

Sh'ynryan extended one gaunt hand to Guile, who clasped it.

"Since the boy so willingly offered his name, I see no point withholding mine. I am called Sh'ynryan."

"Excellent!" Guile said expansively, rubbing his gloved hands together briskly. "Just excellent; this is starting out just fine."

Guile waved a leather-gauntleted hand at the dark forest behind him. "I've taken the liberty to set camp in the shelter of the trees. There we can rest and refresh ourselves and discuss the outstanding matter of my payment. And Vergal looks ready for a warm bedroll. It's nearly morning, and the lad seems set to fall asleep on his feet!"

It was true. The rush of adrenaline that had sustained him through the men's exchange was ebbing. The weariness plaguing Vergal in Gelbrek's tunnels returned with full force. The boy could scarcely believe it had been mere hours since Sh'ynryan had roused him from his sleep and carried him into a waking nightmare, away from the Wayfarer, Alonna, and everything else solid and real in his life.

Guile covered the distance to his mount in a few long strides and swung smoothly into the saddle. "Follow me," he said, yanking the reins to turn the roan toward the forest.

Vergal, who had never ridden before, had a hard time hoisting himself into the saddle. Sh'ynryan, grumbling, pushed the boy until he could swing his leg over.

And, that quickly, Vergal found himself astride the broad back of a horse for the first time in his life.

From his loft, the ground seemed a dizzying distance away. The horse snorted, tossing its head irritably. Vergal gripped the saddle horn in a death-lock. The animal seemed to sense his handler's inexperience and promptly expressed its contempt. The beast pawed the ground, grunted several times, and refused to budge when Vergal gave a half-hearted tug on the reins in a bid to start it moving. The boy looked at Sh'ynryan helplessly.

Now mounted on his own steed, Sh'ynryan leaned in to snatch the reins out of Vergal's white-knuckled fist. "I'll lead you tonight, Vergal," he said, "but we'll be riding hard in days ahead, and I expect you to learn to ride this animal, and quickly!"

Not awaiting a reply, Sh'ynryan set heels to his horse and lurched forward, jerking the reins of Vergal's horse taut behind him. They trotted toward the trees into which Guile had disappeared.

A rough and frightening ride through dense brush, in which lashing branches bent by the passage of Sh'ynryan's mount slapped and stung Vergal, brought them shortly to Guile. The man had picketed his horse in a nearby copse of aspens and stood watching them approach from beside a cheerily blazing campfire in a grassy clearing. A lean-to stood at the edge of the firelight, hastily constructed from a toppled aspen trunk and draped with saddle blankets to break the wind.

The pair picketed their horses and drew near the fire. "I am happy to share my meal," Guile said, pointing to a slab of meat impaled on a spit above the flames. "I don't know if this is a late supper or an early breakfast, but I'm famished."

Guile leaned in to turn the spit, sending the scent of roasting meat wafting into Vergal's flaring nostrils. The boy was suddenly ravenous, but the thought of spreading his bedroll close to the fire and falling instantly to sleep appealed to him even more.

As Guile and Sh'ynryan settled cross-legged in front of the fire, Vergal stretched his blanket near the circle of warmth and rolled into it. The boy almost instantly fell back into the exhausted slumber that had been dramatically interrupted so many hours before.

CHAPTER TEN

"Don't fret so, dear; he'll recover," Gelbrek told Alonna. He patted her shoulder reassuringly. "All of my men appreciate the risk involved in these initiations." He laughed heartily. "Though I dare say, you gave our friend Rostalin much more than he expected from this assignment!"

Alonna looked numbly up into the fat man's face. His shiny features were stretched in a merry smile. She turned her eyes again to Rostalin, the man who had accosted her in the alleyway, who lay prone on a divan in the circular brick chamber beneath Gelbrek's stables. Rostalin's cheekbone was a sunset of bruising where Alonna had kicked him, and the man's knee was bandaged tightly to immobilize a fractured bone. Rostalin's swollen face appeared sullen. As Alonna watched, another man approached him and made a comment that caused the newcomer to laugh and provoked a dark scowl from Rostalin.

Gelbrek nudged her and tipped an outrageous wink. "Believe me; he's thankful you aimed where you did. A little higher, and the damage could have been much crueler."

Alonna did not feel nearly so cheerful. She only half-remembered the jaunt through the warren of tunnels into which Gelbrek and his men led her after accessing a trap door in an abandoned building near the alley where she had encountered Rostalin. The tunnels had dripped with inky water and carried a fetid stench. Gelbrek said they were following an abandoned sewer beneath the street above.

That information had vaguely fascinated her, but the shock Alonna felt at the evening's events made it difficult to register everything happening.

"What is this place?" Alonna asked for the fifth time since Gelbrek had introduced her to his underground sanctuary.

Gelbrek sighed. He seated himself and patted the couch beside him to indicate Alonna should join him.

"I've already told you, dear," he answered patiently after Alonna settled beside him. The couch was comfortable, and the room exceedingly warm. Alonna felt the aches and bruises of the night's adventure keenly. She closed her eyes tightly, savoring the warmth from the crackling braziers ringing the colossal vault beneath the city streets.

"Told me what?" Alonna asked, reluctant to open her eyes and dispel her lethargy.

"I've told you what this place is. It's your new school. You paid us good gold to teach you how to use those keen swords of yours, and this is where your education continues. The fracas in the alley was only the beginning of your instruction."

Alonna's eyes opened but narrowed into hard slits. "You almost killed me! That man—he threatened to rob and ravish me! I was frightened as I have never been before. I was only defending myself."

"And you did an admirable job, never doubt!" Gelbrek laughed. Alonna frowned again. The man's constant jocularity was wearing on her.

"Do not fear," Gelbrek composed himself and continued. "Rostalin had no intention to rob or to ravish. Though, to be honest, had you made no move to defend yourself, he may have killed you on the spot."

Alonna stared at the man, horrified. The gaiety fled Gelbrek's face as he returned her scrutiny.

"You paid a terrific sum to be instructed in swordcraft," Gelbrek said evenly. "That signaled your seriousness about pursuing this training. We investigated you, you see, and we know quite well you are not some spoiled manor wife from the merchants' district, looking to alleviate her boredom."

He sat back again, relaxing. "In fact, Alonna, you've served many of the men in this room now in the Wayfarer's taproom. Rostalin knew who you were when he agreed to arrange this meeting."

Alonna couldn't keep the shock off her face. An appalling thought occurred to her. If these men knew where she lived and the sum she had paid, they might also know where she had stashed her money.

"That is some fine ale served at the Wayfarer," Gelbrek said wistfully. "But where were we? Ah, yes! You see, Alonna, desiring to train, even truly intending it, is not the same as committing. Therefore, it was needful that we test your resolve to learn if you were worthy of our time. Having money to pay is a small thing in comparison. We don't know where you got the money, and we don't care. It's only a part of the equation."

He eyed her shrewdly before continuing. "Possessing the will to fight is the other. Had you submitted to Rostalin, well, perhaps we would not have seen much promise in you. And our blissful little company here cannot be compromised by those just browsing for services. We're in the business of selling!"

Gelbrek paused. When he spoke again, he did so slowly, deliberately. "Had you shown no fighting instinct, perhaps then we might have concluded it better for all involved if you simply were not able to browse elsewhere, hmm?"

Alonna's face grew ashen. She remembered her desperate instinct to flee the skirmish. She sublimated the urge then, but she trembled now when contemplating how near her impulse had come to getting herself killed.

"We do not play games, Alonna," Gelbrek said gravely. "I pray for your sake you are not playing games with us."

Alonna remembered the red-robed man who had stolen her brother. She recalled her satisfying daydreams of hunting down and slaying the abductor. She barely hesitated before she shook her head.

"I promise you on everything I hold dear, I am not," she vowed heatedly. "I want this … I need this! More than you know. I am willing to leave all behind if it is what you ask. I must learn what you can teach me."

Gelbrek looked in her eyes a long moment and then smiled.

"Excellent!" Gelbrek said, cheerful once again. He tapped her knee lightly, fondly. "Your coin is good,

Alonna, and your courage cannot be faulted. You've made the right choice in coming to old Gelbrek. I think you'll find we train complete warriors, not fools who can waggle a sword."

A strange feeling of detachment stole over Alonna. Her old life was dead, she realized. The money had changed it, but her induction into this underground fellowship had completely buried it. She had taken her first step on a path shrouded in shadow, but one she exulted to see end in the death of the man who had abducted her brother. The vengeance she could never take on her parents' murderer would be visited instead upon the man who had stolen their son. And with that, Alonna and the spirits of Teraud and Marillee must be content.

"When do we start? What must I do?" she asked.

"What you must do is appear nightly at the house in the alley, beneath which we entered the catacombs. You will be brought here, and we will instruct you in the use of those beautiful weapons at your waist. And if you prove worthy, perhaps in time, old Gelbrek will allow you to earn back a portion of the princely sum you've paid us, eh?

"As for when you start," he added expansively, leaning back to relax, "well, dear, you have already begun."

—⚔—

Alonna emerged later from beneath the floor of the deserted building to stand alone in the dark. Her mind spun from the gravity of the evening's momentous events. Her recollections bordered on the surreal. Was it possible she had fended off an armed mercenary, won the admiration of a thief prince, and enrolled to learn to train as a killer?

Alonna laughed gruffly. It seemed unlikely, yet as she trudged through the back alleys of Caliss on her way back to the Wayfarer, she realized the surreal had become real.

She was nearing the Wayfarer, wondering how best to sneak through the kitchen past Carek in her surreptitious clothing, when she came under attack once again.

Alonna sniffed the fiery alcohol on the man's breath the instant he exploded from under a pile of rubbish stacked in a nearby doorway. He was a bear of a man, and Alonna read the intent in his bloodshot eyes as he covered the distance between them, gibbering insanely.

With a detachment she thought herself incapable, Alonna unsheathed her scimitar in a fluid motion and set herself for his charge. She sidestepped his rush and lashed out with the flat of her blade as he stumbled past. The blade cracked loudly on the back of the man's head, sending him sprawling. He slid a distance on his belly across the slick cobblestones; his hands splayed in front of him.

Trembling, she tentatively approached the fallen man and checked him for signs of life. He was unconscious but breathing. Blood seeped from a wide cut behind his ear. Alonna turned the man's head to the side so that he could breathe easier. She stood up, gaping in wonder at the silvery blade that had felled the man.

Elation boiled inside her. She had vanquished two attackers in one night. She felt invincible; her course never seemed so sure.

Alonna spun at a sudden staccato noise behind her. Tracking it, she was astonished to see a dark figure crouching at the lip of a rooftop across the alley. She made out the bulky outline of a crossbow straddled across the man's knees. With his free hands, the man was clapping slowly, appreciatively.

Gelbrek, it appeared, had provided his new pupil an escort home.

Alonna smirked and raised her sword in a salute to her rooftop observer.

The man nodded in acknowledgment and vanished behind the overhanging ledge.

Alonna stood alone in the alley, with only the raspy breathing of the fallen drunkard to disturb the silence.

CHAPTER ELEVEN

The sun had cleared the tree line and beat full upon his face before Vergal stirred the following morning. His back ached, and one arm felt numb beneath him. He lifted his head and peered blankly through gummy eyes before realizing where he was and what had happened. Sh'ynryan stood speaking quietly with Guile across the clearing as the man toyed with various straps on his horse's saddle.

Sh'ynryan, a monstrous figure in the dark of night, appeared gaunt and tired by the blithe light of morning. The silver strands of the man's beard made his face appear old. His thin shoulders slumped wearily beneath the rich material of his cloak. Sh'ynryan looked almost feeble by the revealing glare of day, and Vergal felt emboldened as he took careful measure of the man's slight frame.

Then he remembered the terrible strength in those claw-like hands that had pinned him and the resonating power of the voice to which even the natural laws bowed. Vergal's shoulders sagged. It would not do to underestimate Sh'ynryan, he decided. He slumped miserably under his blankets.

The man's threats toward Alonna still rang in his ears: *Both you and your sister will suffer!* Sh'ynryan had warned.

No, it would not do for Vergal to forget with whom he dealt. Tears welled again as Vergal resigned himself to the fact his nightmare could not be banished, like every other bad dream he'd known, by the arrival of a new day.

A booted foot nudged him in the ribs. Vergal pulled down his blanket to find Sh'ynryan towering above him. The man looked at him speculatively, taking note of his tears.

"I thought you'd wept yourself dry last night, boy," he said harshly. "I suppose I was foolish to hope the arrangement we settled on would steel you for what lies ahead."

The mocking tone, despite his fear, angered the boy. He scrubbed his hand under his nose and eyes and scrambled out of his bedroll, fixing an angry glare on Sh'ynryan.

Sh'ynryan caught the boy's dark look. His eyebrows arched. "Was there something you wanted to say?"

Vergal only grumbled and, kicking his bedroll aside, strode purposefully away into the trees.

"Where do you think you're going?" Sh'ynryan called after him in a dangerous voice.

"To piss!" Vergal yelled in his best imitation of the salty sailor language used in the Wayfarer's taproom. "Or do we need an 'arrangement' for that too?"

Behind him, he heard Guile start to laugh.

Strips of left-over venison, eaten cold, were for breakfast. Vergal munched the stringy meat hungrily as they broke camp and prepared to depart. The trail they followed—a worn deer run, Vergal could see—was rugged and rutted. The path followed a rise littered with rock and the exposed roots of trees.

The horses' hooves often slipped on the loose rock. Vergal's horse seemed preoccupied with the steep path ahead and displayed none of the aggressive behavior of the night previous. It trailed Guile's lead horse closely. Vergal took advantage of the horse's passivity to get accustomed to the saddle. After a mile or so, the boy's legs were stiff, and his rear ached from the constant jostling, but he thought he was getting the idea of riding, if not yet becoming proficient. He even allowed himself a private smile of pride at his accomplishment. If Sh'ynryan, following silently behind him, took notice of the boy's achievement, he offered no comment.

The trio rode quietly against a backdrop of constant sound. Birds twittered noisily in the branches above them, and a brisk wind stirred the boughs of the trees, and, several times, Vergal heard branches snapping as something unseen but obviously large crashed through undergrowth back from the trail.

The sudden noises startled, but Guile seemed unconcerned, so Vergal convinced himself to relax. Vergal had only known Guile a short time, but he quickly had come to trust the judgment of the laughing man who led them through the unfamiliar woods. His demeanor exuded confidence. Guile sat straight in his saddle, attentive yet somehow still at ease. The man kept the dark hood of his cloak back from the curls of his carefully coiffed hair. He showed care to duck his head when the horses plunged through dense undergrowth, mindful not to tangle it. His careful affectation did not diminish the man's aura of competency, however. Whenever the crashing back in the brush intensified, Vergal reassured himself with a glance at the longsword riding at Guile's hip. Guile caught him looking on one such occasion and grinned reassuringly. "Likely just deer back in the wood," he said with a wink.

The Watergate Mountains shouldered above the tree line in the distance. Remembering his maps, Vergal placed himself somewhere north of Caliss though still west of the Danea River. His brow knit as he sought to recall a town or village somewhere ahead in their path. However, he could place none and concluded the party was striking deeper into the forested foothills beyond Caliss. He wondered where they were going, but he dared not ask.

The same thought must have struck Sh'ynryan. After an hour of loping along the path, Sh'ynryan suddenly spurred his horse to pull alongside Guile, who rode easily at the lead of their small column.

"Hold!" Sh'ynryan said, pushing his horse in front of Guile's, provoking the roan to flatten its ears and shy backward. "Where are you leading us? I told you we were headed east."

"And we are," Guile said simply, laying a gentle hand on the roan's neck.

"This path is turning north," Sh'ynryan yelled, stabbing a long finger ahead. Indeed, the jagged summits of the Watergates were blotting out more of the northern sky. "You're leading us out of our way!"

Guile's smile never faded, but Vergal saw a hint of the same stoniness that preceded his challenge to Sh'ynryan the night before.

"We must yet cross the Danea, and the river near the coast is wide and flat, but it narrows and is easy to cross further into the foothills. Besides, the most direct path isn't necessarily the fastest," Guile responded with a shrug.

He pointed back down the hill they had climbed. "The road east out of Caliss is thinly patrolled by the Aerie militia, and there is no official presence east of the river at all. The forests there have become refuges for brigands who would attack and kill us on sight, for no more than the clothes we wear."

Sh'ynryan's gaze followed the direction of Guile's finger, his expression thoughtful as he mulled the man's words.

"You hired me to escort you east," Guile said. "And you mentioned a deadline. Trust me when I say our detour will bring you to your destination much quicker than a path fraught with ambushes by the highwaymen infesting the lower road.

"A well-guarded caravan can make it unmolested through the stretch of road from the Danea to the March. A party of three, even if it does include the best swordsman on the coast, cannot."

Sh'ynryan stared levelly at Guile for a long moment, then shrugged. "I'm guilty of underestimating you again," he said. "You're proving yourself an apt guide and solicitous of our welfare. That is heartening. However, the deadline I mentioned is pressing. The need for haste is equal to that of stealth. If this path cannot deliver both, then I fear we must brave the lower road."

Sh'ynryan held up a long hand to ward off Guile's protests. "Now, let me assure you of something," he said. "These highwaymen you mentioned are of little concern to me. I have resources at hand to deal with their ilk. I'm asking you to trust what I say is so."

Guile looked dubious. Sh'ynryan smiled in response and jerked his head in the direction of Vergal. "If my word does not suffice, just ask the boy," he said. "I'm sure honesty compels him to verify what I say is true."

Vergal swallowed and, despite himself, nodded. He glanced up to see Guile regarding him carefully.

After a moment, the mercenary's roguish smile reappeared. Hilarity was never far below the surface in their guide. The thought reassured Vergal. A man who can laugh is a man who can reason, Vergal thought in another of those unformed but intuitive flashes that sometimes visited him.

"Well enough," Guile said expansively. "You are the client, after all. And my father's sword has occupied its sheath far too long these days in any case." He barked one of his contagious laughs. "I think I should like to meet up with a band of those criminals, after all. I would relish the chance to limber my sword arm."

"Just like that?" Sh'ynryan asked shrewdly. "You will take me on my word?"

"Oh, on your word, sure enough," Guile said, equally as sly. "On your word, but more eagerly on the bonus I will require to compensate me for the lumps and bruises your path is sure to inflict." The swordsman laughed again and set his heels to his horse's flanks, spurring it along a stony path.

Sh'ynryan winced but offered no reply. Vergal got the distinct impression Sh'ynryan had just been outmaneuvred in a negotiation he had not realized was underway.

The fight Guile predicted found them in short order.

They continued riding north, paralleling the river Vergal could hear flowing somewhere nearby to the east. True to Guile's word, the river narrowed as the land rose, and they found a ford to cross that soaked Vergal only to the knees of his hose rather than to the neck of his tunic. The land east of the Danea—now officially Arasynian Alasia, their guide reminded them—was wild and broken, thick with evergreens. They waited by the bank of the river while Guile plunged his horse into the trees and crashed about for what seemed a long time. He returned to announce his discovery of a path, and the company struck out on it. Guile ushered his charges through the trampled underbrush to a narrow deer run, then down a steep slope upon which the horses scrambled through hoof-deep leaf litter.

His horse's rump lifted higher than its head as the animal picked its way down the bank, forcing Vergal to lean back sharply in his saddle to avoid pitching to the ground. His impromptu education in horsemanship had been seriously accelerated. He suspected a failing grade in this latest test might result in a broken neck. Grimacing at every slip of his mount's hooves, Vergal gripped the horn of the saddle in one hand as tightly as his awkward angle would allow and held the reins firmly in another.

The ground leveled, then dropped, then leveled again in a series of undulations over loamy soil as the party descended. Sheer rock outcrops crowned by ragged pines butted alongside the path, forming a tight funnel that the party followed down through thick beds of fern.

The long descent gave Vergal time to reflect on how easily Guile had discovered the new trail. A cynic might guess the mercenary had led them astray purposefully, only to eventually bring them in line with this new path. The timing had undoubtedly worked in Guile's favor, with Sh'ynryan demanding to take a shorter route near to where a new overland route conveniently presented itself. Guile had managed to wrest some extra coins from Sh'ynryan before setting out on a course Vergal suspected he had intended to follow in any case.

Vergal's admiration for his new guide increased a notch. Several times Sh'ynryan had asserted how little money mattered to him, yet he appeared to resent it mightily whenever Guile commanded more of it. A glance over his shoulder at Sh'ynryan, who was scowling darkly, indicated perhaps his abductor had reached the same conclusion.

Entertained by these thoughts, Vergal began to relax on his lurching canter, only to have it end abruptly. The trees that had formed a dense tunnel around them yawned open. The horses skidded down a last stony embankment before trotting up a short rise onto a level road.

Vergal assumed it was a road. The broad path curved in both directions around the foot of the hill they had descended, with more of the omnipresent pines lining each side. It was formed of the same pitted, packed earth that had distinguished the deer run, though wider and with perhaps a better camber for drainage. Vergal and Sh'ynryan regarded Guile quizzically.

"Where are we?" Sh'ynryan asked.

Guile raised a hand to silence him. His expression grew grave as he glanced all around, straining to listen. Vergal listened too but heard only the chorus of insect and bird song rising beside the road. After a final searching look around, Guile waved his hand, said, "Follow me," and set heels to his horse's flanks.

The trio rode three abreast, Vergal in the middle. Guile explained how they now traveled the Imperial Arasynian Highway, east toward the fortress called the March. Vergal scrutinized the rutted road as it slid languidly beneath their mounts' casual, mile-eating trot. The road looked anything except Imperial to Vergal. He told Guile this, and the man, as usual, responded with a laugh.

"Oh, it's the Emperor's road, right enough," Guile said. He seemed relaxed once again, but his eyes continued their restless scanning of the way ahead.

"You should see the road on the east side of the March," Guile continued, "all broad and cobbled stones, smooth and even, running straight across the grasslands like an arrow to Speakwater."

"Then why does it look much like the trail we left behind?" he asked.

"For the same reason that the March stands between them," Guile replied simply.

Vergal blinked. "I don't think I understand, sir," he said.

"Call me Guile," the man said automatically. He shifted in his saddle and began to explain. "The Empire holds sway over all Alasia, except west of the Danea. That land remains the realm of the Aerie Coast, but the land between the March and the Danea is mostly this thick forest you see around us and the rocky foothills and mountains north of here. It's not much use to the emperor, at least not for now. There's too much land east of here better suited to Imperial needs."

Vergal fixed his attention on Guile, but beside him, he heard Sh'ynryan shifting in his saddle, watching the exchange.

Guile went on. "So, by decree, the lands west of the March are kept wild. There are a few token garrisons along the road to Caliss, a few villages that have sprung up as well, but it's mostly an uninhabited wasteland, and the emperor likes it that way."

"But why?" Vergal asked, still unsure of what Guile meant.

Beside him, Sh'ynryan snorted. "You are displaying less of that sense I credited you with at Caliss, Vergal," he scoffed. "Think about it, boy; the man has certainly painted a clear enough picture for you."

Vergal glared at Sh'ynryan but nibbled the insides of his mouth to keep from responding.

Guile shot Sh'ynryan a stern look. But when he turned back to Vergal, he wore that same pleasant, crooked grin.

"The March is a defense, Vergal," Guile continued easily. "It was built to defend the mountain pass that was once the border between Aerie and Alasia until the Empire—and I'm talking years and years ago, mind you—pushed its boundaries west, all the way to the Danea. The kingdoms aren't technically at war today, but there is no love between them. The Pirate King shows little restraint when it comes to harassing Imperial ships at sea, and Alasia, for its part, severely taxes the overland routes that the mainland Aerie merchants depend on to get their wares to the markets at Speakwater and Khendyl."

Guile swept his arm grandly to take in the road stretching ahead, which looked muddy and rutted in the bright afternoon sunlight.

"All of this is basically intended as a natural extension of the March," he said expansively. "The emperor discourages development here to keep this land as a buffer between Caliss and the March, even if it is his territory. He doesn't need it right now, so why pay to develop it? Leaving this forest alone and keeping the highway little better than a game trail is a lot less expensive than building fortresses and fortifications across the river from Caliss, is it not?"

Vergal frowned, trying to sort through the scenario. "It all sounds awfully complicated to me."

"Only to folk like us, Vergal," Guile replied with a grin. "To the nobility, it seems to make complete sense. But I'll tell you this, if not for this forest—if Aerie and Alasia butted up against one another at the Danea—I think that river would constantly be running red with blood. Believe me; it's better this ..."

An arrow thudding into the packed dirt of the road ahead suspended the conversation.

A heartbeat passed to register the quivering fletched shaft before the trio instinctively fell low across the back of their horses.

A deep voice bellowed from out of the forest, "Far enough, or the next one takes your skull!"

The three reined their mounts sharply in a noisy jingling of harnesses. Guile swore softly beneath his breath but stayed stock-still in his saddle. His eyelids narrowed, and the pupils under them darted across the road and the forest ahead. Vergal followed Guile's example and remained as still as possible while seated high astride a fidgeting animal.

For a moment, nothing happened. The trio sat like squat statues on the backs of their horses, staring at the empty road. Vergal strained to listen but heard only crickets and the wind sloughing in the overhanging tree branches. Vergal listened so intently he imagined he could almost hear the late afternoon sun beating down upon him. Beyond that, he heard nothing.

His surprise was complete when several figures stepped from the shadows of the trees and bushes at the fringe of the road.

Highwaymen! Vergal's shocked eyes took them in as they filed onto the dusty road. They wore various colored tunics over leather hose, some of which were patched at the knees and rumps. Dark braided leather straps holding pouches and holsters for weapons crossed at their chests and circled their waists and legs.

Arrows bristled from quivers worn by several men, who also carried longbows slung casually over one shoulder. They were a thoroughly disreputable-looking group in Vergal's estimate. Menace emanated from them in near palpable waves as they formed a line across the road.

"Hold there," cried a voice from behind the group. The line parted to allow a tall blonde-haired man to step to the fore.

He wore gaudy clothing strewn flamboyantly over a supple skin of deer leather. Vergal glumly noted the array of weaponry holstered in various scabbards and quivers strapped everywhere on the man: Swords, knives, bow and arrows, even a small studded mace tucked snugly into the front of his belt. How the man walked so silently while draped in all that metal was a mystery to Vergal, yet he made barely any sound as he stepped out to face them.

A broad grin split the blonde hair of the man's unkempt beard. The hair grew thickly on his chin but petered to barely discernible whiskers beneath his nose. The man raised a long-fingered hand to shade his eyes from the sun.

"Greetings!" the man called cheerfully. "Salutations, from a fellow traveler weary of the road!"

A slight rumble of laughter went up from the line behind him. The blonde man shifted his weight slightly from one booted foot to another. He stood watching from beneath his cupped hand. His manner was easy, his grin generous as he looked up at them, but his right hand never strayed from the hilt of a sword at his hip.

"Greetings to you, friend!" came the cheerful retort from their own ranks. The boy started to see Guile returning the man's smile with a crooked grin of his own. "Well met! What say you of the road ahead?"

"Ah, the road ahead, you say?" the man repeated. His grin faded, and his face affected an expression of deep concern. He dropped the hand, shielding his eyes to his waist. It came to rest on the head of a small ax.

The highwayman shook his head ruefully. "Alas, the road ahead is much the same as this stretch, friend. It is lonely, crooked, and dangerous for unsuspecting travelers, honest men such as you and me."

The man gave another slight shake of his head as if truly distressed to share such unfortunate news. Another mocking titter swirled the ranks behind him.

By Vergal's count, nearly a dozen men blocked the road ahead.

"Surely not dangerous," Guile replied. "The emperor's own road? Why, what trouble could befall a loyal subject of the Crown on His Majesty's highway? I can't imagine such a travesty."

The highwayman grinned up at Guile, warming to the exchange.

"Any number of pitfalls await the unwary," he replied in a clipped and cultured voice utterly at odds with the malevolent gleam in the man's eyes. Vergal began to sense the direction the conversation was heading. He wanted dearly to look at Sh'ynryan, who had fallen behind him and whom he could hear fidgeting on his saddle, just out of sight. *Do something!* a silent voice cried in Vergal's mind, but he dared not speak the words out loud.

"Why, a Drakleth could charge from the underbrush and snatch a man right off his mount." The highwayman hooked his hands into claws and vigorously scratched the air as he related this. His men, predictably, enjoyed the pantomime.

"Or, a few stray steps into the bush to relieve himself," he said, holding both hands in front of him as if swinging a great length of rope, "could place him face-to-face with an Obroth!"

More delighted hoots from his cohorts echoed through the forest.

"Any manner of travesty awaits an unfortunate traveler, friend, even on the emperor's highway."

His hands returned to the hilts of the weapons. He frowned as if distressed by a passing thought. "I've even heard tell of encounters with bands of bloodthirsty bandits!"

The laughs and catcalls rose again. Vergal failed to see the humor in the exchange.

Guile paused, pondering all of this.

"A Drakleth or an Obroth, I understand, and your point is well taken, sir." Guile scratched his chin thoughtfully. "But I wonder, who in the realm would be so utterly stupid as to risk the emperor's wrath by attacking innocent travelers? It would require a mental deficiency on the part of the aggressor. Why, only a complete and raving idiot would entertain the idea."

Guile tipped a knowing wink at the man blocking the road.

The smile faded from the mercenary's face.

"You have a smart mouth, friend," he said ominously.

"And you have a foul and malodorous stench," Guile replied briskly. "Perhaps you could remove your band to a stream back in the woods for a cleansing dip? You could personally ensure the cleanliness of their more offensive parts."

Growls went up from the line.

"You stupid bastard," the highwayman said slowly, half in anger, half in disbelief at Guile's flippant tone. "You stood a chance of leaving with your skins. Now I think that be first for the taking, eh what lads?"

A holler of agreement went up. The men in the road drew swords in unison.

A knife materialized in Guile's hand. Vergal, seated directly beside the man, gasped at the speed of its appearance. In one instant, Guile's gloved hand rested lightly on the horn of his saddle; in the next, he held the knife by the point of its blade.

In one smooth motion, the knife—a long, wicked-looking weapon—left Guile's hand and whipped through the air, catching the sunshine in star-point flashes as it turned end-over-end and buried itself in the throat of the rogue.

Guile rolled backward off his saddle and crouched behind his horse's flanks before his target crumpled to the ground, but not before kicking sideways and knocking Vergal off his mount.

Vergal flew off the saddle. It was the tumble he had anticipated since first climbing atop the massive beast, but not the way he imagined it happening. The impact of the fall blasted the breath from his lungs.

"You too, Sh'ynryan! Down!" Guile bellowed from beneath the belly of his horse. Vergal rolled in the dust of the road, fighting to catch his breath. He heard Guile unsheathe his sword.

The warning came too late. The air filled with arrows.

But not before Sh'ynryan uttered a single word.

The strange roaring that had twice overwhelmed Vergal returned with force. The sound reminded Vergal of the hollow, continuous screech when pressing one's ear to a conch shell. However, there was nothing subtle or muted about the noise this time. It exploded through Vergal's brain. The boy's hands left off, cradling his injured stomach to smother his ringing ears.

Prone on his back, half-sheltered by the overhanging flank of his pawing horse, Vergal saw the air swim around him.

The sky changed color—that was the first thing he noticed. The flawless blue above washed out, becoming blurry and indistinct as if seen through a rain-washed window. A confused instant passed until Vergal realized the sky had not changed but that he was now viewing it through a film. A translucent sheet of shimmering air leaped from the ground and arced over them to form a dome.

Arrows slicing out from the concealing trees plunged through the maelstrom of disturbed air, sending ripples of undulating force spreading where they pierced its surface. The arrows' progress slowed to a swirling crawl as they entered the globe. Vergal had the surreal impression of resting at the bottom of a deep, clear pond, watching someone throw sticks into the water from above.

The barbed tips of the arrows twirled tortuously slow as they passed through the barrier, robbing them of their deadly velocity. They slowed and finally stopped, still slightly twirling, suspended in the shimmering air within the globe. Vergal turned an open-mouthed stare through the tangle of horses' legs at Guile, who crouched similarly wide-eyed and astonished.

"What in hell!" Guile yelled.

"Never mind!" Sh'ynryan's strained voice yelled from above, reverberating weirdly through the unnaturally still air. Vergal clambered from beneath his horse to witness Sh'ynryan, his hands splayed over his head, waves of glimmering force pulsing outward from outstretched fingers. The tendrils of force corkscrewed wildly to meet the ceiling of the dome, melding into the mass at large, replenishing it, sustaining it as it spilled back toward the ground.

Sh'ynryan's eyes were clamped shut, his teeth bared. Fine beads of sweat popped on his creased forehead. "I cannot hold this," the red-robed man gasped. "Do something! Now!"

"Do what?" Guile cried. His voice was shrill. It was the first time Vergal had heard anything but confidence in the man's tone.

"The archers!" Sh'ynryan hissed through clenched teeth. "They would be an excellent start."

Guile, still staring incredulously at the forest of arrows suspended and slowly turning in the air around him, shook his head to compose himself. He staggered up out of his crouch.

"What about them?" Vergal cried. Beyond the barrier, the group of highwaymen—initially frozen by surprise—were now charging with upraised swords. More arrows plunged through the sheet of force only to fall victim to the same, slow-rolling stasis that gripped the others.

"We'll worry about them," Sh'ynryan said in a breaking voice. "Get the archers, Guile. Now!"

Sparing Sh'ynryan a final astonished glance, Guile stepped through the watery dome and darted into the bushy fringe.

"Vergal!" Sh'ynryan called in a pained voice. "You have to deal with them. Don't let them near me, do you hear me?"

"Me? I can't..." Even as Vergal opened his mouth to argue, the first of the highwaymen plunged through the dome.

The man instantly suffered the same fate as the arrows. His brisk charge became an impossibly slow crawl as soon as he passed the barrier of roiling air. The fierce expression stamped on the man's scarred face took an almost comically long time to register surprise, then fear, as the static atmosphere seized him. Still, he came on, his limbs moving with the slow, liquid quality of a dream.

"Get him, hit him!" Sh'ynryan screamed. "Take him down!" His words trailed away in a whimper of pain.

Vergal flinched at the agony evident in Sh'ynryan's cracking voice. Without stopping to consider what he was doing, Vergal yanked a hatchet from a loop in Guile's saddlebag and, trembling violently, rushed forward to meet the advancing highwaymen.

It was only then Vergal realized he was still moving freely.

The strange inertia that gripped everything entering the dome did not affect those already inside it.

More highwaymen had broken the barrier. Their windmilling arms, bristling with drawn swords and long daggers, slowed to barely perceptible movements. The long strides that had carried them quickly into the globe now took long seconds to lift and set down again. Their expressions again shifted through those slow range of emotions.

Biting back the bile in his throat, Vergal ran forward, unimpeded by the inert atmosphere.

And for the first time in his young life, Vergal struck another person.

Vergal had once helped the Wayfarer's cook, Malek, chop wood for the firepit. Vergal patterned his swing now after that example. Gripping the hatchet's handle tightly in two hands, he turned the blunt end out and, drawing it over and behind his right shoulder, he swung the weapon with all the might his skinny arms could muster.

The blow was a sound one.

The highwayman—the first who had entered the dome—was hunched over and straining to make headway through the charged air when Vergal rushed him. The man had managed to cover several feet and was angling sluggishly toward Sh'ynryan when the blunt end of the hatchet slammed into his nose.

Vergal leaped back from the shock of the impact, his eyes wild. He initially thought his blow ineffective. The expression on the man's face did not change a whit, and he continued to inch forward in his strange, slow fashion. Vergal nearly dropped the hatchet in terror.

Then reality caught up to the man.

Although the hit from the weapon had happened seconds earlier, the man's nose began to crumple slowly, as if only now being struck.

Fat droplets of blood fanned out from his face, revolving slowly through the air as they spread in all directions.

The man's nose slowly flattened out across his face. His eyelids inched closed, and his mouth crept open in a widening scream. Dark bruising radiated slowly through the puffy flesh beneath his eyes as it swelled with blood.

The same static force that had seized the arrows had delayed the highwayman's response to his wounding, but now the pain was catching up with him.

The man's head moved backward in a torpid pantomime of agony, and his knees began to buckle. He seemed to float back into the air from the force of the impact and took a long instant to land on his back on the bumpy road.

Vergal gaped at the sight of it. His gorge rose at the sight of the twirling blood droplets still hanging in the air. The hatchet nearly slipped from his trembling fingers as the gory results of his handiwork assaulted him. Sh'ynryan's sudden scream jolted him.

"Vergal!" he shrieked. "The others! Now!"

Sh'ynryan was slumped in his saddle, leaning heavily on one arm. Now only one of his outstretched hands fed the pulsing waves that sustained the vortex surrounding them. And that arm was visibly shaking.

The thought of the highwaymen finding release from their torpor spurred Vergal to action. Dashing along the curving wall of the dome, gagging and sobbing as he went, the boy hammered at every exposed piece of anatomy he encountered.

As angry faces thrust through the barrier, he smashed them.

Where men's faces were too tall to reach, he chopped their exposed knees or slammed the blunt end of the hatchet into their unprotected stomachs.

As an afterthought, Vergal darted back around his circle of mayhem and smashed fingers as he went, thinking the assailants would have difficulty wielding weapons in broken hands if Sh'ynryan suddenly dropped the shield surrounding them.

And then he did.

Sh'ynryan cried out once more.

The hazy sky beyond the seething dome of force blinked bright blue again.

Arrows, captured and spinning lazily in mid-air, dropped suddenly to the dusty road, their forward motion spent.

Wounded highwaymen still frozen in various stages of free-fall crashed violently to the ground.

The thick fans of blood rolling slowly through the air spurted in all directions, spattering the men and terrified horses.

Blinded by tears, sickened by the blood and the grisly cracks of shattering bone, Vergal cried out when a heavy hand suddenly seized his shoulder. He spun, his hatchet thrust out in front of him, but a gauntleted hand smartly plucked his weapon away.

Guile stood over him, smiling broadly, a look of genuine admiration softening his eyes.

"Nicely done, Vergal," Guile praised softly. He patted the boy's shoulder reassuringly. "Truly well done."

Vergal, his knees suddenly boneless, fell to the ground sobbing.

"No time for that now," Guile said, hooking his fingers under the boy's arm and yanking him to his feet.

Battered and broken men lay groaning or unconscious.

However, several remained standing. And as their mobility returned, so too did their rage. With screams of mixed defiance and fear, the remaining robbers charged.

Guile shoved Vergal toward the horses. The boy crossed the distance awkwardly, stuttering on his toes, arms flailing for balance. He bounced off the flank of his horse and sprawled on the ground.

"Get behind that animal; I'll finish this," Guile instructed, already turning away.

He raised his sword to meet the few men still advancing. Vergal spotted blood staining Guile's blade and knew without asking that he need not fear a fresh storm of arrows.

The bandits surrounded Guile and lunged, their weapons flailing.

His sword held in front of him, his other hand grasping a dagger, Guile answered the first highwayman with a whirling blur of steel.

Metal rang shrilly through the still air as Guile's sword thrust upward to catch his attacker's descending blade and sweep it aside. His dagger arm shot forward, a quick movement Vergal tracked only by a flash of sunlight off the blade.

The highwayman fell to his knees, his fingers laced over an oozing puncture wound that drenched his tunic in blood.

Guile whirled to meet the charge of the next attacker before the first one slumped to the ground.

The mercenary dropped to one knee to catch the chopping head of an ax between his crossed blades. Pushing the ax blade aside with a sharp dip of his wrists, Guile leaped to his feet in the same motion and whipped his knife blade backhanded across the man's throat, drawing a hair-thin line of blood. The line quickly gaped into a lipless wound. Torn tissue gleamed wetly behind the widening red smile splitting the man's throat.

The battle progressed in a cacophony of clanging steel blades. When an attacker's weapon snaked through Guile's deft parries, the man countered with an abrupt catlike movement—a barely perceptible turn of waist or roll of shoulder—to evade the blow. More often, the weapons clanged off Guile's whirling steel, followed by a sudden flash of the mercenary's sword or thrust of his dagger that pierced heart, lung, or eye. Vergal, awestruck, had never seen the like of the liquid lightning moves Guile put on display.

Men fell, gasping to the road. The dust beneath them turned into a red paste from the pooling blood.

Guile paid them no heed. He turned to meet the next opponent, his features a dispassionate mask. Guile's eyes were flat and unconcerned, as if his attention was elsewhere and he was only distantly connected to the lethal events at hand. Guile grimaced painfully once when a highwayman's blade gouged his dagger hand, but his deadly attacks never faltered.

When the last highwayman fell, his leg nearly severed from a dipping, spinning swipe of Guile's sword, Vergal could no longer contain himself. He rolled on his stomach, retching in one painful body-wide convulsion. He stayed on his face a long time, heaving and crying in a continuous outpouring of fluids that left him drained but strangely cleansed.

At last, he scrubbed the back of his hand across his wet lips and lifted his head. Guile's eyes were there to meet him. The detached gaze was gone, replaced again by the lopsided grin. More than anything, that familiar sight helped Vergal to settle his roiling stomach and calm his violent trembling.

Guile's weapons rested easily in their sheaths as if they had never left. The crickets in the long grass had resumed their chorus. Or perhaps they had never stopped and had only been drowned by the clamor of battle.

A glance at the road ahead broke the sunny serenity. Men lay scattered in heaps, some faintly twitching in their death throes. Even those only initially wounded now lay eerily still. Guile had taken time to dispatch the injured before coming to the boy's aid.

Averting his gaze offered no respite. A turn of his head presented him the grisly spectacle of the boneless body of an archer draped over a tree limb above the road. Blood coursed down the exposed flesh of the arms and dripped slowly from the tips of outstretched fingers, splayed in a seeming gesture of supplication.

The bile threatened to rise again. Guile was looking carefully into his face. The grin was gone; his blue eyes were intent. He nodded sympathetically.

"I know," he said softly. "The first encounter with death is never pleasant. But take comfort in the fact you confronted it bravely, more bravely than some men I've known."

He smiled again, but there was no hint of his usual hilarity, only a sober measure of respect. "You should be proud," he told the boy softly.

The soft thump of Sh'ynryan sliding out of his saddle belayed any response Vergal might have offered. He lay crumpled on the ground, a formless heap of pooled cowl and red robes. He was muttering something.

"Are you hurt?" Guile asked. The inquiry did not hold the same tone of concern.

Guile turned the fallen man over. Sh'ynryan's face was pale, and he trembled violently. To Vergal, he appeared years older, with haggard bruises ragging the pouched flesh beneath his eyes and dirt caked in every crease of his face after a headlong plunge to the ground. Despite himself, Vergal felt a twinge of sympathy for the man.

However, there was nothing sympathetic in Guile's eyes as he hunched over the red-robed man.

"Who are you?" he demanded roughly, seizing Sh'ynryan's thin shoulders in his hands and lifting him slightly off the ground. "No, what are you? That's the better question after this display."

Sh'ynryan's muttering grew stifled. With a long sigh, the man slumped into unconsciousness.

Guile turned to Vergal, who shrugged. "He's a ... I think he's some sort of a magic man," Vergal offered weakly.

Guile looked distastefully at the man collapsed in his arms and let him slide none too gently to the ground.

"A magic man, yes," the mercenary said, standing. He clapped his gauntleted hands together to rid them of dust and gore. "That seems an apt description."

CHAPTER TWELVE

Alonna sat cross-legged on top of her bed covers, sipping a glass of wine by candlelight and exulting in the afterglow of success. She replayed the beating she had administered the drunkard and raised her glass in a silent toast to herself.

Alonna's thoughts wandered into simple daydreams about nothing in particular. She was worrying vaguely about how she had nearly decimated her stash of liquor beneath the floorboards in recent days and was considering when to buy more when a firm knock sounded at the door to her room.

She opened to find Carek in the hallway. His eyes were downcast, and the flesh beneath them was puffy and dark-ringed. He stood with his hands at his side outside her door. He did not raise his head when she stepped out briskly to join him in the hallway. It would not do for Carek to see the expensive bottle of wine on the table next to her bed.

"Carek? What is it?" she asked. She pinched the neck of her nightclothes shut modestly. Carek never visited her bedchamber except to harangue her to begin work whenever she threatened to lag her time.

There was no urgency to Carek's visit this time. He stood for what seemed a long time, dressed in a robe worn open over his bedclothes, scrutinizing the stone floor between his slippered feet. His steady breathing and the pop of the lantern's flame as it greedily consumed its fuel in the hall were the only sounds. He lifted his eyes without raising his head, gawking at Alonna through an unkempt shock of hair. Alonna didn't like the intensity and the silence of that gaze. She clenched the neck of her bedclothes more tightly.

"Carek?" she prompted when the man did not respond. She had never seen him like this, bereft of bluster, introspective, and—she realized with a start—biting back tears. Now she recognized the redness in his eyes that she had mistaken for the play of lamplight on his face.

When at length he spoke, his voice was firm. "Alonna, we must talk. Can you dress and meet me in the taproom?"

Her eyes narrowed. She was in no mood for Carek's histrionics, no matter how uncharacteristically he was launching them.

"What now, Carek?" Alonna demanded, with more iron in her voice than she intended. She did not strictly need her work at the Wayfarer any longer. She privately questioned whether she could endure more of Carek's harassment without lashing back.

She took a deep breath to dissipate the dark, wine-fuelled anger welling inside of her. "It's late," she said softly, stepping back inside her doorway and making to close the door. "We'll talk after my work is done in the morning."

Carek pressed the palm of his hand solidly against the door as she moved to close it. Alonna checked her protest when she noted the melancholy on his face. "This cannot wait," he said, no trace of pique evident in his voice. "If I wait until morning to speak my mind, I doubt I will at all."

"What is this about?" Alonna asked distrustfully, still standing behind the half-closed door.

Carek sighed and lowered his hand. "Just get dressed and meet me in the taproom, Alonna," he said. "Please."

He turned down the hallway toward the stairs without awaiting her answer.

Her curiosity aroused, Alonna was dressed and seated in the taproom soon after. The inn's taproom was not strictly closed late at night, but no customers were about to disturb them. Estanelda, the night maid, sat across the room with an expression of supreme boredom etched on her round face. She reclined in a chair in front of the hearth, warming her feet on the stones and paying Alonna and Carek no mind as they sipped steaming tea from earthenware mugs.

Alonna had never seen such an expression on Carek's face like the mask of regret he wore now. His strange behavior made her uneasy. She flinched when he reached across the pitted table and grasped her hand.

He held her hand for several seconds, his hairy thumb absently massaging the slender knuckles of her fingers.

"I've wronged you, Alonna. I've wronged you and Vergal both," he said at last.

He dropped her hand and laced his fingers around the warm crockery. Carek leaned into the steam rising off his mug, savoring its warmth.

He looked up at her through the veil of steam. "And I've wronged them."

"Who?"

"Your parents."

"What?"

He nodded. "Your parents."

Of all the topics Alonna thought atop Carek's mind, this had not registered. Vergal's abduction had roused in her the most vivid memories of her parents' murder. She wrestled nightly with them—it was like trying to stem the bleeding of a re-opened wound—only to have the horrific images intensify and consume her. After Vergal's disappearance, only alcohol dulled her vivid recollections and protected her against plunging into an open pit of grief from which she might never emerge.

She had tried to focus on her plans for rescuing Vergal, not on her past regrets. Now Carek picked at the wound, forcing her most private and painful reflections into the light, with no stupefying drink at hand to ease her pain.

Alonna's fingers clenched the edge of the table. Her voice sharpened. "What are you saying?"

"What do you remember about that night?" Carek asked. "You were so young; it was so long ago. Tell me, Alonna, what do you recall?"

Her face was a mask. "Nothing," she lied. She drew deep from the hot mug of tea. Her eyes searched everywhere except for Carek's. "I was a little girl, remember?"

Carek observed her expression. "I remember that night," he went on. He reached again for her hand, but she flinched from his touch. His hand returned slowly to his mug. "I remember it all too well," he said sadly.

Carek launched into his account, and by the time he was halfway through it, Alonna could scarcely see through her tears.

—⚎—

In those days, Carek lived in the cramped room beside their own. He had been only too happy to surrender his own large suite to the exotic southerner and his family. Teraud appeared to have an inexhaustible supply of coins at his command and had little compunctions about spending them in support of his family's comfort. Carek had commanded a reasonable sum. The southerner's business had been his salvation as the inn had not been prospering in those days.

Carek had purchased the Wayfarer years earlier. Young and idealistic, seeking an appropriate investment for his inheritance, the notion of owning an inn enchanted him. He fantasized about the respect he would command from the rich captains of the merchant fleets that were put into Caliss, and the money he would harvest from their patronage. He purchased the Wayfarer for an extravagant sum and invested even more into its restoration. He waited out the renovations impatiently, dreaming of prosperous days ahead.

However, Carek soon learned that even the noble merchant princes of Far preferred the coarser delights found in the seedier inns in the quarter—with their barrels of rotgut whiskey and raucous harlots—to the more refined comforts of the Wayfarer.

Customers dried up alongside his coffers after Carek gained a reputation among the merchant and military fleets for running the cleanest inn near the docks. His inheritance had been nearly exhausted, and the money lenders were demanding returns on their investments.

Teraud had been his top customer in those days. He fed his family in the Wayfarer's taproom; he always promptly paid rent on his rooms. Carek felt gratitude to Teraud for his business and budding respect for the silently stoic man who worked without complaint during the day and bypassed the taproom reveling upon his return home at night. Carek had taken to inviting Teraud to enjoy an ale in the kitchen when he returned at night. He would sometimes politely consent to a quick mug before mounting the stairs to spend time with his young family.

Carek believed a cautious friendship had formed when the murderer struck.

He heard Alonna's mother's screams first.

It was late one evening after the first spring merchant ships out of Far had wound their way into Caliss. The piercing screams reached Carek through the thick stone walls separating their rooms, frightening him badly. He heard the soft thud of something banging against the wall.

Pulling on tunic and britches, Carek ran to bang on Teraud's door, calling to him. Only the sound of scuffling came in response. Carek pressed his ear to the door, and below, the noises detected the soft groans of someone in pain.

That decided him.

Rushing down the stairs, he floundered in a kitchen cabinet for the ring that held the master key to the inn's rooms. With the key in his pocket, Carek rushed back to Teraud's door. The noises inside had ceased. A strong draft flowing under the door chilled Carek's bare feet. He turned the lock. The door creaked open, revealing darkness beyond.

The door to the adjoining suite, Alonna's room, was thrown open. In the dimness, he made out the girl's slight form on the floor. Her pale bedclothes gleamed in the watery moonlight spearing between the window's billowing curtains.

A soft breeze moved through the room, guttering candles, lifting the edges of papers scattered everywhere—across the floor and tables, winnowing in the corners of the room.

Carek didn't see the figure standing in the dark corner until it moved.

He stepped backward in alarm. The figure near the wardrobe chose that moment to flee. It covered the distance between the wall and the open window in the space of a heartbeat and dove headlong into the night.

"Stop!" Carek yelled in surprise.

But the figure was gone.

Only the curtains still swaying on the window indicated anything passed that way at all.

Bellowing a curse, Carek rushed to the window and leaned out. The air was clean and bracing, the moons ripe with white light and swinging low on their trek through the night sky. Thunder pealed in the distance, promising more drenching spring rains.

Carek leaned as far as he dared, searching the alley below. The cobbled stones reflected the bright light of the moons. There was no sign of a silhouette splayed on the alley floor, as Carek had expected to find.

Turning away, he started to call for Teraud, but the hallway's lantern light revealed the man would not be answering.

Blood spattered the walls behind Teraud's bed. Carek saw it plainly now in the light from the hall: Black and slick and dripping as viscous as oil. He backpedaled in horror and stepped on something soft and malleable. It was Alonna's arm.

Carek was shocked beyond belief by the scene.

Teraud and his wife were dead, slain in their bed.

The delicate wash of light slanting across the bed showed their throats sliced open. The fingers of their hands were curled and held out before them as if fending off an attacker now unseen.

Carek shook with fear.

On the floor, Alonna stirred. "Mama ..." she groaned.

"Alonna!" He knelt beside her, smoothing her dark hair from her dusky brow. He trembled violently, on the verge of tears. "Alonna, wake up, dear."

She stirred again beneath his touch, and Carek breathed out in relief. An ugly bruise was forming on the side of her face from her fall to the floor. But she lived. He tapped her gently, fearing to move her.

Her eyes cracked open, and she peered into his.

"You're the innkeeper," she said dazedly. Her mouth stretched in a slow smile, a beautiful contrast to her swelling face. "Are you...here? Why are you here?" Her muttering trailed off incoherently.

The child was in shock. She had seen the perpetrator of the crime and had perhaps witnessed the murder.

He lifted her and stood numbly, pondering his next moves. Authorities must be called; the city guard must be marshaled, and a search started. His mind spun when he considered the ramifications of such attention.

As he thought on these things, the child started in his arms. "Vergal!" she shrieked. Carek nearly dropped her in surprise.

"Vergal! Where is he? Where is my brother!" Her thin arms locked around his neck. She sobbed—a heart-rending din that shattered the last of Carek's composure.

"Over there, he's there!" Carek warbled. "I see him!"

A small form lay in a cradle, highlighted in the moonlight. Carek gently disengaged Alonna's clinging arms and lowered the sobbing girl to the floor.

Vergal peered up at him. A smile lifted his bow mouth. Carek's throat thickened at the sight of the new orphan cooing happily in his bed, unperturbed and uncomprehending of the tragedy that had befallen. Scant feet away, blood still seeped from his parents' wounds, drenching the bedcovers.

"Who did this?" Carek whispered to the dark room.

"There was a man."

Alonna stepped beside him, her hands on the cradle. She peered over the rail. Her eyes large and wet, her face white in the moons' light, she said softly, "I heard noises and came in. He was there, standing over them."

She frowned. She reached and stroked her brother's cheek. She went on, hesitantly, as if testing the truth of her memory. "I yelled, and he turned, but I couldn't see his face. He wore a hood. He pushed me away. I don't remember after that."

She stared blankly at Vergal in his cradle. She began to cry.

Carek had rarely witnessed violence beyond sporadic fights in the taproom. The sight of so much blood profoundly shocked him. He could only imagine the impact on the girl. Alonna slumped to the floor, her legs crossed, her body heaving with silent sobs. Her dark, tangled hair fell in a veil concealing her face. He wondered what fate awaited her. In Caliss, only one: Alonna and her brother would join the orphaned waifs on the streets of the port town. There, these children of genteel parents would surely die.

—⚭—

Carek paused in his recollection. The mug cupped in his hands had grown cold in his retelling, but his face flushed hot from the onslaught of vivid, disturbing memories assaulting him: The blood, the bodies, the terror stamped indelibly on the faces of the slain couple. Carek shook his head softly to clear the memory.

When he lifted his eyes again, Alonna was staring back at him.

"But you didn't turn us out," she said in a soft voice. Bafflement in her voice, as if she only now realized this fact after years beneath Carek's roof. "We lived here," she went on. "You gave us a room. You let us stay."

She looked at the table, but Carek could tell she didn't see it. Alonna stared instead at an empty middle distance where images from her memory cavorted. Questions she had not asked herself in years resurfaced: Who killed her parents? Why had the person done it?

Carek stared at her long and hard before lowering his eyes. His countenance fell in abject misery.

"What, Carek?" Alonna urged. The emotions on his face were foreign to Carek, at least for Alonna. The anger she held toward him subsided at that moment. She dismissed the culpability she secretly ascribed to him for her brother's disappearance. For a moment, Carek no longer seemed the bullying innkeeper who bedeviled her. Slumped over his cup, Carek appeared what Alonna now knew him to be: A tired, aging man who carried a great weight on his shoulders.

Carek drank from his mug and made a face. The tea was cold. His voice when he spoke again was subdued and measured.

"It's why I asked you here, Alonna. Given all that's happened..." Carek paused. "It forced me to face the truth. I have wronged you. And Vergal, perhaps most of all. I don't know if it is still possible, but I wanted to try to make things right. I thought perhaps by telling you; things might get straightened out."

"Tell me what, Carek?" she snipped. His stumbling explanations made her impatient. Carek flinched as if she had struck him.

"I stole from you, Alonna," Carek said suddenly. He looked at her. She looked at him.

Then Carek began to cry.

Alonna sat back, confused. Gelbrek's suggestion that his mercenaries had spied on her sent Alonna straight to the loose floorboard upon returning to the Wayfarer. All the coins in her cache were accounted for. Alonna shook her head, not comprehending his meaning.

"You stole what from me?"

The realization hit her before Carek could answer, not like a slap but like a stunning blow from a fist.

"My father's money?" she whispered.

He held his hands in a warding gesture as if she intended to strike him. But Alonna was incapable then of moving. She gripped the mug in her hands so hard she feared it might burst from the strength of her fingers.

"All these years," she said, talking to herself more than to Carek. "There was something left. The intruder didn't take it; you did…something that belonged to us."

She raised her round eyes to Carek, who scrubbed his wet face with the sleeve of his robe.

"We didn't have to stay here," she said, speaking the revelation aloud even as it occurred to her. "At the inn. We didn't have to stay with you."

Carek's nose ran freely. The portly innkeeper, never physically appealing at his most presentable, was singularly unattractive when he cried.

"You must hate me," Carek said miserably. "If you didn't before, how you must now."

Alonna did not reply.

"I'll pay you back, Alonna. Of course, I will," he continued. "I know it is no excuse, but I only ask that you understand what I endured in those days. I was nearly destitute! I had sunk everything into the inn. It was the last piece of my inheritance, and I saw it slipping away from me. Had the moneylenders called their notes, I would have been on the streets, forced to crawl back to my brothers, who would have berated me for wasting my fortune on a foolish dream."

"How much?"

Her tone was icy, impassioned. There was no anger, yet neither was there a hint of empathy nor compassion.

"A scribe's wage for a year, perhaps two—no more than that," Carek offered immediately. "It was almost all in silver and bronze, there was little gold, but he kept it almost in plain sight with a corner of the little strongbox sticking out from under his bed. I saw it there every time I visited your suite.

"Your father had been near ruin himself when he died. He fed and clothed you and kept your family sheltered here in the inn for months, Alonna, and I can only imagine what the journey from Zistah cost him. He surely could not have sustained the four of you on what his salary was adding back."

He paused, considering. Then he went on.

"We were friends, you see. Or at least I like to believe we were close to friendship. There just wasn't enough time, as it turned out. Sometimes we took an ale together in the evenings, and your father would tell stories of his life in Zistah and his plans for his family's future here in Caliss. He was saving every coin he could spare from his salary to make sure he could provide that future for you."

Carek shook his head. "It was plain that he was nowhere near being able to fulfill that vision."

Alonna said nothing. Carek did not know if he should interpret her silence as recrimination for his lies or as vindication for his decision now to be truthful. He did not know what to do. So, he pressed on.

"I took the money, Alonna, but I could not turn you out," Carek said. "I kept you and Vergal here. You became like a daughter to me."

"Oh, but you made me work for it, didn't you, Carek?" Alonna said, with sudden heat in her voice.

She stood from the table, her eyes blazing with anger.

"I was an orphaned girl with a baby brother in my care, and you made me work like a slave for you! You kept me on the verge of despair for myself and Vergal, feeling that the roof over our heads and the food in our mouths could be snatched away at any time."

"I could have turned you out!" Carek pleaded. "I could have kept the money and sent you both away, with no one to question my actions. I gave you a place to call your home, where you were fed and safe and able to care for Vergal."

Alonna shook her head.

"No, Carek. Those are the same arguments I offered you, the same arguments you were unwilling to accept when I believed that your kindness was borne of charity. Had you given us what was rightfully ours, who knows how we might have fared? We would have had a chance. To leave, to stay—the choice would have been ours, and the consequences at least of our devising.

"But you made the choice for us. The mistakes were not ours to make. And now Vergal's been taken from me!"

She gripped the edge of the table as if its counterweight alone kept her on her feet. "My brother's gone," she said, "and that's the consequence of your decisions, not mine!"

Estanelda, near to dozing, started at Alonna's raised voice. She peered at them curiously.

"Alonna, you were a child yourself!" Carek implored. "You were in no position to make any decisions. You were orphaned with an infant brother. Yes, I removed the choice for you but only because you were too young to make it. I don't know how it went so wrong between us since or why I grew so hard toward you. Perhaps I misdirected my own self-loathing. What I did was wrong, I understand that, but it was done with the right intentions. It was done to protect you. Can't you see this, even now?"

Carek slumped in his chair. A tense quiet settled on both: On Carek because he had exhausted his impassioned defense, and on Alonna as she allowed the hot flush of her anger to fade away.

Alonna shook her head. What did any of it matter? Carek's arguments rang true—a young girl and a baby could not have survived alone in Caliss. If her inheritance was the price of their security over the years, then so be it.

Perhaps her wrath was assuaged because sometime over the intervening years, Carek, for all his bluster and tyranny, had become the closest thing to family remaining to her and Vergal. He had undoubtedly been her greatest support since Vergal's abduction.

Perhaps his unspoken repentance in the days since her brother's disappearance also accounted for something.

Or perhaps she was just too weary with the past to allow it to cloud her future any longer.

Alonna sat down. With a sigh, she reached across the table and grasped Carek's hand. He started at her touch, surprised, on alert.

"The past becomes the present for me when I consider these things," she said quietly. "But none of it matters. Nothing matters at all except finding my brother."

She withdrew her hand. Her hands found the lip of the table again, and she composed herself. "I forgive you, Carek," she said at length. "For what it's worth. You had a decision to make, and you made it. I suppose you were honorable in your own way. You kept us when, as you say, you might have turned us out."

She rose to her feet.

"And so, we are even, Carek. We owe each other nothing," She cinched her robe and straightened her back. "I am glad for this conversation. Because soon I'll be leaving this place, and it is good we settled these matters so that the past can be kept properly in its place when I move on."

Carek looked sad but nodded. "You're leaving to search for Vergal."

"How can I not?"

"You've been acting strange since he disappeared," Carek said. "I understand; I know how much he meant—he means—to you. But I worry, Alonna. You leave in the evening and are gone most of the night. I can't imagine what you do so late, and I don't know what you're thinking, staying out so late on the streets of Caliss. It's as if you're begging to be robbed or ravished or worse."

Alonna opened her mouth to respond, but Carek lifted a beefy hand to interrupt.

"No, I think I understand now. You've been preparing to search for Vergal. And I needn't have been worried these past nights because you know what you are doing, right? Please tell me that I am right."

The steel in her eyes and the determined lift of her chin answered Carek's question more thoroughly than her unhesitant reply.

"Yes," she answered. Her voice was strong, uncompromising. "I know what I am doing. It is the only thing I do know with certainty. I am going to find my brother."

CHAPTER THIRTEEN

"Why did you provoke them?" Sh'ynryan demanded. He tried to rise on one arm, but the effort proved too much, and he fell back on his bedroll.

Guile reclined with his feet against the warm rocks that contained their small campfire. He bolted upright at Sh'ynryan's voice. His signature good humor had flown and had not been seen again since before the encounter on the road with the highwaymen. The mercenary looked to Vergal to be spoiling for a fight.

"So, you're awake, are you?" Guile sneered through the embers wafting above the crackling fire. "And showing as much gratitude now as you did civility before, I see. I told you, Vergal, we should have left this wretched warlock where he lay. You are accursedly lucky this boy interceded for you, old man, or you'd have been left for the wolves and Obroths."

Sh'ynryan turned weakly to Vergal, who looked away. Vergal's best chance to escape had been when the thin man had dropped unconscious out of his saddle, but he had not seized the opportunity. He realized with dismay that Sh'ynryan's threats against his sister were only part of the reason. He flinched from the other half of his reasoning. It was not time now to contemplate that.

Vergal pulled his cloak tighter around him. "Then fortunately for all involved, the boy is true to his word," he wheezed. "I assure you, had I awoken before the wolves arrived, you both would have regretted it."

He made as if to rise but left off the attempt, exhausted. "I ask again, Guile," he said, "why did you provoke them?"

"Who?"

"You know full well 'who.' The highwaymen, that's 'who!'"

"Oh, them." Guile waved his hand as if the party's brush with death on the highway had been a trifling matter.

"The truth is, we were in a fight either way," Guile said. He poked a stick to stir the fire. "I've encountered enough ruffians to understand there is no reasoning with them. They are half-starved outlaws, degenerates all. They think nothing of carving out a man's heart, simply to own his boots."

"They only wanted money," Sh'ynryan protested.

Guile scoffed. "We were in a fight for our lives the instant they stepped onto the road. Further bantering would only indulge their egos, so I dispensed with that. Moving first against the leader was prudent to improve our odds.

"Besides, it was you who insisted we take the highway, as I recall," he said. Guile's eyes narrowed. "Something about being equipped to meet any challenge, wasn't it? I'd plotted a safe route to the March along the upper game trail, but you just had to see the sights along the bandit-infested Imperial road to shave a day off your timetable."

Sh'ynryan sniggered. "What happened to your eagerness to limber your sword arm?" he mocked. "You didn't protest when you were gouging me for more gold, just to seek a fight you were looking for anyway."

"I've never seen them so organized before," Guile admitted. "The in-fighting among the bandits is legendary. I never anticipated such a large group of them."

"I'm paying for you to anticipate it, man!" Sh'ynryan bellowed.

The tone didn't sit well with Guile, who jumped to his feet. He kicked a brand protruding from the fire, sending a new helix of sparks whirling into the night.

"You paid me to escort a man and a boy to the March. You said nothing about accompanying a black magician! What sorcery did you perform on the road, Sh'ynryan? What manner of black art was that?"

Guile stamped around the fire to confront the prone man on the bedroll. "What manner of man does what you did?" he demanded, stabbing his finger at the night behind him. "A man in league with darkness, I say!"

Sh'ynryan smirked. "The whores and distillers of Caliss no doubt count themselves fortunate that I did what was necessary and preserved their prized client."

Guile was furious. He drew back and delivered a sharp kick to the meat of Sh'ynryan's thigh. Sh'ynryan clasped his leg and howled. Guile, suddenly recalling the magician's spectacle on the road, prudently leaped back and pulled his sword. He held it, point-low in front of him, watching Sh'ynryan intently.

"Stop it!" Vergal screamed.

The boy stood and tore off his cloak. The outburst shocked both men into silence. Only the snapping of wood being devoured by the fire broke the ensuing stunned quiet.

"What's wrong with you, with both of you?" He pointed at Guile, who winced. "You nearly got us all killed because you fancy yourself the greatest swordsman in Alasia. You can't even imagine the man has been born who can best you!"

"And you," he yelled, rounding on Sh'ynryan. "You take me away from my sister and say how important I am to some plan you won't say anything about. You force obedience through fear and say nothing about if I am even going to live long enough to see my sister again."

"Vergal," Sh'ynryan warned.

"No, enough!" he cried. A deep wellspring of anger had cracked and overflowed the boy. It would not be capped. "Do your worse; I don't care. You have no reason to hurt Alonna if I die because I'll never know what you've done. Isn't that right? So, go ahead, speak the words again, one that stops my heart, if you can. It doesn't matter. I already feel dead inside, so finish what you've started. Hurting people seems to satisfy you."

Vergal lunged as if he too intended to kick Sh'ynryan but stopped short and booted a clod of dirt at the man instead. The spray of earth pattered the man's face.

When he lowered his arms, Sh'ynryan's mouth hung in an astounded circle.

Vergal spun on Guile.

"You saw what he did. It scares you. That's why you're angry. Think how I feel. He sunk me into a stone wall! He took me from home and made threats against my sister, and you've been helping him this entire time. You haven't questioned what I'm doing here. You don't care."

Guile said nothing. He only gaped at the furiously trembling boy.

"Enough of this!" This time, Sh'ynryan made it into a sitting position, though his arms shook from the effort.

"Then kill me; I told you, I don't care!"

Vergal sunk to his knees. He sobbed miserably.

It was a long time before anyone spoke again.

"How did you do it?" Guile asked at length. He lowered himself back in front of the fire, looking at Sh'ynryan. "On the road. How? I've never seen the like. Tell us how you do these things? Make us understand what we're dealing with here."

Vergal raised his head, listening intently.

"You will never understand," Sh'ynryan growled.

"How can we, unless you explain?"

Sh'ynryan hesitated, but only a moment. He sighed. He seemed to deflate, the tenseness in his wiry frame relaxing. Nothing remained to hide. Both had witnessed too much. The boy was clearly close to a breakdown of sorts, and an obstinate determination to receive answers had crept into Guile's face. Sh'ynryan silently marveled this reckoning had not happened earlier.

"I am Magi," he said simply. Then he nodded as if silently affirming he had spoken the word aloud.

Vergal moved closer to the fire. He was fascinated at the change in Sh'ynryan's demeanor and eager to hear his explanation. He drew up his knees and hugged them close. "What's 'Magi?'" he asked.

Sh'ynryan rubbed his thigh. It ached abominably from Guile's pointed boot. "Let's call it a Brotherhood of sorts. That's as good an explanation as any."

Guile scowled. "Let's say you give us more details than that," he said gruffly.

Sh'ynryan considered Vergal's expectant gaze and sighed again. "Yes, perhaps it's time after all."

He brushed the dirt from his face and shoulders. He was exhausted, and the shakiness in his arms persisted. Sh'ynryan longed to curl in his bedroll and sleep again. Instead, he issued orders.

"Vergal, fetch some bread and cheese from my pack and bring it here. I'm ravenous. Guile, why not get the flask I've seen you pulling on, the one under your saddlehorn, and we'll pass it around. Even our young friend could stand a nip tonight. I know I could.

"Then we'll talk," he promised.

CHAPTER FOURTEEN

Alonna danced backward to avoid the strike. She swept her wooden scimitar low to parry the blow and guard her retreat, exactly as Rostalin had instructed. But the blunt side of the warrior's capped sword penetrated her deflection. A stinging pain streaked Alonna's leg, and she fell heavily on her rump.

Rostalin laughed down the length of his sword at her.

"Ho woman! I do so enjoy working your legs," he boomed. "Maybe now you appreciate how I felt when you busted my knee."

Alonna glared at the frowzy little man. "I've apologized for that, Rostalin. A hundred times."

"And you can apologize hundreds of times more until I stop limping every time it rains." He smacked her lightly on the thigh with the flat of his sword and, withdrawing, beckoned for her to rise.

Alonna sighed and climbed to her feet. It had been Alonna's lousy luck to report to Gelbrek for her training only to find Rostalin awaiting her in the sparring quarters. The kick she had administered to the man's knee that portentous night in the alley remained a constant irritation to him, and he took every opportunity to remind her. The other mercenaries in Gelbrek's compound still teased Rostalin mercilessly. Just how does a frightened novice, from her back, in a blind panic, nearly cripple one of the guild's top swordsmen anyway? They asked to know between chortles.

"A fortuitous blow unfairly landed," Rostalin griped in response. Alonna's heart sank when his scowl unerringly turned on her in response. She knew his humiliation in public meant more chastisement for her in private, under the pretense of tutelage.

Still, Alonna enjoyed her sessions in the training hall—a round, bare stone chamber filled to bursting with wooden and cushioned weapons hung from wall racks. Steel or edged weapons were forbidden in the sparring quarters for fear that adrenaline— or just plain bad blood between combatants—might decimate the ranks of the guild's recruits.

Combatants wore leather helms stuffed with padding and with beaten-steel nose-guards to protect their faces and girded themselves with armored coverings. Otherwise, they outfitted themselves in plain clothes. Alonna favored dark, tight hose that accentuated the firming muscles in her slim legs and billowing silk tunics that permitted her arms free range of movement. She tucked the sleeves of her tunic into shining bracers that protected her wrists. Her beloved golden circlet tied her raven hair back in a thick tail that swayed and bounced where it protruded from beneath her helm.

Grudgingly, Alonna came to respect her instructor. Though slight of frame and standing several inches shorter than Alonna, Rostalin's finesse with a longsword was tremendous. Apparently incapable of forgiving a slight, Rostalin nonetheless demonstrated capability as a teacher. Lessons were repeated until apprehended, mistakes were punished until corrected, and the crumbs of praise Rostalin deigned to drop were feasts to Alonna, who felt her skills refining as the weeks progressed.

Alonna had no idea how to go about finding her brother. However, she took heart in the growing realization she would be well prepared to inflict the justice his acts deserved when she at last hunted down his abductor.

Back on her feet, Alonna twirled her wooden scimitars twice expertly in her hands to regain the feel and balance of them. She assumed her battle stance: Feet planted, eyes locked on her opponent, her shoulders and torso turned slightly sideways to present as small a target as possible during the melee. Rostalin nodded approvingly and waded in, his replica swords spinning and slicing the air.

His assault, as always, awed her and reminded her repeatedly of the sheer fortune she had ever caught him unawares on the portentous night of their first meeting. In an instant, Rostalin's measured swings had her back on her heels. The moment she shifted her torso forward to regain her balance, a sword jabbed through her defenses and poked her exposed belly painfully, reminding her to shift sidelong again.

She did so and lost herself, as always, to the swordplay. The dance exhilarated her. Even the pain in her stomach from Rostalin's jab and the ache in her leg from his earlier strike was appreciated as part of the overall cost and experience of attaining new skills.

She swept her wooden scimitars to catch the downward hack of Rostalin's swords. She stepped into the circle of the tangled weapons and, pivoting, threw the instructor's swords high and wide. Her back now to Rostalin, Alonna elbowed her teacher sharply in his stomach and pitched forward on her shoulders to get clear of him. She emerged from her roll in a crouch, spinning to face him, scimitars crossed defensively and rose steadily to her feet.

Still clenching the hilt of his sword, Rostalin rubbed his stomach lightly with the pommel of the weapon. He regarded her shrewdly but said nothing. Alonna smiled slyly and renewed her attack. She pirouetted, sweeping her swords in time, and dropped low to catch Rostalin in his knees.

But the place where he stood had been vacated. Rostalin leaped nimbly over the cutting swords and flattened Alonna to the ground by stamping a boot-shod foot into her back on his descent. The impact of the unyielding floor blasted the breath out of Alonna's lungs, and her arms shot out wide to her sides, sending her weapons clattering out of her grasp on the stone floor.

Rostalin, still pinning her beneath his boot, crossed his swords on the back of her neck and held them there. Vanquished, unable to breathe easily, Alonna spread her fingers—the signal of surrender.

Rostalin stepped off, shaking his head in exasperation. "When will you stop taking such confidence in your lucky strikes?" he asked brusquely.

She rolled on her back. "I thought I'd winded you," she said between gasps for air. "I thought I had won the advantage, and I pressed the attack."

Rostalin made no move to assist her to her feet. He stood evaluating her as she retrieved her lost scimitars.

"Your instincts are sound, but your analysis is weak," he replied. "You had an advantage, but not enough of one. An enemy weakened is not yet an enemy vanquished. You must recognize and understand the distinction. Maintain your composure while whittling away at his! When his reasoning becomes blurred and pain produces anger, then he will make mistakes. It is then he will neglect his defense, and his wounds will sap his strength, and the fight can be won, as I just now illustrated."

Alonna pulled a sour face at that, and Rostalin laughed. "Lift them," he said, slapping her blades with his. "Have at me again. Let's see how quick a study you are."

Alonna fared only marginally better in the next round and, when the session finally expired, she repaired sulkily to her cell to nurse an impressive collection of scrapes and bruises.

She had moved into the guild hall at Gelbrek's insistence. Though she appeared reluctant, she, in truth, was glad for the invitation.

Living at the Wayfarer had become unbearable. Following his late-night confessions, Carek's attitude toward her had bordered on fawning. He lingered in her presence, frowned in consternation when she left the inn in the evenings and angered the other employees by making her unrequested concessions that often added to her colleagues' workloads. A resentful pall had settled over the kitchen.

She had been preparing to move in any case, but Gelbrek's invitation hastened the process. There were tears, vows of friendship, and promises of future visits on the day that Alonna departed. Standing in the common, however, the salty breeze off the harbor flailing her long hair, the promise of open spaces and new possibilities seized Alonna, and she truly wondered if she would ever again visit the Wayfarer.

The decision to move into Gelbrek's compound was irreversible. Alonna realized it before she ever agreed to it. She knew (had been outright told) that Gelbrek would not suffer the secrets he revealed to her ever to be disclosed to the outside world.

The acceptance of lodging simultaneously recast Alonna as a member of what Gelbrek's affectionately called his 'family': A motley collection of some 30 assorted mercenaries and cutthroats. Though disagreeable to outsiders, Gelbrek's family—his guild—was cordial to its own. The comradery Alonna enjoyed among the ruffians of the Caliss company helped fill the void left by Vergal's abduction and provided the first tinges of familial feelings she had enjoyed in months.

Gelbrek prepared her a sparse but comfortable cell in a nearly empty wing of the guild reserved for the few women of his group. The existence of the long annex, accessed from a concealed door in the brazier-ringed lounge, shocked Alonna. Yet that had been paltry in comparison to what still awaited her.

Before entering the guild, Alonna had been restricted to the brazier room and the training hall, a bare fraction of Gelbrek's underground sanctum. She had been utterly unprepared for the sheer size and sophistication of the place once it opened to her fully.

Winding, bare earth tunnels spread long tentacles beneath the city of Caliss, linking up through hidden passages to deserted buildings on the surface, cavernous circular rooms for storage and accommodation, as well as cramped, disused sewer tributaries that Gelbrek's retainers cleaned out, fortified, and incorporated into the complex at large.

The whole of the guild hall turned out to be a series of rooms joined by snaking underground burrows, stretching tendrils across the city and beyond. Stone and wood arch braces shored sodden and interminably dripping earth walls, a keen divergence from the palatial subterranean quarters to which they led.

Though Gelbrek provided for her comfort and permitted her complete liberty within the complex, Alonna understood her introduction to the scope of the fat man's enterprise meant that she had passed irrevocably into an underworld.

She supposed the loyalty Gelbrek demanded of his recruits was the reason why the guild set such an exorbitant price for its service and subjected candidates to such ferocious tests of loyalty. Alonna harbored no qualms about the nature of Gelbrek's business, and that, more than anything, illustrated to Alonna how completely her quest to regain Vergal had divorced her from her former ethical worldview. Gelbrek was transparently a thief. Through his network of mercenaries, he controlled gambling dens and distilleries within the city, he exacted protection money from merchants, and his men weren't above resorting to outright thievery when profits margins softened in other enterprises.

That his massive operation and great underground complex worked the city with relative impunity suggested to Alonna that Gelbrek had more than a few members of officialdom in his pocket. Gelbrek, however, only raised a chunky finger to his lips and winked surreptitiously whenever Alonna delicately attempted to satisfy her curiosity on this point.

It appeared nothing happened in Caliss without Gelbrek's knowledge. Alonna learned this early in her association and held out fervent hope he might illuminate the puzzle of her brother's abduction. She knocked hopefully one evening on the door to the suite of rooms the big man reserved for himself above the stable buildings, far removed from the goings-on in the lower halls.

Gelbrek's corpulent countenance darkened when she related the story of the red-cowled man who had taken her brother and somehow whisked him out of the city without a trace. As she had done with city officials, Alonna skipped the fact the man had left a bag of gold— which Alonna had clandestinely moved to her saferoom at the warehouse after leaving the Wayfarer. After all, she was now living in the thick of a den of thieves. She could not risk losing her means to hunt down Vergal's kidnapper.

She took Gelbrek's sudden frown for recognition and heatedly pressed him for details.

"If you know anything about this—anything at all—or if you know this man or have seen him, I am begging you to tell me, Gelbrek," Alonna said, near to tears.

Gelbrek blinked and shook his head slightly. When he regarded her again, his face was vague, puzzled.

"No, no, you mistake me, girl," the fat thief offered. He held his hands out wide and grinned, his features waxy in the puddle of uncertain light over the cluttered desk of his office. The old oak desk was a study in contradictions: A wickedly sharp dirk lay askew atop a thick, leather-bound text that bore an unknown language on its cover. The entire desk surface was a mess of scattered papers and sharp metal trinkets, many of which Alonna had never seen.

"I've never seen this man or this boy," he said earnestly. He paused. "Certainly, he's never passed my way. I'd tell you if he had, of course, I would!"

Alonna slumped into a chair across the desk from him. In the candlelight, her sudden tears glistened on her cheeks.

"You cannot know what it's been like," she moaned. "I train every day with Rostalin; I keep myself busy all the time to avoid leisure time to imagine what might have happened to him or where he's been taken. For all I know, my brother could be dead. It's a torment, Gelbrek. I'd give anything to have him back. Anything!"

She buried her face in the palms of her hands and wept.

Gelbrek drummed his fingers on the desk, watching her closely. The lies he told Alonna weighed heavily on his heart, and his lips twitched several times as if he were about to say something, but he clamped them firmly shut. *The guild*, he told himself sternly. *Above every other consideration, we must protect the guild.* He shook his head vigorously as if to clear an unpleasant thought.

Gelbrek rose from his chair and shifted his prodigious bulk around the desk to where he could kneel beside the weeping girl. He had grown fond enough of her in the weeks since her brave sojourn into the alley with Rostalin.

"'Ere now, dear," he said soothingly. He stroked her trembling arm lightly. "You're with family now; you understand? Anything you're going through, we're going through alongside you. You've suffered a great loss, but you mustn't dwell on things outside of your control."

He stood and patted Alonna's arm. She smiled gratefully through a tangled mass of inky hair. Not for the first time, the girl's beauty struck him. The flawless skin and the eerily blue eyes behind her wild black tresses sent a vague thrill through him, and the covert glance he stole served to remind him of her womanly attributes. Gelbrek turned back to his desk quickly, lest the girl resume her questioning, and he spill all he knew in rapture at her appearance.

She said nothing more. She rose and walked across the room. Gelbrek watched every step she took.

At the door, Alonna paused and favored him with another brilliant smile. He smiled back at her.

"Thank you, Gelbrek," she said, her voice raw. "For everything. For making me feel welcome here. You don't know what you've done for me."

Gelbrek tucked his fist under his chin and sat unmoving for a long time. At length, he sighed and roused himself. He held by his decision not to tell the girl of Sh'ynryan, the man who once had paid Gelbrek a terrific sum for his services and his silence, and who might one day return to pay him more if he kept his faith.

The sagacity of the guild was its true commodity, the reason why it survived and thrived, Gelbrek reminded himself. He vowed to continue to place his prosperity and the many members who depended on him above one young woman, no matter how comely or genuinely needy she may be.

Gelbrek rose, arranged his rumpled clothing, and padded to the door of his study, lost in thought. He must find Rostalin and ask the weapons instructor to spread the word: No one was to answer any questions Alonna might ask about a small boy and a mysterious man in a red cowl who may have passed through the complex in recent months.

They would obey the order, Gelbrek knew, no matter how fond they too had grown of the raven-haired lass—the latest addition to their sprawling 'family.' Like Gelbrek, the veterans of the guild appreciated the relevance of secrecy to their operation. It was how they thrived; it was the reason the guild prospered. No one would betray that trust, not even for so enchanting a creature as Alonna.

The family came first. Its individual members would always come second. It was the accepted way of life for an institution nearly a century in the making.

CHAPTER FIFTEEN

Water jetted in huge fins as the ship sliced the heaving sea. Jalwyn, leaning on the splintery rail at the bow, was mesmerized by the spectacle. If not for the violent sickness that had seized him, the young man might have taken more time to savor the sights and sounds of his first-ever sea voyage. However, Jalwyn dared not take his eye from the endless stream of spray thrown back by the ship's sharp nose. Only staring fixedly into the constant green-blue geyser of water curling back from the prow eased his malady.

For such a fluid thing, the steady turn of water appeared strangely constant. It went a long way toward settling Jalwyn's seething stomach.

Not far from him stood the masthead of the *Acolyte*—a beautifully carved maiden with blank wooden eyes where the craftsman had neglected to chisel pupils. The masthead dipped and rose in steep step with the waves. Jalwyn risked a glance and immediately felt the sickness rise once more at the sight of the bobbing sculpture. He fastened his eyes again on the spray.

The motion beneath his feet was intolerable. He could not acclimatize himself to the sensation of standing stock still on a solid surface that nevertheless lifted and dropped beneath his feet on the crest of every incoming wave. And though the sun shone brightly in the flawless blue vault of the sky, and only a light wind deigned to puff the *Acolyte's* grasping sails, the rising waves advanced on the ship as if, at least in Jalwyn's overwrought estimation, spurred by gale-force winds. A quick peek at the white-capped horizon stretching ahead confirmed such waves in inexhaustible supply.

He turned and slid his back down the railing until his feet were stretched ahead of him, like sticks poking from beneath his scarlet cowl. The fish-belly white skin of his ankles gleamed unwholesomely in the sunlight. Jalwyn gathered them back beneath the hem of his robe, suddenly ashamed. Even the barbaric northerners, who comprised the crew of the *Acolyte*, people renown for the sallow, pale complexions that were by-products of their lightless winters, seemed ruddy and tanned in comparison to Jalwyn, a man who had dwelled all his life in the tropical city of Zistah, the fairest jewel in the Arasynian Emperor's sprawling realm.

Jalwyn decided that a scholarly life spent locked in the bowels of dim libraries was not conducive to a healthy coloring, and he resolved upon his return to Zistah to spend more time out of doors, in the tropical sunshine that baked the skin of his countrymen to their distinctive hue.

His coloring had been a source of angst for the young man. Though born Arasynian, Jalwyn had, since birth, lacked the tawny pigmentation that defined his southern people. His curling black hair tumbled in an unruly cascade down from a severe part atop his long head, framing a pallid face. Jalwyn was a tall man, slight of build, with a keen aquiline nose that appeared even more pronounced on account of his bad posture, which caused him to slouch when he walked, accentuating his long features.

A rough guffaw caused him to look up. One of the sailors—he had been introduced to this one, he remembered his name was Tael—kneeled near the mainmast. He coiled a length of rope and chuckled evilly in his direction.

"Enjoying the voyage, lander?" Tael grinned, drawing out the derogatory word the brutes aboard the *Acolyte* used to describe all who were not sea-going miscreants like themselves.

"Very much," Jalwyn smiled in return, though the effort of talking made him feel queasy. "Say, aren't you the delightful fellow I saw earlier swabbing the deck?"

"Ayup," Tael drawled, scowling, "'Er', what of it?"

"Then you are likely the gentleman they will call upon to clean up should I lose control and spew the contents of my stomach across the deck, am I correct?"

Tael paused in coiling his rope. "Don'tchya dare, lander!" he exclaimed. "Over the side, if ya be feelin' the urge."

Jalwyn plumped his cheeks slightly as if an eruption were imminent. "I can't make any guarantees," he choked. "All of this engaging conversation has set my stomach churning again."

"Then by the agonies, man—be shutting yer mouth!" Tael cried. He gathered his rope and scampered away, leaving Jalwyn to his misery but relishing his solitude.

What am I doing here? Jalwyn asked himself for likely the thousandth time since the broad transport barge that had made the pleasant trip down the sluggish river from Zistah had deposited him on a stinking and crowded quay at the seaport of Goth.

Unlike the fresh rivers descending from the mountains and through the scented jungles of Zistah, the Arasynian seaport had churned his stomach with its scents of decay and salt. That had been trifling compared to the nausea that gripped him when the northern merchant ship had cleared the long breakwater and set out for the rolling open sea. A man with some talent to manipulate elements with ancient words of power found himself utterly helpless against the ravages of the sea at large. He knew no word he could craft to settle his quivering insides.

As many times as he had asked the question, however, a droll voice somewhere deep in Jalwyn's mind answered it for him: Because the Brotherhood commanded it. When he considered that response, Jalwyn shook his head and drew away from his doubts and fears. As he had been taught since his initiation to the Magi years ago, the Brotherhood's orders were to be obeyed, not questioned. Certainly, not by the likes of him, a novice in the ways of the Words.

Yet that begged another distressing question. Why had the Magi selected him, the youngest and least experienced of their order, for this quest? And to provide him with such sketchy details: A Brother who departed on a mission has not communicated in some time. He was to go where the Brother was supposed to have gone and follow his trail.

He had a name to follow—Sh'ynryan, an elder Brother whom Jalwyn had rarely encountered during his years within the cloister—but nothing in the way of details explaining why this man must be found.

The nagging interior voice told Jalwyn the mission must be important, or the Brotherhood would not have ordered it. The Elders sent him on his way with a generous pouch of gold to cover expenses and a serious charge not to confront the man but send word immediately of his location upon confirming sight of him.

Was he chasing a rogue? Magi who betrayed the Brotherhood and struck out on their own were rare, though they existed. They were powerful renegades, storming across the face of the earth, sowing fear and panic in the populace through the exercise of their prowess with the Words.

But if a rogue, why had the Brethren not warned Jalwyn? And why send a Brother so young in the Words to track him? Only years of experience made a Mage strong enough to exist separate from the Brotherhood. Sending an apprentice after an Elder who could annihilate him seemed less than prudent.

The questions tumbled through Jalwyn's mind without ceasing. Jalwyn felt less assured of his ability to piece together the riddle. Shaking his head to clear the puzzling thoughts, Jalwyn resolved to think less about why he was going and focus instead on where he was heading.

He was aboard a trader's ship bound for Far, the jetsam capital of the Aerie Coast. The Brethren appeared certain that Far had been Sh'ynryan's destination before they lost track of him.

Why Sh'ynryan dispatched there, or where he intended to travel afterward, were mysteries Jalwyn had been sent to unlock.

With every swell it climbed, the *Acolyte* drew closer to the Aerie Coast islands. Jalwyn opted simply to trust in the Brethren's direction. They would not have sent him on an errand beyond his means to complete. If only the bile churning in his stomach would abate and allow him to concentrate!

Intent on these thoughts, several minutes passed before Jalwyn realized a commotion had risen around him. Men were crowding the deck in a frenzy of activity. He spotted his "friend" Tael scurrying among the frantic bodies on the deck and, pulling himself to his feet, accosted the sailor.

"What's happening?"

"Hands off me, lander!" Tael growled, shoving away Jalwyn. "You'll see soon enough."

Before Jalwyn could respond, Tael was gone, having melted into the scramble of sailors all around him.

Sailors hooted and hollered from the rigging that spread between the ship's towering masts. Most of the bustle on the deck was concentrated on the port side railing, where the sailors stood in a seething mass. Gripping the rail, Jalwyn made his way to port on unsteady feet.

"What is happening?" Jalwyn asked again of the nearest sailor.

The man favored him with a grin that was largely devoid of teeth. "Just a little bit o' retribution, lander," he said. "Some fool has strayed out of the shipping lanes."

"What do you mean?"

"Look fer yerself," the man said, handing Jalwyn a spyglass.

Jalwyn peered through the glass. The white-capped waves were suddenly gargantuan and crashing directly before his eyes. He lowered the glass, gulped mightily to chew back the rising bile, and with shaking hands brought the scope back to his eyes.

After a fruitless moment, Jalwyn caught a mercurial flash of something white rocking far out in the pitching sea. Steadying his hands, he spied a ship, not unlike *Acolyte* floundering in the distance. A distinct flag snapped briskly high on its mast.

"That's an Arasynian ship!" Jalwyn exclaimed over the babble of excited sailors.

"Indeed," a sailor replied happily, slapping Jalwyn heartily on his shoulder. "And in a mite of trouble too, by looks."

Jalwyn shifted this way and that, galvanized with nervous energy at the sight of a ship from his native land floundering, uncertain what to do. "We must help them!" he shouted above the thundering spray.

The sailor laughed. "Oh, we'll help right enough. We'll help ourselves to her cargo hold!"

Jalwyn regarded the man incredulously. "What?"

But before the man could reply, another voice interjected loudly, "Ah, I was just looking for you."

Jalwyn turned to face the captain of the ship, a tall man in leather breeches and a silk tunic, with jet black hair salted with grey.

He wore a pleasant smile as he pushed through the milling sailors. A stiff breeze had risen, and it rifled the captain's thick hair and billowed his gossamer shirt.

"Captain," Jalwyn cried, "an Arasynian ship is in trouble. It looks to be listing. We must help them."

The captain placed firm hands on Jalwyn's shoulders. He smiled companionably at him and yelled to be heard above the suddenly gusting wind.

"Please, don't concern yourself, sir!" the captain said, his smile broad. "We have the matter in hand. Don't you think you'd be more comfortable in your cabin until this wind calms?"

Jalwyn shrugged loose of the captain's grasp. "No, I would not! My countrymen are in distress. I'll stay right here and help; just tell me what I can do."

The captain shook his head. "I'm afraid there's nothing you can do. In fact, I'm thinking you'll only be in the way. I suggest you go below to your cabin and let your captain handle this, eh?"

Jalwyn didn't like the steel that crept into the captain's voice.

"Handle what, exactly?" Jalwyn asked.

The captain only grinned and pointed above Jalwyn's head. Jalwyn followed his finger and blanched at the spectacle of a sailor, busy in the crow's nest, pulling down the *Acolyte's* Aerie Coast banner. In its place, a length of black cloth flapped in the wind as the sailor busily drew the ropes.

"Pirates!" Jalwyn spat.

"Only when convenient," the captain replied amiably. "We're a trader's ship, right enough, and we have no qualms about carrying Arasynian goods and people. But we're loyal to His Majesty at Far, and when a chance comes to hit the Emperor, well, the lads and I see it as our patriotic duty to lord and liege."

"You bastard!"

The captain's lips pressed thin. "That's uncalled for. I'm almost certainly my father's son. What you should be worrying about is how your place in this turns out."

When the captain's hands lifted again toward Jalwyn, there was nothing friendly in the man's manner or expression.

Jalwyn cringed and skipped out of range of the man's reach.

"No point in that, friend," the captain said, still advancing. A rapier appeared from a sheath at his hip. His smile grew positively brilliant.

"It's over the side with you, lad. It's a bit of bad luck, I'm afraid, but political leanings are best kept to one's self in mixed company."

Jalwyn turned and fled.

The sailors milling about the deck provided excellent cover. Jalwyn dodged and jagged through the crush of bodies out of the reach of the pursuing captain.

The captain yelled warnings, but few seemed to hear him in the excitement. Jalwyn's eyes cast everywhere, seeking escape. He knew even as he fled that escape was impossible. His only hope was the Arasynian ship, still far off but growing closer. The pirates had tacked the *Acolyte* and swung her girth toward the listing Imperial ship. Concealment was Jalwyn's best bet until his countrymen were within range. He settled on the best defensive spot on the ship: The crow's nest.

Jalwyn ducked behind a stacked row of water barrels to catch a breath and settle his swirling thoughts. He crouched beside the mainmast, upon which the crow's nest perched. The pirate he knew to be roosting up there was out of sight, but Jalwyn decided to settle that problem once it presented itself. Composing himself with deep breaths, Jalwyn began to mutter under his breath and make passes with his hands in front of his face.

The breeze, already growing, thickened around him, writhing in response to its ancient name. Calling the wind was the least of the Magi's ability; molding it to his service was the true test of the Brethren's skill. The rushing wind settled into a turgid column surrounding him. Yet, not a thread of Jalwyn's red robe or black cape stirred. A softly glowing nimbus settled around his body and painted the barrels around him in scintillating blue radiance as it intensified.

The captain's bellowing voice, now bereft of any gentility, warned the Mage he'd been spied. He maintained his composure, as he had been trained, and in tranquil whispered words and motions, he shaped the called power of the Word. His mind envisioned how he wished the wind to serve him; his discipline bent its raw force to his will.

The barrels were thrown aside, and the captain stood imposingly over him, a silhouette wreathed in dazzling sunlight. A brilliant arc of reflected sunlight defined the upraised rapier in his hand.

"There you are!" the captain roared, but the words died in the man's throat as Jalwyn completed the channeling. *Above*, he silently commanded the manifestation.

Jalwyn lifted off the deck, soaring into the air to elevate far above the stunned face of the captain and others who, with yelled oaths and upraised fingers, tracked his path.

As always, the sheer joy of his magic seized Jalwyn: The crescendo of the elemental power building as it rushed to the call of its name, to be crafted, was focused and released by the skill and discipline of the caller in an otherworldly display.

Turning, his long robes flaring around him as he rose, Jalwyn saw the underside of the crow's nest rushing toward him. He stretched his hands ahead of him to receive the gentle impact. He hovered there for an instant, held aloft by the gentle and compliant force, and dug his fingers into the side of the loft. The chaotic activity on the deck had turned its attention from the listing ship in the distance to Jalwyn. Sailors pointed and screamed. Clawing and climbing, Jalwyn pulled himself level with the lip and swung his legs soundlessly over the lip of the nest.

As luck would have it, the pirate in the crow's nest had his back to Jalwyn. He was fixated on the floundering ship in his spyglass and oblivious to the screamed warnings of the men below.

Jalwyn jerked a dagger from beneath his robe and, with grim resolve, drove it to the hilt into the unsuspecting pirate's back.

The man fell chest-first into the rim of the nest. His hands scrabbled furiously to reach the dagger protruding from his back. Blood mushroomed on the fabric of his shirt. Jalwyn, sickened by the sight and sounds of the man's agony, grasped the wailing man's ankles and hurriedly toppled him over the edge. The pirate's shrieking descent terminated in a moist crunch on the deck below. Jalwyn recoiled at the sound of it.

An instant of stunned silence greeted their colleague's bone-shattering arrival on deck before the pirates' cursing and screaming resumed. They waved upraised swords at Jalwyn, who peered nervously over the lip of the crow's nest. Below, the jettisoned pirate's corpse sprawled amid a web of splintered wooden planks. The Mage's fine dagger remained jammed between the pirate's shoulders. Jalwyn lamented its loss.

A horde of pirates leaped for the ship's rigging and, with practiced skill, began scaling the strands of rope.

Jalwyn paced frantically in the close confines of the nest, his mind racing. His seasickness, combined with the light-headedness that accompanied the release of elemental energy, caused the world to spin briefly around him. The pirates' cursing and the creaking of ropes below reminded Jalwyn he had little leisure time to recuperate.

The Arasynian ship grew larger on the horizon as the *Acolyte's* sails bellied in the rising wind. Jalwyn's hope depended on fending off the pirates until his countrymen drew near enough. Even then, transferring from the *Acolyte* to the Zistinian ship would prove a trick, especially if he had upwards of 30 angry pirates harrying him along the way.

The ropes creaked louder, the pirates' cursing grew saltier, garbled though it was by the cruel knives clenched between their teeth as they climbed.

You are Magi! Jalwyn berated himself. *Weakness is for the likes of normal men, not for you! Concentrate now! Focus!*

A pair of tattooed hands appeared at the rim of the nest. A scowling face, contorted with hate, immediately followed. A booted foot hooked over the ledge as the pirate drew himself up. With no time left to consider, Jalwyn waved his hands in front of him and spoke a word. His ears rang, his heart raced, and a gout of fire erupted from the tips of his splayed fingers. The blast wreathed the man's face in flames. The pirate's horrified expression melted and drooped like wax on the stem of a candle. The man's mouth opened in a lipless scream that was lost beneath the furnace of flames jetting from Jalwyn's hands.

"Away with you!" Jalwyn bellowed. The ecstasy of conducting such massive energy battled for supremacy against the severe fatigue stealing into his limbs. He swiveled his hips this way and that, training the billowing sheet of flames on new, astonished faces as they appeared above the rim of the nest.

He screeched with frightened laughter. "Down, you mongrel bastards!" he cried.

He dared not draw a breath or give himself a second to relax lest the strain of maintaining the power flow overtake him. His defiant screaming rolled on uninterrupted as he sheathed the stunned pirates' heads and arms in fire. Men dropped screaming and engulfed in flame.

Jalwyn dug from deep reserves of stamina he didn't know he possessed for strength enough to channel the elemental power further. A few passes of his hand accompanied his cry to fire, and a ball of crackling flame coalesced in his outstretched palm.

Waves of heat emanating from the sphere seared the tender flesh of his nose, yet the flames did not scorch his hand. He pitched the hissing orb over the side to the deck below.

The result was all he could have asked for, given his extreme weariness and his utter inability to defend himself further.

The fireball curled away, trailing a ribbon of licking flame in its wake. It struck the deck and flared mightily, igniting a roaring conflagration. The uprising shockwave staggered Jalwyn but not before he glimpsed the inferno enveloping the massed pirates below. Fire roared up the tendrils of rigging and rope ladders, leaving a tattered, flaming web in its aftermath. Jalwyn slumped to the floor of the nest.

The last thought Jalwyn registered before the darkness settled over him was how beautiful the seething flames appeared around him, turning the sky—his world—into a brilliant canopy of light.

CHAPTER SIXTEEN

Vergal's head swam and a surreptitious glance at Guile, who sat slouched in his saddle with his eyes downcast and his brow furrowed, told him the mercenary was having similar difficulty comprehending Sh'ynryan's long discourse of the previous night.

Magi? Words of Power from the days of Creation that summoned the elemental essence to the call of man? Sorcerors who wielded power to call and mold the winds, the flames, the earth, and even the unseen currents of the deep? A legendary Stone, etched with the true arcane names of all elemental things, since lost to history? Sh'ynryan's stories defied belief. Yet whenever they balked at accepting the Mage's recounting as truth, the boy and the mercenary only need recall the swirling storm that had surged from Sh'ynryan's outstretched fingers to slow the rogues' arrows as if they had been propelled through a wall of water instead of thin air.

Vergal, who had beheld more examples of Sh'ynryan's prowess in past days, had even less reason than Guile to doubt the Mage's word. Yet he wrestled mightily to reconcile himself with the man's explanations of how he could perform such feats and why. It upset everything that Vergal, a practical boy, had ever believed true about the world around him and greatly diminished his own position within it. He was stubbornly reluctant to sacrifice more of his perceptions of the world after a span of time in which so many of his preconceptions had been turned on their side—even in the face of incontrovertible evidence.

Even more difficult to accept were Sh'ynryan's revelations concerning Vergal himself. He shivered to recall them and fell back into his troubled thoughts.

Riding behind the pair, Sh'ynryan wore a smug grin as he studied his companions' drooping postures. Had he realized a simple dissertation on the intricacies of the Words would sap their defiance, he'd have offered it long ago. After all, he had not betrayed anything a diligent seeker might uncover in tomes of lore. Except to Vergal. But that was a separate matter.

"But why did you bring me?" Vergal had asked, and Sh'ynryan launched into the response that he had earlier prepared, the one that offered a half-truth while betraying nothing of his true intentions or reasons.

Sh'ynryan studied the boy gravely before answering. "Not every man can speak the Words," he solemnly explained. "Though the elements of Creation answer to their true names, it is the caller who channels and directs their power. Without a strong will to harness them, they are unrealized energy, present but raw, ineffectual, and rudderless. Whispering its true name can call the wind, but only the strong mind of a disciplined caller can bend it to his will."

He leveled a telling look at Vergal as he said this.

A thought occurred to Vergal. "Is that why you tire so quickly after you do...those things?" he asked, waving one hand vaguely in a gesture intended to look mystical but which seemed to Sh'ynryan as flippant. "Is it because you're working inside yourself to control what you've called?"

The boy was intuitive, undoubtedly so, Sh'ynryan thought. It was further confirmation of the potential his amulet had perceived in Vergal at their first meeting. It pleased the Mage immensely.

"Well done; that's it exactly," Sh'ynryan praised and Vergal, despite himself, felt a flush of pleasure at his words.

"The gathering in, the forming, and the release of the power is incredibly taxing on the caller," Sh'ynryan continued. "Imagine being seized by even the shadow of the incalculable elemental power you have called and attempting to contain it. It demands the utmost discipline to shape these forces, to compel them to execute the manifestation the mind conceives for them.

"Unchecked, the power would rage, emerging in its basest form and consuming the caller in the process. As I say, it is a rare man who possesses a mind even to comprehend the Words, or the tongue to form them, and rarer still one who possesses the mental mastery to act as conduit for their power. Many who believed otherwise have proven fatally mistaken."

"If your Order knows these Words," Vergal asked, "why do you need to find the Stone?"

"We know only the oral tradition of them, carefully handed down through generations,"

Sh'ynryan replied. "However, no man alive has ever beheld them in their original form."

"So?" Guile said dismissively.

Sh'ynryan paused, sighed, then pressed on. "Accuracy of the words is paramount, and this is why the Stone is needed, to refresh our tradition from the original text." His eyes grew distant. "Imagine possessing the Words of Power in their original form, their every inflection unadulterated and absolutely pure…"

Vergal frowned. "Are they not accurate now then?"

"Yes, but no," Sh'ynryan explained, refocusing. He drew a deep breath and pressed on.

"Suppose you read a book from which the text has been translated from its original script," the Mage explained. "Something, as they say, is surely lost in the translation. Then translations get translated again, and so on, as they progress through time. The Words of Power originate from a pure source text but sharing them over thousands of years has undoubtedly altered their precise forms and ultimately compromised them in contrast to their source."

Sh'ynryan went on. "The oral tradition has obviously faithfully preserved the Words of Power—the manifestation of their energy is proof enough of that—but has it exactly recorded them? We have no extant text by which to compare and ensure they are unadulterated. In fact, some in our Order believe the Words have most assuredly been tainted over time, and they point to the immense physical toll it takes on those who call them as evidence of that."

Sh'ynryan paused, pondered, then continued.

"I suppose the analogy is akin to consuming a rotten apple: it remains an apple, and its fruit may nourish still, but the rot threatens illness too. If rot has entered into the oral tradition over millennia, then to possess the Stone would be akin to consuming fresh fruit, with no impurity whatsoever, and only nourishment as a consequence. Do you understand?"

The glazed eyes of his confused but intent audience indicated perhaps they did not.

"The Words of Power in the oral tradition, therefore," Sh'ynryan summarized, "are true representations of the originals – but may have been compromised or corrupted by ages of repetition, if you follow my meaning."

Vergal, who had not learned to read and had trouble grasping the concept of 'translation' as a result, did not necessarily follow the Mage's meaning but pressed on. "But you have not answered my question," the boy said. "Why do you need me here for any of this. Where do I fit in?"

"I'd have thought you would have inferred it," Sh'ynryan huffed. "You perplex me, boy. You provoke me to praise your intuition and curse it within the span of breaths.

"Since you miss it," he went on, "here it is plainly. Given the dangerous nature of the Words, the Brotherhood holds as its highest responsibility its missive to seek out others like unto themselves who possess the gift of understanding them, to instill in them the proper discipline for their use should they encounter them. It would be disastrous for someone with innate capability, but lacking necessary competence, to learn and speak the Words."

Sh'ynryan had leaned forward and poked the fire with his metal-shod walking stick.

"It has happened, you understand, more often than we care to admit. What men consider unexplained phenomena in the world—spirits, demons, and the like—are almost always attributable to novices, who have somehow spoken aloud a Word."

"The Words are in the world," Sh'ynryan said, resting his chin on the butt of this walking stick and watching the fire. "Oh, not the originals, as I already said, but the translations of translations, written on shards of ancient pottery and stone, on fragments of parchments, scattered throughout ancient writings, sometimes accidentally and unknowingly handed down through oral traditions.

"The energy responds to a mind that can comprehend and call it but becomes scrambled when the will cannot channel it. It inevitably unleashes in a haphazard manner, drawing on images in the caller's mind—dreams, nightmares, fantasies, what have you. Some of these incarnations have been truly horrifying, and when the Brotherhood learns of them, they quickly dispatch Magi to contain the situation. It is our most sacred trust, superseding all others.

"We know these people immediately when we encounter them," Sh'ynryan said, looking at Vergal. "We have devised a way."

Vergal blanched; a horrid realization dawned on him. "The amulet," he said weakly.

Sh'ynryan nodded.

Guile, who had sat watching the exchange, leaned into the conversation. "Hey now, what talk is this?" he demanded. "What amulet do you mean?"

"It glowed when you came into the Wayfarer," Vergal went on, ignoring Guile, "and again in my room."

"Yes. The metal forged into the amulet is sensitive to those attuned to the Words. All of this bodes very well for you."

"Are you telling me ...," Vergal stuttered, "do you mean to say ..."

Sh'ynryan threw his head back and laughed. "I do mean to say it!" he said merrily. "And in so many words, I already have. You, Vergal, are one of the gifted. It's unformed in you, true, but the potential is unmistakable. You are a mere boy, and you exhibit such raw potential already, such as I've never seen in one your age.

"And so, we come to the answer to your question," Sh'ynryan proceeded. "You're here with me now simply because my vows as Magi do not permit me to allow one such as you to stumble through the world, flattening forests and rending the heavens with stray words."

Vergal turned his startled expression on Guile, who instinctively flinched from the boy's gaze. He had trouble reconciling the fresh young face before him with the act of sorcery he had witnessed Sh'ynryan perform on the road.

"Vergal," the mercenary said slowly, scrutinizing the boy's face as if meeting him for the first time. "Who are you?"

"I don't know, Guile," he replied softly. "I'm not sure anymore."

Now, the companions rode through the thin bars of sunshine that poked through the leafy canopy above. Sh'ynryan reveled in the silence. A wind rose and with it the scent of promised rain, waving the leaves overhead and shaking the dappled shadows on the road ahead.

The knowledge that the same road stretching ahead terminated soon in his destination thrilled Sh'ynryan. Since his search began years previous, the Mage had never felt so close to his prize. The discovery of Vergal had been a surprise. *The thief had not covered his tracks so completely, after all,* the Mage thought with a grin. He failed to see how he had missed it the first time.

The jingle of harness roused him, and Sh'ynryan looked to see Vergal check his horse and swing out of the saddle. The boy had taken to riding instinctively and now seemed as able horseback as Guile or himself, seemingly able to accomplish everything to which he put his hand. Sh'ynryan advised himself to remember that trait when the boy's training began.

"What are you doing?" Sh'ynryan called to the boy. He thumped his mount's flanks and cantered quickly to join the pair ahead.

"I need to relieve myself," Vergal said. There was no challenge in his voice, no rancor; just a plain statement of fact and much preferable to the venomous rejoinder Sh'ynryan had received in a similar situation the night after the escape from Caliss. The Mage nodded approvingly. The boy's will was breaking; Sh'ynryan had given him matters to mull other than the sister left behind. So pleased was he that he decided not to make an issue of the boy's unscheduled stop.

"Stay close to the road, where we can see you," Sh'ynryan said solicitously. "Remember the highwaymen."

"I remember," Vergal replied, "but this is the kind of comfort break best taken further into the woods, if you know what I mean."

"Ah," Sh'ynryan said simply. He made a motion that Vergal should proceed.

Vergal trudged down the bare dirt ditch beside the road, leaped smartly over the rivulet of brackish, weedy water in the trench, and pushed through the long grass of the steep slope on the opposite side. A few steps carried him out of the knee-high grass and between the slim trunks of an aspen forest.

A glance over his shoulder revealed Sh'ynryan and Guile astride their horses on the road below, whispering. "If I can see them, they can still see me," Vergal grumbled under his breath. He moved further into the woods.

A quick turn and the rows of aspens gave way to a dense thicket of pine. A cloud of mosquitos drifted up from under-hanging branches and the mat of dried needles beneath. They buzzed mindlessly in their eye-watering fashion, fastening to every inch of exposed skin.

Slapping and complaining, Vergal put his head down and crashed through the tangle, seeking escape. When the cloud at last relented, he glanced up to find himself in a mossy clearing ringed on every side by towering evergreens.

A clear brook trickled over polished stones down the center of the clearing, discharging from the forest at one end and disappearing back into it at the other. Vergal realized he had become turned around in his blind dash through the evergreen boughs and was uncertain of the precise direction through the trees that led back to the road. A wall of pines behind him had swallowed the path from which he had emerged. The boy gulped nervously, well imagining Sh'ynryan's reaction if the Mage need come looking for him.

A crashing in the trees behind him indicated the search had already commenced.

"I'm over here!" Vergal yelled, giving his rescuers a reference point to follow through the labyrinth. "I got turned around in the trees."

The distant crashing turned into a nearby din. Wood cracked, and branches snapped loudly deep in the evergreens. Vergal blinked. That was much more noise than two men should be making. Vergal wondered if they were using the horses to blaze a path through the choked vegetation to reach him.

But the head that parted the pine boughs was much larger than a horse's—larger still than the heads of several horses melded together.

It was black-scaled and massive, with ridges of serrated bone that flowed upwards from the elongated snout to end in two obsidian curling horns.

The leathery lips of its maw peeled back in a snarl to display rows of jagged teeth. The monstrous head—slung low to the ground where it emerged from the thicket—lifted on a snaking neck that cleared the uppermost limbs of the ragged pines. Limbs snapped and broke free to tumble to the ground as the beast stepped into the clearing. A clawed foot fell heavily on the ground, thumping loudly despite the mossy floor, followed shortly by another. Its flexing talons churned up stones beneath the loam.

The beast snorted and lowered its neck to examine Vergal. Warty eyelids slid sideways to blink over slit-like pupils. Even from a distance, the thing's acrid breath struck with the force of a bellows. Vergal's hair danced back on his forehead. The boy stood stock still, stunned into immobility by the beast's horrifying appearance.

Then the thing roared.

The ear-splitting scream drowned the sounds of the gurgling brook and sent birds exploding from the trees around the clearing. The monster stood snorting and scratching the spongy earth, turning chunks of sod between its splayed claws.

"Don't move, Vergal!" It was Guile's voice, somewhere nearby, yet out of sight, raised to be heard over the beast's coughs and growls. The mercenary need not have feared. Motion was not presently a viable option.

The beast's head whipped around at the sound of Guile's voice, and it snuffled loudly. Its nostrils flared wide as it pulled in the scents swirling in the air, searching, pinpointing. A low steady growl rumbled in the monster's chest, nearly overpowering Guile's continued shouted instructions.

"It's a Drakleth!" Guile's voice warned from somewhere unseen but nearby. "They don't see well, but their hearing and smell are acute. Move slowly, and it will have trouble seeing you. Back up carefully toward the brook. Get in the water and immerse yourself as much as possible; it will help disguise your scent."

The Drakleth stood sniffing in the direction of Guile's voice. It charged forward several paces, plowing aside tree branches, still noisily testing the air. The rain the wind had earlier promised now began to fall in a light mist that speckled the rushing water of the brook. Despite the sudden shower, the sun shone, though scudding clouds in the distance testified to heavier rain still to come.

Vergal set one foot slowly behind the other, edging toward the rain-spotted brook behind him.

He heard the whistle of the approaching arrow but didn't see it until the shaft had bounced ineffectually off the Drakleth's plated snout. The beast shook its head and roared, lunging forward several ponderous steps. It had now cleared the trees, and Vergal stared open-mouthed at the sheer size of the thing. Its long neck was half the size of its bulky, ebon-scaled body and a quarter that of its lolling, sinewy tail, the tip of which still swished in the underbrush behind it. Had Guile not distracted it, one bounding step would have covered the distance between it and Vergal, and the boy had few doubts about how that encounter would have concluded.

A litany of curses sounded from the trees as Guile lamented his botched shot. Vergal and the Drakleth turned in time to see another arrow slice into the clearing. This one embedded in the fleshy tendon dividing the Drakleth's nostrils, and the monster roared again. The beast dropped its head to the earth and scratched its nose with heavy claws to disengage the stinging arrow.

"Vergal, get to the water! Go!"

His feet were scurrying before he registered the movement. "Where's Sh'ynryan?" Vergal screamed over his shoulder, but if Guile heard him above the angry cacophony of the screeching Drakleth, he gave no sign.

Vergal threw himself face-first into the brook. The icy water sucked the breath from his lungs. He floundered for an instant before realizing his stomach was scraping the stony bottom of the stream. He lifted his head and inhaled mightily, trying to draw breath deep into his spastic lungs.

"It's not deep enough!" Vergal yelled over hitching breaths, but again, there was no answer. He turned his head to mark the location of the Drakleth. He sobbed with relief when he saw it was gone.

Gone, but not departed. Over the babble of the brook, the sounds of rending and ripping trees rose, and an instant later, far across the clearing, Guile bolted out of the woods. His legs pumped furiously across the loamy clearing. Then, the Drakleth burst out of the forest, leaving a tunnel of shattered trees in its wake.

Guile dove into the water, and, as luck would have it, the mercenary chose a spot where the brook widened into a churning pool. Guile disappeared in a loud splash, and quickly after, the Drakleth's open maw snapped down at the place where the mercenary disappeared, sending up a fin of spray.

"Guile!" Vergal screamed, rising to his knees in the fast-flowing water. His teeth chattered from the cold.

The Drakleth's head rose and plunged as it probed the pool for its prey. Water streamed between its teeth, and rocks tumbled from the beast's mouth each time it surfaced. The noisy brook erupted in high jets of water when its mighty head plunged. Vergal, climbing to his feet, found himself running toward the pool before he knew what he was doing.

Then Guile was there, running toward him, gesturing for him to turn back. The mercenary had pulled himself over a rocky overhang, where the brook cascaded into the pool, and his feet churned up geysers as he sprinted down the middle of the creek bed in desperate, wide-eyed flight from the distracted Drakleth.

Vergal skidded to a stop, but his foot slipped on the pebbly bottom, and he fell with a noisy splash. He sputtered, spewing water when Guile grabbed him roughly by the arm and yanked him to his feet at a full run. Vergal cried out and collapsed again. He had turned an ankle in the fall, and the foot would not support his weight.

Soaked, dripping, Guile dragged the back of his hand across his mouth and cursed. "Come on, kid! It will notice us soon. Get on your feet!"

"I can't," Vergal whimpered. "My foot!" Vergal grasped and massaged the offending appendage. "Go on, run," Vergal said bravely, punching Guile's leg with his balled-up fist. "Get away while you still can."

Guile scoffed. "Please, give me credit," he said. Leaning, he hauled Vergal by one hand and drew his sword with the other. Vergal hopped on one foot as Guile dragged him awkwardly through the water. The pain was bearable if he kept the weight off his bloating ankle. Vergal wrapped his arms around the mercenary's shoulders and tried to distribute his weight as evenly as possible for the straining man.

"Where's Sh'ynryan?" Vergal yelled in Guile's ear.

"He's ... about," the man panted between strides. "Just ... shut ... up," he implored. They were following the middle of the brook to conceal their scent from the Drakleth, but their passage was noisy. Vergal, his eyes plastered to the Drakleth at the far end of the clearing, screamed when the creature finally lifted its head and turned its inky eyes directly on them.

"It saw us!" Vergal warned.

"No ... it smells us," the mercenary replied. "The wind's in our face. Damn it all!"

Then the world disappeared.

At least it seemed that way to Vergal. In one instant, the boy's eyes were glued to the creature in the distance. It reared up and stomped over the rocky waterfall and began its pursuit. In the next instant, the beast was gone, obscured by a sudden, shifting sheet of grey.

A torrent of rain erupted from the darkened sky.

It was a cloudburst of a magnitude Vergal had never seen. He coughed, his open mouth suddenly full of water. The slanting rain stung his eyes, drenched his clothes, and streamed in a current down his back. The world seemed composed entirely of water. It was a marvel he could still draw breath out of the saturated air.

"That's your friend Sh'ynryan," Guile crowed, his words gurgling as he spat rainwater. "That skinny bastard's starting to grow on me."

In the distance, the enraged Drakleth screamed. "It can't find us!" Guile rasped. "It can't smell us in this rain. Vergal, get into the trees. Get out from where it can see us when the rain stops."

No sooner did he say it than the rain stopped. It didn't taper or stutter; it merely dried up, its source wholly exhausted.

"Uh oh," Guile said before he flung himself and Vergal into the creek, now bloated and racing even faster from the deluge of rain.

They submerged but couldn't stay that way. The massive downpour had transformed the merry creek into a turbulent torrent that overflowed its banks. The water's current tore them away from each other. Guile emerged sputtering on one bank, Vergal on the other.

Not so far away, the Drakleth sneezed and shook its colossal head to clear its sensitive snout. The air was moist, but the beast soon caught a faint whiff of its quarry. Vergal trembled and could not stifle a scream when the Drakleth, with its head high and sampling the air, bounded toward him.

"Vergal!" came a familiar voice, one faint from fatigue. He pivoted to see Sh'ynryan leaning against a shattered tree trunk at the edge of the clearing. He wearily made a gesture and mouthed the firm instruction to, "Keep down!"

And then the Mage breathed deeply, spread his arms, and spoke a word that carried clearly to where Vergal lay half into the racing stream.

Fire flared to wreath Sh'ynryan's outstretched hands. With a scream of release, the Mage jabbed his fingers forward, and flame spewed forth to strike the ground.

The flames wove a snaking line across the ground, roaring over sodden moss and leaping over inflammable stone. Behind the meandering line, flames crackled heavenward in a great shifting sheet. The wall of fire zoomed overland until it came to the stream, seemed to pause, then reignited on the opposite bank, leaving a gap only where the water flowed along its course.

Across the bank, Guile yelled in alarm as the flames formed a blazing wall near him. He held up one arm to shield himself from the heat.

With his hands pointed at the ground, fire pouring continuously to fuel his wall of flame, Sh'ynryan yelled, "Tell Guile to come! I can't hold this."

On the opposite side of the wall, the Drakleth screamed. Vergal could not see it through the shimmering curtain but heard it skid to a halt somewhere close by. Its jaws snapped angrily, but it kept its head far from the ribbon of fire separating it from its prey.

"Guile!" Vergal bellowed. "Sh'ynryan says get over here. Now!"

His face ashen, the mercenary nodded and climbed to his feet. He waded tentatively into the rushing water, toiling to maintain his balance against the buffeting current. He was slowly making headway when a sudden surge of water drenched the mercenary, nearly toppling him. The Drakleth's monstrous head tapered into view above the brook, in the gap between Sh'ynryan's flaming walls.

The Drakleth jumped into the brook to find the way around the obstacle. It lifted its head and howled triumphantly.

Guile's eyes bulged in terror. He tried to increase his pace through the eddying waters, but it was slow going. The Drakleth's head snapped toward the motion in the center of the stream, and it lunged. Guile disappeared in a violent spout as the Drakleth's open mouth drove forward. The beast's head thrashed beneath the flow as its teeth appeared to pin its prey.

"No!" Vergal howled. He was on his feet, the piercing pain in his ankle forgotten.

Vergal said the Word before he realized it. His thoughts were only to hurt the Drakleth, to save his friend, and in his desperation, he uttered with perfect clarity and inflection the same Word he heard Sh'ynryan speak to summon the flames.

What ensued astonished him.

The roaring he had first heard on the roof of the Wayfarer amplified. It was more vivid than he remembered it. Sh'ynryan's wall of flame seemed to snap toward Vergal, and the boy realized—knew utterly—that the burning barrier had been wrenched fully under his control.

In his rage, Vergal formed a perfect picture in his mind. He imagined the flames surging off the ground in great roiling pillars to strike the Drakleth, to scorch its sensitive neck, to burn its ears. He envisioned the great beast plaited and consumed in a fire of his making.

The flames responded obediently.

The fire jumped and twisted, following the dictate of Vergal's desire, to coil in a glaring wreath around the beast's neck and ears. The beast opened its slathering maw in a thundering scream.

Then Vergal aimed for its eyes.

The fire responded immediately. Tendrils of flame danced away from the fiery collar to flow into the Drakleth's eyes, searing them, turning them to liquid puddles that sloshed in their sockets. The creature roiled and flailed its great neck in a bid to escape the agony, but the flames prevailed. Turning, the wailing creature fled. Fans of fire raced away from the conflagration to follow it, heeding Vergal's wild gesticulations, weaving across the ground in sizzling lines to lunge and singe the maddened creature's hindquarters as it bolted.

The superheated scales of the Drakleth's rump cracked and split apart, revealing pulpy violet flesh beneath. The monster renewed its agonized caterwauling, a haunting clamor that lingered faintly on the air long after it had delved deep into the surrounding forest to seek a place to relieve its torment and, perhaps, Vergal hoped, a place where it could die.

The world whirled around him. A weariness Vergal had not imagined possible settled over the boy and, utterly spent, his knees buckled, and he tumbled to the ground. But not before he saw Guile, favoring one arm but still clenching his sword, rising soaked from the lowering stream. And not before an exclamation of pure astonishment rose from the place where Sh'ynryan had trained his eldritch fire on the spongy ground.

Until Vergal had seized it from him.

Smiling, Vergal let the darkness claim him.

CHAPTER SEVENTEEN

Somehow, amid the ruins of the burned-out ship, they found him.

The man's breathing was labored, and his eyes darted restlessly behind closed lids. The swirling silvery patterns stitched into his robes and the cape fastened at his neck betrayed the man at once as Magi to the astonished Arasynians who discovered him slumped in the destruction of the crow's nest.

They handled him fearfully when they lowered him to the deck. They muttered curses and made gestures against evil at the symbols that marked his tell-tale robes. They stretched him out on smouldering planks.

The captain, grim-faced and astounded at the spectacle of charred bodies aboard the smoking *Acolyte*, joined his men in their imprecations and made signs to ward off evil.

Yet he could not deny the sight of the pirates' black standard flapping from the mast far above, nor the fact that all the dead (so far as he could discern—some bodies were blackened beyond recognition) were northerners—pirates, no doubt, and vassals to the pretender on the throne at Far. The sole survivor of the desolation had been an Arasynian—a countryman—even if he subscribed to the teachings of the detested Brotherhood.

The Mage had quite obviously aborted the pirates' attack on his ship. The small, scattered fires still burning on the deck of the *Acolyte* gave him an unsettling clue as to how he had done it.

The captain grimaced. It would be a simple matter, he thought, to drop the senseless Mage to the sharks that had begun to circle the drifting, steaming ship.

Then he imagined the consequences. He shuddered.

Instead, the captain ordered that the unconscious man be placed on the bed in his own cabin, so the prisoner might be comfortable when he revived.

Until the mysterious man in the arcane robes awoke and could explain for himself what transpired on the *Acolyte*, the captain—a pragmatic man—was not about to risk the ire of the Brotherhood nor the Emperor.

To those who knew him best, Captain Ureld Sanskister had always been an intriguing study in contradictions.

CHAPTER EIGHTEEN

The city appeared beautiful to Alonna from her vantage point atop the manor's high roof. The darkness concealed Caliss's many nasty scars, leaving only the city lights spread out before her like a clutch of diamonds strewn on a sheet of velvet. The lights flooded steeply down the headland, where they terminated at the harbor—though not entirely. A lighthouse on Entry Island, far beyond the breakwater, stabbed its steady beacon through the darkness, warning vessels of the treacherous rocky approach to the port town. The still black waters perfectly reflected the blazing lights of a flotilla of merchant ships at anchors.

A sharp rap on her shoulder shook Alonna from her reverie. "If your daydreaming is near done then?" Rostalin asked roughly.

"Yes," she replied sheepishly.

"Good, then tie off this rope. And, mind you, if I fall climbing down, it's worth your head if I survive the impact. That is my solemn promise."

Alonna sighed. "I think I can manage a knot, Rostalin."

"Be sure you do. This isn't the training hall anymore. This is a drop into a guarded manor house.

If this rope isn't secured on the way out, we're meat for Astareth's hounds and target practice for his hirelings."

Astareth was a minor noble in the city and a legendary money-grubber. He loaned sparingly but collected with voracious usury, often violently. His recent financial predation involved a friend of a friend of Gelbrek's, and thus Alonna found herself on her first official guild outing—to exact revenge on the injured party's behalf by relieving His Worship Astareth of a portion of his precious wealth.

Excitement and trepidation warred inside Alonna as she affixed the scaling rope. She longed to test her newfound skills against opponents who would show no quarter once engaged while at the same time dreading it.

The prospects of dying weighed heavily on Alonna, primarily because it would leave the business regarding Vergal unfinished, his rescue unrealized. Still, her skills required testing outside of the training arena if she was to be confident of them in the field, in pursuit of Vergal's abductor. Though she was confident in her budding skills—Gelbrek and even dour Rostalin had displayed grudging approval as well—she was also cognizant that all warrior eventually met their betters. She wondered how soon in her career she might meet her own.

Rostalin was whispering to her. She tried to still her reeling thoughts and concentrate on the task at hand. The wronged party—a wiry, nervous man with blackened eyes, broken bones, and bloated lips—had provided a precise map to the grounds and the manor. The man had spared no detail in preparing them; he was enjoying his revenge vicariously through

Gelbrek's agents and wanted to make as complete a contribution as possible to its success. The pair had complete reliance on the man's sincere desire to steer them to their destination. It was the integrity of his faculty for recall that disturbed them.

"I'll go first," Rostalin said lightly. "Follow me over the side after I breach the window. I'll be waiting for you just inside."

Alonna nodded and set herself for business.

Swinging his thin legs over the ledge, Rostalin grasped the knotted rope in his gloved hands and gave it a few pulls to test its anchor. He signaled to Alonna the rope was secure and, without hesitation, dropped out of sight.

Alonna peered over the edge. Below, with his fists clenching the rope and his feet pressed to the side of the wall, Rostalin made his way down the rough stone cladding.

The lantern-lit green looked far below the descending man, and Alonna's breath caught when her keen eyes made out the outline of an armed guard entering the circle of illumination spilled by lanterns on the lower wall, but just as swiftly moving out of it. Alonna knew they had chosen their location well. An ancient tree spread its leafy, gnarled arms to conceal the wall on this side of the manor. Alonna realized the sentry would not likely notice Rostalin in the weave of dense shadows thrown by the obscuring tree even should he glanced up.

Bumping his way slowly down the wall, Rostalin stopped at what Alonna presumed to be the target window. From her loft, she could just make out her instructor's hands moving on the glass in front of him. She couldn't precisely see what he was doing but knew from long practice her companion was cutting a circle in the glass of the windowpane and would afterward reach in to unfasten the lock.

Shortly, Rostalin released his hold on the rope and, from Alonna's vantage, disappeared head-first into the wall below, his feet trailing him.

Seconds later, there came a sharp tug on the rope, the signal Alonna should follow.

Her heart pounding, Alonna swung her leather-clad legs over the side of the building. Below she could hear the sentry she had spotted earlier, his boots crunching loudly in the dry leaf litter beneath the tree as he continued his circuit of the grounds. She pressed close to the wall, melding with the shadows, until the noise faded, then began her descent.

In the space of a moment, Alonna swung her legs through the open window, where Rostalin grasped her thighs to guide her inside. She joined him in the shadows of a thick tapestry that covered the near wall.

They carefully surveyed the room by the dim outside light, absorbing every detail of the place.

It was vaulted, as Alonna suspected to find, judging by the profusion of metal-plated domes rising off the rooftop. A colorful mosaic inlaid the smooth marble floor, arranged in a design of sorts difficult to discern in the weak light. Furnishings and lush potted plants lined the round room's walls, leaving the open floor and its mosaic the centerpiece for the whole. Across the way, a door stood slightly ajar. A wedge of light spilled from the hallway beyond across the gleaming floor.

"This is some sort of sitting room or upstairs parlor," Rostalin whispered. "By all accounts, the storeroom is in a chamber below, concealed behind the wall of the master bedroom." He chuckled wickedly and shook his head. "A crafty old miser, isn't he, to take such precautions in his own house? How much must you mistrust your family and retainers when you take such pains to hide your wealth from them?"

"He could be hiding it from the likes of us," Alonna suggested in a whisper.

"Hardly," Rostalin scoffed. "This one's too arrogant, too sure of his security. He cannot imagine the thief who could elude his defenses."

"Is that what we are?" Alonna asked, her eyebrows arching. "Thieves? I thought you were training me to be a warrior."

Rostalin turned a hard look on the young woman. "I'm training you to carry out Gelbrek's orders," he said. "Whatever those orders are, they are for the good of the guild and for the prosperity of us all. What outsiders call us during our duties, however they perceive us, matters little to me. You will do well to adopt the same perspective."

Chastened, Alonna dropped her gaze and did not reply.

The soft-leather boots covering Rostalin's feet made no sound as he crossed the room to the door. Alonna took pains also to keep silent as she followed closely behind. Rostalin peeked through the crack in the door, then lowered himself to the floor. There, he tentatively poked the blade of a polished dagger beneath and slowly tilted it to observe the hallway in both directions by its reflection. Rostalin stood and listened for several minutes. Alonna strained her ears for any sounds she might hear.

The house seemed still and quiet, except for the hiss of a lantern consuming its fuel somewhere in the hall beyond.

Rostalin nodded and carefully opened the door.

The corridor beyond was deserted. Lanterns hung at regular intervals along the curving length of the passageway provided golden light, and colorfully embroidered rugs blanketed the cut-stone floor.

The hallway curved out of sight in either direction. Rostalin did not hesitate, grasping Alonna's leather gauntleted hand and tugging her sharply to the left.

"Stick close to the inside wall at all times," he murmured over his shoulder. "Remember, Gelbrek wants no casualties. We are to exact revenge by hitting Astareth's finances, not members of his household. If need be, we strike to incapacitate, not to kill."

Alonna did not answer. She was suddenly sick at the thought of having to harm anyone in a house into which she had skulked. She was the intruder here; those of the household had every right to defend themselves.

But she also knew she would defend herself if the need arose. Her long months of training had drilled that instinct into her, and it would not be denied. Alonna lifted her gloved hand off the hilt of the scimitar at her hip and reached beneath her cloak to draw forth a small, round-headed mace. A sharp rap in the right spot would render an opponent senseless but leave him breathing.

The passage they followed opened into a wide landing. A fluted stone balustrade across the span indicated a stairway. The same luxurious coverings cloaked the floor, and several overstuffed chairs were pushed up against the walls, next to polished wood tables upon which stood vases of fresh-cut flowers. Candles glowed, their wax still firm near the fiery tips as if someone had only just departed the area after lighting them.

Alonna nudged Rostalin and pointed to the candles, but he only nodded to indicate he had noted them. They glanced quickly about. The shadowy landing was deserted, and the bending hallway behind them remained silent. A gentle wash of light painted the summit of the stairs from somewhere below.

"How will we pass through the lighted area?" Alonna asked in a low whisper. She prowled forward to peep over the railing. The flight of stairs turned back on itself on another landing a level below.

"Carefully," Rostalin deadpanned. He cinched his dark cloak tightly about him. "Now follow me and stick close. Go quickly to the turn in the staircase. We will evaluate from there."

They walked briskly and silently down the firelit staircase, their backs and palms of their hands pressed to the wall. Every step revealed a larger portion of the curving stairwell beyond. At the place where the stair turned back on itself, Rostalin indicated for Alonna to remain still behind him. Crouching, he peered around the stem of the banister.

The foyer below the stairs was dark, unrelieved by the light of a single candle.

Rostalin turned to Alonna. "Empty," he mouthed.

Alonna disagreed. The dark foyer below unsettled her. The silence seemed unnatural, strained, as if something unseen in the dimness listened back hard in her direction. A sensation assailed her that the empty foyer below was not as it seemed. Something down there crouched and waited in taut, predatory stillness.

Without a basis to know it, Alonna's every instinct nevertheless screamed it was true. Rostalin was making ready to rise and step around the banister when Alonna, unable to help herself, seized a fistful of his trailing cloak and wrenched him back. He landed heavily on his rear.

In the same instant, a crossbow bolt whistled of the darkness below, embedding and quivering in a wooden rail.

They regarded each other in wide-eyed alarm. Above and below, bellowing voices and cursing could be heard—a clamor that could only be raised by many large, scurrying armored men.

"Back up the stairs!" Alonna cried, pulling Rostalin up.

"No!" Rostalin countered. "They know we are here; the rope will already have been cut. There's no escape that way." He considered for only a half-second—the time it took for another bolt to plunge itself into the stairs at his feet. "Below!" he cried. "Flare your cloak to help deflect the bolts. Charge them quickly and show no mercy."

Alonna nodded grimly, swirling the black fabric of her long cloak in front of her, grasping her mace tightly in one white-knuckled hand. Rostalin, however, dropped his club and drew his sword. He stabbed her a brief but meaningful glance, and Alonna followed his lead, tucking her small, ball-headed mace into her belt and releasing a wickedly curved scimitar from its sheath to take its place.

Rostalin jumped to his feet, shouting directions even as he burst into action.

"Lunge and roll!" Rostalin yelled, illustrating his instructions bodily by throwing himself face-first down the stairs.

The wiry warrior's head tucked low to his chin, and he absorbed the brunt of the landing on his bunched shoulders, deftly whipping his thin legs over him and rolling the last several steps to land firmly on his feet, sword slashing wildly.

"We never practiced on stairs," Alonna murmured, even as she leaped likewise down the stairs. Her natural agility executed the roll smoothly, and she emerged from her roll unscathed, scimitar at the ready.

She found Rostalin already hard-pressed in the thick of the melee. A knot of chain-mailed soldiers wearing rigid leather helms had hastily dropped their crossbows—their quarry having closed the distance between them in the span of an eye-blink—and were viciously swinging swords. The clamor of steel on steel indicated to Alonna that her instructor was parrying the hurried blows, but the woman wondered for how long.

Alonna made out at least six manor soldiers on the dark landing, but more could have been hanging back in the murk or dashing up the hallway beyond to reinforce their comrades. The battling soldiers gave Rostalin no quarter, and Alonna knew her life and his were forfeit unless they vigorously defended themselves.

Steeling herself, she entered the fray.

Shouldering back her concealing cloak, Alonna's twin scimitar appeared in her hand, and she dropped to one knee, pivoting, the curling blades flowing in response and slicing through the leather breeches of a nearby soldier to bite deeply into the man's calves.

The result was as if someone had cut the strings on a marionette. With his severed tendons unable to support his weight, the soldier cried out and collapsed. His sword bounced free of his hand from the impact, his hands reaching instinctively for the wounds on his legs.

In that heated moment, Alonna did not see a young soldier, incapacitated and screaming in terror and pain; instead, her mind's eye registered a flash of red robes, a hint of greying hair.

The downed soldier became to Alonna the abductor, the thief of her brother, and the root of her torment and grief. Alonna coldly lashed out with her scimitar and opened wide the man's exposed throat before she could discern the difference.

She didn't dwell on the image of the red-robed thief that had overtaken her. Instead, she embraced it. She allowed herself to fall fully into her primal hatred for the man that had abducted her brother.

Alonna rose smoothly, her scimitars weaving in time to parry the heavy blades of two outraged soldiers who loomed in front of her. They screamed in her face as they battered her upraised blades with their swords, but she barely heard their heated vows to avenge the death of their comrade. Alonna's lifted blades caught and deflected every blow with chill efficiency.

Steel rang, and with deft, twisting turns of her blurring swords, she threw their blades wide to their sides and lunged forward with her own. Her scimitars' curving tips sliced into their throats simultaneously, and they slumped, choking, to the floor, their lifeblood pumping from deep wounds in their necks in time with their failing heartbeats.

Alonna's arms vibrated from the crushing impact of the heavy men's pounding sword swings, but she willed them up in front of her, ready to meet her next challenge. None presented; Rostalin stood amid a tangle of fallen, bloodied men, watching her with inscrutable eyes.

"Come," he commanded. "Down this corridor. There are others behind us."

They fled into the dark hall beyond the foyer. Alonna glanced back to see more soldiers rounding the switchback in the stairs. A new hail of crossbow bolts clanged off the bare stone walls behind them as they ran.

"It's so dark!" Alonna panted as she went. The sustaining adrenaline dissipating, she was astonished by how exhausted the melee on the stairs had left her.

"Good for us it is!" Rostalin replied. "They can't hit what they can't see. Faster!"

They rounded a corner, nearly slipping on the loose floor coverings, and found another lighted hallway lined by polished wood doors. They burst through the first one they reached and slammed the door behind them. Without speaking a word to plan it, they each seized the lip of a massive chest of drawers next to the door and tipped it in front of the portal.

In landed with an unearthly bedlam, the loose objects atop it—fragrance bottles, a mirror, a jewelry box—smashing to add to the din.

Hammering fists sounded immediately outside the door. Only then they noticed a slender iron key inserted in a lock higher up the door. They shared a panicked glanced and lunged as one, leaping atop the overturned chest and throwing their full weight against the door.

A muffled grunt sounded on the other side as one of the soldiers slammed into the door and fell back from the impact with a chain-tinkling crash. Rostalin reached and turned the key. The well-oiled lock slid smoothly, and the pair breathed relieved sighs in perfect unison.

"Wish I had seen that sooner," Rostalin admitted breathlessly.

"I wondered why you didn't turn it immediately," said a voice behind them.

They spun in unison to spy a man garbed in a simple white robe standing in a pale wedge of moonlight slanting through the room's mullioned windows. The light in the dark room leaked behind him, obscuring his features but highlighting a thick mop of white hair.

Rostalin and Alonna lifted their swords. The man raised his arm immediately, displaying the outline of a hand crossbow clenched in one thin fist.

"Hold!" the figure warned. "I can only take one of you before the others reach me, true, but the poison on this bolt ensures the first to move dies—quite painfully."

The pair froze, evaluating their options. Behind them, the hammering left off at the door to be replaced by the dull thud of an ax head biting into wood. The door was thick and locked and barricaded, but how long would it keep out an angry mob of armed soldiers?

They needed to act.

"You would choose this room, wouldn't you?" the dark figure was saying, his voice trailing away in a resigned chuckle. "I thought to stay out of the way until my guards had corralled you, yet in you walk, into my private chambers, and bring the adventure to me."

"Call off your dogs!" Rostalin growled. "True, you can take one of us, but we're both dead anyway if those soldiers breach the door. You are making it worthwhile to take our chances."

The man in the moonlight chuckled again. "I would worry more about those men already here," he replied, and on cue, a door on the far wall swung open to discharge a pair of mailed soldiers, also wielding small crossbows. They started toward the intruders, but the white-haired man waved them to himself instead.

"Pity my ensuite has no exit to the hall," the man continued, grinning at the companions' stricken stares. "I'm sure my lads will have that door down shortly. Until then, let's talk."

The poisoned bolt wavered between them. The two grim-faced sentries assumed positions on either side of the robed man at the window.

"Astareth, I presume?" Rostalin said wryly.

The man reached down to a table beside him and pulled the cover off a small lantern. The ensuing bright light washed the man's features. Though not yet old, he was aging, with a head of coiffured white hair and soulful blue eyes. The thin, cruel set of his lips offset the beatific light in his gaze. He was garbed in simple white robes as if interrupted in his preparations for bed.

"You have me at a disadvantage," Astareth said, smiling wanly. "Gelbrek failed to send ahead the names of the thieves he would deliver to my home."

Alonna's eyes darted to Rostalin at the mention of Gelbrek's name, and Astareth did not miss the movement.

"Oh, yes, I know your patron. You may deny it, but that will only draw out our conversation, and, truthfully, you do not have the time. You see, I turned one of Gelbrek's lads. It was he who hired you on. He's a dedicated man. Why, of his own volition, he had one of my guards— a beefy sort, all muscle and mean streak—take him behind the stables and punch him up to make his countenance more suitable to the story he offered. It is unfortunate the man is a traitor and cannot be trusted because he certainly does not lack commitment nor initiative."

Astareth tittered, and the men-at-arms joined in.

"Why this pretense then?" Rostalin asked. If he felt the same anxiety as Alonna, he betrayed no hint of it. Watching him, Alonna noted Rostalin's thin-lidded eyes roving the room. She was sure he was planning a course of action and resolved to follow whatever lead her tutor offered. There would certainly be no time to explain it to her.

Rostalin went on. "Why invite the grief Gelbrek will cause you as a result?"

Astareth laughed. The man was feeling positively merry, Alonna noted irritably. "That is precisely the reason," the noble explained. "Sending your heads back to him in baskets will serve notice to our fat friend that a competitor has opened shop in the market that, until now, he has held as his own."

It was Rostalin's turn to laugh. "You intend to start a rival guild? In defiance of a man who has forgotten more about the business than you will ever know?"

Rostalin's levity didn't sit well with Astareth. His brow knit, and he jabbed his crossbow hand threateningly. "Your predicament is no laughing matter," he said crossly.

Splinters began to appear on the inside panel of the door as the axeman beyond continued his furious assault on the barricaded portal.

"Call them off," Rostalin warned again.

The smile reappeared on Astareth's face as smoothly as if it had never left. "Or what?" he demanded.

"Presently, we are enjoying a pleasant chat," Rostalin said, lowering his hands slowly to his sides. "If they breach, then you force my hand."

Astareth's head tilted back at the beginning of a chuckle, only to be cut off by a gurgling scream by the dagger that suddenly appeared buried in the flesh of his exposed throat. Alonna gaped, having not registered the single fluid motion that had swept the blade from beneath Rostalin's cloak and across the room into Astareth's neck.

Astareth crumpled to his knees, his arms groping ineffectually in front of him. His mouth worked fiercely but emitted only wet, strangling sounds.

Rostalin was already in motion, lunging and rolling with uncanny speed to span the distance between himself and the remaining men-at-arms. The dumbfounded sentries barely recovered from the spectacle of blood fanning from Astareth's wound before Rostalin was on them. Alonna raised her swords and flew after him.

The sentry closest to the charging man dropped his crossbow and reached for a sword at his waist. The other soldier leaped backward several steps and loosed a bolt at the running man.

Rostalin flinched and reached for his neck, where a crossbow quarrel now protruded under his ear. The determined man's charge did not falter, however, and he slapped the sword of his victim out wide, only to reverse the motion and slice backward. A savage crimson furrow opened across his opponent's leather jerkin. Cupping his neck in one hand, Rostalin turned on shaking legs to face the other sentry, who by then had drawn the sword at his own waist.

He need not have bothered.

Alonna was there, her eyes blazing with deadly intent. The rational part of her mind told her Rostalin's wound was surely grave, yet the remainder of her body proceeded unaffected by her surging grief. With calm, measured motions, she engaged the remaining soldier, who barely parried her initial downward hack. Her swinging swords instantly had the man leaning back over his heels.

She barely registered the frenzied yelling in the hallway beyond as the axeman at last opened a yawning hole in the thick door. The battle lust had seized her, not with berserk abandon but with icy resolve, and the image of the bearded, red-robed abductor returned, seeming to superimpose itself over the features of the soldier she faced. He was working hard to regain his footing and take the offensive, but his plan was not working. Alonna's scimitars flashed forward with dizzying speed, one vicious swipe taking the soldier's sword out wide and leaving him hard-pressed to drop his blade in time to shunt the stab from her second scimitar.

His moves became purely defensive. He found no lag in the woman's double-handed attack to set his feet and press for the advantage. Her twin blades whirled expertly, scoring painful nicks on his gauntleted fists as he parried her strikes.

Alonna, her eyes unblinking, pressed her advantage. She kept the man on his heels, intent on wearing him down, giving him time for his mounting exhaustion to translate into creeping despair.

The clamor behind her grew louder. The hole in the door opened wider beneath the axeman's assault, and the curses rising from the soldiers in the hall passed unhindered into the room.

From the corner of her vision, she took note of Rostalin sinking to his knees. His sword clanged on the tiles, freeing both hands to press the wound in his neck. The quick glance filled her with dread.

"You're already dead," Alonna promised her harried, sweating opponent in a flat voice.

Several short jabs of her scimitars worked the man's sword high—he was doing an able job parrying her blows—until finally, his deflections had his elbows nearly level with his shoulders.

Alonna struck, dipping to one knee and thrusting forward with a scimitar, leaving its twin trailing high above her to intercept any countering strike from above.

Muscles toned by months of rigorous training and assisted by the force of Alonna's lunge drove the sword neatly through the man's leather armor and opened a hole in his gut.

His sword clanged to the floor. The man folded up and cradled his stomach, his entrails seeping through his laced fingers.

Alonna paid no mind. She had already turned to Rostalin.

Alonna grimly inspected the wound. Blood pumped from around the embedded bolt. The cruel barbs had punctured and shredded a large vein there, and a sticky dark pool was forming on the floor under him.

An arm reached through the hole in the door and flailed blindly, seeking the key in the lock several inches away. Alonna seized the hand crossbow from Astareth's lifeless fingers and fired. The bolt sailed through the air and thudded dully into the door near the splayed fingers of the questing hand. The arm quickly vacated the splintery hole.

The crashing outside resumed as several men put their shoulders to the stubborn door. The hinges screeched in protest, and the door leaped in its frame, but the lock and barricade still held. She had a minute, perhaps only seconds, before they broke through.

Frantic, she searched Rostalin's eyes. The light there was already fading, but a contented smile stretched his lips.

"You're a quick study, Alonna," he breathed. "You have done me proud."

His mouth opened wide. Alonna expected him to say something else, but he only sucked a copious breath of air.

"The window. Go!" he gasped. "Tell Gelbrek all we learned."

Alonna nodded, tears flowing. Was she cursed to have everyone close to her die or disappear? She squeezed her eyes against the tears. Rostalin never could abide unbridled emotion in his students.

But when she opened her eyes again, she saw Rostalin was beyond noticing.

She lowered his head to the cool tile floor. She hated to leave him there, but she saw little choice. Instead, she grasped his sword and tucked it in her belt. The sword had been as much a part of Rostalin's life as his soul itself. It, at least, would leave with her.

Rising, Alonna rushed to the window and sprung the lock. Throwing the windows wide, she leaned out and surveyed the scene. She was on the second floor now of the imposing stone building, but the grassy common still seemed a long way down. Leaping out the window from this height likely meant a broken limb, but the relentless pounding at the door left Alonna little recourse. Her eyes darted around the room, seeking some means of exit or tool that would assist her in her descent.

There was nothing, only the fanciful overstuffed furniture of a rich man's bedchamber.

She hastened through the ensuite door through which the soldiers had issued but found only a sterile sitting room, more sparsely furnished than the bedchamber. Returning to the main window, her options fleeting, she leaned out again and spotted it …

… a web of ivy crawling up the weathered stone flank of the building, several feet below.

The crashing behind her stopped, and she turned to see the questing hand had returned, this time covered in a steel gauntlet and fumbling awkwardly with the slender stem of the key. Cursing herself for leaving the key inserted, she pulled Rostalin's sword, upraised it, and with a fierce shriek barrelled across the room.

Alonna's sword slashed the exposed forearm just below the protecting steel and severed it nearly in half. A scream sounded behind the door, and the nearly truncated appendage flopped and smacked weirdly against the sides of the hole as its owner hastily withdrew. A stunned silence of several heartbeats was followed by renewed pounding at the door.

Alonna knocked the key out of its lock. The gesture mattered little since the door was bulging weirdly and preparing to give way.

She barely made the window when the door erupted in shards of shattered wood. A knot of furious soldiers appeared in the doorframe, scrambling to clear the fallen chest of drawers.

Her time was gone; her time was now.

Without a backward glance, she jumped out the window.

She plummeted quickly. Her gloved hands reached for and snagged the thickly twined ivy whickering past her. Her arrested momentum swung her forward, and her belly thumped solidly against the unyielding wall.

Ignoring her breathlessness, Alonna willed her arms and feet into action, half climbing, half sliding down the sinewy tendrils that had become a sudden lifeline. Soldiers' angry faces appeared over the windowsill above her, and she heard calls for a crossbow. Others yelled instructions for soldiers to intercept the intruder at ground level.

Panicked, she slid several more feet of ivy, then pushed clear of the wall. She hit the ground with a bump that drove her knees into her already bruised stomach. Alonna writhed on the leaf-littered lawn, winded, longing to draw breath.

Her mind screamed for her to get up. She tried but stumbled and lay again gasping. She sought only to draw the breath that was stubbornly slow in coming. At last, Alonna's stomach ceased flipping, and her lungs flooded with the cool night air. She was up and staggering forward within the span of three frenzied swallows.

And just in time. Torchlight flared behind her. A company of armored men rounded the corner of the building in dogged pursuit. The baying of dogs rose somewhere distant on the grounds. The click of crossbows from above indicated someone had fired from the open window. She didn't see where the bolts landed, but she was thankful for their marksman's botched shots as she careened across the tree-studded lawn toward the looming wall.

"The apple tree," she panted as she dashed. "We entered near the big apple tree."

She turned a corner and spotted the tree. Its umbrella of branches started low to the ground and fanned out as they rose to brush the wall of the house and overhang the manor's outer wall.

"Halt, thief!" came a puffing cry from behind, punctuated by the stomp of heavy-shod feet.

Alonna didn't slow as she approached the tree. She used the momentum of her desperate flight to propel herself to grasp a low limb. Hooking it firmly, she hauled her legs up behind her just as the pursuing soldiers skidded to a noisy halt below, joined an instant later by a pack of snarling, frenzied hounds.

Her feet were just out of reach of the tallest soldier. She scrambled higher into the leafy branches when several guards drew swords and began hacking the limb upon which she stood. The leaping dogs' claws caught but skidded down the trunk of the tree.

She scampered higher into the concealing tangle of greenery. Ridiculously, she plucked an apple and fired it down toward the voices. It crashed through the web of limbs and deflected far short of its target. She took heart that same shield of branches foiled the crossbow man's attempts to target her. She pulled herself higher into the canopy as quickly as her grasping hands and scrabbling legs allowed.

One man began to strip out of his heavy armor, and several of his companions hoisted him to latch onto the lowest bough.

"Go around, outside the wall," he told his fellows. To Alonna, he yelled, "We're coming for you, don't be doubting!"

Alonna swallowed, imagining what the enraged men might do if they laid hands upon her.

She did not intend to give them the chance.

The branches thinned as she reached the upper loft of the tree, and it was there she spied her one chance for safety: A long slender limb, dipping delicately out from the tree to nearly overhang a weathered crenelation on the distant stone wall. She tested her weight on the branch. It drooped but held, supporting her weight.

A straight run across the tenuous limb and a flying leap would take her to the wall and to the grappling hook somewhere beyond they had used to breach the outer defenses.

She winced when she peered down through the maze of branches. A misstep would send her crashing to the feet of her pursuers, where their swords and hounds would rend her. However, remaining still was not an option; the noise of the man scaling the tree in pursuit was intensifying.

And how long had she until the dispatched soldiers rounded the manor to intercept her outside the wall?

Alonna gauged the distance between the limb and the wall. Without a backward glance, she scurried out on the slender branch and used its springy motion beneath her feet to launch herself toward the wall.

The jump was good, if somewhat short. The lip of the ledge struck her stomach, but she thrust splayed fingers forward to grasp creases in the weathered stone, sparing her a long fall backward. Her dangling feet scissored desperately, seeking a toehold in the bumpy wall face. She pulled herself over the lip just as the first whistles of crossbow bolts resounded below her. She rolled on her back atop the wall in time to see a bolt fire past her and over the wall.

Get out of here! Alonna admonished herself. She willed herself to rise on exhausted legs, barely able to support her weight. She bolted down the narrow aisle atop the wall. The babble of excited voices faded behind her. She found the grappling hook still secured where they had left it, and she threw the coil of rope down the outside face of the wall. It stunned her to reconcile the presence of the scaling rope with the loss of the man who had used it to enter the compound alongside her not an hour ago. But now she was leaving alone.

She bounced down the outer wall, the rope sliding quickly through her gloved hands until her feet crunched firmly into dry leaves littering the foot of the wall.

She turned red-rimmed eyes back on the place that would surely have claimed her life if not for the sacrifice of Rostalin, her instructor, and, she realized now, her friend.

"I'll avenge you, Rostalin," Alonna whispered.

She turned and fled, melting into the concealing shadows of the narrow, crooked streets of Caliss without a backward glance.

CHAPTER NINETEEN

"I hope you appreciate the need for restraints until we could properly discern your involvement in all that transpired," the man who introduced himself as Captain Ureld Sanskister was saying, but Jalwyn scarcely heard him.

The Mage had regained consciousness in a shadowy cabin. His wrists were tied loosely yet securely behind his back. The restraints were unnecessary, Ureld could see. The pale man stretched out on the bed could hardly focus his eyes properly, much less strike out magically at him or his crew members.

Ureld nodded at the man he had posted to keep watch. The man's face affected an expression of distaste, but he rose and untied Jalwyn's wrists. The Mage's eyes fluttered open weakly as he was rolled onto his back.

"The Arasynian ship ..." he croaked.

Ureld's eyes narrowed suspiciously.

"What of it?" Ureld prompted. His hand moved to the pommel of his sword. Much of the red-robed man's fate hinged on what his intentions had been for Ureld's *Sea King*, a merchant ship out of Zistah. Had the Mage been friend or foe in the conflagration that claimed the *Acolyte*? Ureld thought it likely that the man in his delirium would speak the truth when questioned and settle the matter for the dubious captain.

"It sails still?" the man asked. He ogled the chamber around him, then laughed weakly. "It must! I doubt I would be resting comfortably in a captain's quarters had the *Acolyte* prevailed."

The captain nodded. It had been as he suspected, then. The Mage had ignited the *Acolyte* in defense of *Sea King*, and not in some botched attempt to aid the pirate ship. Ureld's long-standing loathing of the Brethren warred with a kernel of admiration at the skinny man's sacrifice to protect his countrymen.

The man in the bed fell into a coughing fit. Ureld shook away his musings and turned his attention on the newest addition to his crew.

"What is your name?"

"I am called Jalwyn."

"Well met, Jalwyn. As I've said, I am Ureld, and you are aboard the *Sea King*," he said dispassionately. "We are an Arasynian merchant ship in the service of His Imperial Majesty at Zistah, carrying cargo bound for Caliss on the Aerie Coast."

The captain did not ignore the irony of sailing to a port in a kingdom that had intended to attack him on open seas. Such was the reality of passage through the northern waters. Imperial vessels traveling the well-patrolled shipping lanes between Zistah and Caliss had little fear of marauding Aerie Coast pirates. However, those who strayed risked encountering the profiteering scum who committed thievery and murder under the semblance of patriotic resistance to the Empire.

Ureld longed for the day when the Empire, at last, completed its conquest and drove the pretender on the throne at Far off the Alasian continent and back to his scabrous islands in the Western Sea.

The pirates' nation's ambitious claims on the Alasian mainland, far beyond the territory it now held by treaty on the northwest shelf of the continent, made Aerie a dangerous neighbor. Ureld felt the Emperor would do well to dethrone the expansionist Pirate King before he became more of a threat in coming years.

Ureld shook his head at the sad reality of Arasynian politics and turned his focus back to the man in the bed, who was frowning and shaking his head vigorously.

"No, captain, I must go to Far," the man protested.

Ureld's eyebrows arched. "Really? Why?"

"I was heading there when you encountered us. I am sent by my order to search for someone supposed to be going there, and I must find his trail. It is a matter of utmost importance."

Ureld's nose wrinkled at Jalwyn's veiled reference to the Brotherhood, but he kept his voice civil.

"Regrettably, Jalwyn, Arasynia's maritime commerce with the Aerie Coast is conducted at Caliss, not at Far. Alasia, at least, is neutral ground of a sort for both countries. An Arasynian merchant ship putting into harbor at Far would be looted before it enters its bay."

Jalwyn opened his mouth to reply but closed it again. He knew his history and his current events alike, and he knew the captain spoke the truth. Caliss represented a middle ground between Far and Speakwater, where they conducted trade to their mutual benefit even as each plotted the destruction of the other at gilded capitals far removed.

No amount of arguing with a merchant vessel captain would change the intricacies of the colonial powers' convoluted politics.

But neither did the facts interfere with the urgency of Jalwyn's mission to find Sh'ynryan, the mysterious elder who had become the consuming focal point of the Brethren's interest.

The captain broke the silence. "The best we can offer you is landing at Caliss," he said, dropping into a chair bedside to confer with Jalwyn. "From there, you can board an Aerie Coast vessel to Far if you choose, though why anyone should want to visit that wretched pile of rocks is beyond my understanding."

The captain clasped his hands and leaned forward in his chair.

"I know what you are, Jalwyn," he said gruffly. "By your admission and your actions, I know you to be Magi. I am Zistinian, born and bred. And I know you to be the same.

"Your Brotherhood will find few friends aboard *Sea King*," the captain admitted, "but neither can we deny the service you performed for the Emperor and us. Perhaps many of my crew members' lives were saved by your actions on the *Acolyte*. For that, you have our thanks and my promise of safe passage aboard this ship."

The rigid set of Ureld's jaw warned Jalwyn to take the captain's words seriously when next he spoke.

"But know this. If you in any way cause trouble en route to Caliss, or even the appearance of such, you will be dealt with severely. Do we understand each other?"

Jalwyn, who still felt too drained to lift a finger in his defense should the situation necessitate it, thought he had never understood anything more clearly in his life.

The *Sea King* rounded the headland at Caliss a day later and Jalwyn, who had never seen the city nor the Alasian continent before, leaned wearily on a rail to watch the approach.

The fatigue of his exertions aboard the *Acolyte* still lingered, and the abominable lurching of the deck beneath his feet was not helping matters. But Jalwyn felt himself recuperating.

"Can we expect a hostile welcome?" Jalwyn asked Ureld, who had joined the Mage at the bow.

The captain shook his head. "In Caliss? No, you need not worry. The city belongs to the Aerie Coast, right enough, but the citizens here are more akin to those in Speakwater or Eliard than the rogues out on their island at Far. They share the continent, after all, while the pirates stew in their resentments out at sea. The people here thrive on trade, and few of them allow politics half an ocean away to interfere with earning a few coins. Once you move past the ugliness of the place, Caliss is actually an interesting enough city…"

The captain paused, then added, "Even if it should belong to Arasynia, like the rest of the continent."

Jalwyn grinned. "You say citizens here are willing to sacrifice politics on the altar of commerce, but you don't appear nearly so willing, dear captain!"

Ureld shrugged as if Jalwyn had stated something obvious.

Jalwyn frowned as something occurred to him.

"When first we spotted *Sea King*, she was floundering, and you were far off the trade route," Jalwyn said. "Whatever ailed your ship before the pirates' attack appears to have righted itself in short order. I don't believe I was conscious to witness any necessary repairs, but surely a ship drifting as badly as *Sea King* would require extensive time and work to right itself. And I don't imagine I was out quite that long. Am I correct in assuming so, captain?

Ureld said nothing.

Jalwyn laughed. "It was a decoy! You presented as a wounded target to draw the pirates. Have I the honor, then, of meeting one of Arasynia's legendary pirate hunters, our Emperor's secret counter-measure to Far's unofficial piracy?"

Ureld said nothing. He nodded curtly to excuse himself and walked off.

Jalwyn shook his head, disbelieving. "Merchant ship indeed!" he laughed.

The broken, rocky headland of Caliss slid past as *Sea King* negotiated the choked harbor toward the jetties beyond. They were waved into an open berth at the city's great stone quay. Ureld's experienced helmsman brought the ship expertly to dock.

Lines were cast and tied down, and within an hour, Jalwyn stood before the dock district's gates, opening onto the city proper.

The city's tall, slate roof buildings crawled up the rocky headland, crowning the summit with a bristling irregular skyline.

A large common, the only green space visible from the foot of the incline, broke the unrelieved slate grey mass halfway up the hill. The green rolled in a steep slide from the imposing facade of a manor-like building in the middle of the grounds.

Ureld had pointed out the building from the ship and had informed Jalwyn it housed the Wayfarer Inn, adequate accommodations for lodgings in Caliss.

Jalwyn didn't deem it necessary and had told Ureld as much.

"I'll be finding passage to Far as soon as possible," the Mage explained. Ureld blinked at the red-robed man's assertion as if he held a different opinion on the matter, though he offered nothing in rebuttal.

"Good luck, Jalwyn," the captain said earnestly, clasping the man's thin hand. They stood together amid the bustle of the busy pier. The wind gusting over the open water of the harbor flailed both men's cloaks.

Ureld's grip lingered, and with a final firm squeeze, the captain dropped the Mage's hand and walked away. Jalwyn took the added gesture as a final expression of thanks for the Mage's pre-emptive assistance against the pirates' ship. Or perhaps as a subtle demonstration of approval of a man he had initially judged on his affiliation as opposed to his character.

Jalwyn's search for passage to Far turned up nothing, as he suspected Captain Ureld knew. The crews of the merchant ships, even the fishing trawlers at the dock, all intended to stay at berth for days, some for weeks, unloading cargo and enjoying an extended stay in port to spend their new coins before venturing back out to sea.

A fruitless tour of the docks, during which he was either rebuffed or ridiculed, convinced Jalwyn to take Ureld's suggestion and make his way to the Wayfarer Inn.

Jalwyn decided to make the best of his stay. It stood to reason the trail he had been following to Far—had it not turned up the man he sought—might eventually, in any case, have turned toward Caliss. Sh'ynryan might subsequently make his way off the Aerie Coast islands and toward the Alasian mainland. Jalwyn resolved to use the stopover to lay the foundation for a return trip if the trail turned cold at Far.

The taproom of the Wayfarer was a dank and drafty place, where sailors and other men sat hunched close together at the curving mahogany bar. Raucous laughter and conversation greeted his entrance. Jalwyn slipped quietly into the inn and took a seat at a table where he could observe the bar and the doorway beyond. He savored the relative privacy of the deep shadows thrown by the vaulting stone wall.

The serving girl who approached his table halted in mid-stride at the sight of him. Her mouth opened in astonishment.

"Greetings," he said amiably when she made no move toward him.

The woman shook her head as if to clear a vexing thought. She examined Jalwyn, making no effort to disguise her scrutiny. Her eyes roamed his face, and the silvery sigils stitched into his robe and cloak.

She simply stared, transfixed as if by a serpent that had reared up in her path.

Jalwyn cleared his throat. "Might I bother you to bring a drink?" he asked, careful to keep the annoyance out of his voice. Something about the atmosphere in the bar was tweaking Jalwyn's intuition, unsettling him.

The woman shook her head again. "Of course," she said hurriedly, retreating a step. She smiled disarmingly. "Would you like ale?"

"I think I will take a glass of your house wine."

"Very well," the woman said. She turned on her heel and flew across the taproom, past the bar and through an arch in the far wall.

Jalwyn sat frowning, his feeling of unease growing.

"You!" a voice thundered. Jalwyn, his nerves already on edge, started guiltily in his chair.

A hush settled over the taproom. Every head craned to find the source of the outburst. A burly man with a hawk-like nose stood at the arch through which the serving maid had fled. He gripped a kitchen knife in one hand. The woman peered around the man's bulk, pointing across the room at Jalwyn.

"That is the man, isn't it, Carek?" the woman said excitedly, bending low to gawk around the man's ample girth. "That's the man Alonna described."

"Back to the kitchen, Estanelda," the man called Carek growled, and the woman hurriedly complied. Carek stalked forward, wiping the greasy blade on his stain-splotched apron. His narrow eyes smoldered angrily.

"You have a nerve returning here!" Carek barked. Jalwyn resisted an urge to glance behind him, thinking surely the man addressed someone else.

With his back to the wall, though, only Jalwyn was in Carek's line of vision.

The man stomped forward, and Jalwyn stood quickly, patting the air in front of him. "Sir, I think you have confused me with someone else," he said. Confrontations generally made Jalwyn's stomach weak, and the Mage knew he was still in no physical condition to defend himself should the situation turn sour.

"I remember you well enough," Carek snarled. He was nearing the table now, the point of his knife wavering to-and-fro. Jalwyn backpedaled until his shoulders smacked the stone wall behind him.

"I remember your cloak, those markings," the man yelled, jabbing his knife to punctuate his words. "And that cowl. Well, you will find no youngster here to steal this time! You made certain of that."

"Sir, please, calm yourself!" Jalwyn pleaded. "I know nothing of what you say!"

Carek made short thrusts in the air, maliciously grinning as Jalwyn recoiled at every feint.

"You know well enough," the innkeeper sneered. "You took the boy and drove Alonna away." The veins in his neck stood out like cords. The doughy skin of his face flushed red with rising anger. "She blames me for what you did, you dog!"

This man's knife jabbed forth threateningly. Jalwyn sidestepped instinctively. The commotion convinced several patrons at the bar to take interest and form a small crowd behind Carek.

Desperate, Jalwyn pulled back his cowl, exposing his pallid face to the enraged barkeep. "Look upon me, man!" he blurted. "Surely you have never seen me before, as surely as I have never in my life seen you."

Carek paused mid-stride. The flint in his eyes softened to confusion. His knife wavered.

"You wear the robes, just like him!" Carek said uncertainly.

Jalwyn held his arms out in supplication. "These are only robes, sir, just clothing! Is this cause enough to knife a man in Caliss? If so, point me to your nearest clothier, and I will outfit myself to suit the local tastes!"

The man did not answer. He muttered to himself abstractedly.

The men advancing on the table faltered when they realized there was to be no fight for their entertainment. The excitement passed, they drifted back to the bar and their waiting cups.

Jalwyn barely registered them. The young Mage was deep in contemplation. A man in a red cloak with silvery sigils such as his? Only members of the Brotherhood so garbed themselves. It was Jalwyn's turn to be astonished. Had he somehow stumbled onto the trail of Sh'ynryan in a chance encounter with a hostile innkeeper?

His heartbeat quickened as he considered it further. It could be no other, Jalwyn concluded. No other member of the Brethren was anywhere near this part of the world, at least according to the elders who commissioned Jalwyn for this journey.

Jalwyn thought their intelligence on the matter could probably be trusted.

However, the talk of a boy and an abduction confused Jalwyn. The barkeep appeared confused, like a man waking from a dream. Carek viewed the knife in his hand with something approaching horror. He quickly slapped it on the table. The stout man's anger was gone, replaced by bewilderment.

"My apologies," Carek said. "Your robes, you looked just like him, sitting that way in the shadows."

"Yes?" Jalwyn urged. "Who did I remind you of just now?"

"A man who once passed this way," Carek replied carefully, still taking careful stock of the pale man and his rune-stitched garments. "He kidnapped the young brother of a dear friend. Neither has been heard from since."

Jalwyn blinked away his confusion. A kidnapping? His hopes crashed. Surely Carek mistook him for someone other than Sh'ynryan. Why would an elder Mage abduct a boy? Yet who else could it have been? No other member of the Brethren had journeyed through the northern continent for several years, and nobody sane would impersonate a member of the Magi for two reasons: he would encounter animosity from people on their wanderings, and the Brethren would surely avenge that man's hubris if they found out.

Jalwyn formed his next words carefully.

"Sir, perhaps we can help each other. If you are willing to tell me more about the man for whom you confused me, perhaps I could help identify him. He sounds like a man I am seeking. Though, if what you say is true, I could be chasing a rogue from my order rather than a missing Brother. Either way, perhaps we can unravel this mystery for both of us."

Jalwyn settled later that evening in an upstairs room at the inn. The details of Carek's story mystified him. Lying in bed, staring at the ochre candlelight light playing across the ceiling, the young Zistinian still had trouble accepting much of the tale.

One thing was apparent: the man in question had been Sh'ynryan. Without a doubt. Every Mage wore unique insignias of his own design. Carek's detailed description of the man's embroidered cloak confirmed the man's identity. However, Jalwyn struggled to reconcile the rest of the story: The elder's kidnapping of a servant girl's young brother, a peasant child by all accounts.

What was the meaning of it?

The more he considered, the firmer Jalwyn's suspicion the boy's involvement somehow involved the long-ago quest the Order had given Sh'ynryan to search Alasia for clues to the whereabouts of the Stone.

Though it figured largely in the order's teachings, Jalwyn concluded early in his tenure that the Stone likely no longer existed. Surely it did once exist. The present-day reality of the Words of Power confirmed that. The notion, though, that an ancient artifact employed sentinel cunning to conceal and guard itself over untold generations, as the legends described, proved a road too far for Jalwyn.

He reasoned that the primitive writings would be dust by now, much less actively defying sorcerers' best efforts to locate them. Consigned to history, their loss had forthwith sparked a fable.

Jalwyn shook his head on his pillow. The Brethren hunted a shadow, he feared. The young Mage, always reverent, held the order's practices in the highest regard. However, he sometimes speculated at what progress the Brotherhood had forsaken over centuries by choosing to chase a fanciful legend and its promise of new mastery and power in the Words, rather than more thoroughly plumbing the oral traditions from which the extant Words of Power had descended.

Jalwyn dismissed his musings, none of which answered the essential question at hand: How did the boy—Vergal, as Carek named him—fit in?

Jalwyn swung his legs to the floor and sat miserably at the edge of his bed. Sleep would elude him this night, he knew. Theories and speculations crowded his racing thoughts. He considered dressing and visiting the taproom for spiced wine and some distracting conversation when an arm, suddenly encircling his neck, abruptly changed his evening's plans.

Wrenched back on the bed, Jalwyn felt the cold point of a knife against the flesh of his throat.

Terrified, Jalwyn instinctively flailed at his unseen attacker, provoking the vice-like arm to choke him harder and the knifepoint to press deeper, a hair's breadth from puncturing the skin.

The soft crush of breasts against his back and the flowery scent of the thick, perfumed hair that spilled over his shoulder left Jalwyn to deduce his assailant was a woman. The voice growling from out of the gloom, furiously angry though still somehow musically feminine, confirmed what he still could not see.

"Where is he?" the woman snarled. The encircling arm compressed again, stealing his breath. "Where is my brother? Tell me, or you die here, now."

Jalwyn tried to shake his head, but the sleek muscle of the woman's arm immobilized him. Dark spots flowered in his dimming vision, blotting holes in the stone wall. A deep gulp of air at that moment would have tasted magnitudes sweeter than the wine he had craved. He vied to pry the woman's arm off his neck, but the small, rocky bicep beneath the leather sleeve only tightened on his windpipe. The woman's strength astonished him.

"None of your lies!" she said venomously. "You wear the robes, you bear the markings, and you arrive at this same inn! Do you think us dense that we would not notice? You are in league with him!"

A mirthless laugh followed her accusation. "Did he send you back for the money?"

A strangled mewling from deep inside his burning throat was all the answer the Mage had to give. His hands sunk limply to the sheets beside him. His vision narrowed, dimmed.

Suddenly, the pressure released. Jalwyn's gaping mouth sucked air noisily. He drew delicious, cool draughts of it deep into his searing lungs.

A strong leg scissored quickly over his waist, and, in an instant, his assailant spun from behind to atop him, straddling the Mage's stomach and leaning in close. The silky weight of her hair tickled his face, but he thought it prudent not to protest, even if he had breath to do so. The cruel knife held against his throat from behind now menaced from the front.

Jalwyn's labored breath caught in his aching throat. Even with her features contorted in rage, the beauty of the woman astride him threatened to steal that breath once again.

The candlelight shone full on the flawless oval of her face, her dusky complexion catching it, seeming to mute it. The anger in her face failed utterly to mask its exquisite features. Liquid blue eyes gleamed behind narrowed lids, and the firelight flickering in her wealth of unruly raven hair transformed it to a nearly purple sheen. She wore a dark cowl over a tawny leather cuirass that hugged her taut and shapely form. The hood of the garment was thrown back, and that fiercely beautiful face hovered not an inch from his own, the delicate outward curve of her smooth nose nearly touching the tip of his own.

Her bent knees pinned Jalwyn's arms to the bed and her bottom sat on his stomach. "Speak!" she demanded. "And know that I will not be deceived by the lies you fed Carek. Where is Vergal!"

Jalwyn nodded as much as the knife at this throat would allow. "You, you are Alonna?" he croaked.

"I am. It is good you know the name of the woman who will kill you."

"Then you will spill innocent blood," Jalwyn rasped. "For I only know what Carek told me of Sh'ynryan and your brother."

Alonna blinked. "So," she whispered, "the devil has a name. And you admit knowledge of him?"

"Knowledge of the man, yes, but not his crimes. I came here to find him on order of those we serve in common. I knew nothing of his involvement with your brother, I swear it."

"Your oath is meaningless," Alonna hissed. "By your own word, you serve the same master, the same purpose."

"No. If Sh'ynryan has done this thing of which he is accused, it was not on the instruction of my order."

"You would have me believe you arrived here, after all this time, and happen to be pursuing the same man but with no common goal? You seem to have convinced Carek, but you will find me more dubious. What is your interest in him? Why now?"

In truth, he knew little of the reasons why the Order had chosen him—an inferior in the ways of the Words—to hunt an elder. He reckoned himself a mere errand boy on a mission to deliver messages between men of rank and stature greater than his own.

Staring up the length of Alonna's knife, Jalwyn believed what the elders had neglected to tell him then would get him killed now.

Pinned, fearing the knife held to his throat, Jalwyn related in as calm and convincing a fashion he could muster how the conclave had commissioned him to trail a member who had departed for the Aerie Coast in years past and had not been heard from since. His absence caused the elders to fret, though they did not divulge their reasons why. Jalwyn's task was simply to retrace the man's steps in hopes of finding any sign of him.

"And the trail led you here?" Alonna asked skeptically. At some point in Jalwyn's testimony, the knife had moved away from his throat, though she remained astride him. Something in her expression told Jalwyn his explanation rang true to her.

"Indirectly. I was traveling to Far when I was side-tracked, only today. I could not find passage, and chance brought me here, where apparently, a colleague has left an evil impression for which I am now suffering."

He told her about the pirates aboard the *Acolyte*, and their encounter on the ocean with Ureld Sanskister and the *Sea King*, though he carefully omitted his own actions aboard ship. Something warned Jalwyn that the tempestuous young beauty astride him would not accept the truth of his role in events.

She observed him as he spoke. Slowly, her eyes softened, turned thoughtful. "What would the man be looking for?" she demanded.

Jalwyn saw no reason not to tell her. Though many doubted their powers in the Words, the Magi were not a secret organization. Their traditions were matters of public record. Jalwyn related, in condensed form, the legend of the Stone, its importance to the Brethren, and their unending quest to search the world for clues to its location.

The Mage's tale evoked a wispy memory in Alonna. She envisioned the crowded plaza at Zistah and her father Teraud leading her through the crush of people filling the palm-lined square. So vivid was her recall she could almost smell the scented palms waving in the moist air flowing off the great lake and could nearly hear the background bustle of the masses, the bark of vendors promoting their wares punctuating the overall din.

"They'll find you," the robed man who wore the platinum circlets called after them. "They won't suffer it to be lost to them!"

She heard the words ringing in her ears as clearly as if the man just spoke them. She felt Teraud's firm grip tighten on her hand as he quickened his pace, eager to meld into the swarm of people.

Why the memory surfaced, or what it meant, eluded her. But her recall was total and had been sparked by the arrival of the man pinned beneath her.

Alonna frowned, the immobile man all but forgotten. The Mage could at that moment have taken advantage of her distraction and thrown her away from him, but he did not take his chance. Her wildflower fragrance and her comeliness distracted him. The malleable weight of her curves pressing his body was a sensation he was not eager to interrupt.

Alonna shook her head to clear her thoughts. It was obvious the thin man had nothing to do with Vergal. His emotions and thoughts raced across his features without hindrance, as easily read like an open book.

It was equally as evident the awkward stranger—he was so frail and disheveled, she realized with a surge of pity—presented her best opportunity to find her brother. He knew the man who took Vergal or at least knew of him. He was a member of the abductor's same strange Order, or Brotherhood, or whatever they deemed it, and held insights into the motivations of the red-robed man that no other could hope to match.

In that instant, the trembling man became more precious to Alonna than her secreted gold.

She didn't share her conclusion. She abruptly sheathed her knife and harshly seized the man's thin shoulders.

"You will tell me everything!" she demanded, accentuating her words with a rough shake of his shoulders. "All you know of this man, I will know! You will help me find him."

By the Stone, you are beautiful, Jalwyn thought, transfixed by her clear eyes. His heart ached to look upon her. The immense sorrow and desperation behind the feigned anger now in her eyes needed to be vanquished, and Jalwyn knew he would help her to do so, no matter the cost.

He silently cursed himself for a fool. How, he wondered, had he suddenly become besotted with a woman who despised him, who had threatened him with death and had nearly succeeded with her choking grasp.

Jalwyn could not bring to mind a single magical Word to help him escape this predicament in which he discovered himself. The thought simultaneously elated and disturbed him.

She eased cautiously off him, her hand firm on the hilt of her knife. Looking at her, Jalwyn was suddenly glad that there were still forms of magic in the world even the power of the Words could not counter.

CHAPTER TWENTY

Had he not so terribly missed his sister, Vergal might have enjoyed his time on the road with Sh'ynryan, his abductor, and the swordsman Guile, the Mage's conflicted and confused accomplice.

The two of them observed Vergal's slightest movements warily. When he stopped to rest, or stretch his legs, or when he withdrew into the underbrush to relive himself, as was his wont, they found reason to stand nearby. One of them even hovered when Vergal, a fastidious boy, took opportunities for quick dips in streams and pools to bathe himself.

Wresting the elemental energy from Sh'ynryan's control and deploying it in his own fashion against the Drakleth had surprised and confused Vergal and gave him much to ponder, but not nearly so much as it did his traveling companions. In fact, the Mage and the swordsman regarded him with barely disguised awe. Vergal couldn't fault them; he was awed himself. Not with himself—the feat had somehow seemed strangely natural to him in the aftermath, like a memory of a vivid, remembered dream—but at the new deference with which it afforded him. The change had been dramatic, especially in Sh'ynryan. The Mage's caustic comments to the boy had vanished alongside the magical guttering flames that marked the Drakleth's defeat. A kind of cautious, flustered respect had replaced it.

Sh'ynryan questioned him closely afterward, but the boy had been at an honest loss to explain how he had wielded the power, or how he had remembered and annunciated with perfect cadence a foreign and garbled ancient word he had heard only in passing when Sh'ynryan had beckoned the fire.

The encounter excited and frightened Vergal. Vibrant daydreams of again brandishing the incredible power he had unleashed lightened the drudgery of the trail, interrupted at times by terrified imaginings of the consequences should he call upon the Word again.

What bothered Vergal most in the days following the encounter in the glen, as the companions plodded steadily over broken countryside toward the March, was how the manifestation had shackled him even tighter to his abductor.

How could he escape the sorcerer now, after experiencing the immense force that had possessed him in the forest clearing? His ignorance of its limits frightened him worse than his predicament. Sh'ynryan, he conceded sourly, would be needed to instruct him in this strange skill. The boy's emotions whiplashed between terror at the specter of the power being released, uncontrolled, to exhilaration at the prospect of one day wielding it again.

Sh'ynryan's and Guile's apprehension were no less, as the boy covertly discovered one evening while wrapped in his blankets near the campfire, feigning sleep.

"How could he have done it?" Guile asked, his voice moving between admiration and nervousness. "He's only a boy. You told us that sorcerers of your order spend their lives working on mastering the power, at great personal risk to themselves. Then a mere repeats what one of you says, and—poof!—a full-sized Drakleth goes up in smoke!"

Beneath his blanket, Vergal smiled, recalling the searing pillars of flame he had sent flaring after the fleeing beast. How he wished Alonna could have seen it!

A pregnant silence followed. Vergal could almost hear the confused babble of Sh'ynryan's agitated thoughts.

"It is not unknown," the Mage whispered at length. He was speaking around a mouthful of something he was chewing—another of the Mage's habits that set Vergal's teeth on edge.

"What is?"

"What he did, in the glen. I told you the boy is gifted in the Words. I sensed it; my medallion confirmed it. It is why I compelled him to accompany me, so just such an incident as this might be avoided in the presence of those who would not understand his talent.

"I've told you, it is the preeminent responsibility of the Magi to identify these people, that they might receive the benefit of proper training. Otherwise, an incident like the one we witnessed could be catastrophic for the caller and those around him."

"I tend to believe that," Guile said glumly.

"The thing to remember is Vergal is no different a boy now than he was when you first met him."

"The hell he isn't!"

"No, listen. He is only becoming more fully himself. This ability obviously has always been with him, latent though essential to his nature, in the same way that he will one day grow into the man he always had the potential to become. Do you understand?"

Guile snorted. "I do not understand much of what I've seen since I met you, but, yes, I follow your vein. I suppose I see an example in myself. I had blonde hair as a child; it eventually deepened to black because that is the color it was meant to become. It only grew into that which was already true of me from the beginning. You say these things Vergal can do is like that: His hair is turning black, so to speak."

Sh'ynryan chuckled, a noise that for once lacked its characteristic mockery. "Exactly," he said. "But to extend the metaphor, he also has potential to similarly color the hair of everyone else in the world around him!"

The pair fell silent, listening to the popping logs in the fire, considering.

"I think you see now why I had to take him with me," Sh'ynryan said hopefully.

"I see now why you believed you needed him," Guile countered. "I will never agree it was proper, but I am bound by my vows to Gelbrek to serve you, and my vows to Gelbrek—fat slob though he is—are important to me. He's like a father. I won't betray him, and neither will any of those who work for him. That's why the chunky lout prospers so."

"Though if I believed you intended to harm the boy," the mercenary added after a pause, "my sword would find your guts while you slept—and damn the consequences. I'd be lying if I said I haven't grown fond of the lad. Did you see him smashing the knees of that rabble back on the road! He was scared nearly to death and darting around like a cornered hare, but still swinging his ax and busting everyone's 'caps! Ha! He presents as gentle, but I tell you there is ice running deep in that boy's veins."

The pair shared a laugh at the memory, but Vergal shifted in his roll uncomfortably. He still saw little humor in what had happened on the road. But he brightened when he considered Guile's words; it seemed he had a friend and a protector of sorts on this dangerous venture, after all.

"He's unique; I'll concede that point," Sh'ynryan offered thoughtfully.

"I tell you, the boy has twice saved our lives—on the road and again against the Drakleth. The thing couldn't see or smell me beneath the water, but it kept plunging its head and had rolled me several times with its snout. It was only a matter of time before it got its mouth around me. Had Vergal not ..."

Guile let the statement trail off, the answer obvious.

Another long silence followed, broken by Guile's sudden question. "What is it you seek at the March?"

"I've told you," Sh'ynryan replied quickly. "A stone."

"Yes, yes, a stone, but not any stone. The Stone. That's what you called it. The one you red-robes are all willing to fall on your faces for."

Guile laced his fingers over one knee and reclined slightly, watching the Mage shrewdly.

"I have been thinking on this," he continued. "You're going to the March with a purpose, with no hesitation at all. It's like you know this 'stone' of yours is there. The thing I can't understand is if this order of yours, these Magi, already knew it was hidden there, an army of you sorcerer types would have picked the place apart to find it before now."

Sh'ynryan said nothing.

"So, what's different now?" Guile persisted. His lopsided grin, a rare sight in recent days, returned. "Why can you get at it now when you obviously could not before?"

Sh'ynryan leaned forward and grasped his walking stick to poke the fire. When he looked at Guile again, his face looked haggard and tired.

"You're to the point, aren't you?"

Guile's white teeth flashed in the firelight. "I try to be," he admitted.

"Then please continue. Why don't you share your conclusions? I'm fascinated to hear them."

"Fine, I shall," Guile said. He leaned forward earnestly. "And since you appear to favor plain speech so much, then here it is: I think you know something your order doesn't about the March, and I believe you first needed our little friend there because of it."

In his bedroll, Vergal frowned. He had no idea what Guile meant. His ears strained from beneath his blankets in anticipation of the mercenary's explanation.

"Why else?" Guile continued. "You gave us some story about 'the Words,' and your order, and your sacred mission to seek out those in the world who are skilled as yourselves to keep them from blundering about and harming themselves or others. I know all that. I just don't think it's the whole story."

Sh'ynryan remained silent.

"Think about it. Do you abduct everyone who possesses these skills? That seems unlikely. Surely all those with similar abilities aren't peasant boys like Vergal, and eventually, someone in power would have raised the alarm when a relative, a son, or a daughter, simply disappeared. That would cause discomfort for your cloistered little group."

The cadence of Guile's voice picked up tempo as he postulated. He was enjoying himself, Vergal could tell.

"So why not recruit these people instead? Save your energies, you know? The world already seems wary of men with your, uh, talents, so why kidnap people when you could simply explain the situation and offer help in a civilized way. The logical answer is often the most probable, in my experience, and I can't see reason in an order that effectively built itself by snatching babes from cradles for untold centuries."

"That's unkind of you," Sh'ynryan sounded pained.

Guile ignored him. "That led me to another conclusion. This is not something you've done before, is it? Abducting people. You're obviously not savvy about the entire business. Usually, people conducting crimes don't recruit perfect strangers to help them, no matter the strangers' reputations—too many loose ends; too many ways to be found out. My point is, why did you do so with Vergal? You took a risk. Were you not fortunate enough to enlist Gelbrek, you'd have left a trail a blind man could follow."

"But I did pick Gelbrek. Why do you assume that was an accident?"

"Was it not?"

"Not at all. I needed passage out of the city; I needed a sword such as yourself to accompany us, for the express reasons you have already witnessed. Practicing my craft leaves me utterly exhausted afterward. The passage of such energy through the conduit of a mortal body takes a severe toll. So why expend myself using my talents to depart the city when my coin, of which I have no shortage, works as well?"

Guile barked laughter, an almost appreciative sound. "You are a master of deflection; you realize that, right? I tell you I believe you're not following so blind a trail to this…stone, and instead of answering, you provide a discourse on the effects of sorcery on the human structure. As fascinating as I'm sure the subject is, I am willing to defer. What I need to know is how our young friend fits in? And why you are sure what you seek lies at the March."

Guile paused. He inspected his scuffed boots and, licking a finger, reached down to scrub at a grass stain. "If you haven't noticed yet, I am an Aerian subject, and the Imperial legionnaires are not in the habit of allowing citizens of my nationality through the gates. The March does guard a border for a reason, you realize."

"You must trust me, Guile," Sh'ynryan replied earnestly. His tone was as companionable as Vergal had heard it, as if he wanted to answer the question honestly but was constrained. "I will get us through the March.

"As for your other question, I cast no aspersions on your comprehension, but I honestly say my answer would make no sense. I know what I know, but I cannot satisfy your rational mind based on proof. It's in that same way I knew Vergal was needful. He fits into this somehow. You witnessed him in the forest. That, if anything, should convince you I was not misguided. I said before; he is the same young boy you met outside the walls of Caliss. And that is true to an extent. But he is becoming more profoundly what he is intended to be, more so with each passing day. It was a fortunate happenstance I found him when I did ..."

Sh'ynryan trailed off uncertainly, though he quickly recovered.

"I need him, and I need you. Otherwise, neither of you would be here now. The reasons, I think, will be made abundantly clear in short order, but I cannot offer them to you now.

"Besides," he said, "I paid you handsomely, did I not? You are a businessman, are you not? I have given my word that no harm shall befall the boy at my hand, and I think recent events have convinced you. I need him far too much ever to harm him; he is vital. So, if all the criteria of your contract have been satisfied, why not indulge an old man in his fool's errand, eh?"

Guile stared fixedly at the man across the flames from him. "Most old men I know aren't sorcerers," he said.

The conversation ended at that.

—⚏—

They were on the road early the next morning.

Vergal found, to his relief, that he was growing more accustomed to life on the road beneath the open skies. His body didn't ache so badly when he woke, and the inconveniences of living outdoors grated on him less. Ducking into the brush to relieve himself had become second nature—though he remained wary of lessons learned in the unexpected encounter with the Drakleth—and the food cooked nightly over open fires had acquired a wild deliciousness no civilized table's fare could mimic.

The road behind them had slowly, surely left Caliss far behind. The forest around them had broken and lifted, and their trek veered almost entirely upland now. One evening, a search of his maps showed Vergal that they were now likely deep in a southern spur of the western slopes of the Watergate Mountains.

The mountains dominated—sheer walls of rock soaring above the timberline that lurched closer and taller after every step. Snow-capped peaks flashed brilliantly in the sunshine. As the party curled deeper into the high country, the choking wilderness sometimes opened into grassy alpine meadows ringed by wispy aspen trees. Vergal found the shivering, broad-leafed canopies enchanting after the unrelenting green needles of the evergreen forests.

The meadows were islands in the sea of trees. They inclined gently and were well-watered by turbulent streams spilling from the Watergates' lofts. The green grasses were closely shorn by the deer, mountain goats and sheep, and other animals that grazed upon them so that the whole more closely resembled a verdant green carpet than a wild mountain slope.

Sometimes the bare bones of the mountain thrust from the meadows as boulders, stone outcroppings, or rocky flats. Any number of wild animals could be seen sunning themselves on these granite thrones. Wildflowers sprouted everywhere, their brilliant colors shimmering whenever the fresh wind dropping down the mountain set them to nodding.

The setting was beautiful, serene, and a balm to Vergal's spirits. Often the passing world mesmerized him so completely that Vergal would shake himself from his delighted musings and reproach himself for briefly forgetting he remained a captive, a child taken against his will from his sister—his only family and the only person left in the world he loved.

Still, Vergal had to grudgingly admit, even while sunk in these miserable thoughts, that he was glad to be in the sun-dappled Watergate Mountains. Their ever-changing backdrop outshone the monotonous existence he had endured at the Wayfarer. It brought to life the ink illustrations on maps that not so long ago been his only window to the broader world around him.

Then he would rebuke himself for his thoughts, imagining them disrespectful to Alonna's grief, and the emotional cycle would begin anew.

They journeyed without incident for days after leaving the Drakleth's glen, without sign of highwaymen or any other threat. Sh'ynryan had grown hopeful the path to the March lay open before them and told the party as much.

The Obroths attacked soon after that.

The party rode languidly through another alpine meadow when an explosion of fowl sounded from the surrounding trees. Frantic birds thundered across the path ahead of them. Guile was saying something smart about dinner being nearly served when the howling went up around them.

Vergal experienced an unreasonable though profound stab of betrayal. The sunny alpine meadows had seemed safe havens to the boy since they entered the mountains. To be confronted in one of these sanctuaries robbed him of the growing sense of security he had enjoyed as the journey had progressed.

All thoughts except shock and terror soon flew from the boy when the sources of the howling emerged from the trees.

Guile drew his sword with a steely ring. "Obroths!" he yelled, yanking firmly on the reins to settle his terrified horse. The animal shied and reared, flailing the air with its sharp hooves.

The creatures shambling into the sun stood the size and a half of a tall man. However, they carried considerably more bulk on their towering frames. Matted grey fur covered them completely, but the bulging contours of well-muscled arms and squat legs were obvious even beneath their shaggy coats. The Obroths lunged forward in a strange, hunkering charge that employed the knuckles of their massive fists for momentum as much as their churning rear legs.

Dirt fanned behind them, kicked up by their taloned feet. Massively ridged brows lowered over inky eyes that reflected no light, even in the mid-day sun. Their mouths, still stretched in unearthly howls as they bounded forward, displayed jagged rows of yellowed teeth, each cruelly tipped and slathered in lime-green foam.

"What's the play?" Sh'ynryan yelled. The man wore a grimace of fear and discomfort as the shrill keening drew closer. The veins beneath the skin of his bony hands stood out like cords as he grappled with the reins of his panicky horse.

Vergal counted seven of the creatures. They cleared the trees and ran in their strange, folded gait, up the low swell in the clipped grass, directly toward them.

Even from a distance, the Obroths appeared massive, invincible, and their strength of numbers only bolstered the frightening impression. They advanced with the fearlessness of ravenous wolves. There was no malice in their narrow eyes; only a mindless predatory cunning Vergal found even more terrifying.

In the face of such monstrous adversaries, Vergal knew the response to Sh'ynryan's question before Guile opened his mouth to utter it.

"We flee!" the mercenary yelled.

Setting heels to his horse, Guile plunged down the Imperial highway without a backward glance.

Their horses needed no prodding to follow. The baying Obroths and Guile's sudden flight sent them in swift pursuit. The road plunged out of the meadow and into the pressing forest that whipped past Vergal's vision in a tangled streak. His mount's pounding hooves kept the winding road with deft, sure turns that required no prompting from its handler.

"They're tireless, relentless," Guile yelled over his shoulder. "They want the horses. They'll run them down and rip them apart, and us alongside them if we're foolish enough to be caught near."

"What are you suggesting?" Sh'ynryan shrilled.

"High ground, some defensible plateau where we can meet them one at a time. Otherwise, they'll swarm us before we can set ourselves. It's our only chance."

Sh'ynryan said nothing, only nodded once in response.

The riders' heads ducked in unison to avoid overhanging branches as the desperate flight over the uneven path wore on. Here, on the rising flank of a hill, the highway became little more than a broad, leaf-littered path through an arch formed by the laced canopy high above.

Every time his mount turned a corner or scrambled down a low dip in the path, Vergal ventured a glance back, expecting to discover the pursuing Obroths falling behind. Always, though, he caught a flash of grey through the screen of trees, never distinct but always nearby.

The creatures' baying persisted. As the chase intensified, the creatures' tonguing grew louder, more excited. Vergal had the sickening feeling he and his companions' flight had become an instinctual form of grand sport for the creatures.

They turned a corner and emerged into brilliant sunlight on a bald patch of land crowning the hill. Boulders littered the ground, and grass poked meagrely through an anemic layer of soil stretched thinly over a bed of pulverized scree, laid down by a rockslide in ancient times.

Vergal dared peek behind. The path remained clear. The keening still sounded back in the forest.

The boy turned hopefully to Guile, who shook his head.

"They're flanking, spreading out in the trees to surround us. We either follow the highway back into the trees, where they down the horses, or we make our stand."

The mercenary's eyes darted around the clearing, assessing. He nodded grimly. "The ground's steep here. The boulders will provide an obstacle to them. This may offer our best chance."

Guile looked to Sh'ynryan, who nodded. "The horses can't keep this up," the Mage agreed. "Get behind that outcropping," he said, pointing at a circle of large rocks up the slope. "I'll prepare a surprise for our hairy friends when they stick in their noses."

They turned their horses and galloped hard. They reached the protective circle of rocks, and a frantic survey of the slope below revealed the Obroths had not yet made the clearing. Their howling grew restless in the trees beyond.

"They're getting anxious, hungry," Guile observed, sliding out of his saddle. He lifted a large rock and dropped the reins beneath it as a makeshift hobble for the nervous animal. It was the only picket possible in the cramped, rocky space between the leaning boulders. The others followed suit. The horses bolting free now would prove disastrous. Realizing that, Vergal strained to drag a heavy rock and drop it on the reins. He added more stones to his companion's mounts' reins as the two men stood jabbering.

"Whatever you plan on doing, you better do it soon," Guile told Sh'ynryan. His eyes were round and, if not quite terrified, assuredly apprehensive.

Sh'ynryan peered around a boulder. There was no sign of the creatures, though the howling had swelled to a feverish pitch. Growls and snarls had begun to punctuate the din.

Undermarch

"In all my years," the Mage said incredulously, "I've never seen these things. I've read accounts, I knew they existed, but in the way you know creatures exist deep in the ocean, without any real prospects of seeing one."

Guile joined the Mage at his post. "They're real enough," he said. "A lone Obroth attacked a camp I was in once. We were sitting around a campfire, a real crowd of us, including Torth, a friend since my childhood. We were laughing and drinking when it busted out of the bushes."

Vergal, his errand complete, joined the men behind the boulder, his eyes wide. "What did you do?" he breathed.

"We didn't have time to do much of anything. Fortunately, it made straight for the horses. Obroths love horse flesh. It must taste like the deer and elk they hunt in the mountains, only a lot easier to catch, especially when tied for the night. I remember branches and leaves flying all around us and this huge grey blur hurtling through the campfire, ripping into a horse nearby. It just slashed that animal's neck wide open with a swipe of its arm."

Guile's mouth puckered distastefully as he recalled the scene.

"That horse's head was hanging by sinew alone after one swipe!"

Guile peered anxiously around the boulder again. "Where are the damn things?" he asked himself anxiously.

"What happened?" Vergal urged.

"We needed the horses if we wanted to get out of the mountains. Two of them were dead before we all had swords drawn. It had fastened on a third, taking its time, by the time we reached it. These things are extremely strong and swift; you can't underestimate them. They run on their knuckles and look shaggy and clumsy, but in close quarters, they move like lightning."

Guile leaned with his back to the boulder, his eyes fixed straight ahead as if watching a ghostly replay of past events play out in front of his eyes.

"It was busy with the horse. It had jumped on its back and sunk its teeth in its neck when Torth reached it."

Guile swallowed hard. "Poor Torth," he choked.

The mercenary sighed and went on.

"Torth reached the monster first. He drew back and whacked the Obroth across the back of its leg with his sword, and the sword just bounced right off. The skin beneath their fur is tough. It takes a good deal of strength to cut through. Torth was a strong man, but maybe he was just using that first strike to try to scare the thing off, not really trying to kill it right away. I don't know; I never had the chance to ask him.

"The Obroth turned, and I'll never forget those eyes: little black holes beneath its brow, not even reflecting the firelight. It was on Torth in a blink. It bowled him over, growling and snapping its teeth. Torth screamed once, then gurgled a little bit, and that was it.

"There were six of us left, and we all ran this thing through with our swords while it was atop our comrade. Even with that clear first shot at it, only five of us survived the encounter."

Sh'ynryan licked his lips. They looked dehydrated in the sunlight spilling over the boulders.

Guile looked speculatively at the horses. "I hate to say it, but I think if we stand a chance of getting out of this," he said uncertainly, "we have to sacrifice the horses. That's what they want. It may not be too late to send them out and run the other way while the Obroths chase them down."

Sh'ynryan frowned. "And get to the March how then? Do we fly?"

"Why not? I hear you're good at that," Guile snapped back.

"And better we walk there than be shred into little pieces here. It is a pack of those things! Just one of them killed trained men in our camp."

"You said it jumped right through your campfire." It was Vergal who had spoken. They turned to him.

"Yes."

"Then it has no real fear of fire," Vergal turned to Sh'ynryan. "Was that what you were planning to do? Use fire?"

"Vergal, just because these things aren't afraid of fire doesn't mean it can't hurt them. They're covered in hair! That seems adequate tinder to me."

"My point is they have no fear. What if they charge through it and bury us under like Guile said?"

Sh'ynryan chewed his lip, considering.

"I have an idea," Vergal pressed on. The cautious tone he normally used in conversation with Sh'ynryan had flown, replaced by excited confidence.

"Remember on the road, with the highwaymen? You stopped things, or at least slowed them down, as they came through. Can you do it again? If you can, Guile and I can take care of them as they come through."

Sh'ynryan's eyebrows lifted. "Oh, how will you do that?" he asked. "You heard Guile; these beasts' hides are like armor. You don't have the strength to penetrate their skin. It will likely take time for even Guile to do it. And what if the dome drops? One of these things can tear us all apart."

"Then we don't stab their hides. Guile can stab their eyes or something; that's possible if they can barely move."

Vergal grinned wickedly. "Besides, I don't plan on stabbing them."

Sh'ynryan caught Vergal's meaning immediately. "What you did with the Drakleth could have been an aberration, boy," he growled. "You don't know that you can repeat it. And if you can, you don't know that you can control it."

Vergal started to respond but stopped short. The baying had resumed. None of them had noticed it had stopped. Guile scrambled to his feet and peered over the boulder, then quickly ducked back down.

"They're coming," he said hurriedly. "They smell the horses, and it's driving them mad. Whatever you're doing, do it now!"

Sh'ynryan cast a sidelong glance at Vergal but said nothing. He rose to his feet and blanched at the sight of the seven—no, now eight—Obroths charging across the clearing, their long strides swallowing the intervening span with astonishing speed.

The red-robed man made several passes of his hands in front of his face, composing himself. His racing heart settled, and his mind stilled as he uttered an ancient word—calling it to mind, lingering reverently on its potency and shaping his thoughts to channel the elemental power for the effect he sought. Sh'ynryan grimaced as if discomfited, and beads of sweat rose instantly on his brow.

Vergal listened intently, nodded once, content. Like before, he heard the Word clearly and, though nearly incomprehensible to the ear, he committed it instantly to his memory. It was like a bird in his mind, coming home to roost, blazing like a beacon and twitching on his tongue with perfect inflection. There would be no misstep. His fears dissolved. Yet another Word of Power had become as familiar to him as his own fingers.

The roaring Vergal heard with each utterance of the words filled his ears. He welcomed it, savored the raw power of its volume, and invited it to fill him like an empty vessel. The boy cleared his own exulting thoughts and recalled his previous experience, how he had repeated Sh'ynryan's utterance and made it his own.

Beside the boy, watching the Obroths closing in, Guile nervously licked his lips and gripped the hilts of his sword and dagger. He glanced once at Sh'ynryan. As before on the road, the Mage had drawn great columns of air to himself, molded the eddying winds to his will, and projected it back heavenward in pulsing waves, the winding, fibrous stems swirling from his splayed hands to reach for the sky above.

At its pinnacle, the force sundered and spilled in all directions, cascading to earth again to form a pulsing sphere encapsulating the party and the wild-eyed horses.

The man's thin face contorted painfully. His knees shook visibly, close to buckling. Already the power was taking its toll on the Mage, who had employed the elemental power several times in a span of days. Guile could only hope the Obroths would hit the dome before the toll on the Mage became unbearable.

The Obroths did not oblige.

After skidding to a halt outside of the fluid orb, the creatures cautiously sniffed the air around them. It fairly crackled with energy, and the vitality of it stood their hair on end. Snarling and shaking their heads, they set to pacing the perimeter, eyeing the horses within hungrily but giving heed to primal instincts that warned them of lurking danger.

Vergal and Guile exchanged worried looks.

"Lure them in!" Sh'ynryan demanded through gritted teeth. He wobbled slightly.

"Do it! Now!" he implored.

And in a movement too quick for Guile to counter, Vergal sprinted forward and stepped through the rippling shield of energy separating the companions from the scuffling, grunting beasts massing beyond.

CHAPTER TWENTY-ONE

Periodically, Jalwyn found himself shaking his head uncertainly, trying to stitch together the precise chain of events that led him from the comfort of his tome-lined chambers in far-off Zistah to this dirt trail through the perpetual timberlands of barbaric Alasia. More perplexing was how fate had placed him at the side of a wild beauty who, not long ago, had come to a whisker from killing him in his bed in an ignoble inn in the reeking port town of Caliss.

It had been a disconcerting time for Jalwyn since encountering Alonna at the Wayfarer. He considered it a testament to his innate honesty that he managed to win the trust of a woman who had come to his room to slay him. More distressing to Jalwyn, though, was how in between then and now he somehow managed, for the first time in his life, to fall in love.

At least, he assumed the tumult raging inside was love. He stood on faith on that count since the experience was utterly foreign to a man who had foregone companionship most of his life in devotion to his craft.

All of that had changed, Jalwyn thought, somewhat sourly. The notion of returning to the confines of his book-filled chamber in Zistah left him hollow and unfulfilled unless, as often happened, his imagination inserted the image of Alonna there beside him.

Then the scene changed from the stodgy routines of scholarship he once prized to ardent notions of romance.

A hand brushed by accident during their preparations for the road had been enough to stir the heart. A rare smile tugging her perfect lips raised bumps across the surface of his flesh. And her scent? It was maddening. The clean fragrance of her skin and hair completed a circuit within him. Never in his experience had Jalwyn encountered such an intriguing mystery and that reckoning included his introduction to the Words.

He loved her. Completely. His heart and his intellect confirmed it, yet had someone known and asked him the reason why he could never have articulated it. In the same way, he could not explain how completely he knew the absolute truth of his feelings. It was nothing concrete, yet it was everything real. It was inexplicable and undeniably true. The sun rose in the morning, and he loved the woman named Alonna. These were immutable facts of his existence, and Jalwyn was powerless to influence either reality.

Alonna remained ignorant of his state. Jalwyn took no particular pains to conceal his feelings—surely his slack-jawed stuttering in her presence was indication enough—but she was blinded to anything except her search for her brother and the man who had abducted him. Her focus in that regard was complete.

Alonna's single-mindedness unnerved him. Her thorough interrogation and subsequent plumbing of his background—and the particulars of the Brotherhood—had been relentless, making him into a mere book of information to be opened and absorbed from cover-to-cover, instead of a man trying desperately to aid her. He winced when he considered how many details he provided may have verged on disloyalty, if not betrayal, of the Brethren. He was helpless to deny her anything she asked. His helplessness made him miserable.

She took no note of his eagerness to please nor his fawning looks. Jalwyn did not know whether to be relieved that her preoccupation kept him from being found out or frustrated at her ignorance of his painfully apparent longing.

She visited him by night only, appearing at his ground-floor room window as if in a waking. In the first days of their association, after Jalwyn had convinced her of his fealty and desire to bring the renegade to justice, they spent evenings talking and taking late dinners in his room by candlelight that glittered off the bottles of fine wines he had sent for her pleasure. Jalwyn was not typically an imbiber, but he matched her glass for glass in his eagerness to please.

They talked late into the evenings and early into the mornings. She absorbed every word spoken about Sh'ynryan. She was alternately fascinated and outraged by the man's power. She listened raptly to any speculation about the Mage's possible motives for abducting her brother.

Jalwyn offered all the information she requested without question. He had no choice. He would have done anything for her. And when he provided information she desired, Jalwyn saw confidence in him growing, which filled his heart. In those moments, her focus fastened entirely onto him. There was nowhere else worth existing for Jalwyn except beneath her grateful gaze. The flush of pleasure that accompanied her searching eyes, or the absent touch of her hand on his in animated conversation, provided all the impetus he needed to continue the narrative.

One night when she appeared at his window, as was her custom, her detached manner had flown. Blood flushed the flesh of her flawless cheeks, and her eyes glittered cheerfully. She rushed across the room to where he sat at the edge of his bed, awaiting her. He had half-rose when she reached him and grasped his hands warmly in hers—the feeling of her soft fingers clenching his ignited palpitations.

She smiled at him—an ethereal lifting of her lips that displayed her brilliant teeth in shining rows. She squeezed his hands tighter.

"Jalwyn, will you help me with something?"

The answer erupted from him before he could consider, "Yes!"

She laughed, a clear, beautiful sound.

She smiled. "Do not answer yet," she chided. She sat on his bed and tugged him down beside her. It didn't require much insistence.

As usual, the strange contrast of her coarse leather armor and the exquisite fragrance of her skin and hair permeated him. Their hips touched as they sat together on the bed. Jalwyn's head spun. Never since the night she attacked and pinned him on his bed beneath her blade had she come into such close contact.

She shifted and turned to face him, lifting one knee onto the bed to better situate herself. An unconscious toss of her head sent her thick black hair out of her way and over her shoulder. Jalwyn swallowed hard.

"Do you remember Rostalin and our mission to Astareth Manor?" Alonna asked. Her voice was still eager, though a shadow of anguish veiled her eyes for an instant when she spoke aloud the name.

Of course, he remembered. He recollected nearly every word she had ever spoken. He recalled the fury and the misery that battled in her expression when she related the story of the botched assault on the stronghold of the corrupt nobleman Astareth. He recalled her heat when she related her vows of revenge.

He nodded at her, lost in her shining eyes, captivated by the movement of her mobile lips that talked at length of sad things. She still held his hand, her fingers playing absently with the tips of his.

She smiled again, pleased. "I've found him," she breathed.

"Who?"

"The man who betrayed us. The man who sent Rostalin—the both of us—into that trap."

Jalwyn remembered. They had slain the man Astareth, who had commissioned the betrayal, and several of his retainers as well. The death of Astareth had reportedly left his house in shambles as relatives fought bitterly over his estate and positioned themselves to inherit and repair the crumbling rival guild the nobleman had been in the process of building.

All of this was of scant concern to Alonna, who knew well her guild master Gelbrek would deal with whatever new power rose within the house. However, one matter remained unresolved, and Jalwyn spoke it aloud, "Elnark!" he exclaimed.

She laughed and clapped her hands, an endearingly girlish gesture at odds with the wicked scimitars laying sideways at her hip on his bed. "Your memory amazes me," she said. "I'm starting to think you remember everything I say."

If only you knew! Jalwyn thought, but when he spoke, he said, "I remember you said this Elnark was the agent of Astareth's betrayal, the one who infiltrated your guild on the nobleman's behalf with a tale of robbery and beatings that sent you and your instructor on a mission of retribution."

"Exactly. And now I've found him. He went to sea immediately after learning Astareth's fate, but the fool has returned and in the most obvious of disguises." She snorted contemptuously.

"Why would he return to a city where he angered the existing mercenary guild?"

"As I've said, the man's a fool. He obviously has great confidence in his ability to conceal himself from us."

Alonna shook her head, almost—though not exactly—in a gesture of pity.

"I knew him immediately when I saw him," she went on. "He has been away from Caliss for some time, but I've seen him working on the docks, going about his business as if nothing has happened."

"You reported this to your guild?"

"No!" Alonna replied quickly. "He is mine to deal with. It was my head he threatened by sending me into the trap he laid."

"True enough."

"I cannot tell Gelbrek," Alonna said. "He'd cut me out. He would deal with it himself, under the pretense I've suffered enough. But I know him. He is bent on revenge, as am I. The loss of his weapons master grieved and humiliated him, and the challenge to his enterprise enraged him. His enemies may perceive weakness that Astareth duped him, and that will not stand for Gelbrek."

Alonna spun on him, her eyes fierce. Jalwyn flinched involuntarily. It was not so easy to forget this same woman had come close to killing him. Her sudden movements still instinctively gave him pause.

"I cannot allow that," she said heatedly. "I made a vow that night to Rostalin's spirit that I would finish what these men started, that I would avenge him. It must be my swords that settle this!"

She took a knee in front of him and clasped his hand again. Her face turned up to his was earnest, needful.

"Will you help me, Jalwyn? I can trust no one within the guild not to tell Gelbrek. He may already know Elnark has returned and may be planning his own retribution. I must strike first! Will you help? I need you ... and I am not accustomed to needing anyone for anything of late."

A stray lock of hair came loose and fell across her face as she spoke. Unconsciously, Jalwyn reached out and folded the tendril back behind her ear.

She smiled gratefully. In that moment, he nearly told her everything: That he loved her, that he would do anything for her, that this request she made of him was a tiny thing. He would try to capture the moons if she asked. He'd kill this man himself because he had hurt her.

Instead, he shook his head slightly and cleared his throat.

"You need this, don't you?" he asked gently. "Before we can leave to find your brother, you must finish this."

Alonna nodded. Her eyes drifted closed as if savoring the sensation of his long fingers lightly moving her hair. She laid her cheek on Jalwyn's shoulder. She felt the heat of him emanating from beneath his robe.

The Mage softly caressing her moved Alonna near to tears. It felt so good to be touched in kindness by one willing to take her troubles and burden upon himself. It reminded Alonna of the pure feelings inherent in the responsibility she bore for her brother. The perception stirred a bittersweet nostalgia.

"I do need this," she murmured. "You've been so kind ... you offered the first real hope of finding Vergal. You've agreed to help me do it. But this promise I made Rostalin...

"...I keep my promises."

She turned her blue eyes upon him. It stung Jalwyn to see unshed tears.

"You will help?"

"Yes, Alonna," he whispered. His hand moved in her hair again. He could scarcely stop it from brushing through that thick mass. It delighted him that she allowed it. "Of course. When?"

She smiled, though the smile did not reach her eyes.

"Tonight," she said calmly. "We do it tonight."

***

The moons, pregnant with light, rode high above the docks of Caliss, their bloated reflections rising and falling with the waves in the harbor beyond. The place was filled with sharp smells, sudden screeches, and robust laughs that punctuated the night air.

The dock quarter appeared different to Jalwyn than it did on the day he had disembarked from Captain Sanskister's merchant—pirate hunting—ship *Sea King* at Caliss in full sunlight.

By night, stripped of its veneer of civilization, the gloomy docks seemed a foreboding and savage place. To Jalwyn, the many gruff sailors congregating beneath paltry pools of light thrown by oil lamp standards appeared as ready to knife a passer-by as nod a greeting.

They wound through pillars of wooden crates and jumbles of briny nets, past the creaking ships at anchor on the massive pier. Jalwyn kept alert and recalled a Word of Power he might speak and how he might try to craft it should one of the many silhouettes moving beneath the weak lantern lights prove itself a threat.

However, Alonna walked on, unconcerned. Her passing elicited catcalls and whistles along the pier—not even her leather armor and cloak could fully conceal her lush curves. Alonna's fearless manner and determined stride, together with her firm grip on the hilts of her blades, kept the ruffians at bay, even if she did walk alongside a thin man garbed in what must have looked in the darkness to be a woman's dress.

She pulled her cowl over her head and drew her face back into its shadows.

"We're getting closer," Alonna whispered. They approached a ship rocking lightly on its hawsers near the terminus of the pier.

"This is the ship?"

"It is."

"How do you know he's aboard? You've been at the inn. He could have left for a tavern or any number of those illicit places the sailor folk favor when going ashore."

Alonna's teeth flashed in a quick grin from beneath her cowl. "You sound like a man speaking from experience."

"No! Of course, not!"

She chuckled, unconcerned. Her flippant manner annoyed Jalwyn, who felt queasy at the mere contemplation of Alonna ever engaged in such lusty behavior.

They crouched in the concealing gloom of stacked wooden crates, surveying the ship heaving gently at the end of the pier, their ears attentive to the drone of noise that distinguished the docks at night.

Tatters of fog drifted off the black sea. Its sluggish, clammy fingers caressed their feet and knees. By lamplight, Jalwyn noted a Far merchant flag snapping from the ship's mainmast, but Alonna held no illusions about this ship's maritime activities away from port. A pirate ship, she confided, one wearing the colors of legitimate merchants to disguise itself at port, while fencing their stolen goods in the city.

Jalwyn nodded knowingly. His adventure on *The Acolyte* gave little reason to doubt the woman's words. His eyes had been opened to a whole new world of intrigue and deception since his fiery encounter with the pirates, and Jalwyn had allowed the experience to make a cynic of him. Traveling these new dark circles, Jalwyn thought a healthy dose of cynicism could only prove beneficial.

"The challenge will be getting aboard," Alonna whispered in her whiskey voice. "They post lookouts even at port, in case custom officers arrive for a nighttime inspection of their cargo. Or if a crew from a rival ship pays a visit.

"I think our best chance is to scale the mooring ropes. They're thick and will support us."

She pantomimed a climber scaling a length of rope, hand-over-hand. "Can you do this?"

Crestfallen, Jalwyn confessed to her he could not. Adding to his distress was the fact this wisp of a woman obviously possessed a musculature superior to his if she could perform such a feat.

"I have another way," he said.

Jalwyn offered his hand and smiled when she accepted it without question. Even clad in a glove, the contact of her hand sent a pleasant jolt through him. He shook his head to clear his thoughts. These distracting sensations at her merest touch concerned him. In more pleasant surroundings, it posed no problem, but on the night-time docks, it was different. He needed to remain keen. With her hand in his, Jalwyn slowly rose to his feet.

She pushed him deeper into the shadows of the crates. They watched the ship; silence and darkness prevailed on the vessel. They had not been spotted.

"Don't worry," he whispered soothingly. His hands fell lightly to her waist, and she looked at him speculatively.

"Jalwyn?"

"Shhh." He leaned close, savoring the scent of her hair and the nearness of her. "I've told you I'm a Mage, but I've yet to demonstrate to you any evidence. You've trusted my account. Now I will prove it if you will trust me once again."

She frowned, at a loss to reply.

His voice dropped to a whisper. He bent low to her ear. "I know you think the Mages—when you think of them at all—are nothing more than a scholarly order," he said. "And that is the perception we cultivate. Few know the truth. But there is good reason we dedicate our lives to this order. The power and secrets we share are their own rewards. I'd like to help you now and convince you of my meaning."

Jalwyn's voice carried a note of excitement. Alonna's skeptical frown deepened, and she scanned his face carefully.

Jalwyn sighed. "Ever is it so," he lamented. "I'm unsure why the Order takes such pains to conceal itself when the world is already so entrenched in unbelief."

The hurt in his voice stung her. She opened her mouth to apologize, but Jalwyn's arms cinched firmly about her waist, silencing her. He pulled her to him.

The pleasant shock of sensation as his body crushed hers surprised her, despite her resentment of the impropriety of the action. She pressed her hands to his thin chest and made to push away but paused, distracted by the warmth radiating from him even through her gloves. His frame was like the casing for some ebbing furnace.

Jalwyn's grip tightened. His chin rested on her shoulder now, his face nestled deep in her hair, and his breath was sweet and hot on her ear when he whispered a single guttural noise.

Alonna's feet lifted off the dock.

She froze in shock. Never had she imagined this slight man endowed with strength enough to lift anyone, especially a well-muscled woman weighted with leather armor and swords. Her resentment turned quickly from annoyance to apprehension to numbing fright in a progression as quick as the time it took her to realize her ascent from the dock had moved far beyond the length of Jalwyn's arms.

Confused, her stomach lurching with sudden disorientation, Alonna peered over Jalwyn's shoulder and gasped in horror to see the worn wooden dock and splintery crates falling away from her at bewildering speed. Tendrils of pearly fog rushed to fill the space they had occupied.

"Jalwyn!" she screeched, her arms fastening fiercely to his shoulders. Jalwyn pulled her more tightly to him. Her embrace was borne of shock and fear, he knew, but he permitted himself a fantasy the sentiment behind it could dovetail with his own.

The dock plummeted beneath them. The nighttime vista beyond it curved in all directions, blending into the lights of Caliss and the absolute darkness of the sea beyond. They slowly turned as they rose, the forest of tall ships' masts looming now beneath their feet. The wind whipped Alonna's hair; the roar of its passage filled her ears.

She stayed immobile in Jalwyn's arms, expecting at any moment the inevitable fall to earth. The seconds wore on in a static embrace, and Alonna realized they floated there, turning smoothly together in the buffeting wind. The realization overrode her shock; Alonna pulled back to turn her wondering face into Jalwyn's.

"How?" she stammered.

The Mage laughed easily.

"I am capable of this and more, Alonna," he said. He leaned in to be heard over the nighttime wind. "I am pleased to share this with you."

She risked a worried glance at the world below. Yet the thin man's grip betrayed no hint of wavering, and she realized that whatever force held him aloft had also transferred to her. Her loft depended not on the strength of his arms but the strange aura of buffeting air that enveloped them like a skin.

Amazed, her fear draining away, Alonna threw her head back and laughed delightedly.

"Jalwyn, this is wonderful!' she cried.

"Hush," Jalwyn said gently. "This takes considerable concentration, and we are approaching the ship. It wouldn't do to alert them to our presence now."

It was true. With a movement she had not perceived, they had skimmed above the bristling masts in the harbor and drifted now high above the loft of her quarry ship. Through the rigging mesh, she saw torches above the main deck below, held aloft by men she could not see beneath the glare of firelight. The sentries she had expected were out in force.

"I must set us down," Jalwyn said, his voice strained. Alonna looked at him, concerned. The shimmering swirl surrounding them flickered uncertainly. Alonna fearfully realized the energy suspending them was being held together by Jalwyn's will, one obviously under assault by the strain of his exertions.

She pointed below her. "The crow's nest," she said hurriedly. "It's almost directly below you. It's empty. Can you put us there?"

Always the crow's nest, Jalwyn thought, recalling the refuge he had sought from the pirates aboard *The Acolyte*.

He spotted the loft and turned his thoughts toward guiding them there. The strain was enormous. He had never performed levitation with a passenger in tow. He had underestimated the energy required to maintain the field. He perceived the sustaining power receding.

Several feet above the nest, Jalwyn's vision darkened at the corners. He felt he might swoon. He released the force supporting them, and they tumbled the remaining few feet, ungracefully, into the crow's nest. Their ignoble landing made a dull racket.

Alonna popped to her feet instantly, peering over the lip of the loft. A moment of covert observation convinced her their descent went unobserved. She turned and slid to her bottom, her back against the wall of the nest.

"I don't think they heard us."

"Alonna, I'm sorry," Jalwyn declared between gasps for breath. His exertions had weakened him. He had barked his shin painfully on the rim of the nest when they had fallen. However, their undignified plunge had hurt his pride far more.

Her eyes softened, though he could barely discern her face in the light wash of starlight. "Sorry?" she asked, astonished. "Jalwyn, you are marvelous; you've done a wondrous thing! I can scarcely believe it. It is I who am sorry for my lack of faith in you."

She leaned forward and chastely kissed his forehead. The imprint of her lips on his skin left a fiery stitch of pleasure when she pulled away. He smiled, but the face staring back had turned severe, business-like.

"We have much to discuss, but for now, stay here and rest," she said. She loosened the clasp of her sword and stood up after another cautious peep over the side of the nest. "I will be back."

"No, wait," he whispered urgently. "Give me time to catch my breath; I'll come with you."

She shook her head sadly. "You stay here, Jalwyn," she said in a voice that brooked no debate. "I must do this alone."

And she did.

Back on the trail, the uneven gait of his horse jolting him unmercifully, Jalwyn remembered watching Alonna melt over the side of the nest. He watched her nimbly negotiate the mesh ladder stretched taut to the mast, worried for her.

Then she was gone.

Far below, he had heard disembodied laughs and indistinguishable drifts of conversation rising out of the darkness. It reminded him the ship's deck was full of people. He could not pick out their forms in the shadows between the pools of torchlight, but he knew they were there just the same: People who would not take kindly to stumbling across a skulking Alonna in the corners of their vessel.

He thought to join her. He stood, then slumped; his knees would not support him. He'd called the Words too often in past days. His weariness persisted.

Time slipped by, and the tattered clouds rode furiously across the shimmering bands of light thrown by the full moons. Jalwyn began to despair. The strength he had expended in carrying them began to flow back into him. He had to repress the urge to descend to the deck and spirit her back to the safety of the docks.

She had told him to wait, that she would return. He resolved to trust in her.

His relief nearly overwhelmed him when, soon after, he heard the rustle of her cloak on the ladder below him. Her gloved hand latched onto the crow's nest. He flew to the rim and clasped it, pulling her into the space. Alonna tumbled into the nest, panting from her exertion. They pressed close on the ratty floorboards.

Even by moonlight, Jalwyn clearly saw the flush of color slanting across her cheeks and the glint in her eyes. A dark spatter covered the breast of her armor. Jalwyn considered it for a moment before realizing it was a small fan of blood.

Alonna noticed him noticing and smiled. "It's not mine," she assured him. The blended grimness and gaiety at odds in her tone gave him pause.

But not for long.

Alonna had grasped his shoulder and pressed a firm kiss to the jawline below his left ear, thrilling him. She drew back, her glinting eyes serene, holding his eyes utterly.

"It's done," she whispered in that same conflicted tone of voice, that familiar ghost of a smile playing on her mouth.

"I came upon him in his sleep," she said without emotion. "He got better than his treachery deserved, but it is done. Thank you, Jalwyn. Now we can go after Vergal. Rostalin is avenged; Caliss has nothing more for me."

Her pleasure in him restored the last of the vitality his levitation had sapped. Afterward, it had been an easy thing for Jalwyn to carry them away, soaring rapidly over dark water to the waiting lights of the city beyond.

Their passage out of the city had been brisk. Alonna had astonished him with her organization. Horses awaited them outside the city gate, passed to them by roguish men who winked at Jalwyn. These same men drew her aside to talk in muted voices for several minutes and then embraced Alonna affectionately. They disappeared into the shadows near the rough stone walls.

Jalwyn protested his unreadiness to leave. His possessions remained in his room at the Wayfarer. Alonna offered a knowing smile in response and reached to flip open a saddlebag on his mount. He recognized the neatly folded crimson clothing and the small leather satchel that contained his money and personal effects.

He shook his head, amazed, lamely stuttering as he tried to devise further protests. Alonna laughed at him.

"Believe me, Jalwyn," she said. "We want to be away from Caliss before Gelbrek discovers our outing tonight. The fat man loves me like a daughter, but he's not above disciplining me like one, either. I have no idea what he might do with whomever he catches me. He takes a dim view of insiders knowing the 'family' business, so to speak.

"Besides," she went on. "You promised to help me find my brother. Has that changed?"

"No, of course, not," he replied. "It's only that..."

She cut him short with an upraised hand. When she spoke again, her voice was no longer merry but measured and sad.

"He's been gone a long time," she said. The pain in her voice betrayed the deep intent of her words. *Even another day waiting to find him is too long.*

They had raced together into the woods, beyond the approach to Caliss, with only the swollen moons to observe their passing.

On the road with her now, Jalwyn knew he wanted to help her but had no real reason to think he could.

They were traveling east, on the Imperial Highway, toward the fortress the Alasians called the March. There was an Order House in Speakwater. It seemed as reasonable a place as any to begin the search for Sh'ynryan.

If the renegade had not passed that way, the Brethren there could at least be informed of his crimes. More eyes could join the search for the elder and the boy.

It was a start, at least, though Jalwyn doubted how effective a beginning. Still, Alonna seized upon the information about the Order House with alacrity. In her need for haste, she eschewed the lengthy overseas route south to Eliard, then north by passenger ship on the Vinefruit River to Speakwater, for the more direct though arduous overland route.

They traveled mainly by night when brigands were most likely to have withdrawn to their forest encampments after a day accosting merchant trains. Lately, however, Alonna's impatience to cover ground had forced them back on the trail earlier in the evening, until finally, they were breaking camp in the late afternoon, with twilight only a shadowy promise of the slanting autumn sun.

Amazingly, the road remained clear of bandits as it wound deeper into the foothills, though there were more than a few distressing encounters with wolves and bears and, on one frighteningly memorable occasion for Jalwyn, a tawny, snarling panther.

Alonna managed to defuse these unexpected meetings with the resident wildlife using slow retreats covered by soothing words of reassurance to back out of harm's way. They had surprised the infuriated panther on a leafy bend in the road. Ears flattened, black-tipped tail lashing, the cat had deliberately stalked toward them in such threatening fashion that Alonna had been forced to hurl a small, serrated mace at the spitting cat, catching it expertly on its spine. The cat had leaped high upon impact and disappeared into the enveloping forest, smashing through the underbrush.

"I hope I didn't hurt it too badly," Alonna mused as she swung down off her horse to retrieve her mace.

Jalwyn nodded but secretly hoped the demonic creature had limped off somewhere to die painfully.

The panther marked the most harrowing of their encounters, and soon, Jalwyn began to relax. He tried to enjoy the trek. He was a tourist of sorts, after all, in a strange land, and riding at the side of a dark-haired woman he grew to love more each day.

Every vista that opened, every leaf-dappled brook they crossed, was made more beautiful by the fact Alonna shared it by his side.

The days passed in a blur of ever-changing scenery, in conversation, and in stolen touches with the woman he loved. Finally, the Imperial Highway had crested a dusty rise, where the trees had petered out, and the mountains marched away in all directions.

Below them, a stump-dotted hill flattened into a cropped grass plain that in turn washed against the imposing bulk of the March. The massive fortress looked something like a mountain itself in the mellow northern sunlight.

The sight of the fortress impressed Jalwyn. It was easily the largest construct he had ever beheld, filling a yawning pass in the distant Watergate Mountains like a curtain of solid stone.

"The March," Alonna whispered, as if the spectacle below required description, as if it could be anything other than the most famous landmark in all Alasia.

She turned one of her brilliant smiles upon him, and for a moment, to Jalwyn, the March was dwarfed by the power of her presence. He returned her smile, one of the few actions he was still capable of taking under the distracting onslaught of her joy.

"We're nearly there, Jalwyn," Alonna said. The Mage heard the same hopefulness in her voice he had seen in her splendid eyes. "We're getting closer to him!"

She didn't await an answer. With a whistle to her mount, she set off at a canter down the hill to the plain below, her black hair unfurling like a banner behind her as she rode.

"I hope so," Jalwyn murmured, watching her passage. "If it keeps you happy, if it keeps you here with me, I certainly hope so."

And then, because Alonna was riding hard and opening a wide lead in her excitement, he set heels to his own mount and chased her down the slope.

CHAPTER TWENTY-TWO

His nerve broke. Vergal admitted that later, if only to himself. The sight of the Obroths baring long fangs and snuffling the air outside Sh'ynryan's shimming curtain, combined with the Mage's pained pleas, demanded action, and Vergal's stretched nerves had snapped. Had he waited another instant, perhaps the Obroths would have ventured in, and things might have ended differently. But he did not wait; he could not. Vergal's legs began moving, and he heard the force crackling in his ears as he passed through the dome into unfiltered sunshine beyond.

"Hey!" he yelled. He hopped up and down, waving his arms. Large shaggy heads swiveled at the sound of his voice. Narrowed black eyes transfixed him beneath lowering brows.

"Hey, you bastards, over here! Right here! Come get me!"

An Obroth roared. The sound was deep and enervating and originated directly behind Vergal. He swiveled in time to see the massive creature that had slipped behind him, emerging from around one of the large, leaning boulders. The Obroth held its long arms to the sky, its clawed fingers outstretched in a fan that nearly blotted out the sun. Its head flew back in a primal bellow. The scream excited the other Obroths, who began to batter the ground, snatching clods of earth and stone to throw high into the air. They beat their barrel chests with clenched fists as large as earthenware ale tankards. Showers of dirt and rocks rained down upon them.

Screaming - even the roots of his hair tingling in terror - Vergal spun and scrambled back through the screen of force, steps ahead of the pack of shrieking Obroths that lunged after him ...

... only to be seized by the same static force that had slowed the highwaymen on the road out of Caliss.

It was a sensation outside anything in Vergal's experience. He could only compare the feeling to attempting to walk forward in the teeth of a powerful wind, except there was no movement of air to account for it, only a kind of deep resistance pressed to every part of his body. It was as if invisible hurricane-force winds buffeted every limb and joint from every conceivable angle. The result was a kind of mobile paralysis that dulled even the most frantic of movements into a stalled stutter-step.

The roars of the Obroths were now strangely drawn-out, indicating the monsters had entered the sphere. That part of the plan had worked. What Vergal had not counted upon, however, was being seized by the same force gripping the Obroths. His mind raced back to the encounter with the highwaymen. Why had Guile not been so affected after leaving the dome? Then he remembered: Guile had departed the sphere to dispatch the archers, only returning after the force had already dropped.

An assumption left Vergal's scheme to lure the monsters into the dome badly compromised. With Sh'ynryan concentrating on maintaining the force shield and Vergal slowing to the same pace as the Obroths, only Guile was left to contend with the infuriated beasts. Only Guile, with a pack of Obroths to dispatch before Sh'ynryan's rapidly weakening magic, disappeared entirely.

Vergal did not like the odds.

The chase that had begun outside the sphere continued inside. Vergal had made the done steps ahead of the monsters, but their longer strides were making up the difference, if only by relative degrees.

Unable to move faster than the pursuing Obroths, as he'd counted upon, Vergal knew the monsters would slowly overtake him, as they would have done quickly outside the curtain. He morbidly wondered if the agony of the Obroths ripping him apart would last longer, simply because it would take more time to complete the job.

Then Guile was there. Guile, unaffected by the sphere, moving unfettered and appearing impossibly fast compared to Vergal's own near imperceptible movements.

The mercenary's sword slashed the wrist of the closest Obroth pursuing Vergal, and the beast began an absurdly slow skid to a stop. Before the halting creature could lift its head to meet the new threat, Guile, moving at his normal speed (which was naturally and artfully quick), landed a series of more vicious chops to the beast's wrist, cutting tough skin and sinew until the hand lopped off and started its slow tumble to the ground.

The Obroth began sinking to its knees, falling by degrees. Guile jumped out of reach, watching the creatures close on the Obroth's heels begin a slow-motion collision with their pack leader.

Guile darted back in. Gripping his sword in two hands, he hacked at the neck of the next creature in line. The first few blows bounced off the monster's thick hide. Finally, the blade sunk, and Guile attacked the shallow wound relentlessly, jerking his sword about to widen it and landing a series of more blows after that to cleave the entire way through. The Obroth's severed head tumbled from its shoulders.

Guile was not around to see it. He was busy piercing the breast of the next creature, adding more slowly fanning blood and flecks of gore to the already garish heap pooling at his feet and still lazily suspended in the eerily charged air of the dome.

Now with more space between him and the pursuing creatures, Vergal skidded to a stop. It took what seemed like minutes to do so. When he, at last, got turned around, a fourth Obroth was downed, and Guile was darting and jumping between the remaining beasts, scoring frantic hits on the creatures as they likewise ground to a stuttering halt.

The beasts were difficult to slay. Even the Obroth Guile had decapitated appeared to be attempting to climb to its feet, though Vergal may have been mistaking its death throes for purposeful movement. The other monsters—one missing a hairy hand, another pumping lifeblood in slow-spreading sprays from a wound in its neck—showed signs of trying to return to the fray.

With his tongue lolling in exhaustion and his face bathed in a sheen of sweat, Guile raced in and out of the beasts' outstretched arms, jabbing an eye here, slicing fingers there, in an effort to inflict maximum damage before Sh'ynryan's sphere dissipated.

By the time Vergal's eyes ticked toward the red-robed Mage, the boy realized that time was not long-off. In fact, he realized, the time was nigh.

Sh'ynryan had taken a knee. His face was twisted into a perfect expression of agony as he radiated twisting rods of energy into the sky to sustain the dome of buffeting air. The pulsating force was stuttering now. The glimmering force shield, tinted almost imperceptibly blue, lost some of its radiance. The Obroth's movements, though torpid, discernibly picked up speed.

Vergal opened his mouth to scream a warning. His lips cracked open to form the words, just as the bowl encompassing them flickered once, then disappeared.

Sh'ynryan pitched forward in a dead faint, or perhaps just dead.

The buffeting force vanished, and Vergal's actions caught up to his intent. His arms windmilled to regain his balance as feet previously mired in mid-stride suddenly shot in different directions. The words "Guile, watch out!", which had been laboriously forming in his mouth, erupted loudly from the boy.

Guile instinctively half-turned at the call of his name. He corrected himself almost instantly, but by the time his full attention turned back upon his nearest opponent, the Obroth's swinging arm was no longer inching toward him but flying forward with terrific speed. The great hand caught the mercenary full in the face.

The blow landed backhandedly, or the filthy talons of the beast's hand would have cleaved the man's face open. But its power was fearsome. The protruding knuckles of the Obroth's splayed hand shattered Guile's nose upon impact—Vergal heard it snap even above the roars of the enraged creatures. Guile lifted off his feet, his sword flying free. He dropped in a heap of chain and tangled cloak and lay as still as a corpse entwined in its burial shroud.

"Guile!" Vergal screamed.

That outburst saved Guile's life. The Obroth, falling to its knuckles to finish its kill, swung toward Vergal. Its lips peeled back from foam-flecked fangs. The Obroth stood again, throwing a long shadow across Vergal as it rose. Its nostrils flared. Behind it, the mutilated and injured Obroths were howling again. The rearing Obroth tossed back its head and joined the cacophony, sending its fellows into a fresh frenzy.

An eerie calm settled over Vergal. It seemed as if he were trapped in Sh'ynryan's static sphere again, with the things in the world around him locked in as well. Time seemed to move slower as he considered his options. One of the beasts was uninjured, three others remained standing, though hurt—one missing an eye—while a trio lay spattered in blood and gore on the ground but still moving. Only the decapitated Obroth remained still. Vergal took only vague notice of their many wounds. The mats of clotted hair covering each of the creatures interested him much more.

He considered how nicely that hair would burn.

A small smile on his lips broadened. Vergal lifted his splayed hands, thumbs touching to form a fan. His mouth opened to form a word that would channel the roaring sheet of flame he pictured forming in his mind.

And fire came. The air at once seemed full of it. But Vergal had not called it! He stumbled a pace, startled. Hissing whistles accompanied the darts of fire he now realized were raining out of the sky. Flames erupted on the screaming Obroths, igniting them, wreathing the beasts in red.

Baffled, he turned to Sh'ynryan, but the Mage remained still on his face, his arms sprawled at his sides.

More whistling hisses ensued, and more fire descended in a fiery maelstrom. The flames leaped to life in the beasts' shaggy coats, engulfing the massed and panicked Obroths. The screaming creatures turned frantically all about, howling and slapping with their giant palms to extinguish the fire but serving only to fuel the flames' voracious feast.

Then Vergal saw the truth. Arrows; fiery arrows, arching out of the sky. Few of the projectiles pierced the Obroths' tough hides, but they effectively tangled in the beasts' deep and hairy coats, setting them alight.

Framed by a break in the boulders ringing the clearing, a company of armored men astride horses calmly nocked and released blazing volleys into the air.

Vergal dropped to the ground. The arrows loosed thus far had plunged unerringly toward the Obroths, but he thought it prudent not to trust too blindly in the archers' marksmanship.

The Obroths were now thoroughly engulfed. They lay heaped and unmoving at the heart of a furnace.

"You there, boy! To your feet," a voice called in a commanding note.

Vergal numbly obeyed, rising cautiously. The preternatural calm that visited him when he had prepared to immolate the Obroths had flown, restoring the young and frightened peasant boy - one who, judging by the sharp tone of voice behind him, had landed in a certain amount of trouble.

The men drew closer, cantering toward him on steeds also shod in gleaming steel. The company wore burnished mail and polished feather-plumed helmets. Swords bounced at their hips as they rode, their crimson capes streaming behind them. Arrows bristled from quivers slung over their saddles.

Their bows, now tucked out of sight, had been replaced by triangular shields that concealed each man's left arm. The shields carried the embossed likeness of a fierce half-eagle, half-lion creature.

One of the men held aloft a long pole, from which a banner fluttered. The red banner was embroidered with the same colorful insignia gracing the warriors' shields.

Vergal had seen that emblem once before but could not recall where. He did remember Alonna explaining its significance to him. It was a griffin, a mythical symbol of Imperial Arasynia. The men approaching were Imperial knights. Relief washed over Vergal.

The knights—a dozen of them—jangled to a stop in a crescent surrounding the boy. Vergal returned their gaze wordlessly. Their officious bearing and splendid attire made Vergal acutely aware of his own patched peasant's clothes, tattered shoes, and dirt-caked face. He scuffed his feet on the ground self-consciously beneath the knights' stoic inspection.

"Which one did it?" one of the knights demanded. He wore a green-stone pendant outside his mail the other men lacked. Vergal matched the forceful voice to the same one that had called out to him.

"Did what, sir?"

The man with the pendant frowned.

"'Did what?'" the knight repeated mockingly. He looked at his fellows. "The boy says it as if displays of sorcery were everyday occurrences in the Watergates."

Vergal's stomach plunged. Sorcery, the warrior had said. *Oh no,* Vergal thought.

The man removed his helmet to reveal a distinguished lined face framed by short-cropped silvery hair. A carefully groomed grey mustache bristled above the uncompromising line of his mouth. His blue eyes narrowed in annoyance.

"Let's approach this another way," the man said in a conversational tone, tucking his helm under one elbow. His free hand stirred the air in front of him as if he sought perfect words to frame his meaning.

"Let us assume for a moment my men and I were cresting the hill yonder, and let us say that at the same time one of these two unconscious men did something I, and any other reasonable man in the realm, might deem, shall we say, unnatural—something involving a great deal of hand waving that resulted in a display not attributable to an aberration in the weather.

"Now, we were a way distant, I confess," the knight said, "but we definitely saw a figure—taller than you—at the heart of this spectacle. Given this information, might you now have a more exact answer to my question, 'Which one did it?'"

Vergal's relief at the armored men's approach was quickly turning to dread. He nodded weakly and spluttered a reply. "It's not what you think, sir. I ... I don't think you understand.'"

The man grinned, not kindly.

"I think you'd be surprised at what I understand, lad. I've been in His Imperial Majesty's service a long time, and I'm well-traveled. I've seen performances of this sort before. That is why it is imperative you answer my question." He barked his next words, "Now which one?"

With a guilty start, Vergal pointed at Sh'ynryan.

"Right, tie his hands and gag him," the knight said briskly to one of the patrolmen. The leader waved a hand at Vergal without looking at him. "Bring the boy too."

"And the other man, captain?" a soldier asked.

"Yes, him too, if he's alive," the captain said in exasperation. "Make certain that warlock can't so much as twitch the tip of his tongue, do you understand? This lot is returning with us."

They pried Sh'ynryan's mouth open and stuffed a wadded cloth inside. They tied a second length of cloth around his mouth and knotted it firmly behind the Mage's head. Vergal almost gagged at the thought of the rolled cloth sucking the moisture out of his mouth and how choking it would feel when Sh'ynryan awoke.

One of the knights had thrown back Guile's cloak and stood examining the prone mercenary. Vergal blanched at the spectacle of Guile's ruined nose. His swollen eyes continued to blacken even as he watched. Guile wheezed wetly to draw air, and his mouth worked furiously to compensate for his mangled nose.

The captain joined the knight standing over Guile. He nudged the unconscious man with the toe of his boot.

"Had I seen this mail, I'd have identified the warlock immediately. No wizard outfits himself in this manner. This is the garb favored by the cutthroats of Caliss." The captain fixed a dark scowl on Vergal. "You keep strange company, boy," he said.

"He's a good man, sir," Vergal said softly. "He's saved me from highwaymen, a Drakleth, and now those Obroths."

The captain's eyebrows lifted. "Is that right? Quite a warrior, your friend here? Perhaps. But I'm willing to wager he is a warrior who entered Alasia illegally. I'd double my stake that you did also. Aerians cannot just wander into our kingdom whenever it strikes them. Your party was obligated to pass customs at the March."

"We were headed for the March!" Vergal protested. "We were on our way there when the Obroths attacked!"

The captain laughed. "Were you now? Then why are you in the mountains a league east of the fortress?"

"We are?" Vergal was dumbfounded. He glanced about, trying to get his bearings. He squashed an urge to run to his saddlebag for his maps, fearing the knights would misunderstand his sudden movement.

The captain only laughed again.

The fires devouring the blackened corpses of the Obroths had guttered and begun to die by the time crude litters could be fashioned for Sh'ynryan and Guile. The knights secured the men none too gently and, within the space of an hour, the party was away, trotting down the stony hill in a westerly direction opposite that they had traveled.

Vergal rode his own mount, though the knights trotting alongside him kept a close eye. The remaining horses were led by the knights at the rear of the double-wide column they formed.

The galloping party made a tumult as they crashed down the forested slopes. Vergal decided the noise was deliberate. Even a Drakleth might shy from the uproar raised by a dozen mounted, steel-shod knights.

They made brisk progress, pausing once to water the foam-flecked horses in a mossy glen. There, a welling spring fed a gurgling brook.

With the shadows lengthening and the sun lost above the dense trees, the forest path suddenly opened onto a valley where, in the distance, Vergal caught his first glimpse of the fortress called the March. His breath caught at the sight of it.

The March cut a monumental silhouette. Torches sparked to life along the walls and battlements as the light faded. The fortress blazed brilliantly against a black backdrop of cut stone. The March filled its shallow valley completely, like a drawn curtain, between the steep flanks of two mountain slopes.

A knight riding alongside Vergal registered the boy's expression in the gloom and laughed.

"It's a sight, is it not?" he asked in a voice that carried a hint of a boast. "I'd wager there's nothing to compare in your Aerie Coast!"

Vergal, who felt no pangs of patriotism for his home, nodded mutely. The knight laughed again and slapped him lightly on his shoulder.

"Good lad!" he boomed heartily.

The March waxed larger in Vergal's vision with every jouncing thump of his horse's hooves until it blotted out the mountains and the night sky beyond. A massive portcullis, open and awash in blazing firelight, yawned ahead. The road approaching the fortress had transformed from the rutted trail in Aerie to broad, smooth paving stones, lined on each side by the encampments of merchant trains awaiting their visit from customs and clearance to pass through the March.

"Technically, we're already in Alasia," the knight told Vergal. "The need to build the March in the mountain pass required leaving this territory open ahead of the fortress. That is why all travelers must stick to the road and present themselves at the March—straying from the road and bypassing the March unaccounted for; we will not tolerate. This lot here," he said, gesturing at the merchant camps, "are awaiting their turn to move through."

Vergal noted the resentment etched in the faces of those bivouacked near their wagons. He guessed the wait for passage through the March was a long one. The baleful expressions on the merchants' faces suggested the Arasynian guards made the experience humiliating as well.

The knights passed the encampment without a sideways glance. The horses clattered to a halt in front of the maw-like arch of the portcullis. A man in flowing robes embroidered with the now-familiar griffin emblem stepped out of a squat stone building near the gate to greet them.

"Greetings, Artalen," the robed man said with a wide grin to the captain. He inspected Vergal and the prone men on the litters. "What have you brought in from the wilds?"

"More illegals, Vespen," the captain, Artalen, said sourly. He swung from his saddle, straightened his surcoat and cape with a series of sharp, practiced tugs, and turned his attention back to the gatekeeper. "Two of them, in any case. The third, that one there, might be Zistian, but he is also Magi." Artalen spat after speaking the word.

Vespen had already caught sight of the garments beneath Sh'ynryan's concealing cloak, covered in their distinctive, silvery runes that reflected the torchlight. His brow furrowed.

"Magi?" he said incredulously. "This far north? Did you check him for papers?" Vespen added quickly.

"We did. He carried none."

"Then he is in violation of the Imperial decree," Vespen said with obvious relief. He straightened his robes, composing himself. "The fool," he said at length, "to be found so far from Speakwater when the Emperor has restricted their movements! What do you imagine he was doing in the mountains?"

"Surely nothing good. We witnessed him in the throes of his black arts," Artalen said. "They had attracted the attention of Obroths when we encountered them on our patrol, and the warlock had fashioned some unnatural defense against them."

Vespen was looking curiously at Sh'ynryan's still form.

"Then he has doubly transgressed," the customs official said at length. "This is an excellent night's work, captain. It will not do to have his kind running free in the colony. The Brethren may still hold influence in Arasynia, but the Emperor has been far-sighted in not suffering the fools to take root in Alasia as well. Imagine the trouble if the superstitious barbarians of this rock took a liking to their doctrines!"

"I can well imagine it," the captain agreed.

"Well, then," Vespen said expansively, clapping and rubbing his hands vigorously. He turned his attention to Vergal, "And so, who do we have here, captain?"

"This boy is illegal, by his own admission, and I take this man," Artalen said, nudging the recumbent Guile with his boot, "for one of the pirates of Caliss."

"A good night's work," Vespen remarked again. He drew close to Vergal. "Since you're the only fellow conscious, perhaps you can answer a few questions for me?"

"I'll try, sir," Vergal agreed.

"First, why did you bypass the March to enter Alasia?"

"We were on our way here, sir," Vergal offered hurriedly. "We lost our way in the mountains."

Vespen smiled thinly. "Misdirection appears to be a trait common to most illegals we catch."

"But it's true! We were chased by Obroths and lost the trail. They attacked us until the knights arrived."

Vespen nodded, acknowledging the statement as true based on Artalen's testimony.

"I suppose a pack of Obroths might also convince me to take the shortest route out of the immediate vicinity," he conceded. "Perhaps, then, you are entitled to some leniency for your illegal entry."

Vergal breathed a sigh of relief, but Vespen quickly continued.

"What troubles me, young man, is not so much how you entered Alasia, but why. Such a strange company: a boy, a pirate, and a Mage. Can you tell me where you all were going?"

"Here, sir. To the March."

"Yes, of course, all must pass the March. What was your destination beyond here?"

Vergal lowered his head. "I don't know."

"Really?" Vespen sounded dubious.

"I only heard the March."

"I see," Vespen replied, though his tone indicated otherwise. "Then we shall ask your companions when they can be roused. I assume they possessed a more complete itinerary?"

Vergal shrugged helplessly.

Vespen frowned. "I will have your name, boy," he demanded.

"I am Vergal, sir."

"Vergal?" He sounded surprised. "That's an uncommon name in Alasia. In fact, it sounds Zistinian. Where did you say that you lived?"

"Caliss, sir."

Vespen shook his head as if the information did not resonate. Then he shrugged. "And your friends? Their names?"

"Sh'ynryan and Guile."

"Guile? That is not a name; it is a mannerism."

Vergal shrugged again.

"You're a font of information, Vergal," Vespen said ominously. "Tell me, how do you know these men?"

"Sh'ynryan is my uncle," Vergal lied smoothly. The Mage's threats against Alonna still stood, as far as Vergal knew, so he was not about to compromise his sister's safety until he learned otherwise. "He hired Guile to escort us."

"Ah, an uncle," Vespen said. "That might explain your Arasynian name. At least you have the proper blood somewhere in your line, though your family's choice of occupations leaves much to be desired." The official shot a venomous glance at Sh'ynryan as he spoke.

That ended the interview. Vespen flicked his fingers, and sentries stepped forward.

"Put them into cells until I decide what to do with them," he commanded.

"Aye, sir!" the sentries chimed in accord. They moved to collect their prisoners.

"Have the healers tend to their injuries," he said when they had rounded up the trio. "See to it that the red-robed one stays bound and gagged."

"Aye, sir!"

Vergal's first glimpse inside the March was not what he anticipated when he set out for the place. The yawning portcullis widened into an interminably long and monstrously wide tunnel. Water dripped incessantly from between the arching, rough-hewn stones. Torches flickered from rusted sconces embedded in the walls, stretching in even rows as far ahead as Vergal could see.

They led him some distance through the echoing tunnel before Vergal slowly began to discern other features in the gloom.

Walls that, upon first inspection, appeared bare were in fact set every few yards with barricaded apertures, where the supporting ramparts curved into the convex ceiling. Recessed doors, shod in iron, loomed every so often, set near the top with narrow barred openings that emitted smoky red light.

Vergal began to tremble. The same foreboding that gripped him in the bowels of Gelbrek's guild house beneath Caliss revisited him with alacrity. At that time, his fears of being deposited in a dank dungeon had been unfounded; this time, his fear would be realized. Vespen had clearly described the accommodation he could expect within the March.

At last, the sentries turned into one of the dark recesses along the wall. They stopped to knock loudly on an iron-bound door at its terminus. An unintelligible response sounded from the other side. The clank of a massive bolt being drawn echoed through the alcove. The door swung wide to bathe the corridor in the same malevolent red light Vergal had glimpsed earlier.

Surrounded by sentries, Vergal didn't see who opened the door to permit them, which added to his unease. The sentries ushered him along another long stone passageway. As they walked, Vergal heard Guile begin to moan and stir upon his litter, then fall silent again.

The corridor terminated in a cavernous arched stairwell, where stairs cut above and below the grade. Lifting the litters, the sentries chose the downward stairs. They turned corners onto landings several times on their descent but continued further into the rocky bowels of the fortress.

Eventually, the sentries settled on a deep landing and entered another corridor. They approached a sunken square stone room, strewn with moldering rushes and decaying straw and ringed on all sides by barred cells.

Vergal, nearly petrified with terror, did not immediately enter when a door opened to admit him. A sentry seized his arm and dragged him inside. The man pushed him into a seated position on a splintery wooden bench set along one wall and promptly stepped back into the square room. He slammed the barred door as he went and turned a large key in the lock.

Vergal hugged his legs to his chest. Weak torchlight somewhere out of his line of sight shone dully on the cell bars. Vergal fixed his eyes upon that sole source of illumination.

Outside, the voices of the sentries held hushed conversation. Vergal heard stirring and more soft moans emitting from Guile. He imagined the sentries were laying the injured man on a wooden bench like that in his own cell.

More rustling and more clanging followed, and Vergal realized Sh'ynryan was being placed in his own cell. The Mage made not a whisper of sound during these ministrations. And how could he, Vergal remembered, given the cruel gags both in his mouth and tied over it.

Shortly, Vergal heard a new voice blended among those of the sentries. He assumed the healer that Vespen promised had arrived to tend to the prisoners. He was glad for that. The memory of Guile's shattered face disturbed him.

How the mercenary survived the enraged Obroth's crushing blow, Vergal did not know, but the boy doubted Guile would have lasted the night without proper attention to his wounds.

Gradually, the babble of voices subsided. Vergal discerned fewer people remained outside his cell, and even they were preparing to take their leave. Soon, the voices ceased. He detected only the faint whistle of Guile's strained breathing. The distant firelight that defined the edges of the bars of his cell bobbed away in time with the staccato slap of booted feet upon the masonry floor.

Then the light disappeared entirely, leaving Vergal terrified and alone in the absolute darkness left in its wake.

CHAPTER TWENTY-THREE

They were a day beyond the March on the road to Speakwater, and Jalwyn was glad of it. Passage through the fortress had been tedious, prefaced by a two-day encampment outside the walls (where the merchants proved handy in acquiring a different wardrobe) and followed by a rigorous interrogation inside it. Jalwyn had produced papers identifying him as a citizen of the Empire, though he neglected to disclose his inclusion in the Brotherhood. His superiors warned him of recent Imperial decrees limiting the movement of Magi within Alasia before he left Arasynia for the northern continent. His elders had commanded Jawlyn to move out of Aerie and through the colony only if deemed utterly necessary and to use discretion.

Jalwyn possessed other papers, too, forged Imperial documents that apparently permitted him to move about the land, though he had been instructed to fall back upon them only if it was imperative.

It wasn't. The customs officials at the March had recognized him as a Zistinian and a countryman on sight. However, they had been much more interested in Alonna.

As they rode swiftly on the gleaming Imperial Road east to Speakwater, Alonna still groused about the treatment she had received at the hands of the officials at the March.

"I was born in Zistah!" she complained as they passed through a tidy farming village bracketing the highway.

Villagers at work in the fields alongside the road paused to lift a hand in greeting to the travelers, but only Jalwyn returned their salutes. Alonna was too focused on her annoyance to notice any goings-on around her.

"Who are they to dispute my entrance into the colony of the land of my birth?" she demanded acidly.

"Being born there and remaining there are separate things to the bureaucracy," Jalwyn replied, being careful to conceal a smile. Her pique elicited a pouting expression on her face that he found alternately amusing and adorable.

"But to be subjected to such humiliation!" she fumed. "They looked ready to deny me entry until you told them I was your wife. A fine thing that is!"

"Thanks, truly," Jalwyn replied dryly.

She turned on him crossly. "Oh, you know what I mean, Jalwyn. Don't feel so sorry for yourself! I could have been posing as the wife of a prince, and it would still have been insulting."

"Oh, well, in that case ... thank you? I think?"

They slowed their pace as they passed the village. The Watergate Mountains east of the March were ragged cones on the northern horizon as the continent dipped and began to flatten into the interior plains of Alasia. The plains spread flat as a tabletop toward the Vinefruit River and the colonial capital at the city of Speakwater.

They resolved to savor the last of the sylvan scenery before the monotony of the grasslands swallowed it. The road cut in a broad swath through a mixed wood forest interspersed with extensive, sunny meadows.

Their destination was the Brethren's Order House at Speakwater and possible clues to Vergal's disappearance. Alonna had sent the contents of her storeroom at the Caliss warehouse ahead by a merchant ship, where they would be waiting for her in the Alasian capital.

Each retreated into his and her own thoughts for a time until, at last, Jalwyn spoke.

"I've never passed the March before," he confessed, "but I certainly did not expect that level of security. My elders did not warn me to expect any difficulty at all. Surely, they would have, had they known it would be awaiting. I wonder …" he trailed off thoughtfully.

"You wonder what?"

He blinked and smiled at her. "Oh, nothing really," he said. "It only makes me think of something Erik said."

Their two-day sojourn outside the walls of the March gave ample opportunity to meet several of the Aerie merchants who erected camps along the muddy road. Several of these gathered evenings by the bonfires and shared bottles of beer that one Caliss merchant, aptly named Erik the Brewer, had among stores of spirits, lagers, and ales he was carting to market at Speakwater.

It had been a time of raucous conversation and laughter that wiled the interminable wait outside the fortress and which both Jalwyn and Alonna found oddly enjoyable.

"What did he say?"

"He only mentioned in passing that the queue outside the March had grown longer and the officials more obstinate since some sort of trouble."

"What trouble?"

"He did not elaborate," Jalwyn said. "He made mention of his last trip through the March and an uproar of some sort inside. It closed the border for days, resulting in closer inspections of people and goods once it re-opened."

"And that's why they are still harassing travelers?" Alonna asked dubiously.

Jalwyn shrugged. "Perhaps it was a significant uproar?" He frowned. "Had I not been several bottles deep by then in Erik's wares, I might have asked closer questions."

"Perhaps," Alonna replied, and they rode on in silence.

On their journey east, they stayed by night at the Imperial garrisons that lined the highway, if available, or in an encampment of their own making if not. Jalwyn much preferred the camps since they had only one shelter to share, and they slept—each fully clothed for modesty's sake—huddled together beneath blankets for warmth.

There they talked quietly and joked and laughed as they waited for sleep to overtake them. They listened to the cricket song and the music of the wind in the creaking branches above them.

Sometimes in the reverie state between slumber and wakefulness, when gestures made may as easily have happened in a dream, their hands met in the darkness. Their fingers played absently with the other's. A tremendous sense of peace and contentment deepened Jalwyn's rest on these occasions.

One night, in such a dreamy state, Jalwyn imagined they had been whispering and that he had sleepily confessed to her what was in his heart. In that dazed euphoric state, he thought he had spoken to Alonna of his love and confessed he was a captive to her every request if she only asked it of him.

In this dream—or in reality—her lips had gently brushed his, and her sweet breath carried her words in a whisper he heard over the soft soughing of the breeze in the trees and the crackle of the ebbing fire outside:

I know.

If such an interlude had transpired, neither spoke of it because there had been other nights, too—less pleasant nights. Jalwyn awoke one night with the smooth curve of her cheek pressed to his and had felt the wetness there and immediately perceived she was weeping. Her body convulsed next to his with silent, wracking sobs, and sometime in the night, her hands reached for his and clenched them fiercely. Alonna slept through these episodes, dreaming again of her lost brother.

In his half-asleep state, Jalwyn dared kiss her fingers, her brow and untangled one of his hands to smooth her hair from her tear-damp face. Sleep reclaimed him while he breathed to her gentle reassurances.

He was a slave to her presence yet miserable in it. He knew so long as there was no Alonna and Vergal, there could never be Alonna and Jalwyn. This realization each day inspired anew his determination to find the rogue who had absconded with her brother. The boy was the key to Alonna's happiness, and therefore to his as well.

So far as he could determine, his best chance to help Alonna lay at Speakwater. There the elders of the Order House might know how best to locate Sh'ynryan or perhaps had already heard from him.

Alonna spoke of renting rooms for them at the finest inn in the capital as a base of operations to begin their search. Her color was high, and her voice animated when she talked of finally starting the search that had of necessity been too long postponed.

She had planned for the encounter, she had delayed her search to train for it properly, and she had nearly died in Astareth's manor house while honing her skills in anticipation of it. There she had lost an instructor who also had become her friend, compounding her sense of loss.

"I'll kill him," she promised Jalwyn one day while they trotted along the road. An unseasonably cold wind blustered across the open plains, turning the long grasses and wheat crops into a rippling golden sea. "I'll kill him quickly if Vergal's safe; slowly if he is not. Either way, your friend will die."

"He's no friend of mine, Alonna," Jalwyn reminded her.

She shook her head as if to clear a powerful image. Her eyes slowly lost their impassive flintiness, and she offered a sad smile in apology. Jalwyn's heart ached to watch her.

"No, of course not, Jalwyn," she said sincerely. She reached to pat his hand fondly. "You've more than proven your loyalty. You ..."

She faltered, her attention suddenly diverted. A frown crossed her face. He followed her gaze.

A trio of red-robed men stood abreast in the road ahead.

The figures stood still, unnaturally so.

The deep shadows of their cowls concealed their features. Their arms were crossed, hands tucked into the voluminous sleeves of their robes. The sky behind them seethed with clouds, driven by a growing wind.

"Magi!" Jalwyn breathed.

They stood too far away to have heard his whisper, yet one of the figures drew a hand from his sleeve and raised it in greeting, as if in response.

"Hail, our Brother Jalwyn!" the Mage called.

Alonna's hand strayed to her scimitar. "Who are they?" she growled. "Is Sh'ynryan among them?"

Now it was Jalwyn's turn to reach for Alonna. He drew his mount closer until their legs pinched uncomfortably between the horses' flanks. He placed a restraining hand on the hilt of her scimitar.

"I have no way of knowing," he whispered. "Calm yourself, Alonna. Let us determine who they are and what they are about."

"Hail, Brother," the booming call repeated.

"Stay here," Jalwyn told her. She opened her mouth to protest, but Jalwyn irritably rattled the scabbard of her scimitar. Alonna was astonished to catch him glowering. "I mean what I say, Alonna. Stay here! Let me first see what they are about."

With a final warning glare, Jalwyn set heels to his horse and thudded toward the Magi.

The group conversed on the road. They stood framed by a lowering sky, racing with clouds deepening to the shade of bruises. Fresh bouts of strong wind buffeted her. A storm approached, Alonna knew, and it would not be wise to get caught in the open grasslands when it finally arrived. Storms on the Alasian plain were renowned for their ferocity.

The wind rose—a persistent, chilling stream that snapped Alonna's cloak taut and roiled her long hair—and the conversation taking place in the road grew more animated. She could barely discern above the shrill of the mounting wind, but Alonna thought she heard voices raised in heated debate.

She was mulling Jalwyn's admonishment and preparing to defy it when her companion abruptly wheeled his horse and raced toward her.

"Alonna!" he yelled urgently over the wind.

His free hand waved furiously, warding her away.

He half-stood in his saddle as he closed the distance, his mouth worked furiously, but his words were an unintelligible garble beneath the whistling squall that threatened a full-blown storm.

Alonna clawed her whipping hair out of her eyes, baffled at his change in demeanor. Behind him, the red-robed figures remained motionless in the road, distant smudges ahead of the lowering sky.

She kicked her mount's flank to meet his charge. She closed the space and received his frantic words before the gale ripped them away.

"Turn! Flee!"

The air filled with fire.

When she considered it later, Alonna believed she had glimpsed the inferno's source in her peripheral vision—a small orb of reddish light streaking into the road from the direction of the cowled figures. But there was no mistaking its effect.

Flames blasted the road where the churning hooves of Jalwyn's horse had passed an instant earlier. The concussive force stunned her. A wave of heated air mushroomed from the impact area, knocking Alonna out of her saddle.

The sensation was like a shield slamming into her chest, followed by a painful crack on the back of her head.

Jalwyn, his robes smoking, overshot her to land out of sight in the ditch beside the road.

Alonna lay dazed in the road. Her mind screamed to rise, but her body hesitated to respond. Pain bloomed like a poisonous flower inside her, unfolding nightshade petals and shooting ugly roots into her skull, back, and chest.

She fumbled for the sword at her left hip only to close over empty air. Confused, she clutched at the empty mouth of her sheath. She realized she was looking at the curving blade in the road, several feet away.

Someone was screaming—a ghastly sound ripe with terror and agony and accompanied by a staccato slap. *Jalwyn!* Alonna thought distantly, attributing the tormented wailing to her companion.

But it was not the Mage. The sound rose ahead of her, not from behind where Jalwyn had rolled off the road. It was Jalwyn's horse. The animal was enveloped in crackling flames and pounding a mindless circle in the road, insane with suffering and screeching like a maddened woman.

The bright flower in Alonna's head was wilting. The sharp flare of pain settled into an aching throb. The woman breathed in relief to realize she was not incapacitated, though she was surely hurt. A sharp bolt ripped through her abdomen when she moved, and Alonna feared she had broken a rib.

She ignored it; she had to because, beyond the thrashing torch that had once been Jalwyn's horse, the Mages stood in silent repose, watching her dispassionately through breaks in the animal's fiery wake.

She had little time before the frenzied horse finally dropped and the way cleared for the Mages to pass. Jalwyn was out of the fight, perhaps dead, and she had learned enough of Mages in her short experience to understand time and space were wizards' allies and the bane of their opponents.

She needed to close the gap dividing them and remove the time and concentration they required for their deadly evocations.

Her second scimitar remained in its sheath, but she ignored it. With the dying horse still providing a screen, she saw a chance to help even the odds. Wincing, she pulled the short bow she wore slung around one shoulder and drew an arrow from the small quiver at her belt. Most of the arrows had spilled in her rough tumble to the ground, but she only needed one. She fervently hoped so, in any case.

Nocking it, she took aim. The Mages flinched, glimpsing her through an eddy in the smoking charnel and raising their long-fingered hands instinctively, in unison.

The arrow took flight. It flew slightly wide of the middle figure, but the near-miss was enough to send the Mages scattering. However, they quickly regrouped.

Alonna leaped to her feet, her scimitar in hand, careful to keep the eddying smoke in front of her as she covered the distance separating her from her enemies. Every joint ached, every muscle stung as she ran, but the alarm on the wane faces she glimpsed between the Mages' cowls lent her strength.

One Mage's pallid hand began making passes in the air.

She moved fast, but she feared not quickly enough. The Mages had advanced toward her after unleashing their fire, but they remained a respectful span from the carnage. She saw the Mage's hands splay and his mouth open wide...

...and with no alternative, Alonna drew her scimitar behind her head in a two-handed grasp and hurled it end-over-end.

The Mage's eyes grew wide at the spectacle of whickering steel hurtling out of the smoke toward him. Whatever the Mage had been set to say died in his throat when the scimitar's blade sunk deep in his torso. His companions instinctively grabbed the stricken Mage to prevent him from falling. Alonna, charging hard, screamed in sheer hysteric relief.

Then she was upon them.

She leaped into the knot of them, leading with both her feet. Her rib lit up with pain, but she delivered the hard soles of both boots straight into the mid-section of the nearest Mage. The man folded and fell, forcing his companion to accept the full weight of the stricken Mage. Alonna bounced back, landing on her back, but she was on her feet again in an instant, grimacing away fresh waves of pain and yanking her scimitar from the Mage's chest.

Her scimitars preceded her into the fray, opening a red line on the remaining Mage's warding arm. The Mage screamed, panicked. He let go of his wounded companion, who slumped to the road. The Mage raised his good arm defensively in front of him. He stumbled back, mumbling in a strange chanting voice thick with fear.

Alonna flinched, expecting more deadly fire. Nothing happened. Frantic snatches of conversations with Jalwyn tumbled through her fevered mind. She recalled pieces of his explanations of his magical craft, of how clarity of mind, poise, and proper inflection of voice was necessary to channel the power of the ancient words.

Alonna pressed her attack. She did not intend to give the Mage time to follow the formula.

The Mage she had kicked scrambled to his feet and fled down the slope of the road and into the long prairie grass. The distance he was placing between them concerned Alonna, but she focused on the task at hand. She heard the strange chanting rise from the fleeing figure.

He was fleet of foot; Alonna gave him that. Encumbered by her stiff leather armor and weapons, she knew she could not hope to catch the lightly clad Mage in a foot race.

She considered her bow, but she had dropped it in the road. By the time she retrieved it to fit an arrow, the Mages would be out of range, and she would stand exposed between two enemies.

She opted instead for the dagger strapped to her leg and let it fly. The blade tumbled and sunk into the fleeing man's buttock. She grimaced. It was not quite the vital target she had intended, but at least the effect was similar. The Mage dropped to his knees in mid-flight and sunk out of sight in the long waving grass.

The delay allowed Alonna to tend to the Mage she had sliced. He stood crouched over his fallen companion, holding his bleeding arm. He looked up in time to catch the hilt-end of Alonna's scimitar solidly in the bridge of his nose. He pitched forward with a groan.

Alonna knew the other Mage still lurked about, but she could not see him in the long grass. Her instincts screamed for her to keep running before he could renew his magical attacks.

But her consuming concern was for Vergal, her brother who had been stolen by a man such as this. Pent-up questions, anger, and grief boiled over at the sight of the Mages, one surely dead and the other insensible at her feet. She dropped low and ran, crouched over, deducing that if she could not see the remaining Mage in the tall grass, then he could not spot her either.

She found him quickly, prone on his stomach and groaning, his hands clenching the hilt of the dagger still impaled in his buttocks.

Alonna seized the fallen man's robes and rolled him over. That elicited a howl when the sudden motion sunk the dagger further. Alonna ripped the cowl off his head, exposing a thin, sunken face. Doe-brown eyes darted frantically in their sockets. Flecks of saliva spotted the man's trembling lips.

"Don't kill me!" he begged in a voice that spanned octaves in the space of three short words.

"Where is he?" Alonna demanded roughly above the wind. She pulled free her dagger, provoking a fresh scream from the Mage. The first cold pellets of rain pattered in her hair. "Where is Sh'ynryan?" she demanded. "Where is my brother?"

"Spare me, I beg! Oh, please, mercy!" The man wept openly now, thoroughly overcome.

She balled her fist and punched him. The Mage's head rocked back, and his gibbering ceased. His eyes glazed with pain, and he lay still and unblinking beneath her.

"Your life depends on your next words, so consider them carefully," Alonna warned. The man managed a weak nod.

"You know of Sh'ynryan and my brother, Vergal. And you know we are pursuing them; otherwise, you would not have attacked. You would not have tried to kill one of your own. Now you will tell me everything, or I promise your death will be a torment. Do you understand?"

The man nodded again. But now, his lips were moving. Alonna thought he heard him mumbling. Enraged, she drew back and punched him squarely again. A sharp crack sounded behind the man's lips.

"None of that!" Alonna spat. "I know all about you, Mage, and I am prepared. Breathe one syllable strange to me, and it is worth your tongue."

She held her blade to the man's cheek to accentuate her point. The Mage nodded frantically in response.

"Where is he?"

"I don't know," the Mage replied. "We lost track of him in Caliss long ago."

Alonna nodded. She had lost the trail in Caliss too, after all, and she had lived in the same city. Not half a continent away in Speakwater.

"It is why we sent Jalwyn," the Mage offered hurriedly. "We needed a report of Sh'ynryan's progress in his task. Our auguries have been dark. I..."

"What task?" Alonna interrupted.

"You must know. To find the Stone."

"What has my brother to do with this Stone? He is an eleven-year-old ..." she paused, stricken as it dawned on her how Vergal would have turned a year older by now. A boy of twelve, on his way to thirteen.

"He is just a boy," Alonna went on fiercely. "He knows nothing of this Stone of yours. He can't even read! What would Sh'ynryan want with him?"

The fear in the Mage's eye receded momentarily, replaced by a flash of predator cunning.

"If Sh'ynryan abducted the boy, then he is vital to his cause," the man said. His demeanor grew sly and his voice, though quavering, rang with mockery. "The cause is everything. There can be no wavering, no turning aside!"

"Speak plainly! How can a child be vital to Magi?"

But the Mage did not reply. His face instead regarded Alonna's keenly, and an incredulous recognition unfolded there.

"By the Stone," he breathed. His hand clutched weakly at Alonna's arm; the fingers dug in. "I can see him plainly, reflected in your features. And it was your brother that Sh'ynryan abducted. It makes sense now!"

Despite the Mage's predicament and Alonna's hovering sword, he laughed aloud. "You are the thief's daughter!" he exclaimed. "You are Teraud's!"

A blow with a mace could not have stunned Alonna more in that instant.

Her father's name, formed by the lips of an enemy who was in league with the one who abducted Vergal.

Teraud.

A voice rang in her mind from the passages of the misty past: The rich voice of a man in robes and a circlet, pealing above the bustle and drone of a busy street on a sunny day in Zistah ...

They will find you, Teraud. They will not suffer it to be lost to them!

The battered face beneath her had aged over the intervening years, and the white robes worn then were scarlet now. But the image in her mind of the librarian that long-ago day in Zistah vividly superimposed itself over the Mage pinned beneath her. Except for deeper age lines and bloodied features, the match was exact: The same drooping right eye, the same slight lisp to his speech! Alonna's sword slid off the Mage's cheek and out of boneless fingers. She stared at him in disbelief.

"If you permitted me, I would kneel before you," the Mage said earnestly. His fear had flown entirely, replaced by wide-eyed adoration. "You are royalty. You are sister to the One. He would wish for you to be kept in good care. I realize it now! Oh, that I nearly missed it!"

Alonna did not answer.

The Mage's eyes searched her face restlessly, drinking her in. "It can be the only explanation," he softly offered as if Alonna had contradicted him and must be gently corrected. "The son of the thief is the One. Why else would Sh'ynryan take him?"

"Where?" Alonna asked, weeping. Her self-control had fled, and a dam threatened to break deep inside her. "Why do you call my father 'thief'? Where is my brother? Where is Vergal?"

The Mage nodded, almost sympathetically. "Sh'ynryan will take him to the Nay'fein, of course. And among them, Vergal will be instructed—surely his education has already begun—and once complete, he will reveal the Stone."

Before she could reply, a gruff voice called out, "Step away from him. Now!"

Alonna and the Mage turned in the direction of the new voice. In the distance, out of range of swords, stood the other Mage. His hood was thrown back, revealing a fleshy face capped by a shaggy shock of greying hair. The Mage's eyes blazed balefully. He held one arm in front of him, the fingers of his hand hooked into the semblance of claws. The other arm hung useless, dripping blood, at his side.

"No!" Alonna and the Mage cried together. The man standing waist-deep in the thrashing prairie grass blinked at them, confused.

"What are you about, Krynerus?" the Mage called urgently. "Has she tortured you?"

"I am not tortured, Deren; I am ecstatic," the Mage called Krynerus cried happily. The Mage shocked Alonna by winking at her. "Do not come a step closer, Deren!" he called in warning. "Not until I've had a chance to explain."

"She killed Aphelen!" Deren protested, although he made no move forward.

"Then Aphelen died in service to the Stone, as we all have vowed. Trust me, friend. I have received a revelation, and I see the fingerprints of fate upon it. We must explore this!"

Turning to Alonna, he quietly asked, "Will you explore this with me? If it means finding your brother? Will you give me a chance to explain?"

"Why should I trust you?" Alonna said. "You tried to kill me. Jalwyn, one of your own, may already be dead. If he is, I promise your life is forfeit."

"You cannot hope to understand, though perhaps Jalwyn might," Krynerus said hurriedly. "The Order had declared him *Jalk'la*—renegade—for abandoning his mission to find Sh'ynryan. By all reports we received, Jalwyn was assisting a woman known to be seeking the death of Sh'ynryan.

"We knew nothing at the time of Vergal's abduction, nor Sh'ynryan's reasons. But I have beheld you and know you to be Teraud's daughter and this Vergal, his son. This changes everything, everything! Sh'ynryan has found the One and has taken him to find the Stone. All along, it was the thief's own son! This is a truly portentous thing. Jalwyn has more than succeeded in his errand, and we pose no further threat to him, nor to you!"

"Empty words! Words to deceive and save your life so that you may kill me at your convenience."

"They are not!" Krynerus yelled. "You understand nothing of what transpires around you! We can no more harm you than command the moons to fall from the sky. You are blood to the One, who will reign when he returns with the Stone! You deserve honor. We are pledged to protect you for his sake!" He reached again with shaking hands. "Oh, please," Krynerus pleaded. "Allow me time to explain this all to you!"

Lies ..." she wailed. "He's a peasant boy! He knows nothing of magic or words of power or this Stone. He is the son of a scribe. Where is he! I want him back."

"He will be back," Krynerus offered soothingly. "If he desires to see you again, no force in this world will prevent his doing so."

Alonna stared at Krynerus numbly. Her mind shied from the implications of the information the

Mage presented her, and she could only fall back on the lone assertion that seemed in her jumbled mind to sum up all the arguments against the Mage's reasoning: "He's only a boy!" she objected weakly.

Krynerus's swollen, bloodied lips widened in a beatific smile. "A boy, yes, but a crown prince also—and soon a king."

CHAPTER TWENTY-FOUR

Sometime during the night, other prisoners had been delivered to the cells. The noise of their entry roused Vergal from a deep sleep, and he spent a miserable hour listening to the bawling and shouted protests of those freshly incarcerated before he again drifted away. When he awoke later, Vergal felt refreshed, as if he had been asleep for an inordinate amount of time, but in the lightless belly of the March, he had no sense of whether it was morning or if another entire day had passed again into night.

Torchlight around a distant corner bathed the walls beyond his cell. He heard a familiar voice that he at once associated with the most animated shadow of the lot. He was instantly alert.

"I will remove your gag, Mage, but be warned," the official, Vespen, was saying. "Answer my questions directly and do so slowly in words I clearly understand. If I detect even a hint of an incantation, the guards will have no alternative except to defend us. And I promise you will not find the experience pleasant. Do you understand?"

There was a pause during which Vergal assumed Sh'ynryan had been nodding because shortly after came a rustling sound, followed by wretched, hacking coughs.

"Might I have some water?" It was Sh'ynryan's voice, though cracked and strained.

Vespen laughed. "Let's keep your voice something less than refreshed for a few moments longer, shall we?"

"What crime have I committed that I should be mistreated in this way?" Sh'ynryan rasped. Vergal detected the customary edge in his tone. "I am a proud citizen of the Empire and His Majesty's most loyal subject."

"Your citizenship is not in doubt, but your loyalty, for the moment, must be scrutinized. Surely you are aware of the Imperial decree that restricts the Magi's movements within the colony."

"Of course," Sh'ynryan said.

"Then where, sir, are your travel papers bearing the governor's own seal?"

"Lost, I assume, in the fracas with the Obroths."

"Ah," Vespen said dubiously. "Your party finds the Obroths a convenient excuse for all its misdeeds, doesn't it?"

"What do you mean?"

"You were found in Alasia illegally, in the mountains east of the March. The boy Vergal contends the Obroths chased you across the border."

"We crossed the border at the Danea River weeks ago," Sh'ynryan replied.

Silence, except for the crackling of the torches, settled for several seconds before Vespen said acidly, "Your sophistry won't work, Mage. You know the March is the only border that matters, at least for now."

"Can't you see the logic of the boy's argument?" Sh'ynryan demanded. "Wouldn't you take the most direct path away from Obroths?"

"Indeed, I would," he admitted. "However, I do not possess the resources you do to defend myself."

Sh'ynryan said nothing. *How could he?* Vergal wondered. The Imperial knights had witnessed his sorcery in the boulder-strewn clearing. Vergal perceived that Vespen had reached the crux of the interview. Sh'ynryan had no defense to offer.

"I'm willing to accept there were mitigating factors involved in your decision to employ your craft," Vespen nearly spat the word, "in defiance of Imperial law. Being a reasonable man, I can even see occasion for bypassing customs, given the pursuit. But I am afraid my leniency cannot extend beyond two of your three transgressions. I have men combing the clearing and its environs as we speak. If they find the traveling documents you claim to have lost in the flight from the Obroths, then all should be well with you and your strange company. Otherwise ..."

Vespen's voice trailed off ominously.

A tense silence resulted. Sh'ynryan finally broke it.

"Then I will await your knights' return with my lost satchel," the Mage said confidently. "In the meantime, I must relieve myself, and I require water to drink. You speak spiritedly, sir, of honoring Imperial laws, so surely you are familiar with His Majesty's decrees concerning detainees. I ask that you remove these bonds and allow me to visit with my companions, whom I assume are being kept nearby."

"I need no lectures on Imperial laws from your likes, Mage," Vespen said heatedly. "You will receive water and be permitted to tend to yourself, but the bonds and the gag remain."

Vergal could imagine the evil smile twisting Vespen's lips when next the man spoke.

"His Majesty permits those he trusts broad discretion in dealing with your ilk."

A clamor ensued as the armored guards assisted Sh'ynryan. Vergal heard the Mage greedily sucking water. Some more time passed, and then a rustling as apparently Sh'ynryan's bonds were secured again. Suddenly, Sh'ynryan's voice boomed loudly in the cell chamber, "Vergal, are you here? Are you well?"

Vergal's name echoed weirdly about the cold stone chamber. He opened his mouth to respond but stopped short when he heard a sharp smack followed by a loud groan from Sh'ynryan.

"That was foolish, Mage," Vespen growled. "I would not venture to attempt that again. The boy is fine, and your mercenary has been attended to as well. We are not the barbarians for which you obviously mistake us."

Then Vespen yelled, and it startled Vergal to realize the official was addressing him.

"Good lad, Vergal," came Vespen's reverberating voice. "You'll stay quiet in there, won't you? You don't want any part of this man's trouble."

Vergal dashed back to his cold bench in his dark cell and huddled with his knees drawn close to his chest.

"Good lad!" Vespen's voice rang out again.

Another bustle transpired in Sh'ynryan's cell. Vergal suspected the guards were fitting the Mage's gags again.

"Wait," Vespen said suddenly. "One more question, one which might clear some of this affair. What is your relationship to the boy?"

There was a brief pause, and Sh'ynryan answered. "He is family."

"Is he now? And what is your relationship to him?"

Another pause. And then, "He is my grandson."

"Ah, I see," Vespen retorted, sounding pleased. "You may wish to explain the distinction to Vergal, however, who believes you to be his uncle."

The guards laughed, and Sh'ynryan's gags were roughly reattached. Vespen was tutting sarcastically. "None of this bodes well thus far for the integrity of your word," the official said. "I certainly will anticipate the knights' return from the field to banish any last remaining doubt."

They departed Sh'ynryan's cell. The door clanged shut, and the other prisoners in the chamber, who had fallen silent during Vespen's loud questioning, erupted in a confused babble of protests. They wailed and cursed as the cortege passed. "Quiet, the lot of you!" a guard bellowed. An instant later, the door to the chamber banged, and a bolt slid. The chatter faded away to be replaced by faint discordance.

"Vergal?"

The voice was so weak, so pained that Vergal barely perceived it above the background noise.

"Vergal?" came the call again, stronger this time.

Vergal walked to the bars of his cell. Unrelieved darkness shrouded the room beyond.

"Vergal, answer me."

"Guile?" Vergal said hopefully.

"Yes, yes," came Guile's response, relieved. "How are you, boy?"

"I'm not hurt, but I am scared."

"Then you have me bested. I'm both scared and hurting."

"Is the pain very awful?" Vergal asked.

"Moderately awful. It's somewhat difficult to breathe through my nose. That beast cracked me square in my beautiful face. Do I sound strange when I speak?"

"Moderately strange," Vergal replied, and Guile laughed, a nasally, gravelly sound.

"Ouch. Oh. It hurts to laugh." But Guile laughed again anyway, followed by a stifled moan of pain.

A sudden clanging shattered the silence from the direction of Sh'ynryan's cell. Vergal imagined the Mage kicking the bars of his cell in a desperate attempt to communicate with them.

"Ah," said Guile, "our warlock hears us. Don't fret, Sh'ynryan," he called. "I know what you want to say; I know what comes next."

The other prisoners in the cell chamber had fallen silent again, listening intently in the darkness.

"What comes next, Guile?" Vergal asked.

"I thought it would be obvious. Next, you extract our sorry selves from this rat hole."

"Me?" It came out as a whiny squeal.

Guile sighed somewhere deep in the darkness. "Do not bother with the 'why mes' or the 'I cannots' boy! I think you have known since the moment they locked us in here that only you can spring us."

"Why not pick the lock?" Vergal countered. "Aren't all you mercenaries, thieves?"

Guile chortled but stopped short with a painful gasp.

"No," he wheezed. "Not all mercenaries are thieves. It just so happens that, well, I am. But without my picks and tools, I have little to contribute. They conveniently stripped me of all my paraphernalia."

"Para - what?"

"No matter. Listen, boy, it is up to you to release us! As much as it makes my flesh crawl to watch, do whatever it is you do with the fire to get us out of here."

"What good will the fire do?"

"I don't know. Can you not melt the lock?"

"That would just get it stuck."

"Maybe. Melt the bars then."

"How?"

"You are asking me?"

A muffled choking sound came from Sh'ynryan's cell as he apparently attempted to offer the solution through his gags.

"No help there," Guile said ruefully. "You will have to puzzle it out, Vergal. But hurry! I do not know if Sh'ynryan truly lost a satchel in the forest, but it will not go well for us if the knights return with or without it. He has legitimate travel papers in the same way I have my mother's blessing for my occupation. Get it?"

Vergal sat, contemplating what to do. A young girl's voice startled him out of the darkness. "Sir, what does he mean?"

Vergal froze, surprised by the lilting, disembodied voice issuing near to him.

"What fire can you make? Can you get us out of here?" Weeping began to accompany the lilting voice. "Oh, please, sir, if you can open our doors. Get us out of here, please. It's so dark."

Vergal's heart hurt to hear the girl. He last heard a female voice on the night of his abduction, when Alonna had whispered into his ears her sweet assurances he would never be harmed. The memory made his throat husky with suppressed emotion when Vergal replied.

"I'll try," he told the little girl in the darkness. "I've ... I've never done something like this before."

The girl may have responded, but if she did, her voice was drowned beneath the sudden pleas and screams rising out of the darkness from the other prisoners. They raised a cacophony, all simultaneously begging for release, for salvation. The tears that threatened Vergal now fell freely. The prisoners' misery matched his own. Clinging to a new shred of hope, none of them bothered to question the ludicrousness of a boy in a cell possessing means to wield a fire hot enough to melt steel.

"Come, Vergal," Guile yelled above the din. "Time is wasting. Hurry!"

"I will, Guile," Vergal responded, though the mercenary could hardly have heard him over the renewed pleas from the prisoners.

I need to focus now, Vergal thought, and instantly, his ears were shut to the prisoners' supplications.

Vergal comprehended without knowing how the feat would be a simple matter of perspective, a change in his focus.

Previously, when he wielded the power, he had simply released it. Now he needed to direct it in a new manner to serve a rigidly specific purpose.

What had Sh'ynryan once said? That the words turned the elemental energy into the form molded by the caller's will? If those had not been precise words, it had been their meaning. So Vergal gripped two of the bars of his cell and imagined them filled with fire. He imagined them as they must have appeared on the day of their forging—transformed from molten to solid steel. It was a simple reversal of an order, Vergal decided. He found it supremely easy to fix the image in his mind.

With the image set, Vergal spoke the word of power. He remembered it vividly and spoke it without hesitation. The energy arrived immediately to his call. It was as if the power had been crouched in anticipation of leaping to his service. The bars beneath Vergal's hands instantly grew warm. Vergal concentrated, willing the heat through every part of the cold cylinders.

The bars grew uncomfortably hot, and Vergal released his grip. Within seconds, he found himself backing into a corner of his cell, forced away by the intense heat baking off the bars, which now glowed fiery red.

He watched, fascinated, as gobs of crimson-black liquid began to slide off the bars, like wax down a candlestick.

He willed more heat into the bars, sending more of the fire racing through it even from a distance until solid white-hot light encompassed them. The radiating heat was terrific. Vergal savored the feeling of it on his cheeks, exulted in the knowledge his will alone directed this miracle. He felt invincible. He wished for a guard to enter the cell chamber at that moment that he might witness the awe and fear on his face.

One bar crumpled and bent, drooping to the floor. Another simply liquefied and collapsed in fat, blazing lumps. More bars followed in quick succession until a large smoking hole gaped in the door. A spreading puddle of burning metal sizzled and hissed as it consumed the rushes strewn on the floor.

Vergal stepped through the portal to a chorus of resounding cheers. The dying light of the molten metal showed Vergal a forest of arms reaching through the bars of neighboring cells, grasping in entreaty. Sobs, laughter, and fresh pleas for deliverance filled the chamber. He skipped nimbly over the fiery pool on the floor and went in search of his companion.

He found Guile nearby, hooting and laughing, with no care for his mangled nose, his face ruddy in the fading glow. Vergal grinned and clenched the man's outstretched hands through the bars.

"You are an absolute wonder, boy! I watched, and I still cannot believe it!" The mercenary's laughter sounded high and hysterical and, fed by the chorus of prisoners, trembled on the verge of relieved tears. "I would hug you if I could reach you!"

Vergal smiled. "Stand back, Guile."

The fire came faster, easier, hotter. It veritably rushed to his command. The bars reddened immediately, and the prisoners shrieked again when the barriers slumped to the floor scant minutes later. Guile emerged from the cell, shaking his head in astonishment. It hurt Vergal's heart to see the mercenary's swollen eyes and mouth and the flattened nose under his bandaged face, but Guile gave his injuries no mind. True to his word, Guile folded the boy in a grateful hug.

"Now spring the old man," Guile said, mussing Vergal's hair.

"This feels like a parlor trick," said Vergal, grinning back.

"A hell of a trick, I'd say! Worth seeing time and again."

The bars of Sh'ynryan's cell began to glow, revealing the bound Mage by their soft light, crouching in the space beyond. The man's hands were clinched behind him, and a gag covered his mouth. But his eyes were keen and glittering. He utterly ignored the spectacle of the blazing metal. His attention riveted on Vergal alone.

Guile stepped through the ruin of the cell door and loosed Sh'ynryan's trusses, and removed the gag from over his mouth. Sh'ynryan spat out the rolled cloth inside, sinking to his knees, hacking and retching. Vergal and Guile watched impassively.

"I will let out the others now," Vergal told Guile. On the floor, Sh'ynryan held up a warding hand.

"You cannot," the Mage grated.

"I think he has fairly conclusively proven he can," Guile replied harshly.

Sh'ynryan fixed them with cold eyes. "Do not be fools; use your wits," he hissed. "Vergal releases them, but to what end? How will they escape the March? The penalty for attempting to escape will be much harsher than for the various minor charges these people now face. Some may even be put to death if any sort of confrontation with the guards ensues. Do you want that on your conscience?"

The wailing beyond them continued unabated. Vergal and Guile exchanged helpless looks.

"We will be hard-pressed to escape this place ourselves," Sh'ynryan pressed. "It is a fortress, remember? Do we really need a stream of stragglers slowing us down?"

Both glared hard at Sh'ynryan, but Vergal spoke first. "I hate you, do you know that?" the boy declared venomously.

Sh'ynryan flinched as if struck but composed himself immediately. The Mage's mouth set firmly, and the cunning glint returned to his eyes as he rose to his feet.

"Yet neither of you deny my words," the Mage said.

"No, but maybe I can wipe them out of your mouth," Vergal said with heat.

Sh'ynryan smiled thinly at the boy.

"You think yourself my superior, Vergal?" Sh'ynryan asked, leaning close. Guile placed a restraining hand on the Mage's thin chest, but Sh'ynryan batted it aside.

"A few experiments with a handful of words of power, and you fancy yourself a Mage?" Sh'ynryan went on coolly. "You're talented, true enough, and I'll not deny it. But you're raw. When I look at you, I see an infant in its cradle. I see the rough-hewn stone before the mason shapes his masterwork. I could destroy you a dozen ways before you collected your thoughts enough to muster a defense."

"Not if I throttle you where you stand," Guile interrupted. His expression was flat, his eyes merciless.

Sh'ynryan ignored the mercenary. "Do not think too highly of your station, boy, and do not take false confidence in what you called a 'parlor trick,'" he advised. "The prisoners remain, for their safety and ours. Ignore your heartstrings and consult your heads, and you will reach the same conclusion."

Guile's smile was hard. It accentuated the unfriendly sheen of his eyes as he stared down the Mage. Vergal stepped in front of the mercenary to separate the men.

"Someday, you and I will settle all of this," Vergal promised harshly.

"Perhaps time will change your perspective, Vergal," the Mage countered.

"Or realize it," the boy rebutted.

Vergal spun away. Guile allowed his malicious smile to linger on Sh'ynryan a moment longer before he followed.

Neither of them noticed Sh'ynryan's violently trembling hands.

CHAPTER TWENTY-FIVE

Jalwyn's next reunion with his Brethren went much more smoothly, at least after his initial consternation vanished.

Jalwyn awoke stretched on his back in a brackish ditch, his head groggy and pain blazing a hot course through both of his legs. When his vision cleared, the image of two grey-haired Mages bowed over him fell into focus and startled Jalwyn into coherence.

Gasping, Jalwyn began to scurry backward, kicking slimy ditchwater at the grim-faced older men to cover his retreat. The Mages held their arms crossed to shield their faces as Jalwyn thrashed.

Jalwyn covered several feet in this manner before he realized the men made no move toward him. More shocking, Alonna sat serenely on the grassy slope behind them, watching with distant, narrow eyes. She was dripping wet, and only when looking at her bedraggled hair did Jalwyn realize a pounding rain was falling.

"Alonna?" he said uncertainly.

The two red-robed Mages turned to Alonna, and she waved a hand toward Jalwyn. "Help him up," she said curtly. The men hastened to obey.

One of the Mages approached Jalwyn with a distinctive hitch in his stride. The other favored a bandaged arm. Both of their faces presented a sunset of bruises. It was grotesque to see them smiling reassuringly at Jalwyn from behind the mask of their injuries.

"Alonna?" Jalwyn said again apprehensively as the Mages hoisted him to his feet.

Alonna stutter-stepped down the side of the steep ditch and splashed through the water toward him, taking stock of him as she came.

"They promise you will be fine, Jalwyn," Alonna said. Her expression was distant and slightly bemused as if she wrestled with weightier topics than the one at hand. "You've knocked your head and banged up your legs, but at least the ditch water snuffed the fire before it could catch hold."

She turned a hard look on the Mages, who released Jalwyn and stepped away. "Fortunately for them," she added ominously.

"What happened?" Jalwyn demanded, alarmed. "These men tried to kill us." His head swiveled, searching. "Where is the other?"

"Oh, I wouldn't worry about him," Alonna said. She turned a cruel smile on the Mages, who dropped their heads.

"As for the rest of it," she continued, "circumstances have changed... for now. But Krynerus and Deren will explain it all to you. Thinking about any of this for long makes my head ache."

They spent a miserable night huddled away from the storm in a large tent pitched away from the road in the sodden grass, eyeing each other uncertainly. Jalwyn tugged more frequently than usual at the bottle of port that made its way around the cheerless circle.

As Krynerus took pains to explain to Jalwyn the revelation that had perhaps saved all their lives, Jalwyn found himself increasingly unable to wrench his eyes away from the object of the old man's sudden fierce reverence and affection.

"Stop staring, Jalwyn," Alonna said irritably. "I am having as much trouble and more absorbing this."

"How?" Jalwyn stammered. "How can your brother be the One? You said yourself he is only an ignorant peasant ..."

"I'd use more care in future in how you speak of the One," Krynerus warned in a lofty tone. Jalwyn ignored him.

"...you said he has not even learned to read. How can a boy such as this be the powerful One who is to come? How can such a one master the Words of Power and find and read from the Stone?"

"Perhaps I can shed some light."

Everyone turned at the sound of Deren's voice. The Mage had said little since dragging Jalwyn out of the muddy ditch. Now sprawled with his back to the tent, resting on one elbow, he toyed absently with the neck of the bottle.

Deren's sharp cheekbones and sunken eyes formed deep pools of shadow on his face. He regarded each person in turn and slowly began to speak.

"I've pondered these same questions. As much as my heart would deny Krynerus's revelation, my reason cannot. The pieces of this puzzle fall too solidly into place to permit outright dismissal. To understand what I say, you must know Sh'ynryan, whom you do not. So, learn of him, our Brother, the one who has always pursued the Stone."

Deren paused and hefted the bottle; his throat worked to drain the fiery fluid. He pulled away with a contented sigh and resumed toying with the bottleneck. He showed no intention of sending the bottle back on its circuit of the tent. Deren scrubbed his moist lips and went on.

"It was Sh'ynryan who found the tablet. Did you know that, Jalwyn? Perhaps not, since you were not then within the Brotherhood. Why, you were likely only a lad at the time. The Brethren never gave Sh'ynryan proper credit for the discovery, so perhaps our itinerant Brother's accomplishment is not common knowledge among acolytes.

"It is only fitting that Sh'ynryan found it, since from his days as a novice, he dedicated his life to searching for it."

"What tablet?" Alonna demanded. "What is it he found?"

"Patience," Deren cautioned, holding up a hand. "Any story worth telling is worth telling in its turn. And I am patching parts of this together as I go.

"All Mages know of the Stone," Deren continued. "But knowing of the Stone does not imply belief in it. Every member of the Brethren will attest to its historical authenticity—how else to explain the power of the words extant today? The relic's continued existence in the world, however? That leads many to doubt.

"And with good reason. After all, a segment of the Brotherhood has been searching the world since our inception without a trace of it.

"Many respected scholars have concluded that records which speak of the Stone being placed for safekeeping in a hidden place, forever out of reach of man, were in fact parables for the relic's destruction. The imagery tends to suggest it.

"Still, something missing is always discovered in the last place in which one looks, is it not? This drives true believers to continue the hunt. Those Magi who believe in the Stone's preservation faithfully perpetuate a search that has spanned generations.

"I admit I was among those who counted the records as legends. I was content to perfect my craft in the known Words of Power, not spend my life in a fruitless search for that which has long been lost."

Deren sighed. "At least I was content until Sh'ynryan returned."

"Returned from where?" asked Jalwyn. His heart was hammering as he listened to his elder's account, ensnared in the story's weave.

Deren smiled at Jalwyn from above the lantern's glow. "From Undermarch," he replied softly.

"Undermarch?"

"Don't frown so, trying to place the name. I'm certain you've never heard it before. Only contemporaries of our friend Sh'ynryan know of it, for he coined the term. It was the name Sh'ynryan gave to the great subterranean city he discovered in caverns far beneath the lowest dungeons and vaults of that monstrous Arasynian construct called the March."

"A city beneath the ground?" Alonna asked dubiously.

"Not a city as we know cities," Deren added hurriedly. "But a city right enough, in the proper translation of the word. It is the community of the Nay'fein, a people unknown to us before Sh'ynryan found their lair beneath the earth."

Krynerus smiled, nodding encouragement for Deren to continue his account.

"We could consume days theorizing what Sh'ynryan encountered; he offered only the barest descriptions. He made a pact with its inhabitants not to reveal their existence or their location to any except the most trusted of our order.

"In what he did reveal, Sh'ynryan spoke of a marvelous city sculpted from stone, where temples and towers were cut from a massive cavern.

"It was a gloomy place, Sh'ynryan said, illumed only by the incandescent lichens and moss that cover the cavern floor and walls. The Nay'fein cannot endure the light of the sun; it is almost certain they have not beheld it since near the start of time!"

"What are they like?" Alonna pressed. The tale engrossed her. "These Nay'fein, I mean. What manner of creature can live hidden from the light of the sun, in the cold depths of the earth?"

"You are mistaken," Deren said. "Undermarch is anything but cold! Heat currents rise from molten stones that flow through the heart of the earth. It pulses through the vents and seams of the underworld, delivering warmth throughout. There is no passage of seasons, at least none the Nay'fein discern, only a stifling heat and oppressive blackness in which the Nay'fein have ignited the lone spark of light, to keep at bay the creatures that share their darkness."

"'Other creatures'?" Jalwyn pressed.

Deren raised his hand again. "I will not speak of them; I cannot, for I know nothing concrete. I know only that the world beneath the world supports a wilderness of its own, and within it lurks beasts we can only imagine.

"Sh'ynryan's encounters with these beasts were few, but they terrified him. He would not talk long about them. It was as if he sought only to forget they had ever occurred.

"But of the Nay'fein, Sh'ynryan was more forthcoming. He described them in some detail to our official artisans, who painted them based on his detailed observations.

"We have portraits of these beings, based on Sh'ynryan's descriptions, concealed in the vaults of our Order House at Zistah. Sh'ynryan swears they capture the Nay'fein's true likeness. I have studied them and so can speak of them with some confidence.

"The Nay'fein are like us, though slighter of frame. Their features are delicate, and one might say beautiful, but for the alien quality of their eyes, which are enormous pupil-less orbs and most unsettling.

"Their bodies are stark white and completely smooth and hairless, except for thick locks atop their heads. In appearance, by light, they seem carved from ivory."

Deren paused. He licked his parched lips and prepared to drink, but Jalwyn reached forward and plucked the bottle from his hand. He tipped the bottle and made to have a draught, but nothing came forth. Alonna rustled through a pack; two more bottles appeared in her hands. She broke the seals and sent the bottles around the circle. Deren resumed his narrative only after satisfying his thirst.

"I've wandered in my story, but only to say the Nay'fein are fey and mysterious creatures, as I understand it. I should very much like to encounter them one day and witness for myself the spectacle of their strange kingdom.

"But where was I? Ah yes. I don't know what ancient clues or texts Sh'ynryan uncovered that led him to Undermarch. Perhaps Sh'ynryan himself has lost the exact thread? I do not know because he would not tell us. He is protective of these beings and his pact.

"Sh'ynryan said the Empire inadvertently built the March over an ancient entrance to this underworld. But where exactly in the fortress lies the portal to their lair? And which paths does one follow through the maze of twisting corridors into the dark below if one were to discover it? We have no answers to these questions, though we have had agents placed within the March who have been covertly investigating ever since.

"We do know the Nay'fein received Sh'ynryan warmly. They astonished Sh'ynryan with their claims he was expected. Some lore or prophecy of their own foretold a time when an otherworlder would seek them, one who knew the Words of Power as did they.

"The elders claimed to know of the world above, and they proved it when they admitted Sh'ynryan to their temples. There, statues and icons depicted figures of men such as they appear in the world today, in every aspect like us! These statues stood side-by-side with the strange idols of their own spirits and immortals as if the men of the surface world were somehow objects of religious significance to them.

"Sh'ynryan soon discovered why. The Nay'fein knew of the Stone. Indeed, they claimed it was an ancestor of their own who was commissioned to hide and guard the Stone when ancient man removed it from his grasp for the sake of the world.

"We all know the surface legends, and there is no need to repeat them now, except to say no mention exists in the records of those who carried it away.

"The Nay'fein claimed to be the progeny of this leader and his tribe who departed the world of sunlight to hide the relic in the underworld."

Jalwyn emitted an involuntary sound. Deren grinned and nodded.

"Yes, it's true! Everything that happened afterward confirmed it. The Nay'fein furnished Sh'ynryan with a small stone tablet bearing a passage of their prophecy of the One. This person would return to uncover the Stone. They instructed Sh'ynryan to seek out this person in the world, for their auguries promised the time approached.

"The One would be known by an understanding of the incomprehensible words of the Nay'fein included on the tablet. The Stone would call to and instruct the One. The Stone sought to be wielded by the one instrument of its choosing who would not abuse its power, as men had in ages past—one whom it had foreknown since the time of its descent."

Deren paused and considered his next words before uttering them. "The Names of Creation, it seems, long desperately to go about in the world again."

"How can this thing 'desire' at all?" Alonna asked. "How can something not alive crave anything?"

"You misunderstand," Krynerus chided gently. "The Stone is the vessel for the Names recorded thereon. These Names represent life itself. They are at the essence of every force that binds our world.

"What can be more vibrantly alive than that which sustains existence? The universe is self-sufficient, requiring nothing from us; it is we who depend on it. Something so vital, so quickened and life-giving, must surely desire to manifest the life itself possesses. Indeed, it already has in the act of Creation."

Alonna considered that, but Krynerus used the break in the conversation to comment.

"I can pick up the story from here. Sh'ynryan brought the tablet back from Undermarch, to the elders at Zistah. None of them could understand it and turned it over to the order's scholars at the Imperial library. Teraud was among their number, and, for whatever reason, he took the tablet for himself."

"No!" Alonna yelled, startling the Mages. "My father was a scribe," she said heatedly, "an honest man! He was no more a member of your order than I."

"I knew your father, Alonna," Krynerus interjected. "Deren and I both knew him. I saw him in the Order House; I sat next to him during the rituals, pored over the tablet alongside him in cellars beneath the library. And I tell you Teraud, though an initiate, was a member as surely as was I! Truly, it was your father who took the tablet. Think! You know my words to be true."

The call rang once more in her mind: *They will find you, Teraud. They will not suffer it to be lost!*

Krynerus's words rang true. There could be no other explanation. Alonna's beloved father, the cheery, bright-eyed scribe, had suffered a thief's death for his temerity in stealing a relic of utmost importance to a powerful order.

Teraud's actions had cost Alonna's mother her life and her brother's freedom.

One question remained.

"Why?"

Krynerus's expression lost its flint. His sunken face grew weary. "He was frightened," Krynerus explained. "And he reacted."

"Frightened of what?" she asked. "If what you say is true, he was a Mage in good standing, no? An initiate allowed to work at translating the tablet alongside his superiors. What dangers did he face if he had not taken it?"

Krynerus looked at her sourly. "Not all Magi relish the prospect of the One's appearance," he said.

"The faithful—Deren, myself, many others," he went on, "anticipate a new order, a better world. The One will appear and wield power to remake the world and share knowledge with those who will command the Words wisely."

The animation in Krynerus's voice was transparent. His eyes gleamed from out of his bruised flesh.

"Others, like Teraud, feared the undiluted powers of the Names returning to man—a time of chaos to rival that which was. Man, in his ignorance, once exploited the Words for his own ends, and Teraud truly believed that history would repeat."

Jalwyn frowned. "Doesn't our own tradition teach that this will happen?" he asked. "Man's avarice is cited as the reason the Stone desired to be hidden. What changed? Is man today any more responsible than his ancestors? Does our quest to regain a power so long ago denied us not suggest our selfishness persists? The power that seduced us in the beginning is sure to do so again when loosed, this time in the hands of one person, with none to check him."

Krynerus puckered his lips. "You leave little doubt which side of the debate you favor, Jalwyn."

"Is it a debate or a lesson in history? Do any truly believe the power of the Words returned to the world will result in an outcome different than that recorded?"

"You forget, young one," Krynerus said, his tone patronizing. "This time, the Stone calls to the One! It has chosen the instrument by which it will be made whole. Can we question the right of Creation to manifest? The powers are prepared again to be fully wielded by man!"

Jalwyn pondered that. Then he said softly. "It seems to me Creation chose wrongly once before."

Silence ensued, then consideration.

"What became of the tablet?" Alonna asked at length.

Jalwyn reached for her hand, knowing where the questioning was heading. She gripped his hand briefly, warmly, then released it.

Krynerus watched her carefully. "No one knows. At least none knew at the time, though following our meeting today, I believe I have an idea," the old Mage said mysteriously.

"You claim my father had the tablet, with its hints of where lies the Stone," she said forcefully. "You claim he took this precious thing from you. I am willing to cede the possibility. Now tell me, what was the Brethren's reaction once it was discovered missing?"

Krynerus answered her plainly. "Your father was pronounced *Jalk'la*—renegade, as I've explained—and he was dealt with summarily."

Alonna winced. Her eyes clamped shut as if Krynerus had struck her. "How?" she croaked. "How was he dealt with?"

"You know the answer," Krynerus answered softly.

"Who then?" she screamed. "Who did it?"

Krynerus shook his head softly. "I cannot answer that."

"You cannot, or you will not?"

"I cannot because I do not know."

"Liar!"

"I am not lying. Jalwyn, confirm this! The Order has contacts... associates ... those who provide solutions to problems. Or it can deal with problems itself, as we were delivered to do this day with Jalwyn.

"Either way, the number of those who can be called to service is enormous. Those not immediately involved are not privy. It only means more mouths to slip secrets and more witnesses to cause complications. Your father's killer could have been anyone. A hired sword? An elder Mage? I simply don't know."

"He butchered him," Alonna said. She trembled with suppressed rage. "Whoever did it drew a knife across his throat and my mother's before fleeing. I saw him—a hooded man who exited the window of our room. How he escaped maiming himself on the flagstones below, I knew not then, but I surely know now!"

Krynerus and Deren exchanged a brief glance. "Alonna, please," Krynerus offered at length. "Please do not pursue this."

"Yes," Alonna said in a monotone. "Perhaps no answers are to be had after all."

Her scimitar appeared in her hand. It flashed without warning, opening Krynerus's throat.

The Mage tumbled backward, his lifeblood spurting.

Jalwyn cried out in astonishment. Deren spat his wine. But she continued, slicing Deren's mouth, widening his lips into a bloody grin. The man screamed, plastering hands to his wounded mouth in time for Alonna's second swipe to remove most of his fingers.

Jalwyn choked.

Alonna leaped from her crouch to knock Deren prone and, growling, plunged her sword into the Mage's breast.

CHAPTER TWENTY-SIX

Sh'ynryan's torch trailed a curdle of oily black smoke. A bare stone corridor stretched ahead, fading into blackness beyond the wash of firelight. They walked briskly down the passage, one of a dozen they had entered since fleeing the cells. Sh'ynryan led them through a twisting labyrinth of hallways that seemed to lack any pattern. Yet the Mage walked with purpose.

The screams and curses of the prisoners left behind had long since faded, but Vergal heard them still. The tear-choked voice of the girl in the darkness he had promised to release—yet left behind—echoed in his ears. It hurt to dwell on it. He glowered angrily at Sh'ynryan, who seemed oblivious to the boy's reproach.

Guile padded alongside Sh'ynryan, his face expressionless, his eyes scanning restlessly.

"Where are we going?" Guile asked harshly for what seemed the hundredth time.

"I've told you," Sh'ynryan answered acidly. "I'll know it when I see it. Be quiet and allow me to concentrate."

"Concentrate on what? They'll kill us if they find us. We've escaped custody. They won't bother to subdue us next time after they see the cell doors and that rabble tells the guards how we escaped."

The Mage grunted irritably.

"And I am fairly certain by now you have noticed we remain bereft of our weapons and gear," Guile pressed. "Yet here we are, wandering, unarmed, the bowels of the March, the greatest fortification in Alasia! No doubt with a well-armed patrol formed up close behind."

"All the more reason for you to close your mouth and allow me to find what I seek!"

Sh'ynryan lapsed into stony silence again. Guile shook his head angrily.

Vergal, walking at the fringe of Sh'ynryan's torchlight, was first to register the lightening of the darkness behind him. He spun to see several blobs of firelight. A barked command shattered the silence.

"Prisoners! Halt!"

Guile spun and swore, his hand reaching reflexively for a sword that was not there. Sh'ynryan dropped his torch to the floor, where it rolled and spluttered on the verge of extinguishing before blazing to life again, fed by a cool draft sliding across the stones. The Mage lifted his hands and closed his eyes.

"Vergal, to my side," Guile ordered, but the boy was already stepping toward the man. "I'm sure you will want out of his way."

A chorus of clicking sounded in the distance, and a heartbeat later, several crossbow bolts thudded to the ground near the guttering torch.

Vergal jumped, though the bolts had skipped in along the floor far to his side. The soldiers were too far for the volley to be effective, aiming in the direction of the fallen torch—the only thing visible from their position far down the corridor.

Sh'ynryan muttered something and, for an instant, nothing seemed to happen, though Vergal heard the tell-tale roar.

The lights down the long corridor were jolting frantically now as their wielders set out running toward their quarry. The roar in Vergal's head continued, gaining strength until the boy realized the sound was not only in his head but in his ears.

Behind them, a fierce wind blasted out of a bisecting corridor and, so far as Vergal could tell, turned sharply, unnaturally, at an angle to fly down the hall in front of them and assault the approaching soldiers.

The wind barely fluttered their clothing and left their fallen torch alight, seeming to part and split around them as it passed, but the noise of its advance was a keening shriek.

The approaching lights down the hallway ceased their advance, froze, then extinguished. The still unseen soldiers seemed to make no headway into the teeth of the buffeting wind.

Guile and Vergal watched in astonishment, neither having before witnessed this manifestation of Sh'ynryan's power.

The small circle of light from their still-burning torch showed the hallway ahead filled with debris that left them untouched—dry leaves, papers and parchments, and several wraith-like items of clothing. It suggested the conjured wind originated somewhere outside the keep, only to collect and impel objects it encountered in its path into the depths of the March ahead of it.

Vergal could only imagine the havoc the occupants of the upper levels were being subjected to as the mindless gale obeyed Sh'ynryan's call.

Vergal imagined the sentries above straining without effect to close the keep's enormous doors against the alien, invading wind. A new dread of Sh'ynryan blossomed deep inside him. The boy realized the truth of the Mage's warning in the cells: *I could destroy you a dozen ways before you collected your thoughts enough to muster a defense.*

Shouts and curses stabbed through the thunderous gust. The battered soldiers relented before the onslaught. A resounding crash and accompanying screech of metal indicated that the armored company had been thrown to the stone floor and pushed relentlessly across it.

With a wave of his hand, Sh'ynryan left off his conjuring, and the wind ceased at once. The Mage whispered gutturally and stabbed the fingers of his hand toward the floor before him. Up rose the familiar chorus in Vergal's ears; his gaze followed the direction of the Mage's hand.

At the edge of the torchlight, the paving stones cracked and groaned, shifted and buckled.

The destruction rippled like a wave out of the circle of light, heaving toward the soldiers.

The stones gave way to the earth bulging beneath them in an ear-splitting retort in the darkness ahead.

Heartbeats later, the surprised screams renewed. The surging stones reached the faraway soldiers and lifted them like boats on the crest of a wave, knocking them off their feet—those who had regained their feet from the crushing tempest.

"Come," Sh'ynryan ordered breathlessly. He surprised his companions by scooping the fallen torch and running ahead into the gloom toward their pursuers.

Too shocked for questions, Guile and Vergal followed.

The tortured stone impeded their progress. Several times they encountered yawning holes ripped in the earth by Sh'ynryan's conjuration. They were forced to circumvent them or leap over their dark expanses. Sh'ynryan labored to breathe. Vergal wondered if the stress of his spellcasting would overcome the Mage, but Sh'ynryan persisted. After a moment of crossing the buckled terrain, their torchlight fell upon the first of his victims.

Soldiers lay in various states of repose, unconscious or nearly so. Many moaned and turned their heads slowly, eyes open but distant, and many had sustained injuries. Sh'ynryan's summoned windstorm had buffeted the armored men into one another, and many remained in a tangled heap, bruised and battered, sliced and pierced by their own brandished weapons.

What the wind had not bashed, Sh'ynryan's rippling earth tremor had felled.

As in the corridor beyond, the stones here were cracked and uneven, and in spots, the earth had split into chasms into which men had slid, leaving slicks of blood on the rocks. The destruction here appeared total.

Vergal thought again of Sh'ynryan's dire warning not to think himself too far above his station. The boy's heated challenge to the Mage in the prisoner's cells seemed ludicrous considering this new display of power.

Guile emitted a low whistle as he surveyed the carnage. He turned a wary eye to Sh'ynryan, his face half cloaked in shadow. "Impressive," he said.

"Yet not complete," the Mage responded. "Those still alive will raise a new alarm and return with even more soldiers. We must dispatch them."

Guile frowned. "I'll not butcher injured men," he said. "Especially members of a company of Imperial soldiers."

"As you said, Guile, our lives are already forfeit," Sh'ynryan countered. "By now, Vespen has learned of Vergal's display of what he calls sorcery, and it has surely disquieted him. He'll have branded us all warlocks and without Imperial leave to be at large. We have transgressed their ridiculous laws. As you said, they will come after us to kill, not to subdue. If you value your own skin, you will respond in kind."

Guile's lips pursed. "I'll not kill men who were acting on their orders."

Sh'ynryan stared hard at the mercenary. "Fine," he said at length. He looked around himself and said, "Perhaps there is another way."

Hiking his robes clear of his feet, Sh'ynryan shuffled awkwardly down the steep slope of the deepest pit his tremor had opened. Loose earth slid down noisily after him. A soldier lay sprawled at the bottom, his limbs at awkward angles. The ashen, fixed expression on his bruised face indicated the man suffered more than mere injury from his fall, but Sh'ynryan kept his observation private.

Stepping around the prone figure, Sh'ynryan knelt and pressed his hands to the floor of the pit. He closed his eyes, concentrating.

Guile moved about the fallen soldiers, stripping them of items of gear and weapons. He took a sheathed longsword and added it to his belt—not so beautiful a weapon as his own, but a quality blade nonetheless—and added a long-handled dagger to the loot. Rummaging still, he relieved a dazed soldier of his quiver bristling with crossbow bolts and slung it over his shoulder. The man's hand crossbow also went on his belt.

Thus equipped, Guile selected a small mace and knife and handed these wordlessly to Vergal. A few of the men wore satchels at their waist—these contained food rations. Plenty of waterskins lay about as well. These were patrolmen, provisioned for lengthy rounds of the extended catacombs beneath the March. He tossed several of these into the growing heap at his side.

Watching Guile sort gear, Vergal felt a stab of loss for some of his own possessions. Vespen had relieved him of his map cases. He suddenly missed them desperately. Another comforting link to his former life had been ruthlessly severed.

Crisscrossed with straps and buckles, laden with weaponry and equipment, including a new hooded cloak that he swept over his shoulders, Guile joined Vergal at the mouth of the pit. Below, they watched Sh'ynryan paw about in the earth. Guile handed the boy a few of the lighter satchels. Vergal silently looped these over his shoulders. They stood staring down at Sh'ynryan, who continued scratching at the earth.

"What is it you seek?" Guile called.

Sh'ynryan didn't answer. He straightened and beckoned them to join him. They slid cautiously down the slope and stepped tenderly around the downed soldier to join the Mage.

"I don't know why it did not occur to me sooner," Sh'ynryan said. The cadence of his voice betrayed excitement. "I was so absorbed in finding the exact path I took last time; I never considered another might be as readily at hand."

"What are you babbling about?" Guile demanded. "Need I remind you a patrol could round the corner at any time, with us deep in a hole to greet them?"

The Mage smiled thinly. "You need not worry about another patrol."

The Mage fell again to scratching in the dirt. He was muttering to himself excitedly, in a hurried voice utterly at odds with his usual dour personality.

"You see," he said in the same brisk tone, speaking to himself as much as his companions, "I opened the portal in a deep chamber where the emanations were strong. It was my one visit here, and I assumed until now that was the lone entry. But the emanations are everywhere, running like a current under the surface of a river. When I stop to feel for them, I can detect them, some strong, some weak, but undeniably there! The entire March overlays a vein that can be entered from many quarters if you know how."

Guile and Vergal looked at each other. They found equal confusion in each other's eyes.

Sh'ynryan rounded on them. "Think!" he demanded. "I've been telling you since the beginning what I seek and where I would find it. Are you both so dense that you do not realize we have now nearly arrived?"

"I thought you meant the March itself!" Guile protested. "Do you mean to say this fortress is not the place with this Stone of yours? That it is only a doorway elsewhere?"

"Not a doorway, a barrier, constructed in ignorance over the one known portal where the world above meets that below."

Guile and Vergal offered more questions, but Sh'ynryan held up a hand for silence. He closed his eyes, patted his hand in the scratched earth, and set up a chant.

Vergal strained to hear the Mage's words but could detect only foreign syllables. He began to suspect Sh'ynryan of purposefully obfuscating his speech to avoid having Vergal glean more words than he had already acquired. He felt vaguely resentful toward the Mage for it.

The thunderous ringing rose again in Vergal's ears and, when Guile's hand suddenly closed on the boy's shoulder, Vergal realized that this time, even the mercenary's unattuned ears had discerned it.

"Do you hear that?" Guile whispered.

Vergal smiled. "I hear it every time. The question is, how do you hear it now?"

"I don't know. But it's an awful sound. Will it stop soon?"

"Soon enough. Watch."

Energy vibrated in the air, and the silent roaring intensified. For an instant, the gloom of the pit lightened, and the loose earth walls seemed to bulge.

A maelstrom formed where the Mage's outstretched hands touched the earth.

The ripples of force concentrated on the space beneath Sh'ynryan's palms, the distortion swirling outward. Soon the pool of force widened until a sizeable hole appeared in the bare earth floor, ringed on its boundary by an eldritch blue glow.

Transfixed, Guile and Vergal stepped to the swirling lip and looked within. Darkness looked back.

"In with you!" Sh'ynryan yelled. His voice had lost its earlier mounting exhilaration and now carried an edge of discomfort and annoyance.

The pair stepped back from the hole, shaking their heads in unison.

"Will you force me to endure this again?" Sh'ynryan demanded. "I cannot maintain this! My previous exertions taxed me greatly, and if this portal closes, I will be unable to open it again before another patrol arrives. Perhaps you'll have time to regret your foolishness before the hangman's noose tightens on your necks!"

Exchanging helpless glances, Guile and Vergal fell to their knees and crawled cautiously toward the mouth of the glimmering portal. They leaned forward, craning their necks to peer inside.

That's when Sh'ynryan kicked them: A good hard thrust of his booted feet delivered soundly to each of their protruding backsides.

Caught off balance, Guile and Vergal pitched into the hole, sounding twin yelps of fear.

There was a brief sensation of falling, as if into a deep void, but an instant later, they lay on their sides on a rough stone floor, unhurt.

Instinctively, they looked up and saw far above them the shifting enchanted hole rimmed in light.

Sh'ynryan's face appeared framed therein, impossibly far away. The light strobed deep in the whiskers of his beard. Then the Mage, too, pitched face-first into the hole. Instantly, he disappeared. Guile and Vergal scanned, trying to track his descent, only to find the Mage had materialized behind them, unscathed and standing in a composed fashion.

Guile found his feet in a flash. "You dare!" he began to yell but stopped when Sh'ynryan plastered a hand over his mouth.

"Believe me when I tell you," Sh'ynryan breathed in the mercenary's ear, "these caverns are no place for raising your voice. Am I understood?"

Guile's eyes darted nervously about. He calmed and nodded affirmation, and Sh'ynryan removed his hand.

A gasp from Vergal alerted them. They followed the boy's gaze above, where the faint glow of torchlight above the gyrating portal was dwindling to a pinprick. In a moment, Sh'ynryan's conjured aperture spun shut and winked out, leaving the party engulfed in absolute blackness.

At least for a moment.

They stood in darkness, hearing only the ragged sound of their own breathing. In time, however, Vergal realized the blackness was not complete.

As his eyes adjusted to the murk, he realized he was, in fact, seeing the outline of something directly in front of him: A thin veneer of moss limning a mound of pointed stone that shrugged up from the uneven stone floor. The clinging moss emitted a faint luminescence.

Vergal made out the contours of a stalagmite by its near imperceptible glow. He turned all about. Everywhere, faint features began to present themselves, rimmed by streaks of the same curiously glowing moss.

These forms and profiles started to solidify beneath their thin glows. Perception of depth began to fill in the void. The spectacle eased the suffocating sensation that had enveloped him when the portal closed.

Bathed in such dim radiance, the silhouettes of his companions and the wet gloss of their dilated eyes began to emerge.

A massive cavern slowly materialized all around them out of the oppressive gloom. A dry, warm current of air wafted across its length. A wilderness of stout stalagmites jutted from the rugged floor to meet an equal host of stalactites stretching down like stony icicles from a vaulted ceiling lost in blackness. The rocky floor of the cavern unfurled unevenly, stretching into the inky black and out of sight in all directions.

Vergal turned in wonder to Sh'ynryan, who had approached and laid a comforting hand on the boy's shoulder. The Mage's face, an indistinct plane of curves and bumps in the not-light, tilted toward him expectantly.

Awed, Vergal whispered, "What is this place?"

A lightening of the darkness near his mouth indicated the Mage's ensuing smile.

"Welcome to Undermarch," Sh'ynryan murmured in reply.

Vergal began to respond, but Guile's sudden grip on the nape of his neck silenced him.

"Listen," the mercenary rasped, alarmed.

The trio fell silent. They strained to hear above the maddening rhythm of unseen, dripping water and the rush of their own blood in their ears.

A new sound emerged—a chitinous clacking, like the rapid striking of sharp flint against bare stone.

The clamor sounded alternately near and far, distorted by the weird echoes of the underground realm.

"What is it?" Guile whispered.

"It's still far off," Sh'ynryan replied, his tense posture relaxing slightly.

He turned to face them. "I warn both of you to use the utmost stealth," he said. "This is a place such as you have never seen, more purely wild and filled with more exotic dangers than any untracked forest of the surface. I visited once before and still relive the denizens of this place in my worst nightmares. The beasts here can kill in any number of ways. We must make all haste to the Nay'fein. There we will be safe, and this long journey can begin to reach its end."

"You didn't answer me," Guile whispered fiercely. "What is that thing? I think I can still hear it."

"It's not safe to remain," Sh'ynryan deflected, though he could not conceal a shudder. "I assure you; you do not want to meet it. It is this world's equivalent of the Drakleth, though more horrible by far, in my estimation."

"What is the 'Nay'fein?'" Vergal whispered.

"Eh?"

"The Nay'fein. What is it? You said we were going there, that we would be safe there."

Sh'ynryan pressed a hand to the small of Vergal's back and pushed him along in front of him. Guile quickly fell in step beside the Mage.

"All your questions will be answered," he quietly promised as they picked a path across the undulating cavern floor. "This is no place to loiter. We must be off and find a concealed place to take shelter and rest. I am unsure how far we are from our destination. I need to get my bearings...

"...But our journey has begun."

CHAPTER TWENTY-SEVEN

It took all Jalwyn's powers of persuasion—which until then he thought considerable—to prevent Alonna from turning back for the March that same night.

Sickened by the murder of men who were his brethren, yet concerned for Alonna's increasingly unstable state of mind, it was a conflicted Jalwyn who employed equal parts reasoning and subtlety to convince the young woman not to depart.

Alonna raged and wept and, in a singular storm of emotion, fell to kicking the lifeless body of Deren as it lay slumped against the tent's bulging canvas wall. Deren's sightless eyes stared, his torn mouth grinning, as Alonna set upon the corpse. Jalwyn, on the verge of vomiting, intervened to stop her.

He kept a wary eye on the woman's scimitars. She was skirting the precipice of hysteria, and Jalwyn contemplated how best to defend himself should she step off that ledge.

However, through it all, a silent part of the Mage sympathized with Alonna and forgave her. She had endured much in her life: the murder of her parents, her instructor Rostalin, the abduction of her brother, compounded by years of wretched and unrelieved poverty and hopelessness. That she held herself intact at all through her various trails astonished him.

The supreme sadness marring the woman's glorious eyes made even a brutal murder seem venial. After all, Jalwyn reminded himself, these same men had earlier attempted to kill them both.

Jalwyn's promises of a more complete revenge ultimately swayed Alonna. Leading her gently by the arm out of a tent now transformed into a charnel house, he explained that riding to the March would serve no purpose. Remember, he reminded, they had no means of finding the entrance to Undermarch, even if they went.

We must continue to Speakwater, he concluded, and salvage clues from Sh'ynryan's writings.

His measured tone and soft voice calmed Alonna. She objected, but her protestations grew thin. Alonna shivered and clutched Jalwyn's hand in a soft embrace meant to convey an apology and plea as the violence of her acts fully dawned on her.

"Surely, they will seek revenge!" Alonna said. The two stood facing each other in the whipping wind. The rain had ceased, and they stood now beneath a vast vault of cold stars.

"Yes," he admitted, surmising her meaning though she had not stated it. "The Order will learn of what we have done. Not immediately, perhaps, but soon after these men fail to return."

He trailed off. She was smiling at him, and the vision of it stole his breath.

"What?"

"You said 'we,'" Alonna breathed. "Your order will know what 'we' have done, you said." She raised her hand and gently caressed his cheek. "I killed two of your Brethren this night, and yet, you take the burden of my guilt upon yourself."

"Of course, Alonna," he replied. "I am for you in this. Have I not yet made that plain?"

She did not answer. Instead, she pulled his face close and parted her lips to press a soft, lingering kiss upon him.

When they parted, the words spilled from him. He could contain them no longer.

"I love you," he declared.

She smiled. "Believe me, Jalwyn," she whispered, leaning in to renew their embrace, "I know."

They departed that same night, leaving the dead Mages in the tent far back from the highway. They took nothing except for Krynerus's horse, a replacement for Jalwyn's mount that had perished in the Mages' attack. They thundered away, not in the direction they had come—back to the March—but to the east and the colonial capital of Speakwater.

The days of travel passed uneventfully. They passed merchant trains heading west but stayed ahead of any traffic trailing them from the March. An Imperial patrol occasionally approached on the road, and they spent nervous moments contemplating their course of action should the knights attempt an arrest, but the soldiers in their burnished platemail ignored them utterly. The famed Arasynian haughtiness that so annoyed Alonna at the March now relieved her. She felt invisible to the arrogant authorities.

That suited her, especially since, surely by now, someone had discovered the murdered Mages.

"I'm sorry," she told Jalwyn often. She sat miserably in her saddle. "I do not know what overtook me. They as much as said how the means justify the end in the murder of my parents, for the abduction of my brother. They tried to kill us! I could not endure it a moment longer."

In these moments, Jalwyn would extend his hand to grasp hers. He had little to add. He nodded his sympathy.

They spent evenings in Imperial hostels or crossroad inns, enjoying hearty meals and sharing a bottle of wine before quietly retiring to separate quarters. Alonna and Jalwyn had grown bolder in their willingness to embrace one another in the days since the Mage's profession of love, but by unspoken agreement, their affections fell short of any more physical demonstrations.

And Jalwyn was painfully aware Alonna had acknowledged his profession of love but had not returned it.

At night in bed, the Mage laced his fingers behind his head and stared blindly into the darkness, chasing sleep, uncertain and distressed by what her omission meant.

In time, Speakwater appeared on the horizon.

It was mid-day when they passed the ornate gates onto the broad streets beyond. Speakwater had grown considerably in the years since Alonna had passed through, but the city, in her estimation, had retained its sober and stuffy character.

The streets were wide, neat, and flawlessly paved—lined everywhere with imposing houses, monuments, and basilicas of gleaming marble. Ample park-like lawns, manicured gardens, and splashing fountains fronted the massive homes. The size of the city was about all that had changed in the intervening years.

Though impressive in its grandeur, the oppressive sameness that offended her taste for diversity as a child was still evident.

They made for the river harbor—a district as uniform and scrupulously clean as the rest of the capital. It presented the exact opposite of messy, polluted, chaotic Caliss. Immaculate warehouses rose beside the docks. Polished stone market buildings lined the stone quays and wharves jutting into the waters of the Vinefruit River as it flowed past the capital on its way south to the port of Eliard and the ocean beyond.

The vine-clad hills that gave the river its name rose on the opposite bank. Only the palatial estates of winemakers, wealthy producers of foodstuffs, and lumber barons interrupted the vast tracts of greenery across the way.

None of the babble, scents, excitement, nor undercurrent of menace that marked the docks at Caliss were evident. Here the shopkeepers waited for customers to patronize their stores and stands rather than bawling stridently to attract them. The richly adorned residents, all clad in subdued pastel shades, moved in an orderly and dignified fashion through the streets, inspecting merchandise quietly, keeping their own counsel.

Jalwyn had taken to pointing out the sights of the capital with interest, pronouncing on the evidence of the Empire's investments to civilize the northern hinterland. Alonna smiled and nodded at his observations but kept her opinions on the matter to herself.

Alonna's belongings had traveled upriver from Eliard following an ocean voyage from Caliss. Alonna paid to have the goods—mostly her trunks full of clothing and sundries amassed in Caliss—moved to a suite of rooms she rented at an inn named simply The Griffin. The Griffin was a mythical beast—half lion, half eagle—that dominated the themes of the city's architecture and a symbol of the Empire at large.

If Speakwater was ostentatious in its facades, it somewhat redeemed itself in its interiors. Their suite at The Griffin—which took in the entire top floor of the square, marble-clad building—was richly appointed with a variety of colorful furnishings, artwork, tapestries, and drapes, so the whole presented a delightful clutter to absorb the eye and engage the mind.

Jalwyn balked at the expense of the suite, but Alonna paid it no mind. She had deposited the bulk of her gold with a moneychanger in Caliss and had watched her holdings modestly grow through the man's shrewd investments. Anything she spent in Speakwater would barely scratch her principle. She laughed in response to Jalwyn's sober recriminations of her lavish spending and opened her money purse even more freely.

"Jalwyn, I've lived most of my life in a bare-stone room and, recently, in a below-ground chamber," she told the fretful Mage. "Allow me to enjoy this now. Stop worrying about money!"

"You permit me to pay for nothing!" the Mage protested. He jingled the fat purse at his belt to punctuate his point. "I'm not without resources, Alonna."

"How much longer do you think you will have access to such funds?" she asked gravely. "When your Order learns about the Mages, do you believe you will be held blameless? What happens to your chambers in Zistah, to your stipend, to your possessions? Do you think you can still call upon the moneychangers in the Order's name then?"

Jalwyn looked startled at that as if only considering the possibility now.

"No, Jalwyn, save what money you have," Alonna said seriously. "You sacrificed to help me, the depth of which I do not think you even realized. I have plenty at my disposal, and I am happy to share it with you."

They spent a week in the capital but did not pass the time idly. Jalwyn made nervous, covert inquires of his Order House and was relieved to learn the elders had no news concerning the trio that had accosted them. Indeed, from what Jalwyn gleaned, nobody had any hint that the murdered sorcerers were missing for any reason other than the pursuit of their own studies. If the Mages of Speakwater had received word of their colleagues' deaths, they betrayed no hint.

This development confused Jalwyn, who had been told by the Mages they had been sent to hunt him, that the Order had declared him a renegade—*Jalk'la*.

"They must have lied," Jalwyn said one evening as Alonna and he reclined in divans outside her chamber. Alonna had lost none of her taste for her evening wine, though certainly, she had restricted her intake compared to the lonely nights passed above the Wayfarer. The pair had grown accustomed to enjoying a glass together before retiring to their quarters.

"They presented themselves as agents of your Order House, yet everyone seems oblivious to their agency. They have not sent anyone to round you up yet. Would that not have been their first order of business upon your return to the city?"

"Then they were working alone, without sanction," Jalwyn reasoned, more relieved than he let on.

"So it seems."

"But why?"

Alonna shrugged. "You heard them. Zealots, the lot of them! By their admission, they were part of a minority that believes this 'Stone' is lying about, waiting to be found. It is becoming clear they were acting on their own behalf, no doubt in league with Sh'ynryan. They knew your elders had sent you to find the bastard. It appears they considered the road to Speakwater—before you could reach your Order House—their chance to stop your search."

"Then you believe me in no danger from the Order at large?" Jalwyn asked her, hopefulness in his voice.

"The Order at large sent you to find Sh'ynryan; those we met on the road tried to stop you. I believe they had separate agendas."

Emboldened by his conversation with Alonna, Jalwyn decided to present himself before the ruling council. His relief was palpable when he was favorably received.

CHAPTER TWENTY-EIGHT

The network of tunnels beyond the huge cavern by which they entered Undermarch astounded Vergal. The meandering corridors connected caverns great and small, and progress over the uneven stone floor was difficult. Vergal began to detect a slight downward grade to the smooth path they followed, and the intensifying dry heat in the air confirmed the small party was delving deeper into the earth, away from the cool air of the surface and closer to the furnaces beneath the world.

Vergal had no comprehension of how Sh'ynryan followed his course. As their journey progressed, however, the Mage's steps became brisker. He even breathed once, in relief, Vergal thought, and exclaimed, "Ah!" before deciding to take a tunnel entrance to his right rather than left.

Vergal, for his part, was completely turned around. He could not distinguish one lichen-covered rock from the next until, at length, they turned a corner and found themselves in a cavern very unlike those preceding it.

The sound of dripping water sharpened as they walked, but the intensity of it did not prepare Vergal for the sight that greeted him as he rounded a cleft in the rough passage.

The party found itself atop an outcropping jutting precariously over the black, still water of a subterranean lake.

Glowing algae coated the slope of the lake, thinning in intensity as it submerged to steeper depths. The shimmering play of water and radiance cast faint rippling light on the cavern roof and walls. A ribbon-like shore of crushed rock and gleaming minerals circled the lake below. The far wall of the cavern receded into darkness, but the small pathways lining either side gleamed dully—smooth arcs reflecting the unearthly light shed by the dimly glowing minerals and growth.

Vergal gasped at the spectacle while Guile absorbed the vision in silent contemplation. Sh'ynryan surprised them both by laughing aloud.

"Yes, this is the way," the Mage cackled, forgetting his earlier admonition for quiet and slapping a hand over his mouth at the sound of his own voice. The echo of it rolled around the empty space.

"I've passed this way before," he followed in a whisper. "We are close."

"Close to the Stone?" Vergal asked.

Sh'ynryan smiled at him. "Perhaps more accurate to say close to a grand adventure."

Vergal considered that; his imagination formed fanciful scenarios to frame the Mage's words.

"What do we do now?" Guile asked. The smooth face of the lake below lay like a still bed of velvet.

Sh'ynryan looked around. "We descend this slope to the ledge, just there, and find a niche in the cavern below to make camp and rest. But I caution you, despite appearances, this is no haven. Surface game trails near water attract predators, and so too do the hunters of Undermarch prey upon creatures coming to slake their thirst."

Guile nodded. The Mage's example made sense. Given the comparison, the gloom surrounding the party assumed a sinister aura, ripe with the hushed menace of a stalking animal.

They picked their way carefully down the scree to the cavern floor. Loose rubble, disturbed by their passage, poured noisily down the slope to splash in the water below. The noise skipped Vergal's heart a beat. Sh'ynryan winced at the racket but offered no comment, knowing his companions were taking care to move quietly in conditions that did not allow.

Minutes into their awkward descent, the talus began to lift, then leveled, and Vergal stood on the rocky margin of shoreline they had spotted from above. Minerals mixed into the crushed rock glinted in the glow from the lake. The broken shoreline made passage uneven and footing difficult, but the vision of it stunned the onlooker.

Now at water level, Vergal picked out the gentle lapping of the lake against its shore. A slight wind off the water stirred his hair. The tenebrous interior of the cavern had not allowed him to spot it from above, but the lake was fresh, not a stagnant pool, and the far-off sound of moving water exiting the cavern through some unseen outlet intensified as they approached the lake.

Guile spotted a small depression a short way up the side of the cavern and climbed up to inspect it, expertly finding handholds in the rough wall. The shallow cleft appeared deserted. He beckoned, and Vergal and the Mage climbed to join him.

They erected a crude camp but dared not light a fire for their meal for fear it would attract predators. They devoured a cold repast of cheese and bread, recovered from the staples Guile had scavenged from the fallen soldiers and went eagerly to their bedrolls soon after.

It seemed only minutes later that Vergal started awake, Guile's hand plastered over his mouth.

The mercenary's face hovered close to his, nearly indistinguishable in the dim light.

"What is it?" Vergal whispered worriedly when the mercenary pulled his hand away.

"Lights. Across the lake but circling toward us."

"Let me see."

He threw back his cover and moved to the mouth of the cave for a look. He spotted them immediately—pinprick clusters of light, shining brilliantly through the encompassing murk. The lights jerkily moved as if held aloft by beings on the march.

"Why didn't you wake Sh'ynryan?"

Guile shrugged. "I never know how much rest he needs after his sorcery. And I think before long, we will need him fresh."

Vergal stared at the lights, pondering.

"Maybe whoever they are will pass by," he ventured.

"Maybe." Guile didn't sound convinced.

"What should we do?"

But the problem of the approaching lights quickly became moot, overshadowed by the more immediate problem of a clamorous din erupting from the high ledge.

Panicked, Vergal seized Guile's arm. "What's that?" he squealed.

Sh'ynryan's silky voice rising suddenly in the darkness caused them both to flinch.

"It passed us earlier in the tunnels," the Mage whispered. "I feared this."

"There's something over there too," Vergal pointed to the lights.

Sh'ynryan did not spare a glance. "I know. Don't worry about that for now. The Kastneth is our immediate concern."

"Kastneth?"

"Yes, a giant, predatory spider, plated as if in armor. It is a feared hunter of these depths. That racket you hear is its simple movement. It gets much louder in full attack."

"Wonderful," Guile offered drily.

"We have to leave, now. We can't have stone to our backs if that thing finds us." The Mage began gathering his possessions.

"Are you insane?" Guile whispered harshly. "We wait here and let it pass. With any luck, it meets up with whatever's on the other side."

Sh'ynryan sighed. "If it corners us, it will dispatch us at its leisure. We stand a fighting chance in the open."

Guile frowned, considering that. The mercenary didn't exactly know what a Kastneth looked like, but he imagined it was well equipped for digging prey out of shallow cavities in the walls of its hunting grounds.

"So, we fight?"

"Ah, no," the Mage replied. "The thing wears its skeleton outside its body, and it is as hard as the stone of its lair. I like your idea, though. Let it fight whatever is approaching from the other direction. And I think I know what that is as well."

"What?"

"Goblins," Sh'ynryan replied. "Misshapen denizens of the subterranean world. They are bipedal and humanoid, like us, though possessed of leathery skin that is difficult to puncture and canine fangs that can pierce flesh with ease."

"A real garden spot you found here."

"Save the humor, such as it is. I suggest you gather your equipment while that Kastneth is still content up on the ledge. We will move toward the lights and hopefully time it in such a way that the two confront each other and allow us to slip away. We must hurry, though. The Kastneth sounds as if it is whipping itself into a lather."

The chitinous clanking blasting from the ridge had boomed into a true cacophony. As they listened to the tumult, Sh'ynryan's face blanched with sudden realization.

"It sounds as if there might be a pair of them up there."

"That's it," Guile stated with finality. "I'm getting out of here." The mercenary quickly stuffed his bedroll into his purloined satchel. He swung his legs over the edge of the cleft and dropped out of sight. Vergal and Sh'ynryan grabbed their belongings and followed.

They picked their way quickly down the wall, throwing nervous glances over their shoulders as they went. They could discern nothing beyond the dim glow of the enveloping moss, but the Kastneth's clacking had swelled to enormous proportions above.

They reached the rocky strand below and set a brisk pace toward the bobbing lights in the distance.

"Slow down, slow down," Sh'ynryan cautioned. "Believe it or not, you do not want to range too far ahead. Kastneths aren't noted for their speed. We need to give it time to catch up, so it meets the group ahead at the same time we do."

With an effort, they abated their pace. The black lake lapped faintly against its dimly glowing shore as they proceeded. Behind them, the clanking increased, now joined by the grating din of falling rock as the Kastneth hastened down the rubble.

Ahead of the party, the light-bearing creatures rounded an outcropping of honeycombed stone onto the rocky strand.

Though still only silhouettes beneath the soft glowing spheres they held aloft, Vergal perceived the approaching figures were man-height, not the squat goblins Sh'ynryan had described. He didn't know if that was an improvement. Though man-like in form, the things might well be creatures more horrible than the Kastneths. He had no way of knowing.

Guile yelped, giving Sh'ynryan and Vergal a start.

"There they are," he croaked.

Vergal turned and, for the first time, beheld a Kastneth.

It loomed at the margin of darkness and light, horrible in its enormity. Towering on massive, segmented legs, its body appeared sheathed entirely in a bulky suit of armor that dully reflected the phosphorescence. More dreadful still was its head. Set like a boulder at the apex of its curving body and crowded with a bulbous mass of jelly-like eyes, the head was dominated by curving, articulated fangs, each fully longer than daggers and clanking raucously. Its plated joints made an uproarious racket as it advanced.

A second beast materialized out of the gloom from behind the first.

"Now we run," Sh'ynryan commanded, raising his voice to be heard over the Kastneths.

His companions required no further urging.

They bolted until the figures beneath the approaching lights fell in focus. With a surprised oath, Sh'ynryan slid to a halt and stood gaping. The group ahead returned his disbelieving stare.

Bathed in the soft shimmer of strange crystal orbs they held aloft, stood slender, bone-white likenesses of men.

Luminous eyes set beneath unruly shocks of tangled hair dominated their slender faces. The creatures wore few articles of clothing save for lengths of what appeared to be spun silk, tied negligently around their loins. Circling their waists and looped around their bare, well-muscled chests hung what appeared to be belts and holsters that bristled with exotic-looking weapons. Granite-capped maces, strangely worked in the shapes of spiders and other curious creatures, were set upon slim handles of smooth bone.

The groups stood regarding each other in stunned silence for a heartbeat. The shocked faces of the creatures turned wary and then threatening. The blazing eyes narrowed to slits and the fists hefting weapons tightened their grips.

"*Ast noth, arake'cil sutay, Nay'fein!*" Sh'ynryan cried, holding his hands, palms-open, in front of him imploringly.

By Vergal's quick count, there were a dozen of them. Surprise registered on each face at the sound of Sh'ynryan's strange utterances. But their disbelief swiftly changed to resolve when the clamor of the approaching Kastneths sounded again in the darkness.

One of them—the leader, Vergal assumed by the being's lofty bearing and excessive ornaments of gold and precious stone—growled in a guttural tongue Vergal did not understand. The warriors behind him set themselves grimly. One of their number stepped forward and seized Sh'ynryan by his wrist.

Guile lifted his sword in response, but the Mage quickly warded him.

"No, Guile," Sh'ynryan breathed, "they mean us no harm. Just follow my lead."

Guile and Vergal watched, astonished, as the warriors who had grasped Sh'ynryan shoved him roughly behind his fellows. Others stepped forward to corral the boy and the mercenary, pushing them to join the Mage. They then stood abreast to form a wall. They held their glowing crystals aloft to better survey the gloom ahead.

The Kastneths emerged into the circle of light, their chelicerae crashing hungrily, their hard limbs sending up a racket.

The adorned leader of the group stepped fearlessly forward. He lifted his glowing crystal in one hand and his spider-head mace in the other. He shook both menacingly in the direction of the Kastneths.

"*Al bol, Kastneth,*" the creature cried. He shook his implements again at the beasts.

The monsters froze at the sound, chattering loudly at him. The creatures stood side-by-each, filling the space between the cavern wall and the waterline on the rocky strand. Vergal's body quaked to behold the monsters. He reached unconsciously to clutch the hem of Guile's cloak for reassurance.

Guile spared him one worried glance but said nothing. The Kastneths had unnerved him badly, and it took all his self-control not to flee, screaming, into the darkness.

"*Al bol!*" the pale creature screamed again. He knelt and thumped the head of the mace on the rocks of the strand before standing to shake the weapon at the beasts again. "*Al bol, terrak noth qualthalel!*"

The warriors behind the leaders raised their crystals and began to chant, punctuating the adorned man's shrill cries with staccato counterpoints of their own.

"*Al bol, Kastneth,*" they yelled, "*Al bol!*"

The Kastneths snapped their pincers and pounded their spike-sharp legs into the rocks. But they did not advance. Each of the beasts' multitude of eyes glinted with reflected crystal light.

Perhaps emboldened by the beasts' indecision, the leader stepped forward, his voice rising to an angry crescendo.

"*AL BOL! AL BOL!*" he screamed. He struck the ground again. Bright sparks leaped from the head of the mace, which had begun to glow with a soft nimbus of white light.

"What is he saying?" Vergal breathed.

Sh'ynryan did not turn from the spectacle in front of him. "He is telling the Kastneths to begone," he whispered over his shoulder.

"And they're listening?" Guile asked incredulously.

"We shall see."

The man had worked himself into a frenzy. He dashed forward, within easy reach of the Kastneths' deadly legs, screaming imprecations at the creatures while whipping his mace in short, vicious arcs, in a pantomime of a battle. Each pass of the mace head trailed long streaks of white light. The Kastneths gave way a step, chittering loudly.

The men's accompanying drone swelled to a roar, "*AL BOL! AL BOL, KASTNETH! AL BOL!*"

A dangerous moment passed in which the Kastneths appeared poised on the brink of attack. The beasts' legs twitched, and its chelicerae thundered. The mace-wielder did not waver. He continued to shake his glowing weapon and held his crystal aloft. The chanting of the men behind him rose to the edge of a shriek.

As one, the Kastneths clanked their bony appendages and, turning, scuttled away into the concealing darkness.

Vergal blew out a pent breath he had not realized he was holding.

The leader of the group sunk to one knee, apparently exhausted by his efforts. His companions stepped forward to collect him, helping him carefully to his feet and straightening his holsters and silks solicitously. The leader flashed a grateful smile at his friends. But his expression turned hard when he turned to regard Sh'ynryan.

The Mage held his hands out again, fingers splayed, palms forward. "*Arake'cil sutay, Nay'fein,*" he said again hopefully.

Vergal reeled as if struck when he realized he understood the leader's reply.

"I remember you, Sh'ynryan," the leader said in a thickly accented voice. "And to save you from stumbling over the few words you command of our language, I will address you in your own tongue. I remember it from the instruction of our ancients, refreshed by your sojourn with us."

Sh'ynryan's mouth opened in surprise.

The man smiled ruefully. "You do not remember me?" he asked in a mock-injured tone. "You were long a guest in my father's house, Mage."

Sh'ynryan frowned uncertainly. "Ker'alstil?" he ventured.

The smile broadened, becoming brilliant, unguarded. "Ah, your memory serves," the one named Ker'alstil said delightedly.

"Ker'alstil," Sh'ynryan said again, smiling now too. The Mage sunk to one knee on the rocky strand in front of the man. He bowed his head respectfully. "My greetings to you and your father's house."

"And my father's greetings to you, Mage," Ker'alstil responded solemnly. "Now tell me," he said, "why have you returned to the realm of the Nay'fein and chased by hungry Kastneths, no less?"

Ker'alstil turned expectantly to Vergal and Guile. "And who are these accompanying you?" he asked.

Sh'ynryan straightened, pausing to nod respectfully at the impassive faces of the grim men in formation behind Ker'alstil. To the leader, he replied, "I have returned as I promised your father. I have returned because I have completed the quest."

The countenance Sh'ynryan turned on Vergal froze the boy's blood. The medallion at the Mage's throat began to strobe with muted light as it had that long-ago night in the taproom of the Wayfarer.

Undermarch

Vergal cowered behind Guile's cloak beneath the weight of the Mage's cold stare.

"I have returned because I have found the One," the Mage said.

CHAPTER TWENTY-NINE

"Jalwyn!" cried Harbesh Neomonitis, the eldest of the five Mages who composed the ruling council.

The Mages sat in plush, wing-backed chairs set in shallow alcoves. A great expanse of polished, mosaic-laid floor separated the entrance from the alcoves across a largely empty hall. Harbesh's wrinkled hands reached for a cane next to his chair, and he began to rise on shaky legs. Jalwyn hurried forward to assist him. He didn't want to be responsible for any nasty spill the elder took off his pedestal. Harbesh's mastery of the Words was formidable, but the old sorcerer was less adept at controlling his trembling legs.

The other four Mages seated in the room cast sneering glances behind the elder's back, unimpressed by Harbesh's undignified greeting. Jalwyn ignored them. "No, elder, please, do not exert yourself on my account," he said, gripping Harbesh's wrist and elbow to guide him back into his chair. Jalwyn stepped away and bowed respectfully. When he looked again, the elder's pendulous white beard cracked in a broad grin.

"I'll hear none of this 'elder' business from you," Harbesh said in mock vexation. "We are Brothers here, each of us." He darted crafty glances at the Mages seated near him. "Too many of us forget that."

Jalwyn smiled. "Yes, Brother," he answered, though the familial address felt awkward upon his tongue when directed at an esteemed patriarch of the order.

"Better, better," Harbesh said jovially. The old man's bones veritably creaked and groaned with the motion of settling back into his seat.

"What news then, Brother?" Harbesh said expansively. "I have not seen you in years, not since leaving Zistah for this post. The Mother House, of course, sent word of your mission. We knew you were somewhere in Alasia, and I wondered if you might appear. Have you tracked our itinerant Sh'ynryan?" The old man laughed in a booming bass that belied his frail appearance. "How goes our Brother's pilgrimage to collect his beloved Stone?"

That last statement drew grumbles from Mages seated on either side of him. Harbesh paid the complainers no heed. Jalwyn hurried to change the subject.

"No news, I regret to inform the council," Jalwyn lied smoothly. Not long ago, the Mage would have trembled at the prospect of deceiving the elders. However, nearly being killed by members of his own order had given him a new perspective on the merits of unrestrained candor.

Jalwyn was shocked by how seamlessly the deceit poured from him as he continued.

"It is, in fact, why I am here," he said. "As the Mother House informed you, the Zistah elders seek news of Sh'ynryan's progress. He has been absent for several years, and they sent me to learn of his whereabouts. My mission has not been fruitful. But I learned in my travels that Sh'ynryan might have left behind writings during his sojourn in Speakwater. For this reason, I come before you."

Several old Mages shifted in their chairs.

"I hope by examining his journals, I might gain insight into where he might have gone or what clues he may have left as to his destination. My own investigation is at a stalemate; I believe this my only recourse."

Harbesh appeared confused by the request, but before he could reply, a portly Mage interrupted.

"Brother, Sh'ynryan's writings are not common knowledge, especially not to brethren so young," said the Mage. Jalwyn did not recognize the man. The Mage's voice was clipped and cultured but carried an unmistakable edge. "Since you report having found no indication of Sh'ynryan, perhaps you could explain how you learned of them."

"Forgive me, Brother; the fault is mine. I did not intend to leave the impression I have learned nothing about Sh'ynryan. I only meant I have not yet found him and that I don't know where to resume my search. I have, in fact, confirmed Sh'ynryan has within the past year been in Caliss, on the Aerie Coast."

"How have you confirmed this?" the Mage inquired. He shifted again in his seat. Looking at him, Jalwyn got the sense of a hunting cat, tamping its rear paws.

Jalwyn coughed politely and asked, "And you are, Brother?"

The red-robed Mage drew himself up in his chair, scowling.

"I am Danyalius," he answered harshly, "an elder of the ruling council who has asked a direct question of you. I would appreciate an answer."

"Danyalius," Harbesh admonished. "Even the barbarians of Alasia announce themselves before the blood-letting begins. Surely you will show our visiting Brother at least as much courtesy as they."

Danyalius opened his mouth to respond, but Jalwyn intervened.

"Well met, Brother Danyalius," Jalwyn said quickly before returning to his narrative. "In Caliss, I encountered an innkeeper who positively identified Sh'ynryan. Our Brother had taken a room there for many days and, in the course of his visit, he mentioned journals he kept of a previous trip he had made across the continent."

Danyalius snorted. "I highly doubt that."

"Yes, well," Jalwyn continued, trying to affect a sincere yet slightly offended expression. "In any case, your own admission confirms the truth of this man's words. As for how he came by the information, I can only speculate."

Danyalius opened his mouth as if to respond, but it closed again when he realized he could not refute Jalwyn's words.

"So, I come to you, Brothers, to ask your permission to peruse these journals. It would aid me greatly in my search, I am sure. And," he added easily, "I am certain the Zistinian elders would appreciate any assistance you afford me."

"I am certain they would, and I am sure we will!" Harbesh responded expansively. He turned each way to the Mages beside him. "Truth, Brothers, I had no idea Sh'ynryan kept journals. Obviously, Danyalius knows of them, so if you would be so kind, Brother, to arrange for Jalwyn to receive these so we can send this young man back on his way."

Danyalius's face was composed, but his eyes blazed. "Surely this matter should be put to the vote of the council, Harbesh."

The elder Mage blinked. "Why would we do that, Brother?" he asked, sounding bewildered. "This is no matter of policy, but a simple request for materials. Name a time in which we called a conclave on a matter such as this?"

"Not all the Brethren will be pleased to release Sh'ynryan's journals," Danyalius replied.

"Again, I ask, why?"

"Come now, Harbesh," Danyalius spat, rising to his feet. The other seated Mages looked at the portly Mage, astonished.

"We both know the schism in the Order over what you so flippantly call Sh'ynryan's pilgrimage," Danyalius said heatedly. "Those of us who support our Brother's quest prefer to keep his observations on the Stone among those who respect it, those not so quick to mock our hopes for the future."

Harbesh's bushy eyebrows lowered. "Hopes for the future? Danyalius, what exactly does Sh'ynryan advocate in these writings? You declare two camps within a single Brotherhood; this suggests nothing beneficial to the unity of our order."

"Exactly, you said it!" Danyalius exclaimed. "Two camps, that's exactly what this order has become. A house divided! Those who deny the existence of the Stone are blind, ignorant, or both. You are heir to the legacy of the Stone yet fail to comprehend the entirety of what has been bequeathed to you. I tell you some believe there is more, and we stand on the edge of uncovering it!"

Harbesh rose to his feet. This time, nothing flagging presented in his stance. The elder addressed Jalwyn, though his eyes never left Danyalius's face.

"The journals will be brought to you, Brother Jalwyn," he said in a calm voice that belied his flashing eyes. "The Mother House has directed you be assisted as needed in your search for Sh'ynryan, and judging by what has transpired here, I find wisdom in Zistah's ruling. The sooner we find Sh'ynryan, the sooner we may address the cancer that has been revealed."

Danyalius's eyes bulged dangerously. "Cancer? You dare call us a cancer upon this Order?"

"No, I name your duplicity and your contentiousness toward a Brother as such."

Jalwyn watched the exchange in open-mouthed astonishment. Harbesh turned to the young Mage. "Brother, I give thanks for your diligence and your obedience to your elders' orders. You will receive the materials you seek, I assure you. I only ask that you report to me what you discover therein, that we may uncover the truth of this distressing matter."

Fuming, Danyalius said, "You have made no friends here this day, Jalwyn!"

"Enough!" Harbesh roared. "Contain yourself, Danyalius, or would you force your Brethren to compel your good behavior?"

Shaking with rage, swinging his angry glare between Harbesh and Jalwyn, Danyalius spat and stomped off the pedestal. The hard heels of his boots clicked loudly as he crossed the polished stone floor toward the broad arch door and the hallways beyond.

CHAPTER THIRTY

Vergal saw things he never imagined following the fey creatures Sh'ynryan named the Nay'fein deeper into the earth.

The exotic sights that lined the winding way made the long journey pass as if in a dream. Vergal thought himself inured to shocks following his abduction and flight and ensuing encounters with a Drakleth, Obroths, and, most recently, the subterranean spider-things called Kastneths. But the preternatural vistas unfolding in the maze-like corridors of Undermarch convinced Vergal his long flight across the Aerie Coast had poorly prepared him for the strange realm of the Nay'fein.

Led by the stern-faced Nay'fein warriors, the company padded stealthily across heaving terrain. One turn in the winding tunnels might lead to a chamber of fractured crystal, upon which the aura from the pervasive moss refracted in scintillating beams. The next step might plunge into darkness so absolute it threatened to suffocate.

Craggy stone pillars and knife-like stalactites formed leering and grotesque shapes in the gloom of one chamber, only to smooth suddenly to bare and polished rock in the next. At times, they followed tabletop flat passages smoothed by long-vanished waterways, and at others, they negotiated ankle-turning expanses of lumpy lava fields.

Echoing caverns of amphitheater-like vastness soared into all-encompassing darkness, only to abruptly narrow into slender ducts through which party members wriggled uncomfortably on their stomachs through a close and winding labyrinth.

The going turned alternately easy and hard. In a span of minutes, the company might skirt the narrow ledge of a yawning chasm, only to soon trudge effortlessly across a natural highway of pulverized rock, laid down by some ancient collapse of stone.

The domain of the Nay'fein, though at its heart a desolate rock, was as feral and motley as any wilderness of the world above.

Slowly, the boy began to pick up sounds in the otherwise funereal silence of the passages.

Water constantly dripped, though its source was impossible to pinpoint behind the distracting screen of echoes.

Rock rumbled and stone grated in far-off places, and dust sifted and pattered to the cavern floor from the ceiling above. A warm gust of wind whipping through the tunnels might blast past a startled ear, registering like an unearthly scream upon the overwrought mind.

Overlying the whole was a nearly palpable sense of menace that emanated in slow, cruel waves from the surrounding shadows. It left Vergal with the impression of an awful predator tracking his progress with a hunter's cunning eyes.

It surprised Vergal to find life thriving everywhere in the barren Undermarch. Sometimes as Vergal walked, absorbed by the strange realm emerging around him, a Nay'fein might suddenly seize his arm or shoulder to freeze him in his tracks. At these times, the Nay'fein stood stock still and opened wide their oddly luminous eyes to the surrounding darkness. Vergal strained to listen and sometimes detected sounds—a clacking, a skittering, or, perhaps most ominously of all, a bass rumbling that could have been a harsh growl rising from the shadows.

If these encounters disturbed the Nay'fein, they betrayed no hint beyond their abrupt stops and harsh demands for stillness. They moved quietly always, but sometimes the beings became even more furtive. These sudden bouts of Nay'fein wariness always sent a worm of fear burrowing through Vergal's guts.

However, the frequency of these pauses lessened as the journey progressed and soon disappeared entirely.

Though the paths they trod appeared as formidable to Vergal as any previous in the trek, the Nay'fein became more confident, less wary, as they went. They began to talk and laugh among themselves in their strange guttural dialect. Their manner was that of men returning home, entirely at ease with their environment, taking the last few familiar steps more by instinct than observation. Vergal took his guides' cues and allowed himself to relax as much as his taut nerves permitted.

The voyage through Undermarch had alternately frightened and delighted Vergal, but it had completely unhinged Guile.

The formerly roguish mercenary had lost all vestiges of his carefree manner. The watery radiance from the Nay'fein's glowing crystals showed Guile's wide and nervous eyes dominating an increasingly pale and sickly face.

The mercenary forced a thin smile when he noticed anyone watching. Covert glances indicated something else, however: His companion was suffering in mind, if not yet in body, from the stress of their lengthy delve into the underworld.

Vergal drew close to the mercenary and asked in a whisper, "What's wrong, Guile?"

Guile started but quickly composed himself and offered Vergal another of those unconvincing smiles in response.

"Besides the obvious, you mean?"

Vergal did not smile in response. "This place is strange to me, too," the boy said. "I think even Sh'ynryan is nervous. Look at him. He hasn't said a word; he's barely looked at us since we took up with these fellows." He touched the mercenary's hand briefly, reassuringly. "This is a very different place for people like us. It's all right, you know, if it feels frightening."

Guile's scowled. He pulled his hand away. "Take care who you call a coward," he said gruffly.

"I didn't call you a coward. I said you might feel frightened. That's not the same thing. We are all scared, aren't we? Even these Nay'fein looked nervous passing through some of these corridors. There's more to this place than presents itself. I think our guides are picking the safest path they can, but... well, it's hard, not knowing what waits around each corner."

Guile shook his head. "It's not that," he murmured, and all trace of his mounting hostility had flown.

"I'll put my blade against any man or beast. It's something else."

"What?"

Guile sighed. "It's not what lives down here that bothers me, Vergal; it's where they live. A few of those tunnels we had to squeeze through reminded me just how far below ground we've come. And now that I've considered it, I can't get the thought out of my head."

He chortled once harshly, without mirth. "I've darted through more tunnels and sewers in my time than I can remember, and I never once gave being underground a thought. Now, for whatever reason, the darkness, these weird glowing stones, the closeness of everything, it's all a trial. Men were meant to walk the face of the earth, not crawl through its belly. Every step we take removes me farther from the light."

The mercenary tilted his head to take in the cavern ceiling above, then quickly averted his gaze. "How much rock do you think is above us?" he asked. "Miles of it by now, I would wager."

Vergal considered that. "I don't know," he replied shortly. Guile's observations did not bother him in the same way they distressed the mercenary. The ceiling looked solid enough—razor-sharp rocks and all.

When Vergal turned again, the mercenary was glowering at Sh'ynryan, who was oblivious to the stare. "Remind me when I get the chance to properly thank the Mage for pushing me down that glowing hole he made," he growled.

A loud call interrupted their muted conversation. An instant of silence was followed by a responding call from the lead warrior. In response, the party, its guides smiling and chattering animatedly now in their strange language, increased the pace. A few steps more carried the company around a rocky outcropping, and Vergal and Guile issued instinctive gasps.

The dwelling place of the Nay'fein opened in a stunning vista beneath them.

Far beneath, a vaulting natural cavern curved gently down from the precipice upon which they stood. The shape of the cavern was the only thing natural about it. All else, every shelf of rock, every fang of stone, every mound, had been sculpted and set ablaze with the muted pastel brilliance of the underworld. Curving spires gleamed with pale radiance where the Nay'fein had incorporated their strange glowing crystal as art or accents. Capering lights shimmered throughout, shifting hues before onlookers' eyes, delineating the crafted dwellings of the Nay'fein, and even marking deep fissures and cracks radiating across the cavern floor with a baleful, warning gleam.

The Nay'feins' structures were divided by wide, spacious avenues that bisected the bowl at regularly spaced intervals, dipping and rising to follow the primeval contours of the cavern floor. These broad streets bustled with activity. Hundreds of the beings crowded the boulevards, entering and exiting the smooth-hewn doors of busy buildings that could only have been merchants' shops. Most shocking of all, traffic moved on these boulevards, mounted on the broad backs of enormous spiders. These monstrous creatures appeared like the Kastneths, though smaller and obviously more benign than the horrors that had harried the party in the tunnels.

The sultry air rising from the vast expanse below carried the distant drone of street noise and blended exotic scents.

The orderly bustle below him comforted Vergal. Any creature capable of such organization and culture must also be endowed with reason, Vergal thought, though not precisely in those terms. His initial impressions of the Nay'fein were too scattered to form any certain turn of phrase, though his instinctive conclusion remained the same.

The vision of the Nay'feins' domain had an alternate effect on Sh'ynryan, who slapped and rubbed his hands gleefully. He laughed out loud, without malice, without restraint, in a tone different from anything Vergal had yet heard from the Mage.

The Mage kneeled in front of Vergal to clasp the boy's shoulders. The eyes searching Vergal's face had lost their flinty indifference. They were wide, earnest, and, to Vergal's surprise, decidedly moist.

"Vergal, Vergal," Sh'ynryan said, his voice thick. He paused to compose himself, turned his head to wipe his eyes on the sleeve of an outstretched arm. The thin fingers tightened on the boy's shoulders, not meanly, but in honest response to the depth of feeling that had risen close to the surface in the Mage.

"Vergal, we have arrived!" Sh'ynryan said. "We have safely come, and I can tell you now our arrival here was by no means certain. Yet here we stand, and you helped bring us here! Now all can be revealed. Soon your education will begin. Everything that you are and still are meant to be will be made plain, for we now have the Nay'fein to guide and assist us."

Incredibly, Sh'ynryan sobbed, though he still smiled gently. Vergal felt his own throat grow thick with emotion at the display.

"Such a birthright you stand to claim!" the Mage rejoiced, drawing Vergal into a brief, rough embrace. Vergal stiffened as his abductor held him. The Mage held Vergal at arm's length, showed him a sad smile.

"Don't judge me too harshly," Sh'ynryan pleaded. "My only concern above was to bring you below, and I could brook no dissent nor be swayed from that path. I promise it will all be made clear to you, and the end will be better than the beginning. Please believe what I say."

Vergal could do nothing except stare. Sh'ynryan was acting out of character, all signs of his bellicosity gone. If Vergal needed further proof of this, Sh'ynryan supplied it when he rose to his knees and firmly clenched Guile's hand.

"And you!" the Mage said expansively, flashing the mercenary the same disarming smile. Guile grimaced as the Mage pumped his hand. "You have been a truly worthy road companion. You honored your word and remained at our side on a path that must have surely seemed strange. Thank you, Guile. I truly mean it when I say this; hear my words: Thank you!"

"Yes, you're welcome, I suppose," Guile stammered. He stared at their clenched hands, vaguely fascinated as if seeing entwined snakes instead of clasping fingers.

"The small matter remains, though," Guile said once he had regained himself, "how do I return home? You have reached your destination, and I am convinced that you mean the boy no harm. My contract with you is more than fulfilled. I am eager to be away from here, back to more ... congenial surroundings."

"Oh, that!" Sh'ynryan exclaimed, releasing Guile's hand and waving his hand as if the mercenary's concern was an insignificant matter.

"Of course, you will be taken home," Sh'ynryan went on. "Did you think I meant to keep you here?" The Mage laughed. His color and spirits were high. "The Nay'fein will escort you back through the tunnels, as they did me those years ago. And, believe me, it is not a journey you wish to commence without them! They have means by which to open the portal to the March, as I did. I'm afraid I will not be available to help you escape the fortress, but I have confidence in your abilities to do this thing alone."

The Nay'fein had begun to follow the twisting stone path that curled toward the city below. Sh'ynryan tossed one arm easily around the mercenary's shoulder and guided Vergal with his other. "But stay with us a while," Sh'ynryan urged. "Many delights await you in the city of the Nay'fein, many wondrous sights that few eyes born to sunlight have ever beheld."

"Really, I should not," Guile answered uncertainly, though he allowed himself to be pulled along. "The journey home to Caliss is long. I should be underway."

"Your guides will not be eager to return so quickly to the road. They have patrolled the outer tunnels and caverns many days—what we call days in this lightless world—and desire time with their families and for leisure before returning. Can you blame them? As eager as you are to return home, so too have they."

With only a little more prompting, and because Guile could not refute Sh'ynryan's logic, the mercenary agreed to stay. "Only a day or so, mind you!" Guile warned sternly, and the Mage nodded his agreement.

The switchback ramp of worked stone was a boulevard, so broadly and gently did it snake to the cavern floor. They soon stood before the gates of the city of the Nay'fein.

Massive constructs of dark metal, the gates gleamed in the city's glow. Guards hastened to open the portals at the party's approach, exclaiming loudly in their indecipherable tongue to their fellows when they caught sight of the surface beings accompanying them.

Vergal found himself surrounded by greater numbers of Nay'fein. They wore variations of the same silk garments that clothed the patrol soldiers, and they talked excitedly in their fluid tongue. They gathered around, their odd eyes unabashedly examining the newcomers. Vergal flinched at their scrutiny but reminded himself of Sh'ynryan's promises they would be safe among these beings. With an effort, he brought himself under control and returned the scrutiny his hosts were affording him.

They were slim and well-muscled beings, their sparse garments insufficient to cover all except their most private portions completely. They favored ornamentation and wore little crafted works of metal and gemstone, woven into the long braids of their hair or hanging from strands of the spider silks that fashioned their raiment.

The features of their faces were slender, delicate, and their countenances and bearing exuded unearthly beauty. This trait seemed common to them all, though with incredible variations of composition. Their teeth gleamed white when they smiled, and Vergal noticed the sharpness of their eye teeth, like the piercing fangs of a small predator. All of them wore weapons crafted of metals and stone and bone—appropriate in an underworld devoid of the wood of trees.

The jabbering guard sentries waved the party beyond the gate area. They proceeded into the city proper, where the cavern floor had been made into a highway as smooth as anything constructed on the surface world. This road was shared by a multitude of people, all hurriedly engaged in their own business, and all of whom froze in astonishment when they caught sight of the strangers moving mong them.

They walked through the milling crowd, marveling at those who marveled at them until, at last, the way became blocked. Word of their arrival had preceded them throughout the cavern, and the press of Nay'fein, who had come to satisfy their curiosity, became an obstructing wall.

Their guides spoke roughly and tried to open a passage through the crowd, but to no avail. Vergal had begun to entertain fears of being crushed by the jostling swarm when the path forward abruptly cleared.

Vergal soon saw the reason why. Paces ahead stood a trio of the great spiders he had glimpsed from above the city. Ornamented Nay'fein warriors sat astride the beasts, their gossamer capes of thick spider web stirring in the cavern's dry, swirling air. The spiders' huge legs carefully but firmly pushed the last of the stragglers out of their way as they advanced.

Trembling, Vergal edged toward Sh'ynryan, who rested a reassuring hand on the boy's shoulder.

"Ah, at last," said the patrol leader, Ker'alstil, with noticeable relief. "Our escort will clear the rabble, and the way to the Drolanjan will be clear. My father must be eager to see you."

"What is a Drolanjan?" Vergal whispered to Sh'ynryan.

"It's their word for both palace and king, and here he refers to both. We are to receive a royal welcome, Vergal."

The spider riders reached to pull their new passengers onto the backs of their mounts. Double-seated saddles with room to spare for themselves and their scant possessions awaited them. The saddles were fashioned from what appeared to be cured leather, from the hide of what beast Vergal could not tell. Ker'alstil and his company continued to march vanguard for the riders.

The crowds continued to part before the tall-stepping spider mounts, but not without much shouting and finger-pointing at the exotic visitors to their realm. Vergal revised his estimate of the Nay'fein population from hundreds to thousands as they wound deeper into the city.

The palace's impressive facade overlooked the city from the sheer wall of the cavern from which it had been cut. The same shining multi-colored crystals that graced most features of the city highlighted its huge statues and monuments. The minerals shifted through spectrums of colors as they danced: Red, violet, orange, white, black, then back through the progression. It mesmerized the eye.

Another gate opened, and the spider-riders directed their mounts into the palace courtyard. The building's glistering facade loomed above, carved into the sheer face of the cavern wall. Pinpricks of what appeared to be firelight shone from many small windows dotting the exterior—a glaring contrast to the muted radiance of its softly shining exterior.

Guile, staring at the windows, asked, "How can they have fire here? What manner of fuel do they burn?"

Sh'ynryan followed his gaze up, then away. "They burn the stalks of the great fungus that grow in the region. These also provide food, materials for their furnishings, tools, fibers for their garments, and much more," he explained.

Guile thought about that, pondering the ingenuity of their hosts.

They dismounted. Grooms appeared to take the long silk reins from the riders and lead away the spider mounts. Vergal watched them go with mounting relief. He didn't share the Nay'feins' faith in the ugly beasts' domestication.

They straightened themselves and their possessions under the detached eyes of their escorts. They had finished with their primping and were preparing to climb the embellished stairs to the wide palace doors when a fanfare sounded. A curious buzz rippled through the Nay'fein, accompanied by plainly incredulous looks.

Before Vergal could inquire, the palace doors opened wide to discharge a company of soldiers onto the wide terrace atop the stairs.

Startled gasps rippled through the gathering. The assembled Nay'fein dropped to one knee as the fanfare sounded again, this time much closer. Wide-eyed, Sh'ynryan also knelt and motioned with his hands for Vergal and Guile to do likewise.

They complied just in time. The bedecked soldiers on the terrace parted. From their midst stepped an elderly Nay'fein man. He wore a simple wrap of thick, gossamer spider silk. Unlike the soldier who had accompanied him, or even the members of Ker'alstil's small group, the only baubles the man on the terrace wore were a simple collar of what appeared to be beaten silver in addition to thick gold bands on the long middle fingers of each hand. The man's long hair was pulled back and tied tightly behind his back. His round eyes flared as he fixed the newcomers beneath a penetrating glare.

"*Ast noth*, Sh'ynryan!" came the call from the man on the palace terrace.

The Mage lifted his chin at the sound of his name. He smiled broadly. "*Ast noth, Drolanjan!*" he answered heartily, his tone measured as he carefully vocalized the thick Nay'fein syllables.

Drolanjan, Vergal thought in amazement, remembering Sh'ynryan's earlier words. The king! The boy dipped his head lower.

The Drolanjan on the terrace laughed. "Still struggling with our dialect, I see," the king responded in words Vergal understood. The king's speech was accented but perfectly decipherable.

"And you still a master of my poor tongue, Drolanjan," Sh'ynryan replied, bowing his head.

"Only with practice, friend. I have had much time to practice awaiting your return." The Drolanjan's smile remained, but his eyes narrowed as he scanned the assemblage. "Where is he?" the Drolanjan asked simply. "Have you brought him?"

Sh'ynryan straightened proudly. "I have, Majesty. It is this boy, here," the Mage said, hooking one hand under Vergal's arm and hauling the boy to his feet.

The Drolanjan's eyes widened. "A boy?" he asked, surprised. "Are you certain of this?"

"Of course, Majesty. Otherwise, I would never have risked your displeasure by bringing outsiders to your realm. I remember my solemn oath and have guarded your secrets. I have shared the knowledge of you only with those like-minded as myself, as we discussed and as you approved."

"Indeed," the Drolanjan murmured, nodding. But it seemed he had only barely heard Sh'ynryan. The Nay'fein king eyes were intent on Vergal. The king wore a perplexed expression that indicated he did not quite believe the evidence before him.

"Boy, rise," the king commanded. Vergal lifted his head to see the Drolanjan crooking a beckoning finger. "Come here."

Vergal cast a worried glance at Sh'ynryan, who nodded reassuringly.

Rising unsteadily, Vergal moved slowly forward. He felt every eye boring into his back as he climbed the broad stairs. The wizened king at their summit grew larger with his every step. At last, Vergal stood before the Drolanjan. Not knowing what to do next, he made to kneel again.

"Not necessary," the Drolanjan said hurriedly, reaching to stop Vergal in mid-crouch. But the instant his hands met Vergal, the beaten silver collar spread across the man's breast flared with light. It was a brilliant, scintillating radiance that momentarily stole Vergal's vision. He had seen that revolving glow before when Sh'ynryan had crept in the manner of a thief into his room to abduct him.

The Drolanjan swore an excited oath and stepped away quickly as if burned.

Vergal groaned. That variety of swirling light had meant nothing but trouble for him thus far. He imagined nothing had changed no matter how far underground he had retreated.

The Drolanjan's wide eyes sought Sh'ynryan. "Surely you have spoken the truth, Mage," the king said breathlessly. "This is he. You have found the One."

Sh'ynryan said nothing, only stared forward, his chin high, his expression sublime.

The Drolanjan drew himself up, pulling his silken garment tighter around his body.

"His instruction begins immediately," the Nay'fein king announced crisply. "My palace is at your disposal, Sh'ynryan. You are all my honored guests; my servants shall be your servants."

Vergal said nothing, offered no thanks or refusal in response to the Drolanjan's words. He only continued to stare at the flashing collar at the Drolanjan's throat. The colors ebbed and faded, and Vergal's lingering hopes of an imminent end to Sh'ynryan's mad quest faded alongside them. There were no tears to mark the death of his dream, no crushing grief to wrestle or to overcome. It simply did not seem important anymore. Those emotions were distant—they were the concerns of someone he had once known.

Because in the instant that the light died, Vergal had witnessed something, a revelation as immense in its scope as it was simple in its message.

The Stone existed, and it called to him.

Vergal fell senseless at the Drolanjan's feet. His lips wore a blissful smile even as his head thumped the unyielding ground.

CHAPTER THIRTY-ONE

A light knock at the door roused Alonna from her unhappy thoughts of Vergal. Much of her sorrow centered on the vividness of the image of him she held in her heart. At times, this memory visited her with startling clarity—a dusky-haired boy with a sad round face and injured eyes, an expression that haunted her since his abduction.

At other times, the image blurred and ran as something glimpsed faintly through a sheen of rippling water, and she struggled to retain it. This frightened her immensely. Alonna wrestled with ordering her thoughts when these unwelcome gaps in her memory intruded. She strived to set the image of her brother firmly in her mind until, at last, her mind relented, and his face fell sharply again into focus.

The fact that she sometimes struggled to accomplish this distressed Alonna. So much time had passed since her brother's disappearance. Her fury at his abduction plagued her still, but she was startled to find the grief that numbed her in early days had begun to fade, ever so slightly, with the passage of time.

This she could not allow.

She stared without seeing at the plastered ceiling of her room when the sudden soft rapping sounded. Sighing in irritation, she swung her legs off the bed and went to open the door.

Jalwyn stood there, a roll of parchment held in one hand.

"Jalwyn, come in," she said, stepping aside to admit him. She brightened at the sight of the parchment. "You've finished your reading then!" she exclaimed. Her melancholy flew in a sudden rush of excitement. "You've found the way to Undermarch?"

Jalwyn did not answer. He stepped inside and gently closed the door behind him, his face bleak.

"What?" Alonna asked warily, sensing his mood. "What did you find?"

"I've found much," the Mage said slowly. It was as if he was testing each of his words before speaking them. "There is nothing specific in the journals, of course, since Sh'ynryan had made vows not to reveal the entrance to the Nay'feins' realm.

"But I have information I did not possess before, and I believe we are ready to leave soon for the March."

"Oh, Jalwyn!" Alonna cried happily. She rushed forward and embraced him. But Jalwyn's arms remained limply at his sides as she held him. Alonna frowned. That had certainly never happened before.

"What is wrong?" she asked, stepping back a pace to regard him. "This is good news! We can leave immediately! We can leave tonight! We've found their trail."

Jalwyn sighed. Almost reluctantly, he moved forward and dropped the scroll on Alonna's bed covers.

"Yes, we can leave tonight if that's what you desire, I have made the necessary arrangements," Jalwyn answered. "But not until you have read this."

"What is it?"

The Mage moved to the door. "Read it, Alonna. Then come to my room when you are done. I will have completed preparations by then, and we can discuss it."

"Discuss what?"

"Read it," Jalwyn urged softly. He stepped out the door, closing it quietly behind him.

Alonna shook her head, annoyed, puzzled. What was the mystery? She hefted the parchment—an ordinary cylinder of papers, tied in the middle by a thin length of silk. She unraveled the silk and let it fall. She gently smoothed the parchments flat on her bed and began to read the words written there.

It was a journal, written in a spidery slanting hand, self-identified as the writings of the Mage Sh'ynryan. Alonna bit her lip. Her eyes darted across the pages, seeking mention of she knew not what, until she forced herself to calm and begin her reading anew, deliberately at first, but soon with dawning horror:

What I have taken to calling "my mission" cannot rightly be regarded as such since it never enjoyed the sanction of the Order. I am confident of the importance of my quest to those in the Brotherhood who are of like mind, however, and so I pursue it in the same manner I might a direct order from the Conclave itself.

There is nothing so important as the path I now follow. It hurts my heart to know not all my Brethren agree on this point. I pity the deniers because they have embarked on the broad path of unbelief and eschewed the narrow path that leads to knowledge. Soon, though, the evidence their doubts require will manifest, and what they perceive now as unreasonable disobedience will be hailed as rewarded faith once my tasks are complete. Perhaps then this sense of guilt will abate, and these hands will again be made clean.

I record these words that my Brethren might one day rejoice that we are again of one mind going forward and learn from this sad chapter of history during which we contend. My own heart, for now, is devoid of joy. I long for the day when our Order's schism is mended. My work to accomplish this sustains me on my road.

Brethren, I have related to many of you in person and recorded elsewhere the marvelous realm I discovered in the course of my search for the Stone. I need not repeat those adventures here, even if I still thrill to recall my sojourn beneath the earth and the secrets it revealed.

It is enough to say my discoveries in that strange place spurred me in a new direction. I returned afterward to Zistah, land of my birth, home of my Brethren, to reflect on what I had learned, and to study alongside my Brethren the tablet that had been entrusted to me.

It was a comfort to savor again Zistah's fragrant breezes and watch the sunset gleam on the inland sea. Inspiration fired me upon return to the sights and sounds of my home; memories of the same had sustained me in my quest. It brought me near tears to return where my heart resides after my journeys across the detestable northern vassal we call Alasia.

The joy I felt at my homecoming turned quickly to despair. My Brother Krynerus awaited my arrival one day at the Imperial library, where I had come armed with new experiences and information, to renew my studies into the ancient history of the Stone.

Imagine then my horror to learn this was not to be. A thief—a traitor—had emerged from within our ranks to flee with the tablet!

This thief—an accomplished scholar, yet an acolyte in the Order—used his position of trust and standing to steal the relic. Only as he made final preparations to flee did Krynerus learn of his treachery. He hesitated to remedy the situation forthwith, lest the tablet be lost.

This misguided acolyte was fearful of our quest, Krynerus explained.

He had been entrusted with the glorious revelation of a renewed Creation and had turned away from its light.

Like so many, he preferred the wallow of his cowardice to the heights of possibilities.

He despaired of a second age of Chaos descending should the prophecies be accomplished. And in his ignorance, this thief purloined the writings central to the auguries and claimed to have destroyed them.

In a rage, I swore revenge.

I booked passage north to Alasia, where the thief was believed to have fled. I made landfall at Eliard. I will not relate here again the wanderings that began with my first step onto that accursed shore, except to call them long and fruitless.

For too long, I scoured that place. I moved through the unbroken countryside and through the pens that pass for its cities. The trail always eluded me, and, despairing, I often returned to Eliard to regroup and begin the search anew.

But after so much fruitless searching, I found him at last.

It was in an unusual place he had managed to elude me. A city of the Aerie Coast, not in Arasynia, where the thief had fled.

He proved resourceful. Starting his trail in Eliard, he trekked slowly outside of the Empire to the city of Caliss, if such a flotsam place can lay claim to such a title. It was there I caught my quarry.

He had accepted employment as an Aerian tax collector! Such a disgraceful fall in station for a brilliant scribe, who once had at his fingertips the wealth of the Empire's knowledge and the catalog of man's secrets. But not a position entirely unsuited, I suppose, to his thievery.

He toiled by day in the vaults of the governor's squalid palace, crammed alongside others of his ilk, counting coins, preparing official records for the treasury.

He was miserable. I know this because I spied on him daily. I watched when he left the drudgery of the offices at day's end, and I followed him through the crooked streets when he returned to rooms he had taken in a nearby inn.

His expression betrayed his dejection each evening as he trudged home over slushy streets, bundled against the raw spring wind.

His wife and children awaited his return each day. Their eager reception was the one thing that seemed to relieve his misery, and I raged at even this small respite. His family seemed oblivious to the destruction he had wrought through his theft.

I knew the time of my vengeance was drawing near. I savored my mounting rage. I was eager to give way to it. First, though, I required knowledge of the disposition of the tablet. Thus, I bided my time, continued to spy.

Unknown to the thief, I often disguised myself to slip into the taproom and watched as he took meals or sometimes to hoist a drink with the insipid innkeeper who appeared to be his casual friend. Cowled in rough *plain garb (the red vestments of my Order would have drawn too much attention), I appeared as any other dock hand taking his evening meal. And so, I surveyed the thief as he went about his routine.*

I listened. I learned. And when I could no longer abide my wrath, I moved against him.

I remember the night vividly.

He had spent the evening with his family as I, unseen, clinging to the rough-hewn stone wall outside of his room, observed them through his windows' gauze draperies.

Soon his children were put to bed, and his wife made to retire.

With a kiss, he left his wife for the taproom downstairs. "I'll be back shortly," he told her.

I hurried to the roof to wait. Even condemned men receive a final meal. I allowed the thief to pass the last hour of life with drink, food, and companionship, unmolested.

It was more than he deserved.

I waited in a chill and drizzling rain. I savored what was to come and sunk in my imaginings of how it would transpire. I was therefore caught unaware by the sudden flare of light in the window below that marked the thief's return.

I searched my heart for one last hesitation against my course. I found none.

Over the wall, I went, held aloft by a silent, conjured wind, and I watched through a seam in the curtains as he prepared by the light of a candle to retire for the night.

He undressed, settled into bed, and kissed his sleeping wife. He rose on one elbow and licked his thumb to snuff the candle beside his bed.

Darkness enveloped the room.

I waited. How long, I don't know. But after a span, I entered the room.

A whispered word unlocked the window's clasp, and it silently opened wide.

I stood in the darkness, listening to the deep breathing rising from beneath the blankets.

My anger galvanized me. Here lies the thief, comfortable, unconcerned, content beside his wife. I had chased him across an ocean! I boiled inside; I was incensed as never before.

I advanced upon the bed.

I pulled a dagger from beneath my cloak. Afterward, I recall being mildly surprised to see it. It was something I noticed from afar.

I had planned first to accost him, I swear I did, to rouse him and demand answers. Why his betrayal? What misplaced morality had moved him to such treachery? Why those he trusted and loved, and who had loved him in return, had he made into his mortal enemies?

I believe I wanted to hear pleas for forgiveness upon his lips. And above all, I wanted to know what he had done with the tablet.

The dagger was in hand. I gripped the hilt tightly and tested its edge with my finger. I smiled to feel the keen blade draw blood.

It was as if I was only remotely connected to the actions of my body.

I observed but did not feel my hand draw back the covers.

"The thief's face was serene in sleep. His wife nestled in the crook of his arm, her face lost beneath the tangle of her dark hair.

His eyes opened.

He looked at me without comprehension for a dreamy instant before recognition dawned.

"Why?" I screamed.

"Where is it?" I raged.

"Do you know what you have taken from me?"

He had no opportunity to respond.

Each of my questions had been punctuated by the thrust of my blade.

His blood spattered my face. I did not feel it. I only know because later, I washed it away.

Blood poured from the wounds in his neck, pooled on the mattress of his bed.

I was dimly aware of his wife's screaming. I turned the blade on her and her cries dissolved into a choking protest.

She slumped on the bed, blood welling between the fingers clamped to her throat.

I turned my fury back on the thief. I stabbed him again, repeatedly. The bed rocked beneath the force of my thrusts. The headboard slammed the wall.

He was dying. His lips moved, but no sound issued forth. His last words, whether a plea or a curse, went unheard by any denizen of this world.

The sound of weeping filled the room.

I stared blankly, uncomprehending, at the motionless figures in the bed. The woman made sounds deep in her throat, but her eyes were fixed and clear, devoid of tears and light.

No, not them ... the sound had risen behind me.

I turned, brandishing my knife. A child stood in the shaft of moonlight slanting through the open window. She shivered and wept, her hands clutched to the side of a cradle that I had not noticed before.

A cradle.

The gulf that had separated my deeds from my understanding narrowed, disappeared.

I stared in disbelief at the bloody dagger held in my shaking hand. Bile rose in my throat.

The heap of blankets in the cradle began to stir slightly. The little girl stood trembling; her hand clamped protectively to its rail.

She stared with eyes that betrayed no fear, only shock and incomprehensible sorrow ... and a single question: "Why?"

I shook my head to clear it. I looked at the dagger. I turned to the bed but shrank from the sight there. Their blood spattered the wall. The light from the street slanting through the open window highlighted their garish wounds.

The child slumped to her knees, and her long hair veiled her face. She descended into a heart-rending shriek of loss.

I wanted to say something, anything, to mitigate that despair. At that moment, however, noises arose outside the door. A voice urgently raised. I heard a key fumble in the lock.

There was no time for words. In my confusion, I ran, inadvertently bowling over the girl. She fell heavily to the floor. I concealed myself in the shadows until the bulky figure in the doorway fully entered the room, noticed the carnage on the bed. I plunged out the window. I spanned the alley to fasten on a wall opposite the inn. Clinging there, I watched the window across the way for the pursuit I knew would follow.

Within a span of heartbeats, a face appeared at the window. I recognized the innkeeper. His eyes were wild with fright and disbelief as he scanned the alley *below for some sign of an intruder that, seemingly, had escaped out the window.*

Finding nothing, he clasped the window and closed the drapes.

Finding the roof, I remained there for some time, my heart tripping.

I recalled the cradle and the small formless figure that had stirred beneath the blanket. Above all, I remembered the face of the child. Her anguish matched my own when I realized what I had done, what had been lost to the dictates of a rage I could not control.

Removing myself to the street below, I tightened my cloak against the rain and returned to a place I had secured earlier for myself. A place I could rest far from the scene of the crime I meant to perpetrate.

But, of course, I returned.

It was several days later. I allowed time for the uproar to abate. Though sick at heart and haunted by the devastation in that child's face, I intended to complete my search. I did not mean to leave the city until I had uncovered the tablet or learned of its fate.

I found the room much as I had left it, with the exception that the walls had been cleaned and the cradle removed.

Moving stealthily through the room, I brandished the medallion given me by the Drolanjan of the Nay'fein. By its light, I searched for some trace of that which I sought.

The stone brightly flared when I approached a small coffer resting upon the dressing table.

I lifted the lid with trembling hands. It was empty. I patted the cushioned lining with impatient hands but soon stopped as the medallion's radiance flickered and then died, plunging the room back into darkness.

The thing I sought lodged in that casket once, but no longer.

My teeth gnashed in frustration.

I crept that same night into the room where the children of my victims were quartered. They had been moved to a different room but still accessible by a window. And through the window, I entered again.

The girl had slept fitfully, her twisted sheets and blankets testifying to her restless slumber.

I felt a stab of pity as I leaned over her, at the fresh tracks of tears beneath her closed eyes. I swept these emotions from my thoughts and concentrated on the task at hand. Carefully, so as not to rouse her, I placed the cool disk to the flesh of her face. The colors flowing over the medallion continued to shimmer but did not intensify.

I think I nodded to myself, my suspicions confirmed. The thief may have studied the tablet in the presence of his child but he had dared not share the writings explicitly with his daughter. The Brethren committed the Words of Power through oral tradition to acolytes within the Order, their timeless energy implanting upon the receptive minds of their listeners. The medallion would betray any who had knowledge of the Words.

The thief had well understood the risks involved in initiating such an untrained mind to the mysteries. The disc's cold indifference to the girl confirmed no such tutelage had taken place.

A sudden wail from the cradle startled me. This time, I had noticed the infant's bed upon entering and had given it a wide berth. I did not want to look upon that innocent's face and see reflected there the consequence of my rage.

The girl stirred, pulled toward consciousness by her brother's cries. Convinced that there was nothing more to learn by remaining, I fled back the way I had come.

The tablet had left an ethereal trail around the city that I followed for days. It proved a pursuit of a ghost. The phantom resonance had embedded in the earth and air upon their arrival in Caliss, for the medallion continued to shine. But the faint impression of their long-ago passage from the harbor, about the city, and especially throughout the inn, offered no solid thread to follow.

I spent much time in the city, following every lead, investigating every possibility. By night, I broke into what passed for a royal library in that barbaric land and ransacked the collection. I sought any clue the thief had hidden the writings there. I found nothing. The governor's residence, in which the thief had toiled, I also visited. There was no place the thief might have visited where I did not follow, covertly by night, gaining entrance to secret places, searching for that which had been stolen.

I could only conclude the thing was nowhere in Caliss.

Somewhere, in his long flight across the northern continent, the thief must have concealed it in another place.

There was nothing left except to retrace my steps, to begin the search anew.

And so, I continue in my quest, always lamenting how the intemperate fear of one misguided man had foiled the ambitions of a new age.

I curse myself for a fool when I remember how close I had come to ending my journey that fateful night in Caliss, how my reason had given way to rage before it could receive its answers.

And as I journey, I sometimes dwell on those two children, so brutally orphaned. The liquid light of the medallion strobing on the smooth flesh of that girl's face, the cry rising from the nearby cradle ...

In those times, I am torn between my righteous anger and pity for those innocents forced to suffer for the thief's malfeasance.

But even in my regret, I do not deceive myself. For my desire will suffer no distraction. I would gladly carve the hearts from them both this very today if it somehow led me to that I seek.

The weeping had overtaken Alonna early in her reading. Through a veil of tears, she had pressed on, drawn by the Mage's omissions, an unsettling sense of fulfilment blossoming in her breast.

Years of agonizing questions were being answered in an abrupt and dramatic fashion, and she refused to shy from the horrible details.

Having reached the end, she collapsed, sobbing. An all-pervading grief invaded her: For the loss of her parents, for Vergal, for her own life's dreams wasted in connection to the intrigue that had nothing to do with her yet had cost her everything.

Consumed by anguish, Alonna failed to notice she was no longer alone until a gruff voice proclaimed, "That is her. She has the writings."

Alonna blinked, immediately registering red-robed men standing at the open door to her room.

One, a portly man whose robes billowed around him like a stage curtain, stood slightly in the lead of the group. His lips lifted in a disdainful sneer.

"Kill her," the man said.

CHAPTER THIRTY-TWO

They padded soundlessly through the eternal night of Undermarch, as even Guile now called the otherworldly realm.

They were days out of the city now, in a warren of caverns more exotic than anything Guile had encountered before in his wanderings alongside the Nay'fein hunters.

Shattered columns of quartz and crystal, ablaze with the profuse fluorescence, jutted from the cavern floor and stabbed like the points of knives from the cavern roof above.

The pale light cast deep pools of shadows behind every rocky outcropping. The Nay'fein watched these black basins warily as they passed, their senses attuned for any sound or movement, though none was evident beyond the barely perceptible whisper of their own footfalls across the rubble-strewn floor.

The mercenary was now dressed after the manner of the Nay'fein, having long-ago abandoned, at his companions' insistence, the chattering mail that presented more of a handicap than protection in the hushed realm where only the silent survived.

Guile now wore the light, silk-spun garments peculiar to the Nay'fein. Both the flexibility and the protection the garments provided astonished him. The Nay'fein applied finely ground minerals of some alien variety to the spider silk and wove in mushroom fibers that added surprisingly to the garments' toughness. It was akin to wearing supple leather but without the rigidity of that armor.

Guile carried his longsword still. He refused to part with it. Though the stone-capped maces and hammers the Nay'fein favored were formidable instruments in battle—as Guile had many occasions to witness—they, nonetheless, felt unwieldy in hands that for years had brandished blades. Guile had successfully argued, through example, the advantages of allowing the mercenary to keep the simple blades he had taken from the downed Imperial soldier during their flight through the March—an episode that, to Guile's reckoning, now seemed to have happened to someone else, in a different lifetime.

As a concession, Guile agreed to pad the sword's holster and black its blade, so his surface weapon would not betray them to the hearing nor keen vision of the predators that roamed the interminable maze of Undermarch.

Save his ruddier complexion, Guile might have appeared as any other Nay'fein. His time underground had impressed upon him their mannerisms, especially their all-pervasive awareness of their surroundings when traversing the dangerous caverns. Despite the outward similarities, Guile felt anything except close to the creatures who shared his company.

Guile had realized long ago that the Nay'fein, despite their amiableness, were no friends but his captors.

And the realization grew sharper with every passing hour.

He had not seen Vergal nor Sh'ynryan for a long time. The Nay'fein had failed to uphold their long-ago promise to escort Guile out of Undermarch after the Mage and boy were settled. Instead, they offered excuses. Vergal was deep in his studies with the Drolanjan, they advised, learning swiftly to read and master his growing magical abilities with each passing day. The boy was far too absorbed in his education to be interrupted, though Guile was always promised the day would arrive when they would reunite.

As for the mercenary's desire to be out from Undermarch, it was out of the question—for the time. The hunting season was upon them, the Nay'fein explained, and the creatures roaming Undermarch were too numerous and dangerous for any small contingent of warriors to handle. Guile had seen the many dangers of the dark beyond on the road to their city, they reminded. The mercenary was urged to show patience, to wait for the annual cleansing, in which the city's warriors poured into the tunnels to rid the passages close to the city of the marauding creatures that had grown bold enough to draw near. Then the path to the surface would be clear, they promised, and Guile could safely return home.

Besides, his companions countered, did Guile not enjoy their company? Had they not received him as a revered guest, his every comfort unquestioningly provided? Did not his eyes behold wonders that the surface masses had no hope ever to see? Was he not privy to secrets and knowledge surface scholars would kill to possess? Was it not enough to fill the hours in challenge and sport until he could return to the surface?

There was no arguing. The Nay'fein alternately dismissed or ignored his concerns, countering them with renewed invitations to hunt, or yet another dalliance with one of the eager Nay'fein women, many of whom seemed to delight in Guile's exotic and—in their words, "otherworldly"—appearance.

Guile had to admit his lot was not entirely unfortunate. The Nay'fein provided him sumptuous quarters. Guile enjoyed a massive suite of rooms, hewn from the walls of the city cavern, in the finer section of the community, secured behind beautiful wrought-metal gates and manned by a personal retinue of bodyguards to deter any curious citizenry who might entertain notions of pestering the odd surface dweller.

The Nay'fein informed him that the huge rooms were his as long as he desired them. He began to feel an odd attachment to his suite. He had never owned a home, and it was a satisfying sensation to have a private space larger than Gelbrek's cells—especially one so richly adorned and furnished—to hang his sword at the end of a day.

He grew comfortable with his surroundings and at ease with the creatures who frequently invited him to one feast or another at this or that noble house or- as on this day- to join the hunting parties in search for game.

If Guile was captive, he was a well-kept one, but a captive, nonetheless. He perceived the Nay'fein had no intentions of releasing him from Undermarch. He began to despair of ever seeing the light of the sun again.

Guile had come far in conquering his fears of being deep below ground. He barely felt the suffocating panic that seized him in those early days. The vaulting ceilings of most caverns rose so high and were lost in such complete darkness that he sometimes imagined himself a surface dweller still, wandering beneath a black and starless sky.

Only when their paths led through the inevitable tight passages—narrow arteries between the veins of larger tunnels—did the smothering dread return. These moments convinced Guile that, even if he could somehow find them in this subterranean maze, he could never alone navigate the twisted paths to the surface.

Guile's misery intensified. He could not stay, yet the Nay'fein would surely never allow him to go. Only by ignoring his predicament could he endure it. And thus, Guile continued to accept invitations to feasts, to follow the warriors on the hunt, having convinced himself that with patience, he would see the realms of sunlight again, even as an unquiet portion of his mind screamed curses for deluding himself.

If only I could see Vergal, Guile thought as he followed the hunters through the quartz chamber. His companions had assured him of the boy's well-being, and Guile had no reason to doubt their truthfulness. He had witnessed the esteem and reverence with which the Drolanjan regarded Vergal when the strange band at the king's neck had exploded in color, and Vergal had fallen senseless at the Drolanjan's feet.

They had carried the boy away, and that had been Guile's last glimpse of him. He received informal updates into the boy's progress at the palace, where the royal tutors and scribes instructed him. It was rumored Vergal had learned in short time and with supernatural swiftness to read the words of not only his own language but that of the Nay'fein, absorbing every lesson put to him, reading, writing, and commanding dialects it took scholars lifetimes to master.

The Nay'fein whispered in awed tones of Vergal's growing competency with the Words of Power. They talked among themselves of ancient prophecies Vergal's arrival had convinced many Nay'fein were now on the cusp of being fulfilled.

Guile smiled when he recalled these reports. He sheltered no doubts that the incredible magic the boy had manifested on the trail had only grown in potency under the proper tutelage. He felt a stab of longing to see the lad.

Of Sh'ynryan, Guile heard little. It was common knowledge the Mage was quartered in a wing of the Drolanjan's palace. But it was rumored that the Mage had been given no part in Vergal's training, and the snub had angered the Mage.

It was a comfort to know Vergal and the Mage were near and well, even if he could not see them.

The hunting party halted in a crooked tunnel. The Nay'fein warriors suddenly relaxed, opened flasks and skins, and drank heartily of the mushroom brew they favored. They chattered easily amongst themselves in loud tones punctuated by unguarded laughter.

Confused, Guile dropped his gear in the quickly growing pile at the center of the clearing and searched the milling warriors for Ker'alstil, the party's leader. He found him talking earnestly amid a knot of men. The conversation died as Guile approached. Ker'alstil, tall for his people, nodded above the heads of those surrounding him and gestured Guile aside to speak privately.

Ker'alstil offered a benign smile, but Guile thought he caught a hard look in the man's glittering eyes. The mercenary suddenly felt ill at ease, though he knew not why. Guile had come to count Ker'alstil as the person closest to a friend among the Nay'fein. The two had broken bread, drank, laughed, and hunted together, but never in that time had Guile spotted such flintiness in him.

"Ker'alstil," Guile greeted, speaking slowly with his imperfect command of the thick Nay'fein tongue. He slipped into his own language when the strange dialect failed him. "Why are we stopped? Is it wise to relax the guard and make such noise in the tunnels?"

Ker'alstil's smile did not touch his eyes. "Our runners have reported back. The tunnels are clear all around. This area was recently purged. The scouts attest to our safety."

"Purged?" Guile replied, frowning. "I don't understand. If there are neither game nor predators to be had, what are we doing here? I was told this is a hunting party."

"It is."

"Then what do we hunt?"

"There is quarry about, right enough, but perhaps not the variety you imagine."

"You speak in riddles, Ker'alstil."

"For your protection, Guile," the Nay'fein answered solemnly. "For now, trust me and do not concern yourself. We have journeyed long to reach this place, and now we will rest. Let us eat, drink, and sleep. When we awake, you will be refreshed, and I will share all you need to know."

With a final penetrating look, Ker'alstil turned away, leaving the mercenary to his increasingly anxious thoughts. Something was amiss; his instincts screamed it. The Nay'fein hunters cast him sidelong glances as they prepared camp and diverted their gaze when they caught him looking.

Despite his unease, Guile ate well and partook his share of the mushroom brew as it made a circuit of the company. The warriors talked loudly and often laughed, raising their flasks in hearty toasts to one another as the intoxicating beverage took effect. Guile allowed himself to relax and join in the comradery. Later, he went to his bedroll—a soft affair fashioned from the omnipresent spider silk that provided cushion from the rocky cavern floor—and fell immediately into an exhausted sleep.

How long he slept, he did not know, but a light kick to his leg woke him. He opened his eyes to find Ker'alstil looming above him in the half-light.

"What is it?" Guile said hurriedly, blinking away sleep. He jolted upright. "Is there danger?"

Ker'alstil did not reply.

Grim-faced, the Nay'fein warrior dropped Guile's sheathed sword on the ground beside the mercenary. It landed with a clatter, shattering the silence.

Coming fully awake, Guile noticed Ker'alstil's pale companions fanned in a half-circle behind him. All vestiges of their previous humor and ease had disappeared. Their features were set in stony dispassionate masks; their enormous eyes flashed eerily in the murk.

Guile's hand closed instinctively on his sword. "What is it?" he asked again, truly alarmed. The campsite seemed in order; no sign of danger presented itself. The Nay'fein stood at rigid attention, watching him coldly.

"Are you refreshed, Guile, was your sleep sound?" Ker'alstil asked in an imperturbable voice.

"Yes," Guile answered distractedly, rising and looking around uncertainly.

"Did you eat enough? Do you require anything more?"

"I'd like to relieve myself," Guile said, smiling dubiously. "And I'd like to know what's going on."

Ker'alstil did not smile in response. "First, tend to your needs," the warrior replied. "Then all shall be made clear."

It was a highly-strung Guile that disappeared around a cleft of rock to empty his bladder, his mind racing. He returned to stand in front of the stiff-backed assembly, his expression questioning.

"Ah, I see you've belted on your sword," Ker'alstil said, pointing. "Excellent. You will need it. You asked me what quarry we sought in these empty tunnels. Now you will have your answer. I regret it, Guile, but our quarry is you."

Guile barked a laugh that immediately died when he realized the Nay'fein had not spoken in jest.

Guile stepped back, his hand on the hilt of his sword. Eyes wide with disbelief, he scanned each impassive face. "Ker'alstil? What nonsense is this? I am your friend!"

A hint of an expression that might have been sorrow touched Ker'alstil's eyes, though it quickly vanished. "Yes, Guile, I counted you as a friend. But my Drolanjan has called you an enemy. Therefore, we declare you an enemy as well."

"What crime have I committed against your Drolanjan?"

"It is his right to judge who lives and dies amongst us, and it is our duty to serve his wishes."

Ker'alstil shook his head as if angry.

"Why could you not submit, Guile?" he said in a rush. "Why was it so needful that you depart this place, where we kept you in luxury and offered our friendship?"

"You hold me against my wishes," Guile said, anger rising to replace his alarm. "Gild the cage as you will, but its occupant remains captive. I am not of your blood; I cannot endure this lightless place forever. My desire to be home is as natural as anything you might feel if I forced you to the surface! How can you fault this?"

His angry glare turned to encompass his fellows. "How can any of you fault me?" he demanded heatedly.

"You desire to be away, to make a report of us to the surface dwellers," Ker'alstil accused.

"I would not!"

"The Drolanjan has examined your heart and seen the truth of the matter. He knows your distaste for the Mage and your zeal to protect the boy. These things distress him; they run contrary to his intent." Ker'alstil stood to his full height. "Our king passed judgment on the deceit in your heart," he declared. "Now, we must deliver his sentence."

The Nay'fein slapped his war hammer across an open palm.

"You mean to strike me down, dishonorably, beneath the weight of numbers?"

Ker'alstil shook his head. "We offer you an honorable death. We offer you the opportunity to defend yourself, to die with your blade at hand. It is a tradition of my people. You are allowed free rein in these tunnels. We shall seek you out, individually, thereby giving you the opportunity to meet us in singular combat."

"Perhaps you will elude us or kill us," the Nay'fein warrior added grimly. "We all respect your prowess with your weapon. Honor demands the outcome of the hunt by no means be certain."

Guile shook violently, in rage or fear he did not know—perhaps a mixture of both. He fixed a venomous stare on Ker'alstil but offered no reply.

"Do you accept our offer of an honorable death?" Ker'alstil asked. "Or is the sentence executed here, now?"

"Have I any real choice?"

Ker'alstil shrugged. "The choice is yours. I offer no judgment on your options."

There was no choice but one. Through pursed lips, Guile responded, "I accept."

"Excellent," Ker'alstil said, his voice suddenly brisk, business-like. He waved at the pile of gear. "Take as many belongings and provisions as you can carry. As I said, our warriors recently purged these tunnels of predators, though I cannot with certainty say none have since returned.

"The caves and tunnels are extensive," he went on. "Even our people can become lost in their web.

The labyrinth may lead back to your world. I cannot vouch, but the possibility should please you."

"Leave, now," he said glumly. "Soon after, we shall follow. We will not know the passage you took, so we must divide in search ..."

"This is all sick sport to you!" Guile interjected.

"This is our way," Ker'alstil replied simply. "You do not understand, so I will not attempt to convince you nor make apology for our traditions to an outlander. Know this, though: We offer you an honor valued highly by our own people who receive it."

Guile sneered. "Are thanks in order then?"

Ker'alstil ignored that. He motioned to the tunnel. "Go," he said. "Swiftly."

Sweat beaded Guile's forehead. His tongue flicked over dry lips. He took a hesitant step back, eyes roaming the assembled Nay'fein warriors for any hint of movement. They stood still as the stone surrounding them, watching.

Bending, never turning his back, Guile swung a satchel and waterskins over his shoulder. He stood straight, hesitating, a final plea in his eyes.

"Begone!" Ker'alstil roared.

The uncompromising timbre of the Nay'fein's voice decided him. Sparing a final baleful glare, Guile turned and ran into the tunnel beyond.

CHAPTER THIRTY-THREE

"Kill her," said the red-robed man standing in Alonna's doorway.

Alonna dove to the floor, landing hard on her stomach in time to hear the roar of rushing flames and feel the baking heat. A gout of fire immolated the bed where she sat an instant earlier.

Alonna darted her hand beneath the bed, her fingers closing on the hilt of the scimitars kept there.

She found her feet in time to leap and avoid the fierce jab of a red-robed assailant's dagger.

She flailed with her sword and knocked the blade out of her attacker's hand. The man stepped quickly out of reach of her other scimitar.

"You prolong the inevitable," the red-robed man called above the crackle of flames.

The heat was staggering; it singed Alonna's hair, her eyebrows.

"Who are you?" Alonna cried, swiping her sword again to force back another menacing red-robe.

The fat red-robe sneered.

"Someone who knows your crimes," the man snarled. "Someone bound to avenge his Brethren."

"They accosted me! I defended myself!"

"Is that so?" the man laughed, a sound without mirth or warmth. "Then given your record, I suppose my actions then might also be construed as such."

"Who are you?" she demanded again.

The red-robe dropped a short bow—no easy task, given the ample waist he needed to fold. "I am Danyalius. It pleases me that you know the name of your executioner."

It dawned on Alonna that the red-robed fellows, though similarly clothed, were not Magi. They had her cornered but made no effort to speak their strange words against her. That some of her attackers were mere mortals relieved Alonna. But the Mage worried her greatly.

Still, she saw cause for hope. Despite his confident demeanor, Danyalius appeared unsteady on his feet, his face blanched and sweating. Alonna remembered the exhaustion that claimed Jalwyn after each exercise of his power and saw her opportunity. The Mage's release of fiery energy had staggered him and bought her precious time before he could repeat the feat.

Danyalius's companions harried her, her back to a wall on one side, a blazing bed on the other.

The men dropped their daggers only to replace them with swords, pulled from beneath the concealing folds of their robes. They brandished the blades and advanced threateningly.

The closest red-robe thrust forward his sword. A swing of Alonna's left blade knocked it aside, followed by a jab forward with her right scimitar. Her attacker leaped beyond the sword's tip but, set off-balance, fell back into his fellows.

Alonna pressed her advantage. She fell to her knees, driving one blade into the meat of her opponent's inner thigh and lifting its twin to stab his exposed stomach. She shifted her weight forward against the blades, propelling the screaming man away from her, then quickly leaned backward, pulling free both blades.

Danyalius bellowed from somewhere behind the remaining red-robes, but Alonna paid him no mind. She was too busy countering the expert strikes of the infuriated red-robed warriors swarming around their fallen companion.

Alonna rocked on her heels as the larger, stronger men worked her uplifted scimitars. Vicious, two-handed swings of their swords nearly jolted the hilts from her hands. The space Alonna gained by felling the first man closed as the warriors banged at her defenses.

It was all Alonna could do to lift a sword to deflect the strokes. Her arms grew numb from the jarring blows. She felt the composure Rostalin had instilled in her begin to drain away. She saw the promise of a painful death in the bared teeth, half-lidded eyes, and relentless battering of the red-robes.

Walls and an inferno confined her on three sides. Alonna knew her salvation depended on moving forward, on finding room to maneuvre.

Wheezing from exertion, she allowed her attackers' next ringing blows to drive her back against the wall. She slumped there, exhausted. The red-robes braced, expecting a countermeasure, but when Alonna offered none, they jumped forward in unison, seeking to complete their advantage.

It was the tactic Alonna expected.

When the red-robes lunged, Alonna pitched forward in a roll. Her trailing scimitars opened bloody lines across the men's exposed legs. She regained her feet instantly and, battling her mounting exhaustion, pivoted to confront the assailants now standing behind her and boxed in on three sides!

The red-robes moved to turn, but their injured legs would not fully support them. They labored. Alonna seized the advantage, driving her heel smartly into the wounded leg of one red-robe. The leg snapped to the side. The red-robe screamed and pitched to land on the blazing bed. The flames instantly caught the man's robes, engulfing them.

Danyalius screamed behind her again. His voice was less shaky, much stronger than before.

Her remaining assailant found his back to the wall. The wound in his leg looked shallower than his companion's, and he remained standing to meet Alonna's charge.

Steel rang. The red-robe deftly turned his blade to parry Alonna's rapid attacks. He pushed off the wall on his backswing and kicked Alonna in the stomach. The man used his injured leg for the strike, and so it lacked power but was sufficient to stagger the depleted woman.

Alonna's arms ached; it hurt to lift her blades. Her breath escaped in gasps, and a burning stitch in her side warned of impending cramps. Her forearm bled profusely, where one of the red-robes' swords nicked her. She took consolation, though, in her attacker's similar exhaustion. The red-robe had his back against the wall, his chest heaving, watching her warily from behind the length of his sword.

"You die now!" Danyalius yelled, his vigor restored. He shook his hands free of his voluminous sleeves and raised them in front of him, fingers clutched like the talons of a hunting raptor.

He chanted something, swiping the air in front of him ...

...and Alonna abruptly soared off her feet.

She smashed first into the ceiling before plunging to land hard on the floor.

The world whirled around her. Her rib, still tender from her encounter on the road to Speakwater, screamed in fresh agony. Her head pounded, and her back and knees ached abominably where they had each been driven into the ceiling and floor.

She lifted her groggy head. The room swam in her vision, but she spotted the Mage, laughing and moving into the room. Behind her, she heard the panting warrior push himself off the wall.

Then Jalwyn was there.

He veritably flew through the open door, his legs pumping in a running stride. Yelling an angry oath, he tackled Danyalius from behind.

His rush staggered the big Mage, who lurched sharply forward but did not fall. Jalwyn bounced off the much larger man. Danyalius turned to meet Jalwyn's renewed charge in time to envelope him in a bear-like clinch. The two staggered off-balance on the tips of their toes, struck the window, and disappeared outside amid a resounding smashing of glass.

"Jalwyn!" Alonna screamed, rolling to rise, making to go to him.

She did not get the chance. Growling, the remaining red-robe materialized from the pall of smoke, his sword uplifted. Alonna rolled aside, but the man's downward chop clipped Alonna's shoulder, eliciting a gasp of pain.

The stench wafting from the blaze was revolting as the corpse of Alonna's initial victim charred within the heart of the magical furnace. The red-robe paid it no mind. He advanced on shaking legs. Alonna scooted on her rear to place her back to the wall. She lashed at him feebly from her seated position, but the red-robe easily batted her sword aside and thrust forward for the kill.

She pivoted her head in the same instant of the jab, and the sword tip thudded into the wall a hair's breadth from her earlobe.

A primal scream erupted from her. Her second scimitar flashed out, driven by the last of her remaining strength.

A blow the red-robe missed.

Jarred by his sword's impact with the wall, the red-robe had no time to react to Alonna's second strike. The blade's hooked tip sliced neatly through the flesh of the man's abdomen and into his organs beyond. The red-robed pitched forward, gurgling. Alonna slid sideways down the wall to avoid his slumping body.

Bloodied, weeping angrily, and hurting abominably, Alonna forced herself to stand. The smoke roiled out the shattered window, siphoned by the cool night air. She stumbled toward it, dreading the sight she expected to see below.

What she saw instead stunned her.

The Mages contended still, though not on the ground.

Undermarch

The pair twisted and writhed in the air, suspended just beyond the broken window.

Their red robes billowed and snapped in a growing wind as the pair wrestled in a spinning, airborne pirouette that might have appeared comical were it not so lethally earnest.

The elder Mage, Danyalius, worked his mouth furiously, but no words issued forth as Jalwyn, who appeared to hold the upper hand, gripped the puffy flesh of the man's fat throat.

Danyalius's hands blindly alternated between Jalwyn's wrists, in a vain attempt to pry the younger Mage's fingers off his throat, to Jalwyn's face, where the elder raked bloody gouges down his cheeks.

Alonna heard Jalwyn's screaming even above the roaring wind of their melee. "You dare touch her!" he thundered. "You would put your vile hands upon her! I'll kill you!"

His fingers dug so deeply into Danyalius's throat that they disappeared into the overlapping flesh of the elder's doughy neck.

The pair spun rapidly in space, locked in their violent embrace, dim figures growing darker as they drifted farther into the blackness.

"Jalwyn!" Alonna cried, reaching in vain for the Mage.

Jalwyn hesitated at the sound of Alonna's voice, and Danyalius spotted his opportunity.

With a desperate surge of energy, the larger man bent back Jalwyn's grasping fingers, eliciting a cry of pain from him. Danyalius struck a sound blow to Jalwyn's face and shoved the younger Mage away. The force sent the Mages spinning away from each other until the energy was expended, and they faced each other again across a vast expanse of the empty night air.

"Traitor!" Danyalius shrieked. "Ignorant cur, blasphemer! You violate your oath."

The man threw back his head and laughed.

"You do not yet comprehend your defeat," he shrilled. "Sh'ynryan's silence can only mean he found the Stone. He stands ready to usher a new age, and the folly of those who defy him will be justly rewarded!"

A crowd had collected on the expansive lawn beneath the circling Mages. People drawn by the fireglow emanating from the inn windows gestured in shock and disbelief at the spectacle of the red-robes hovering and drifting in wary circuits opposite one another, far above their heads. The air crackled and sparked in the Mages' revolving wake.

"You are insane!" Jalwyn yelled across the gulf. "You would kill innocents in the name of their salvation!"

Danyalius ignored him. "I am honored to begin the punishment of the unbelieving today!" the Mage snarled.

His mouth worked in the syllables of a strange word that Alonna could not hear above the wind. Danyalius thrust his hands forward. The gesture impelled a screaming force before it, unseen except for its effects. The force smashed Jalwyn, throwing the Mage backward and whirling away into the deepening dark.

Alonna could watch no longer. The stinging smoke funneling around her and out the broken window nearly blinded her. She bent, hacking and coughing, ducking beneath the smoky pall to clear her stinging throat. The heat from the blaze behind her intensified, cooking her back through the thin material of her nightclothes. The flames set up a crackling chorus. Above their song, she heard the raised voices of people nearby, yelling into the smoke-filled room, calling for survivors of the conflagration.

"With your death," Danyalius yelled above the din, "the first of those to oppose us are dispatched."

She lifted her head. Danyalius floated outside the splintered window frame, wheezing as he drifted forward. The exertion of his magic seemed evident on his face, yet he wore his mouth in an evil grin.

Alonna met the Mage's gaze. She said nothing. But when the Mage lifted his hands in the gesture she had learned only too well, Alonna reacted.

She ran, stepping once on the sill to launch herself through the window.

Her scimitars led.

Both blades whickered down in overhand descending arcs.

Alonna's blades buried to their hilts in Danyalius's chest.

She hung from the protruding handles, her legs scissoring over empty air, the upturned faces of screaming onlookers far below.

The Mage reached with trembling hands for the steel in his chest.

Alonna, struggling to keep her grip on the damp hilts, wrapped her legs around those of the Mage, reached one hand for his neck, and hauled herself level with his face.

"You are dead," she whispered softly—as gently as a lover—into the Mage's staring eyes.

With the light in his eyes fading, the Mage slumped in her grasp.

The magical force suspending them released, and they fell.

But only for an instant.

Alonna numbly watched as Danyalius continued his tumbling descent.

She did not immediately understand why she had not fallen alongside him.

A bleary second passed in which she realized the ground and the people below were growing smaller, not larger.

She rose swiftly, steadily into the night.

Arms looped around her waist pressed her close. A familiar voice whispered in her ear, faintly above the gusting night wind and the passage of their own ascent, "Alonna, brave Alonna."

Alonna turned in his arms to face Jalwyn, throwing longing arms around his neck, the blades still in her hands clanking loudly as they met behind him, and smothering his mouth with grateful, passionate kisses made wet by her own tears.

"Carry me from here," she whispered. "I know now. I know who Sh'ynryan is, and I know what he has done."

Another soft kiss on Jalwyn's eager mouth, another urgent whispered demand, "Take me to him," she murmured. "Let this be done."

The city's highest spire fell below them now.

They drifted as do eagles, with their wings spread to the wind. The magical skin of swirling air carried them as if along a swift current.

The lights of Speakwater spilled in all directions beneath them.

"Yes, Alonna," Jalwyn answered. The young Mage felt alive and in love. He felt angry and invincible. He did not flag nor grow weary as he commanded the night's winds. Fury and passion stoked the furnace that powered his magic now, and he wondered if all the power of the Stone could match the potency of the magic cast in defense of his beloved Alonna... if any force could rival that called to protect the ruined, broken, beautiful and perfect woman who had become his all-consuming love.

They would soon see.

They moved west, borne on howling winds.

Jalwyn vowed to test the limits of his abilities against the elder Sh'ynryan, who had bereaved his love.

And upon all others who dared stand in her way.

CHAPTER THIRTY-FOUR

His stumbling flight carried Guile awkwardly over the uneven stone floor. The contents of the waterskin sloshed; the food sack shifted, and his sheathed sword jounced gracelessly at his hip. His uneven load nearly knocked him off balance several times, but he straightened and continued his flight.

His rapid footfalls echoed like tumbling stones through the empty caverns. He increased his speed until the noise of his labored breathing also reverberated off barren walls, sounding in his ears like the panting of a pursuing beast.

Guile turned corners blindly and slid down slopes haphazardly. He had no option but to trust in Ker'alstil's vow that the dark chambers ahead had been cleared of predators. He thought only to put as much distance between him and the Nay'fein camp as possible before their pursuit began. Guile had no idea when the chase might start—an hour, a day, mere moments later? His life depended on the honor of his would-be executioner, an alien creature possessed of reasoning and morality he could not hope to comprehend and who had betrayed him utterly.

Guile cursed himself for a fool. He had humanized creatures without humanity; he had projected upon them the ethics and empathy of men. He resolved not to repeat the mistake.

Guile skidded to a stop, heaving for breath. Resting, the mercenary took stock of his surroundings. He found himself near the edge of a bowl-like chamber. Sharp-edged rocks spiked up from an undulating floor of crushed minerals. The ubiquitous luminescent moss cast its weak and glittering sheen upon the bare stone.

Above the bowl, Guile barely picked out several protuberances that might have been narrow ledges. His ears, made keen by his new hunter's instincts, detected the faint rush of air emitting from somewhere above.

Guile paused. Continuing his flight held little hope; the Nay'fein knew the terrain better. He needed to make a stand. Guile determined to reach the upper terrace, to claim higher ground should the Nay'fein pursue him into the cavern. He hoped—however unlikely—that some seam in the wall above might somehow open passages leading to the surface. The presence of the whimpering wind above at least gave reason for hope.

The serrated rock of the floor shrugged up into cavern walls worn smooth by time. Finding handholds proved no easy task. He made it halfway up; his limbs splayed, his body pressed tight to the cold stone when he detected a noise behind him.

Guile craned his neck to peer over his shoulder. The sharp cave floor appeared far below, though Guile could discern little beyond the leering stalagmites in the faint wash of light.

Drawing a steadying breath, the mercenary focused his attention back on his ascent. His fingernails, abrading the unforgiving rock, chipped and cracked. His wrists and ankles ached abominably from the stress of squeezing shallow handholds. His satchel and waterskins threatened to pull him off balance, and his sword sheath tangled in his legs.

Eventually, though, Guile was rewarded for his efforts. Gasping for breath, he finally hauled himself over a rim of rock and collapsed onto a narrow, natural ledge perhaps twice the length of his outstretched arms. The space was cramped, but Guile settled gratefully into it, his limbs trembling from exhaustion.

He had little time to rest. Forcing himself to his feet, the mercenary surveyed the ledge. It was a slender ribbon of rock, curving unevenly—narrowing and broadening—almost the length of the entire wall before disappearing into the distant blackness. He could still hear a soft whistle of wind somewhere above, indicating an unseen opening. There appeared no way to access his perch without an arduous climb. He allowed himself to relax a little. The Nay'fein would corner him if they could reach him, but first, they would have to find him. His climb at least bought time to think.

Guile slaked his thirst with water, though he sipped it sparingly. He didn't know how long he would be stranded on the ledge, away from a water source, and intended to preserve his stores.

Guile gathered his silky cloak around him, pulled his knees to his chest, and stared blankly at the cavern floor below. Time passed—impossible to know how long in this lightless hell—before Guile realized he was watching faint movement on the lower level. Barely perceptible at first, he discerned at length a silhouette nearly lost in the tangle of shadows thrown by the spires of rock.

Guile bolted to attention. His eyes explored the murk for the barely glimpsed figure without success. He was ready to turn away when he saw it again: a mere darkening of the shadows between two leaning pillars of rock.

"I see you, bastard," Guile whispered.

The flitting figure proceeded through the darkness, tracked by Guile's narrowed eyes. At last, the figure encountered an open expanse drenched in a condensed beam of moss luminescence. The figure stepped tentatively into the illumination, its head turning to rapidly scan the surrounding terrain.

Guile recognized the figure immediately—Calvith, a young hunter from Ker'alstil's band. The slender Nay'fein wore the dyed spider silks favored by trackers and blended easily with the rock backdrop. He might have been a flitting shadow against the rock, his white hair a wash of reflected light off the marble. He gripped the haft of a granite-headed mace in one hand as he crept.

Guile remained utterly still, daring to draw breath only when necessity compelled. The young tracker was a renowned scout and hunter, among the band's finest, and obviously following a trail detectable only by himself. What kind of markings Guile left in the barren stone for the Nay'fein to follow, he did not know, but the mercenary respected Calvith's skill enough to assume his stealthy pursuit was not blind. The Nay'fein had traced Guile's steps perfectly and would soon stand at the base of the ledge beneath the mercenary.

Guile eased himself until he lay face flat on the ledge, out of sight of any probing eyes on the cavern floor. If Calvith followed the trail up the wall, the Nay'fein would not see the mercenary until he peered over the rim. The advantage would then belong to Guile.

Gripping his sword, still and sweating, Guile strained his ears to detect any stray sound. His heart beat quickly and, to his overwrought nerves, too loudly.

Guile concentrated so fiercely on gleaning sounds from below that he did not hear the one from above until the last instant.

Booted feet thudded lightly on the ledge in front of him. Guile cried out and rolled in time to avoid the downward stroke of a granite hammer.

Guile looked up into the stern face of Ker'alstil.

"Guile," the Nay'fein said reproachfully, shaking his head. "I expected better of you. Following you was like trailing a herd of Kastneths through the tunnels. Did you learn nothing?"

"You lied," Guile growled, rising on one knee, keeping his sword point thrust ahead of him. "You gave me no time to set my defense; you hunted me in a group when you vowed otherwise."

Ker'alstil laughed. "And you made straight for a fissure leading to the surface," the Nay'fein replied lightly. "You followed the freshening air, without realizing, I'm sure. Were we to allow you to scale halfway to the surface before beginning our pursuit? The Drolanjan would have taken a dim view of us had we permitted you to escape, I fear."

Guile looked at the ledge above. A sickly mix of despair and exhilaration greeted the realization a portal to the outside world lay within reach.

But Ker'alstil stood to block the way, his wicked hammer outstretched.

"I have nothing to lose, Ker'alstil," Guile warned, rising smoothly to his feet. "Move, or I'll cut you down where you stand."

Ker'alstil straightened to his full height, made a few expert passes with his hammer, testing its heft and balance. "You will not leave this place, Guile," the Nay'fein said without rancor. "Even now, Calvith scales the wall and, as you see, my companions have arrived."

It was true. Shadowy figures appeared on the upper ledges. Guile could not distinguish their faces in the gloom, but their tense postures indicated their rapt interest in the scene unfolding below.

Guile blocked them out. They were a secondary problem. Ker'alstil, standing armed and dangerous ahead, was his immediate concern. Guile pulled a long dagger from his belt, gripped it fretfully in one hand, and held it aloft alongside his longsword.

"I value this opportunity to meet you in singular combat, friend," Ker'alstil said sincerely. "I have admired your prowess since first I met you. I am eager to see how your blade fares against my weapon."

"Don't talk to me of singular combat, Ker'alstil; don't imagine yourself an honorable warrior," Guile snapped. "You've brought reinforcements. Should I gain an advantage, your companions will surely rectify it. What honor in that?"

Ker'alstil frowned at Guile's words. Turning, he made a series of exaggerated hand gestures toward the ledge. One of the dark figures across the cavern lifted its arms and gestured in return. Ker'alstil turned back, grinning broadly.

"The battle is our own,'" Ker'alstil said expansively as if a great favor had been granted. "Should you dispatch me," Ker'alstil's said, his grin growing wider, leaving no doubt how he believed the encounter would end, "you will then contend with my brethren, but not before. Does this satisfy honor?"

Guile's replied in an explosion of movement. As Ker'alstil spoke, the mercenary had hooked his foot under one of the fist-sized rocks that littered the ledge. He kicked it forward now, sending the rock hurtling toward his opponent's head. Ker'alstil lifted his hammer in time to block a blow to his face, but the rock caught him partially on the fingers of his weapon hand, and the Nay'fein gasped in mixed surprise and pain.

"Ah, well done!" Ker'alstil boomed happily. But his words were swallowed beneath the clash of weapon strikes as Guile followed the hurtling rock with a blinding series of blade swipes that set the Nay'fein back on his heels.

The spectators above whistled and shouted appreciatively. Guile's flashing sword and darting dagger battered and nicked Ker'alstil's massive war hammer but could not elude the weapon to strike its wielder.

Ker'alstil worked his weapon expertly, hands sliding deftly up its length to cross-block a descending sword stroke, then sliding as quickly to the middle to deliver a forward jab or round-house attack that painfully jolted Guile's arms when he parried.

Guile abandoned his intention to penetrate the weapon's defense and focused instead on the hands holding it. Chopping with his sword to freeze Ker'alstil in a defensive posture, Guile used his dagger to open several slices on the Nay'fein's exposed hands as they maneuvred the hammer hilt.

Blood as red as any Guile had spilled spattered from the wounds, dotting the Nay'fein's sweating flesh, blossoming like crimson flowers on his hands.

Death by a thousand cuts, Guile grimly thought as he proceeded to score a series of nicks on the Nay'fein's bleeding hands.

Enraged, Ker'alstil changed tactics. Choosing a moment when both Guile's blades were driven high, the Nay'fein dropped into a crouching, roundhouse kick that caught Guile squarely on his shin. The strength behind the blow snapped the mercenary's leg back and staggered him a pace. Ker'alstil pressed the advantage, pounding Guile's upraised sword with two-fisted, overhand swings of his weapon.

However, Guile's nicks and scratches had begun their work. The hands clutching the hammer were raw and bloody and losing their strength. Though Ker'alstil's downward strokes still rattled the bones in Guile's arm when he parried, at least the force behind them no longer threatened to crack his blade in two.

Guile cinched the head of the Nay'fein's war hammer between his crossed blades, stepped between the upraised weapons, and kneed Ker'alstil sharply in the meat of his thigh, narrowly missing the man's groin. Ker'alstil grimaced and retreated a step, by luck avoiding a forward thrust of Guile's trailing dagger.

Limping, breathing heavily, the warriors faced each other warily from behind their brandished weapons.

"Had we scored the bout, I would give you first advantage," Ker'alstil wheezed, his lips stretched between a smile and a grimace. Blood dripped freely from several long cuts in Ker'alstil's hands.

"Absolutely," the mercenary grinned between pulls for air, "but the victor is the man who remains standing. That remains unresolved. Patience, though, I will rectify that blunder straightaway."

Guile transformed into a helix of blurring steel.

His life at stake, with everything to lose, the full skills secured over an adult life of violence and mayhem unleashed.

Blades dipping and stabbing, metal ringing and sparking on polished stone, Guile danced inside Ker'alstil's shunting to score several telling hits. A chop of his sword incised the flesh of his opponent's right arm; a poke of his dagger punctured the thick muscle of the Nay'fein's left leg.

Exclaiming in pain, Ker'alstil gripped the butt and head of his war hammer and, turning the weapon sideways, dropped and drove the length of the handle solidly into Guile's mid-section. The blow launched him backward against the rock wall of the ledge. He gasped for air.

Despite his wounds, the Nay'fein advanced, snarling, hammer held aloft, two-handed. Guile pivoted—his tortured lungs protesting the movement—and pistoned his heel into Ker'alstil's exposed stomach, blasting the wind from the Nay'fein and knocking him flat.

Crumpled against the ledge wall, Guile swung his sword feebly but was gratified to strike the fallen man's leg and lay open the pale flesh. Ker'alstil screamed and drew his legs back, blindly, seizing and throwing rocks to cover his scampering retreat. One sharp rock struck Guile's face, ripping the flesh off his cheek. The skin hung in a grisly flap.

Faint from pain, Guile pushed the wall to lever to his feet. Every movement ignited his tortured lungs. Favoring his throbbing shin, Guile commenced a staggering advance on his fallen foe. He awkwardly kicked aside Ker'alstil's fallen hammer. The Nay'fein continued to fire rocks, but the projectiles grew progressively smaller as he exhausted those within reach. Guile ignored the stinging barrage.

Guile stepped on his opponent's wounded leg, provoking a clarion cry of anguish from the fallen warrior. The mercenary's sword hovered over the Nay'fein. He grinned down the length of the blade at his victim.

"You lose; you die," Guile said, his voice choked behind a cocksure smile.

The dread in Ker'alstil's blazing eyes softened, then disappeared. He met Guile's determined gaze levelly, offering a knowing smile of his own.

"No, friend," Ker'alstil whispered. "I win. You die."

Ker'alstil's eyes darted slightly. Guile realized the betrayal, but too late. A wicked blade pierced his back, skewered his heart; in the same moment, Calvith's evil chuckle sounded in Guile's ear.

Guile's eyes widened. His lips parted slightly, a rebuttal behind them. Only blood came forth. He slumped to his knees. His hand reached weakly for the sharpened stone protruding from his back.

The mercenary's eyes never strayed from Ker'alstil, who hoisted himself on his good arm and intently watched Guile's dying gestures.

"You lied," Guile burbled, his voice wet with blood.

Ker'alstil smiled. "Yes," he admitted, "but it is a lie I will live with."

CHAPTER THIRTY-FIVE

"Is this the place?" Alonna asked impatiently.

"Perhaps," Jalwyn returned hesitantly. He stood and clapped the dirt from his hands and the dust from the knees of his vermillion robe.

The Mage stood at the bottom of a crater, examining the fissures and pits marring the face of the cavity's sloping walls. Alonna crouched at the lip of the basin, peering anxiously down at him. Vespen, the Imperial administrator of the March, stood apart, scrutinizing them both with a grimace of pure distaste.

The Mage stumbled over the loose scree littering the crater floor and groped his way up the slope to join them. Alonna took his hand to assist him. Jalwyn straightened, flapped the dust from his robes again, and stared speculatively back into the hole.

What other holes have you two crawled out from? Vespen thought, regarding them stonily.

However, the administrator kept his thoughts silent. After all, the Mage had arrived at the March bearing documents signed by the Emperor's continental Governor and the elder Mage of Speakwater, one Harbesh Neomonitis.

Those documents requested—in an officious vein that brooked no denial—that Vespen place himself at the bearers' disposal as they searched the tunnels beneath the March for some obscure purpose of their own. The thin Mage and the lush, leather-clad woman had been most fascinated by the large crevasse they discovered shortly after commencing their investigation.

Vespen sighed wearily. He held a hand to his brow in a vain attempt to soothe the fierce headache developing there. He had spent much time trying to forget another red-robe and the motley crew accompanying him who had been the originator of the sinkhole in the lower corridors of the fortress. That same crew had initially been in his custody but had somehow escaped to wreak havoc.

And now, a second adherent of the detestable red-robes stood before Vespen, poking around the scene of his most spectacular failure, tirelessly asking probing questions in addition.

Vespen opened his eyes, distantly comprehending he was being addressed.

"Ah, begging your pardon, Sir Mage," Vespen stammered. "I'm feeling unwell, I'm afraid. I missed your question."

A hard look passed over the Mage's features, but his tone, when he continued, stayed neutral. "I asked you to tell us again, please, exactly what transpired here."

Vespen sighed. It seemed he had related the story a hundred times already to the damnable sorcerer. If not for the eager anticipation marking the red-robe's features, Vespen might have thought the man was tormenting him with his constant questions, rubbing

Vespen's face in the ashes of his most monumental failure as administrator of His Imperial Majesty's March.

But Vespen could not say as much. He certainly could not protest the red-robe's redundant request. The wording of the Governor's correspondence had been precise: Co-operate in any way the Mage asked.

"As I've said, sir," Vespen began, careful to keep his tone conversational and not accusatory, "the three of them were found in the wilderness, miles east of the March. When the Imperial patrol encountered them, the trio was being harassed by a pack of Obroths. The company commander instructed his men to dispatch the Obroths, then took the three—a Mage, a mercenary, and a young boy, as I've indicated—into protective custody. There were two reasons for this: They were discovered illegally in Arasynia, and for their own safety, because the wilderness through which they were traveling was rife with beasts, such as they encountered."

"Yes, yes," said the woman impatiently and, Vespen thought, testily. "We've heard this. Please, just tell us again the details of their disappearance!"

She was a beauty, Vespen had to concede, with her flowing mane of black hair framing a flawless face, exquisite for the sum of its parts rather than any singular trait. However, the woman's irritable demands for information—a near-constant since the pair had arrived— had begun to wear on the administrator.

The Governor's correspondence had been clear, Vespen reminded himself. So, he pressed on.

"Yes, to recap," Vespen said. He couldn't quite keep the exasperated tone from his voice, but the man and woman did not seem to notice.

"The three were being held in custody until we could sort out the details of their entry into Alasian territory," Vespen went on. "They somehow escaped custody."

Vespen paused and coughed uncomfortably. "I believe I've covered the particulars of that incident already."

Jalwyn shot him a firm look. "Indulge us, please, and cover the details one more time. For the sake of clarity."

Vespen bit back the retort he would like to have given. Their documents bearing the Governor's personal seal indicated smart remarks that might not be the wisest course of action to pursue.

Drawing a settling breath, Vespen rehashed what he had come to call, simply "the incident." He had not personally witnessed any of the mayhem, Vespen noted, but accounts provided by the garrison troops indicated the scene had devolved into one of tumult.

The guards tracking the escapees through the vaults had been ambushed and attacked, Vespen said. He omitted the official report that guards had first fired upon the fleeing prisoners. A strong wind had begun to howl through the corridors, buffeting the soldiers and driving them away from the fugitives. The resulting impacts with the walls and floors had injured many Imperial soldiers, Vespen made certain to note firmly, knocking several men senseless and breaking bones in others.

Those who endured the initial battering had bravely pressed on. However, the red-robe leading the company, the man called Sh'ynryan, had not finished his assault. According to reports, the floor in front of the advancing soldiers appeared to shimmer and swirl, and the solid rock rose and fell like the swell of ocean waves. Chasms opened in the flagstones, and many pursuing soldiers had fallen into the spreading pits. Several more were injured, incapacitated, and, in a few cases, Vespen added grimly, died.

Jalwyn listened intently, often nodding in response to the dialogue. The Mage betrayed no regret and offered no apology for the soldiers' plights. Vespen expected no less, but the red-robe's indifference toward the men his vagabond colleague had killed infuriated the administrator, nevertheless.

"Yes, please continue," Jalwyn said hurriedly, "What happened next is of great interest to me."

Vespen sighed. "Well, as I said, the accounts vary after that. Some men report the fugitives climbed down into one such hole. One soldier fallen into this pit feared for his life, for the mercenary had earlier stripped weapons from their fallen comrades. Instead of dispatching him, they clawed around in the dirt as if looking for something. Apparently, they found it, because they either disappeared or dropped out of sight down another hole, depending on which version of events you choose to believe."

"And this is where I have difficulty," Jalwyn said, ignoring Vespen and turning his attention to Alonna. "What hole? I've inspected the floor of the crater, and there is no hint of any portal or fissure through which they could have passed."

Jalwyn turned again to Vespen, who was by now silently fuming at the Mage's abruptness as much as the man's earlier attentiveness. "Is it possible," Jalwyn asked, "that they later escaped the March?"

Vespen drew himself up proudly. "Impossible!" he declared, his chest puffing. "The fortress was locked down as soon as their escape had been discovered. They were cornered in these corridors, an entire company advancing on them, with more scouring the passages that lead to the upper levels. They did not pass those soldiers.

"The survivors," Vespen laid particular emphasis on the word, "agreed the fugitives somehow disappeared down this hole, even if they could not say how this was accomplished."

Jalwyn rested his chin in his hand and considered. "Then there was only one way," he said.

"Excuse me?"

"Nothing." Jalwyn straightened. He held out his hand to Vespen, who, astonished, shook it.

"Sir, thank you for your attention to this matter," Jalwyn said. "Please extend my thanks—no, the thanks of the Governor—to your soldiers for their bravery and sacrifices in defense of the March. They have performed admirably in defense of the Empire, in trying circumstances. I assure you, their part—and your own—will not go unnoticed by the Emperor."

Vespen twitched. He stammered when next he spoke. "The ... the Emperor, sir?"

"Indeed, sir," Jalwyn said effusively. "You saw the seal upon my documents; you know whom I represent. Upon receipt of my report, the Governor will surely extend his gratitude for your service to the Emperor. I am confident he will requite in kind."

Vespen's smile positively beamed. His surliness toward the red-robe melted away—rain clouds dissipated by the burning sun.

"Sir," Vespen said gratefully, "thank you for your kindness. Please inform the Governor I am His Excellency's most humble servant!"

"I shall."

"Is there any other way in which I can be of service?"

"No, thank you for your patience in relating this difficult account to me. If you will, please give us a moment to speak privately?"

"Of course, of course," Vespen's shocked expression indicated he wished he had suggested it himself. "If I can be of any other assistance..."

"I think that will be all," Jalwyn smiled. "If there is anything else, of course, we will ask."

"By all means!" Vespen enthused. He was backing down the length of the corridor. With a final ingratiating nod, he turned a corner, his Imperial bodyguards falling in step behind him, and the retinue disappeared behind a turn in the wall.

Jalwyn waited until the long shadows of the departing men had disappeared before he turned to Alonna. She was giggling behind her hand, and, at the sight of her, Jalwyn began to chortle too.

"Expertly done," Alonna said. "I thought he'd never stop hovering, then with a little name-dropping and flattery, poof, he disappeared."

Jalwyn laughed again.

"But you said something," Alonna said, taking a serious turn. "I asked you if this could be the place you sought, the entrance to Undermarch, and you said 'perhaps.' What did you mean?"

"Exactly what I said—perhaps. The soldiers' accounts of the incident are convincing; I have no reason to doubt them. But where is the evidence that this is the portal to the Undermarch of Sh'ynryan's papers? His journals included nothing so specific as a particular portion of a subterranean corridor."

"Yes," said Alonna distractedly, "his journals." She remembered her revelations while reading the Mage's journals—writings that revealed the red-robe's role in the murder of her parents.

Alonna shook her head and motioned for Jalwyn to continue.

"I have a theory," he said. "I believe we are not seeking a specific portal. We are in the place above the Undermarch, according to Sh'ynryan's writings, and to a Mage of his abilities, that may well have been enough. He may well have opened a new portal, rather than combing these corridors to find the particular place where he opened a passage those years previous."

"So, what do you propose?".

Jalwyn sighed. "I suppose I propose doing something that I have never done before. I propose to open a portal in that same way I suspect Sh'ynryan did."

"And how was that?"

"Through the Words, of course," Jalwyn said offhandedly. He held out his hand. "Come," he said, pulling her to the crater. They picked their way down the rubble-strewn slope to the bottom.

Jalwyn stood still; his chin lifted, his face alert. He appeared to be listening.

"Do you feel it?" Jalwyn asked softly after a long pause.

"What?"

"No, I suppose you would not. But I do. It is so faint, but it's there."

"By the Stone, Jalwyn!" Alonna exclaimed, borrowing one of the Mage's favorite imprecations, "just tell me what it is!"

"It's a residue, an imprint; call it what you will. It's the fading shade of powerful magic wrought here in the past."

"Vespen said as much," Alonna replied. "Sh'ynryan obviously used the Words of Power in his encounter with the garrison soldiers. Isn't it likely you sense his evocations from their battle and not the portal?"

Jalwyn stayed hunkered on his knees, clawing in the dirt. After a moment's frantic digging, he replied, "No, it is something else. Something more concentrated, precise. It emanates here. It's so very faint, like a breeze that caresses your brow but is not strong enough to stir your hair. But I feel it!"

Alonna knelt and joined the Mage as he clutched at the earth. She scooped a fistful of dirt and let it strain slowly through her fingers. Clapping her hands to clear them, she tipped Jalwyn a wry glance. "I will have to trust you on this."

Jalwyn ignored her. His color was high, and his expression excited as he continued digging.

"Yes, yes," he said with a widening smile, "That's exactly what he's done. He opened a doorway. He must have! The foundation stones of these lower corridors must rest above but near to the caverns below."

"You're certain of this?"

"Let's find out." Jalwyn pushed his sleeves up his arm and rubbed his hands together briskly.

"You mean to open a portal?" Alonna breathed. "Do you even know how?"

"No, but I am near certain he did not know either. Not precisely how, in any case. He made an educated guess and took a risk. I believe it paid off."

Jalwyn stared at the pit floor critically, like a fighter taking the measure of an opponent before battle.

"How do you know how to begin?"

"The Words call the elemental power, Alonna, but the caller's mind and his will channel it, giving it form and purpose. If I can strongly conceive a use for the power, I can attempt it. If the mind and will are strong, the power can manifest the intent."

Alonna blinked at him.

Smiling, Jalwyn patted her hand patiently. "Trust me," he said. "Besides, a door has already been opened here; I am only trying to reopen that which now exists. The energy I expend will be much less than what Sh'ynryan mustered."

Jalwyn stepped back and stood looking at a spot in the earth. Muttering beneath his breath, he held his hands spread in front of him and closed his eyes.

Initially, nothing happened. Alonna heard nothing except the distant spluttering of a torch set somewhere on the wall above the crater. It was her eyes that captured the first inkling of Jalwyn's success. A dot of light so faint at first that she thought she imagined it, blossomed in the middle of the bare earth at Jalwyn's feet. The dot mushroomed, became coin-sized, then plate-sized, then quickly swelled into a pulsing oval of blue-ringed light. Loose rock and earth began spilling over its sides as it widened.

Alonna gasped. She peered cautiously into the breach and noted a broad tunnel fading to blackness.

"Jalwyn!" she piped joyously. "There is something down there; I can see it!"

Jalwyn said nothing. A frown creased his brow, his lips pressed in a bloodless line to maintain his concentration, and beads of sweat formed beneath the Mage's hair and dripped down the length of his nose, reflecting in the intensifying light spreading at his feet.

Alonna bent over the opening, peering deeper inside. The light ringing the hole beamed between the gaps in her splayed fingers.

"Something is reflecting back," she reported excitedly. "I think I see the bottom, but it looks very far away."

"Get the gear!" Jalwyn croaked, silently berating himself for not dragging the equipment down with them before beginning his incantation. The oversight would add to the time needed to hold open the portal, and the strain was significant.

"Right," Alonna said, leaping to her feet. She sprinted up the steep slope, her sheathed scimitars jouncing noisily, and began pushing their gear over the edge. It tumbled to a rest near Jalwyn, who by now trembled violently. Jalwyn hoped his knees did not buckle under the spasms wracking him.

Alonna skittered after her rolling gear. She watched the Mage expectantly.

"Get in!" Jalwyn demanded in a pained cry.

"Just jump in?" She balked. "We'll kill ourselves!"

Jalwyn did not have enough strength to argue. His knees crumpled, and he fell heavily on his side.

The light-ringed hole in the earth immediately began to shrink.

"Jalwyn! It's closing!"

Jalwyn clawed the earth, trying to find his knees again. "Get in ..." he moaned.

There was no time to argue. Alonna kicked the gear over the lip of the portal, which continued its insidious constriction. She tried to ignore that she heard nothing strike anything solid below.

Grasping Jalwyn behind his elbows, she dragged him forward. The Mage had lost consciousness and offered only dead weight. With a fierce effort, Alonna yanked Jalwyn to the opening and, breathing once deeply, pulled him alongside her into the darkness.

Vespen, choosing that moment to return to request clarity regarding a timeline for the Governor's future correspondence with the Emperor, appeared at the crater's edge in exact time to see four legs disappearing down a glowing circle in the ground.

In a span of heartbeats, the circle collapsed to a slit before vanishing.

Vespen stood staring blankly for a moment.

Only the spluttering of torches in their sconce disturbed the silence and the darkness.

He spun on his heel.

He walked away, whistling.

You did not see that, the administrator's panicked thoughts advised him sternly. *You will forget you ever saw that.*

Vespen turned the corridor, resolved never to return to that portion of the fortress's tunnels. That stretch of dark catacomb had offered him horrors enough to last a lifetime.

CHAPTER THIRTY-SIX

Vergal wore soft clothing. He possessed shining jewelry and enjoyed fine food and a spacious suite of rooms, richly furnished, reserved for his private use.

Above all these, though, Vergal had books and maps.

And for the first time in his life, he could comprehend the marvels they contained.

Vergal bubbled inside with pride. The boy's life-long desire had been to learn to read. His parents had not been there to teach him. Nor could he fault his sister for this gap in his education; nobody knew better than Vergal how her long years of servitude at the Wayfarer Inn allowed neither time nor means for such instruction.

The education deprived of him as a child the Drolanjan now bestowed in abundance.

More than a year had passed since his abduction, the flight through the storm, and the subsequent journey through Gelbrek's underground lair.

Sometime early in his journey to the March, a birthday had passed, unnoticed. Then in the long sojourn underground, yet another birthday had come and gone. Considering the math while lying in the comfort of his bed, Vergal had been startled to calculate he was now thirteen years of age.

A newly minted teenager, Vergal had so far enjoyed the first flush of young manhood. Things were changing as he grew older, internally, as well as in the world surrounding him.

He stood noticeably taller now; that was one thing and the most obvious. Vergal's skinny frame had fleshed out considerably. The rigors of the road had given his lean arms new, knotted muscles, which Vergal prized and had become quite vain. His dark hair no longer lay flat and wispy upon his skull. It had thickened, gained texture, and acquired fresh, luxurious waves and curls, which Vergal believed flattered him immensely. His skin radiated good health. A ruddy blush painted the smooth cheeks of his face, accentuating his tangled hair and flashing eyes. His jaw seemed thicker now; the cheekbones above it strong and pronounced.

There was no denying it. The boy Vergal had become a young man.

And such a young man! The Drolanjan and Sh'ynryan, on the rare occasions when the former permitted the latter to visit, praised his new, robust stature. They did not restrict their approval to his outward development. Above all, they commended Vergal's internal progress.

Vergal hungered for such praise. His lifetime of uneducated ignorance taught him to most dearly prize intellectual improvement.

As naturally as he had grown, Vergal had learned to read. He conquered the intricacies of his native tongue, and that of the Nay'fein with an ease even Sh'ynryan confessed had not marked his own education. Vergal now wrote as fluently as he read, in a prose that charmed his tutors.

Vergal's mastery of magic, however, delighted above all else those charged with his education.

The student quickly outstripped his teachers in the early days of training. The power Vergal merely kissed in the wilderness manifested itself now as intimately as a lover. His command of the Words of Power grew daily until his tutors despaired of having any more to teach. The Drolanjan intervened. The next stage of the boy's education, the king decreed, now fell to him alone. Sh'ynryan's visits following this declaration grew rare until they stopped entirely.

The royal court whispered. The people exclaimed among themselves. Never in the Nay'feins' history had it been so, they declared, a king instructing a commoner! And a surface creature at that! The unprecedented move caused a stir among the populace as word spread. However, the Drolanjan ignored the gossip. Perfecting Vergal's education mattered most to the king.

Vergal, too, heard the rumors. He sometimes wondered why the Drolanjan found the need to fast-track his studies, but he did not complain. The magic simmered inside of him, pent up and seeking release. It rushed easily, like a fast stream over sharp rocks, when permitted to manifest. The faster he learned how to control it, Vergal thought, the better for all involved.

The Drolanjan's motives were not unadulterated, Vergal realized. Though the king's pending role had never been explained to his satisfaction, Vergal realized he played a significant role in whatever was to come.

A perfunctory rap at his door startled Vergal from his deliberations an instant before the door banged open to admit the king. Vergal suppressed a grimace of irritation. The Drolanjan saw no need to observe customs of propriety. Vergal supposed he understood why. The king did, after all, rule all he surveyed in his underground realm, even those spaces given over to a guest. The knowledge never suppressed the faint lance of annoyance he felt whenever the Drolanjan exercised his prerogative and burst in unannounced.

Vergal rose and bowed. The king smiled at his obeisance; the expression nearly lost in the flickering shadows thrown by the moss globes lighting the room.

"Vergal," the Drolanjan said expansively, stepping forward to enfold the boy in the folds of his soft-spun robe. Such displays of affection by the king had become common. Vergal suffered them stoically.

"Drolanjan," Vergal acknowledged with a nod.

"Still growing, I see," the king exclaimed, scrutinizing him. As usual, the king's scrutiny unnerved Vergal. He feared what might happen if those probing eyes somehow found him wanting and if approval switched suddenly to disdain.

Guiding Vergal into a nearby chair, the Drolanjan also seated himself. He leaned over his knees and said, "I have a surprise for you."

The words blurted before Vergal could consider them. "I am to see Guile, then?" he asked eagerly.

The Drolanjan's smile faded. His brow fell. He looked briefly over his shoulder where a knot of royal bodyguards and advisors stood near the door. When he turned back, the Drolanjan's face was smooth and neutral.

"I had hoped to spare you this news, Vergal," the king said sombrely. "You have been pressing for some time to see the mercenary, and such expectation fills your voice that I thought to deflect you and spare you pain."

The Drolanjan sighed deeply and studied the folds of his robe.

"What is it?" Vergal asked, alarmed. He had not seen Guile in the lengthy time since they had arrived among the Nay'fein. The Drolanjan explained how Guile was being indoctrinated into the ways of their underground race, as was Vergal, and those lessons required time. He was learning their customs, that he might survive and thrive among them. But the lessons, by all accounts, had not been proceeding smoothly.

"Drolanjan, what is it? What happened?" Vergal pressed. A worm of panic worked through him. "Has Guile been injured?"

The Drolanjan raised his hands. "Calm yourself," he said soothingly. "Your friend is well. At least, we assume."

"You assume? What does that mean? Where is he?"

Another deep, regretful sigh. "We do not know precisely."

"I beg your pardon?"

"He has departed," the Drolanjan said simply.

"Departed where?"

"To the surface, I presume. Returning there was his only concern while a guest among us."

Vergal's expression was stunned. "How?" he demanded.

The Drolanjan frowned, not appreciating the boy's tone, but he allowed the slight to pass.

"It was during a routine patrol," the Drolanjan explained. "As part of his induction, Guile had joined the patrol groups securing the outer tunnels. It is a position of high honor among our people, and by all accounts, Guile performed admirably. His stealth and efficiency in battle equaled our own warriors'. He earned my men's respect.

"The patrol moved far beyond the usual perimeter recently. They found themselves, quite by accident, near those same tunnels where we first encountered you. Guile began to recognize the terrain and became excited."

Vergal's rapt eyes locked on the Drolanjan, who stifled a smile. No disbelief, only trepidation, marked the boy's expression. Excellent, thought the Drolanjan.

He went on.

"Guile said he felt a lightening of the air, fresh winds in the caverns. Ker'alstil—his patrol leader and my son—assured him he did not, that he and his company entered our realm by way of a magically opened portal.

"Guile would hear none of it. The deeper they traveled into the tunnels, the more he insisted he recognized his surroundings, that the surface was near."

Vergal nodded. He remembered Guile's dread at the prospect of miles of rock above his head and how it increased with every step deeper underground. It seemed natural Guile would feel as if he was ascending back toward the surface as they moved farther from the city.

The Drolanjan smoothly continued his account.

"Ker'alstil thought he had convinced the mercenary of his folly because Guile's enthusiasm faded, and he fell quiet. It proved a ruse."

The Drolanjan sighed again. He lifted sorrowful eyes to meet Vergal's.

"When the patrol took its rest," the Drolanjan said, "Guile slipped away."

Hot tears rising in Vergal's eyes threatened to drop. He lowered his head.

"Ker'alstil searched for him, of course, but Guile had a long start. Ker'alstil could not be sure of the direction he had taken. The camp was at the large crossroads near the lake chamber where you encountered the Kastneths, do you remember it?"

Vergal doubted he would ever forget. The huge armor-plated predators still tormented his dreams. He nodded once, curtly, but made no reply.

"Tunnels branch in all directions from the crossroads, and Guile covered his tracks. They searched for days but found no sign."

The tears flowed freely now, but Vergal wore a hopeful smile. "Do you think he made it out?" he asked. "Is it possible Guile made it to the surface?"

The Drolanjan eyed him carefully. "The tunnels are dangerous, Vergal. I do not want to offer you false hope. Predators range the outer tunnels in great numbers. The odds stood against him, and, as I said, the portal that brought you here was magical in nature. He could not possibly reopen it.

Vergal slumped, but the Drolanjan raised a hand.

"Having said that, let me also say this," he added. "Natural apertures do open onto the surface, far distant from our city. They are difficult to find, and

I would suppose, treacherous to navigate, but they exist. Judging by your friend's talents, if anyone could beat the odds, Guile would."

Vergal allowed himself a brief, sad smile at that. His tears still dripped steadily. "He only wanted to go home," he said in a small voice. "Why could he not go home?"

"You already know, Vergal," the Drolanjan answered sternly. "Our existence is unknown to the surface world. Our safety, our society, depends on our secrecy. In time, Guile would have been allowed to return, of course, but only after we had assured ourselves of his fealty, as we did Sh'ynryan's those long years ago. Acclimatizing Guile to our ways, giving him time to befriend our people... these are means by which we would earn his fealty and have him hold sacrosanct our secret."

The Drolanjan's face grew sad. He reached and clasped Vergal's hand warmly. "He simply did not give us enough time."

A long silence stretched between them, each sunk in his own private thoughts.

The Drolanjan broke the silence, slapping Vergal's knee lightly. "Come!" the king said, rising to his feet. He held out his hand to Vergal, who stared blankly before accepting. The Drolanjan pulled him to his feet. He threw a long arm over the youth's soldiers and guided him toward the door.

"Where are we going?" Vergal asked.

The Drolanjan smiled, his teeth brilliant by the light of the moss lamps. He did not answer, only beckoned once more for Vergal to follow.

They emerged through the stone doors of the palace onto the terrace above the broad plaza. Below, a crowd milled restlessly around the flagstones, and in the center rose a hulking spider, harnessed and outfitted with a royal litter secured to its back.

Vergal turned to the Drolanjan. "A journey?" he asked hopefully.

The king smiled. "Of course," he replied. "Did you think we meant to keep you in your rooms forever?"

"I sometimes wondered."

"Wonder no more. Come, a friend awaits you below."

They descended the curving stairs to the plaza, where the vanguard soldiers cleared a path through the milling Nay'fein citizenry to the spider mount waiting beyond. Vergal caught a glimpse of familiar red robes. The figure turned, and Vergal was shocked at the relief that flooded him to see the dour face that always before flooded him with fear.

A broad smile and genuine expression of happiness melted the stern mask of Sh'ynryan's face. He moved through the press to greet him.

"Vergal," Sh'ynryan greeted him gladly. "You've grown!" he exclaimed, his eyes scanning every inch of his frame.

"I hear that happens," Vergal replied, grinning, unaccountably glad to see the old Mage.

"Indeed. It also illustrates how long since our last visit." Sh'ynryan cast a reproachful glance over Vergal's shoulder at the Drolanjan, who watched the exchange keenly.

Vergal's grin faded. "Guile is gone."

The Mage nodded grimly and placed a comforting hand on Vergal's shoulder. "I know; they've just informed me. I am sorry, Vergal."

"Do you think he made it out, that he is going home?" Vergal asked hopefully.

Sh'ynryan smiled wistfully. "Imagine him, as I do, astride a purloined mount, riding hard on the western road, the wind in that dark curly hair of his and that grin wide on his face at having added another daring escape to his life's long list of them."

Vergal nodded, his eyes shining, "It is my fondest hope for him," he said, his voice husky.

"Good lad," Sh'ynryan said softly.

The Drolanjan broke in irritably. "Come, both of you," the king bade. "Our escort awaits, and time is wasting."

"Where are we going?" Vergal asked the Drolanjan again, but Sh'ynryan replied.

"To the outer caverns," the Mage said. His voice quickened, rife with barely suppressed excitement. "The time has come, Vergal; the king has declared your education complete. We depart on the journey you were born to make."

The Mage smiled, and the Drolanjan joined him. Vergal watched them both expectantly.

"At long last," Sh'ynryan said in a whisper nearly lost beneath the clamor of the crowd. "We seek in earnest the Stone."

CHAPTER THIRTY-SEVEN

They traveled for what seemed days, the harsh beauty of the realm opening before them banishing the need for prolonged delays. A new vista and a new marvel awaited every curve of the twisting corridors.

The place they entered Undermarch had been, to Alonna's reckoning, typical of any subterranean passage, save for a strange, glowing moss carpeting the bare rock. A faint but all-pervading scent of rot and mildew filled the damp chamber. She had never ventured below ground, but the sparse environment matched her imaginings of how such a place appeared.

But the environment changed with nearly every step they took deeper into the gloom.

The sound of running water intensified, then grew faint. The chill dampness permeating the darkness faded, replaced by a dry warmth the companions found in turns comfortable and suffocatingly hot. A wind sometimes moved through the tunnels as if thrown by some enormous though unseen furnace. The breeze stirred exotic scents from the luminescent moss and carried hints of something else, far distant but sulphurous.

They quickly learned the unsuitability of their surface attire and began to strip themselves of various items. Alonna removed her leather armor, leaving her only a light vest over a white sleeveless tunic. Her leather leggings also disappeared, leaving only form-fitting hose to cover her sculpted legs. The sight of her half-clad body might have driven Jalwyn to distraction had not the surroundings demanded every bit of his attention. The Mage, his robes peeled back and tied at his waist in what resembled a makeshift skirt, walked bare-chested through the tunnels, his ears and eyes attuned for any hint of danger.

Trouble had yet to present itself, but the Mage feared an imminent encounter. Several times they heard the clamorous passage of some living creature in the distant darkness. The mounting sense of unease at being watched stretched Jalwyn's nerves taut. He walked with a dagger in hand, murmuring beneath his breath to himself.

The bizarre beauty of her fey surroundings fascinated Alonna, capturing her eye and scattering her thoughts. Like Jalwyn, she walked with a blade at the ready but held its point low. She took note of the threatening sounds that sometimes rose, but only distantly. The voices that had risen to whisper incessantly in her head were so much more interesting and absorbed her attention.

Discover ... darkness ... come...

Faint but insistent, the litany repeatedly played in her ears. Jalwyn was saying something, but his soft whispers barely penetrated the murmuring chorus filling her ears. She turned to him, puzzled, frowning. The worried expression on his face amused and annoyed Alonna at the same time.

His hand grasped her wrist now, pulling her to a stop. She shook her hand free. "What?" she barked, irritable at leaving off the voices' soft refrain.

Echoes of her loud response ricocheted around the gloom. Jalwyn, his eyes bulging, instinctively clapped a hand over her mouth. That proved too much. Instinctively, she straight-armed the Mage, shoving him to the ground. He stared through perfectly astonished eyes. His head whipped fearfully from side to side.

"What is the matter with you?" she demanded. "How dare you cover my mouth!"

She fixed to admonish him further when she became aware of the clamor rising around her. Several dark, squat shapes flitted between the stalagmites shouldering up from the cavern floor. The clashing grew louder.

Alonna raised her scimitar in one hand and groped with the other for Jalwyn. She hauled him to his feet, never taking her eyes off the figures, at least a dozen of them, emerging from the murk.

The figures grew distinct in the glowing moss. Alonna recoiled at the sight of them. She thought immediately of the tales her father told her as a child. The tales never badly frightened her, though they had sometimes raised the flesh on her arms—a tribute more to her father's flair for storytelling than any genuine fear of its subjects.

Not now, with mythical creatures from her childhood imaginings loping out of the darkness. Now, Alonna felt true fear.

"Goblins," she rasped.

Jalwyn, trembling beside her, his knife defensively in front of him, nodded. Alonna drew her other scimitar from its sheath and gripped it tightly.

In her father's stories, the goblins presented an almost comical creature with flopping feet, pointed ears, and long, tapered jaws full of crooked yellow teeth.

Not these creatures ambling toward them, however. Not these fiends emerging from the darkness and banging crude weapons against cruder shields, raising an unholy racket.

These beasts bore only a superficial resemblance to the monsters of myth. Though squat, the brutes approaching betrayed no hint of flat feet or pendulous bellies. These massively muscled creatures possessed long knotted arms far out of proportion to their compact torsos. Coarse black hair framed their inhuman faces, bristling like lions' manes. Their skin shone sickly green by the moss light. Weeping sores and protruding carbuncles covered their bodies, gleaming wetly.

Alonna found nothing remotely comical about the baleful red sheen of their squinting eyes nor their sharp jutting teeth when they snarled.

The creatures growled and danced on the balls of their feet, viciously clanging their shields, working themselves into a frenzy.

"Do something, Jalwyn!"

The Mage was already in action. Jalwyn crossed his open palms a few times in front of his face and whispered something that set off a faint roaring in Alonna's head, not unlike the cacophony of soft voices that had recently bemused her.

Harsh splintering, like the sound that wood makes beneath the cutter's ax, resounded. Alonna searched anxiously for an outward manifestation but saw nothing. Nothing until the monsters leading the pack set up a sudden pained howling.

Many of the beasts dropped to the cavern floor. Alonna, amazed, watched the creatures' strong legs shattering like dry twigs snapped between strong hands. The sharp retort of splintering bones reverberated across the cavern. Jalwyn, his face a mask of concentration, passed his hand across the line of gibbering goblins. Creatures caught in his span fell screaming.

Sharp thin spears of rock twisted out of the cavern floor amid the massed goblins, rearing like serpents to plunge into the advancing creatures. The ensorcelled stone rods blew clear through the creatures' legs, pulverizing bone and rending flesh.

Alonna thrust her scimitars above her head, gripped by ecstasy and a smoldering passion for the slight, red-robed man at her side. "Jalwyn!" she cried.

The Mage ignored her. In the distance, the creatures continued falling to his devastating assault, their leg bones hurtling out at unnatural angles to their hulking bodies as rock spears skewered them and writhed to find fresh victims. The unaffected beasts began to scream in outrage and charged across the sloping cavern floor.

Jalwyn's outstretched hand pulsed palpable waves of force. Bones continued to snap, and goblins tumbled. But the Mage was clearly flagging. There would be no fight left in him once the creatures drew within reach. Alonna flew into action.

Her scimitars chopping, their blades capturing the weak light, she leaped forward to meet the beasts' charge. Infuriated beyond reason, intent only on the Mage, the goblins registered Alonna only after a trio of their mates had already fallen to her blades.

Her offense barely dented the horde. For every goblin at the forefront of the swarm, two more poured out from the gloom. They had stumbled into an encampment of the beasts. How many other unseen creatures were responding to the screams and calls of their fellows?

Alonna's blade relieved a charging goblin of its head. Three more of the creatures emerged behind it, running hard. Alonna guessed running might prove a fine strategy as well. Jalwyn's waves of force had dwindled; the thin shafts of stone seemed stunned now and merely stabbed instead of shattered legs as they whickered and whipped in the midst of the throng. Painful injuries, but minor. His power failing, the Mage scrambled back in the face of the enraged creatures' onslaught, training his hand on those beasts which drew too close. He panted with exertion, and he trembled visibly.

Flight... darkness... daughter... come.

The voices raised their clarion song, and something in their urgent tone gave Alonna pause. *Flight,* the voices advised. *Yes,* Alonna concurred, and, cutting down a pair of goblins blocking her path, she bulled through the press to reach Jalwyn. He slumped against a wall, the creatures surrounding him but capering at a respectful distance, leaping and snarling, afraid for the moment to approach the red-robe who had felled their companions but steeling themselves for a final surge.

Flight. Daughter. Come!

Two more creatures fell to Alonna's overhand chops before those surrounding Jalwyn realized a new danger had entered their midst. They surged to face her, but her charge had served its purpose. Reaching Jalwyn's side, she swept her scimitars in long, whistling arcs. Nearby goblins jumped out of her reach.

Flight. Rise. Come.

"Jalwyn!" she yelled over her shoulder. "You must carry us out of here like in Caliss! It is the only way."

No response. A goblin shuffled forward and swiped with his sword. Alonna's darting scimitar knocked the sword away and opened a long gash on the beast's arm on her follow-through. The goblin, wailing, fell back into the crowd. Two of its fellows leaped forward in its place. The ring tightened. Alonna's blades parried a pair of clumsy strikes, chiming loudly. She thrust the blades into the attackers' chests on the counterattack, and the goblins fell backward, their lifeblood spurting from ruptured hearts.

The beasts' screams of outrage rose to a deafening crescendo. The wall of monsters pressed on three sides.

Jalwyn remained collapsed against the wall, unmoving except for the slow rise of his chest.

No time remained.

What happened was not what Alonna intended.

She only reached for the Mage on an unformed urge to gather him and flee—hopeless as that course seemed—or to die with him in her arms.

But she felt a wrenching sensation deep within herself...

...rise... flight... free...

...and found herself cradling Jalwyn's still form, high above the circle of goblins the instant it crashed in upon the place where they stood bodily before.

She looked into Jalwyn's face, puzzled. The Mage was unconscious, his face slack against her breast.

She had carried them above their attackers. It was she who held them aloft.

The goblins howled and hooted; their sickly upturned faces tracked her progress across the soaring vault of the cavern. They leaped and gestured and screamed in a spasm of primal rage. Several dropped their weapons and took up rocks to throw, but Alonna's swift ascent carried them out of range, and the projectiles fell short of their mark.

Rise... daughter.... sister...

Below, the goblins took to the walls. Their taloned fingers easily found handholds in the rough stone, and their clawed feet propelled them effortlessly. They scaled columns of crumbling rock with the speed of spiders, spreading out in a fan, climbing over one another to cover the cavern walls in an outer skin of writhing monsters.

No weariness, wonderment, nor sense of strangeness bothered Alonna. Bemused, she skimmed effortlessly above the horde, deaf to the goblins' shrieks, listening only to the chorus of voices. The lassitude that overtook Jalwyn when he summoned the wind bothered her not. She felt only mild curiosity to learn how she had done it, and, contemplating that, a cruel smile touched her lips.

She turned back on the goblins—a solid mass of them now, Alonna could see. Many had cleared the cavern walls and now crawled across the vaulting stone ceiling.

Fire... come, daughter... sang the voices, the notes sharp and clear.

The power leaped, seemingly of its own accord. Alonna felt a spasm behind her eyes, a dull throb that was not precisely pain, and the walls and ceiling surrounding her erupted in burning goblins.

Utterly engulfed, the clinging beasts dropped and tumbled, trailing spewing flames and smoke, lighting the darkness, crashing like meteors to the cavern floor.

The voices exulted: *Daughter, we call... we love. Seek him.*

Alonna sent out the power. It was like a knife thrown by her mind. It flared outward, traveling like a flaming snake to ignite the dry cavern moss, branching out in tendrils to overtake and destroy the frantically retreating goblins. The cavern shone; the heat of the inferno baked Alonna's skin and reflected in her eyes.

She laughed and exulted alongside the caroling voices, flinging the power again and again.

Rock cracked loudly, and fissures marred the stone walls. A massive crag of jutting rock tore free of the wall, crashing to the floor to obliterate the fleeing throng below.

Dust and rock rose in a choking plume. Jalwyn, insensible in her arms, coughed and spat. Alonna breathed deeply, savoring the sharp, powdery scent of utter destruction.

The voices remained, full-throated in a pure anthem. Images joined the voices to flit through and fill her mind, a book surrendering its story in a flurry of speedily turning pages.

Alonna saw the darkened cabin of the ship to Eliard and a blanket-shrouded figure lying in the narrow bed. Teraud sat bedside, his lips moving slowly and deliberately as he read from a tablet easily, reverently, his eyes weary, frightened, but intent with purpose. The words he read had frustrated the best efforts of learned scholars, yet he spoke them effortlessly in the dim, rolling cabin without pause. They fell on the ears of the sleeping girl beneath the blankets.

Another page flipped in her mind; the scene unfolding in front of her shifted. Now rain flecked a tall, arched glass she recognized instantly as the window of their room at the Wayfarer. The chamber was illuminated faintly by the glow from streetlamps beyond. The blankets again, drawn tight to the chin of a still young face composed in sleep, yet her eyes wide and unseeing. Teraud leaned forward in his chair, the tablet in his hand, whispering the secrets revealed there into his daughter's ear.

More scenes, more fragments of a distant past. Surroundings melted, shifted, morphed, and blended, but always Teraud emerged at their heart, reading, whispering, smoothing her hair, and speaking wonderful, alien words in a fluid cadence that soothed her now to hear.

Months of nights spent in this way. And she had never known! The man hunted by Magi had wiled the hours of his daughter's slumber, confiding to her sleeping ears the secrets etched on the fragment of tablet. Not tutelage, but transference. Safekeeping. Preservation. The runes etched there sometimes flared, their embers rising, drifting, flowing to fill Alonna's ears, her eyes, her mouth, seeking passage to imprint on her heart. In this way the thief Teraud concealed that which had been stolen.

No, not a thief! Her father's voice rang, faint but discernible above the canticle in her mind. *Steward, custodian, servant...but never a thief!*

There was no anger in her father's tone—Teraud never succumbed to such base emotion—only disappointment, sorrow, profound hurt that unknowing minds had ever labelled him such.

The words, plain to behold yet indecipherable to the Magi, revealed themselves to me. How then have I stolen what they never possessed? How am I blamed for heeding their call, this relic that engraves their invitation? What penalty, then, for delivering them home? I share them now with you, daughter, caretaker...to hold, to preserve, to bestow in the fulness of time.

Alonna frowned, considering this ... but the singing! How distracting, these joyous, pealing, incessant refrains! Her name repeated resoundingly.

Alonna continued her swift passage through the caverns, rising and dipping to follow the contours of the chambers she entered and as quickly left in her shining wake.

Her empty hands stretched in front of her in the gloom. Somewhere in her flight, she had released Jalwyn. She did not fret; she felt him near, locked in the same force holding her aloft—a crimson fleck towed in her turbulent wake. She easily read his blaze of emotions: Love, fear, awe, lust... all lavished wholeheartedly and singularly on her. Alonna smiled but did not turn to him, content for the time to permit Jalwyn's somnolent mind to marvel alone.

A journey of days through Undermarch passed in a span of minutes. Alonna's surroundings materialized, then faded as she entered and departed the space between all things to make enormous strides in her journey.

The dark beauty of Undermarch that so captivated her now seemed mundane compared to the celestial sights she glimpsed passing through those distant spheres. She longed to enter that shining realm forever but could not while the voices remained without. They beckoned still, and their call took an urgent quality. They offered reward and rest, an end to the burden of body and heart she had carried since that night.

The realization drew her cry of elation: The voices promised her Vergal.

Alonna emerged from the space between spaces into the largest cavern she had yet encountered.

It stretched for miles, a massive bowl sprawling in all directions. And the realization that the cavern beneath was filled to bursting with the stone edifices of a subterranean city released Alonna from her musings. She sailed to the center of the city, where she hovered still, oblivious to the distant cries and trumpets rising below.

The streets below bustled with activity. Strange, pale creatures milled about, their faces turned upwards in expressions of perfect astonishment, their long and delicate hands splayed in her direction. Gruesome creatures were strewn through the crowd: massive spiders, outfit in tack and harness. Legions of goblins resembling those she had dispatched in the outer tunnels here wore the shackles of captivity and cowered at the end of chains; their dispirited demeanor devoid of the fire inherent to their wild cousins.

Her appearance high above the cavern and burning with light caused an uproar. A fanfare sounded, and projectiles flew from the ramparts below. Alonna laughed to watch the great javelins crack asunder against the pulsing nimbus surrounding her.

Prodded by their handlers, several of the giant spider-things reared on towering legs and spat streams of acid and venom high into the air—a sheet of deadly reversed rain. Others jetted lines of gummy webs to ensnare her. These fluids and strands either missed and fell to earth again upon the shrieking populace or encountered her fiery cocoon and burned harmlessly away.

Alonna laughed delightedly. She had raised defenses without being aware. Or perhaps wards had been raised on her behalf. The answer did not matter to her since the outcome was the same.

The voices had led her here. They demanded a course of action, and she intended to obey.

CHAPTER THIRTY-EIGHT

The company moved across a wide field of sharp, broken rock, but the Kastneths' long legs easily cleared the obstacles. From the vantage point of his litter, Vergal silently watched the terrain flowing past.

Vergal felt bored and surly. They were days removed from the city and traveling, aimlessly it seemed, through the labyrinth of connecting tunnels that composed the wilds of the Nay'fein's realm. A mostly unseen vanguard of warriors scouted the way ahead. The Kastneths, surrounded by their small army of handlers and guards, followed in noisy procession. The royal party had no need for stealth. No creature of Undermarch would confront a pack of Kastneths and their armed Nay'fein guards.

The Drolanjan and Sh'ynryan shared Vergal's spacious litter, watching him almost constantly. Their constant scrutiny and expressions of expectation compounded Vergal's annoyance. He knew they waited for some grand pronouncement that he had pinpointed the artifact they sought. They seemed to believe the thing would call to him and reveal a hiding place it had occupied since near the dawn of time.

Had their conviction not been so strong, Vergal might have scoffed. However, he stewed in a state of low agitation, biting his tongue against bitter words. Instead, he tried to focus and stay alert for a call he did not hear and watch for a sign he doubted he would see.

The tension among the occupants of the royal litter swelled as the trek progressed. At last, the Drolanjan called a halt. "I weary of the sight of him," the Nay'fein king muttered irritably as his servants helped him dismount. The king's comment was directed at Vergal, though not intended for him to hear. Vergal heard it anyway. And the feeling was mutual.

Standing on solid ground again, Vergal stretched his legs and arms, working out the stiffness. The royal litter's soft couches and gossamer carpets were fine, but the lack of mobility in such a confined space made his limbs ache more than any long hike. He wanted only to walk and work out the soreness.

The Drolanjan had other ideas. "There are hot springs nearby," he said, drawing tight his web-robes. He appeared exhausted. His long hair hung in dirty, unkempt locks. "The opening is too small for the Kastneths, but our guards will escort us," the Drolanjan went on. "We can relax and bathe and take something to eat. Come."

The Nay'fein warriors formed up around them. Scouts melted into the darkness to inspect the cavern ahead. Vergal marveled again at the utter silence in which the Nay'fein moved and how easily they blended to the darkness. The scouts returned shortly, proclaiming the way clear.

Vergal stood at the entrance of a remarkable cavern.

Steaming water churned in pools that pocked the floor of the cavern in profusion. The gleaming moss on the walls was interspersed with columns of exposed minerals and clusters of jutting gemstones. These gathered the weak light and reflected it brighter, purer. Shafts of scintillating light danced around the chamber.

The bright chamber surprised the eye, but the boiling pools captured it. Utterly clear beneath a thin film of foam, Vergal easily spotted the rocky bottom. Luminescent algae hugged the basins' rocky beds. The algae's pale violet light fractured and danced in rippling sheets atop the water. The play of moss-, algae-, and reflected gem-light merged to golden radiance, reminding Vergal of a sun-drenched afternoon. He half-expected to see the molten disk of the sun high above. Only light-dappled rock greeted him. A crushing fear of never seeing the sun's light again seized him: a flash, a quick, sad memory of restless Guile.

The chamber's beauty failed to impress the Drolanjan. He shaded his eyes and complained of the glare. His servants and warriors likewise squinted in the brilliance, a natural enough reaction for creatures shut away from the sun. Once again, it illustrated the difference between Vergal and the alien, cloistered Nay'fein.

"The light is initially unbearable," the Drolanjan griped, "but the eyes adjust. The warm spring waters outweigh the sacrifice and are a balm to aching bones."

"Bathe, relax," the king bade them, "and afterward, we eat. I am famished!" His retinue led him into the steamy chamber in search of a suitable pool.

Vergal sought a private pool of his own away from the others, who appeared to have little compunctions around disrobing and bathing communally. There were plenty from which to choose—cauldron-like holes, hissing and popping from the heat of their crystal water, abounded. Entering one took all Vergal's resolve. The bubbling, steaming water threatened to lift the skin from his bones! However, the initial discomfort faded, and the water settled into a soothing roil around him. A narrow shelf rimming the pool just beneath the surface provided a perch for Vergal to sink into the seething water. The pool clouded briefly, the furious water stripping the dust and grime off his body, but soon dispersed, leaving the water flawlessly clear as before. Vergal scissored his legs happily in the churning water, watching his feet cut silhouettes in the light cast by the radiant algae below.

Clean, refreshed, and freshly clothed, it was a hungry Vergal who wandered into the midst of the Nay'fein preparing to take a meal.

A polished stone slab had been erected, and servants bustled about, setting places and dropping heaping platters of food. Vergal had learned not to look too closely at the roast game offerings that were a staple of the Nay'fein. He knew it was sustaining and often delicious but preferred not to think too deeply about the type of creatures the Nay'fein harvested in their underworld realm.

A contented sigh announced Sh'ynryan's arrival at the table. Wound in a gossamer robe following his bath, his usual red robes discarded for the time, he stood behind his chair awaiting the Drolanjan's leave to be seated. The pale cast of the Mage's skin jolted Vergal. He realized his flesh must appear much the same after such time locked away from the sun. The Mage's chest was sunken, and his belly protruded in a slight pot, but hard muscles corded his arms and legs. The sight dredged a memory of the strength in the Mage's hands the night of his abduction. A hot ember of anger flared inside him at the recollection. Vergal examined the growing muscles of his own arms and wondered how they might soon fare in any such future contest.

The sight of the Drolanjan's body shocked Vergal most of all. The king, wrapped in his after-bath robes, was now revealed as a lithe, muscular creature. If his thin body contained an ounce of fat, Vergal could not detect it. The satiny white arms and legs were long, like Sh'ynryan's, though better sculpted. Coal-black nails capped exceedingly long fingers and toes. The king's exposed arms and legs seemed to reflect the light of the cavern.

The Drolanjan approached the table and motioned Sh'ynryan and Vergal to take seats next to him. He bade his servants and guests to eat, and the meal commenced.

They ate heartily, taking their fill after a long journey and stocking up for the road still ahead. The conversation rose and fell around the table, then split into groups, and Drolanjan took the opportunity to wave his guests to move their chairs closer.

"We have traveled many days' journey," he said conversationally, leaning over his plate. He spoke softly, his words reserved for his guests alone below the drone of conversation. "Assure me once more, Vergal, you have no inkling of the Stone?"

"Nothing. If I knew what I seek, it might help me find it." He could not keep a note of reproach out of his voice.

"You know," the Drolanjan replied, unperturbed.

"A tablet, of some sort, what you call the Stone. I have no problem imagining its appearance—Sh'ynryan has explained it enough—but it is an idea only."

The Drolanjan lifted his head. "Is this so? Since no living man has seen the Stone, I wonder then how Sh'ynryan describes it?" The king sounded amused.

"No less accurately than you," Sh'ynryan put in sardonically, drawing a surprised glance from Vergal. One did not address the king so flippantly.

The Drolanjan allowed it to pass. "Ah, but our people carried the Stone below. Our traditions owe their descriptions to observation, though millennia old."

Vergal eyed the Drolanjan with renewed interest. "Tell me," he said. "Why have you not told me earlier? Surely any information you can offer would help?"

"The One will know the Stone," the Drolanjan replied as if this was self-evident.

"And you believe I am the One?"

"Certainly. Why else are you here?"

"Then why can't I find it?"

"Fear not, the One will hear the Stone. It is written."

"Where is it written? Tell me."

The Drolanjan laughed. "Vergal, have your procession of tutors been in vain?"

"I know the teachings," Vergal replied sourly. "'The One shall find and wield the Stone that was hidden. The Stone shall call to the One in the fullness of time.' Yet I tell you truly; I have no inkling of what I seek or how to seek it. The tutors taught me theory and left me to wrestle with the facts."

The Drolanjan regarded Vergal thoughtfully for a moment. "Well enough, Vergal. There is time. Listen then, and I will share a tale."

And this is the tale the Drolanjan told:

CHAPTER THIRTY-NINE

"In ages past, the Nay'fein appeared as you do now," said the Drolanjan. "We were human, like you, and suppose we still are, though our search over the ages for the Stone distinguished us in custom and temperament from the race, even as our appearance today separates us physically. We were men in those days, no doubt, who took upon ourselves responsibility for the salvation of the world.

"Our forefathers were Magi, the men who wielded the great powers of Creation in days when the world was new. The ignorance and folly of man wrought awesome devastation. Fire fell as sheets of rain. The earth opened to swallow cities. Oceans rose and swallowed the margins of the world, and a continuous pall of smoke rose from man's relentless destruction, hiding the sun. The world groaned in agony at man's affront, but man paid no heed, continuing blindly in his pursuit of power.

"Our account mirrors yours in that measure, according to Sh'ynryan. Upon seeing the destruction, man repented of his folly and grew to fear the power of the Words. Man could gain no advantage so long as his neighbor wielded the same power against him. Only ruin and death resulted.

"Man elected to destroy the Words of Power. However, the Stone—the manifestation of the Words—rebuffed every attempt. A great conclave of Magi resolved then to put away the record of the Words. One man, Nay'fein, took upon himself the responsibility to execute the conclave's will.

"'Where shall we conceal the Stone, where those who covet it still will not come by stealth nor take it by force?' the elders asked.

"'We see the chaos wrought by the Words, and we tremble. But this age will pass. The earth's wounds will mend, and men will yearn again to master Creation. How, then, to keep the Stone from the generations and prevent them from smiting the earth anew?'

"'Because no man shall know the place,' proclaimed Nay'fein, entering the circle of the elders. 'I will conceal it and surround it with great and terrible wards. I will curse the ground under it. No man shall find it. And my family will guard the way to its resting place forever.'

"And the conclave was exceedingly jubilant and commended Nay'fein for his bravery and his sacrifice. But one among their number stood apart, troubled still.

"Nay'fein begged this elder to speak his mind and name the sorrow that so marred his countenance.

"And the elder replied, 'Because the Words are vessels only, frames man gave the powers of Creation, that one might be distinguished from the other. We hide the Stone, and Creation suffers it to be so for it wearies of man's destruction. But I foresee the age when Creation will call again to man.'

"And the elder dropped his head and would speak no more of the visions he beheld.

"Then Nay'fein scoffed and, angered by the elder's words, proclaimed, 'Then I shall carry The Stone beyond the reach of any man. I shall hide it below, in the bowels of the earth, beneath the great mountains that spew fire, deep in the secret places of the world that my visions have revealed!'

"And the company of elders voiced acclaim, and many among them vowed their loyalty and promised to follow Nay'fein into the Great Below to aid him in his quest.

"And the elder marveled at their lack of understanding and spoke contrary to the face of Nay'fein, though without rancor.

"The elder warned, 'Time will erase the purpose of this conclave. It is against that day we now bury the Stone, but a generation will rise that seeks it again. Its children will scoff at the example of their forefathers, and their scorn shall doom them to share our fate. The Stone will call to the One of its choosing and emerge into the world again.'

"And Nay'fein, despiteful of the elder's prophesying, turned and received the Stone reverently from the conclave.

"Nay'fein held the Stone aloft. 'Remember, Brethren, the Words of the Stone!' he pronounced. "We are the faithful, who will remember the words of Creation. It is given us to call upon them in truth and wisdom, to preserve them in the world even as we remove them from its knowledge, thereby sharing their truth only among those faithful to our pledge.'

"Rallying his family and his faithful, Nay'fein led the great company into the mountains of the vast north.

"Beneath ragged peaks, Nay'fein read aloud Words of great potency. The flank of the mountain shuddered and quaked. Rock and ice hurtled from lofts above to dash the earth below.

"And Nay'fein exulted at the spectacle of Creation's power unleashed, and read again from the Stone, and the unquiet face of the mountain sundered to collapse upon itself, revealing through the haze a portal to the Great Below.

"The people followed Nay'fein beneath the ruin of the mountain. There he sealed the rift that no man without might find entry, and none inside might turn back.

"And it is written, the people moved deep into the darkness of the earth. Courses carved by ancient rivers and the shaking of the world in millennia past opened unto spectacles such as man never beheld, visions of beauty but also of horrors.

"Where the bones of the earth barred the way, the Stone created a path. Fissures cracked and widened in the wake of Nay'fein's years of wandering, leaving behind a labyrinth to both conceal and defend Nay'fein's realm.

"And Nay'fein remembered the promise he made the elders. And departing from his people, Nay'fein delved deeper into the Great Below. In a secret place, he raised a shrine for the Stone, that it might spend eternity in a place pleasing. For Nay'fein discerned the Stone was aware and wise and lamenting its need to hide from man.

"In its enormity, the cavern of the Stone was like unto the surface places, with rises and valleys and a preponderance of gushing water that coursed in a pleasant melody beneath the vaulting arches.

"And Nay'fein cultivated the glowing growth of that sacred place into beautiful arrangements. And he carved semblances of man and animals and other living things of Creation and infused these with the guise and blush of living beings so that the Stone might contemplate these and be content through eternity.

"For Nay'fein gave no heed to the elder who had warned of the One whom the Stone would beckon. With mighty magic, he laid great wards and curses upon the hidden place. And seeing his task complete, this chamber too did Nay'fein seal. He returned to settle his people in the Great Below, where they might forever guard the way to the vault of The Stone."

The Drolanjan fell silent.

It was Sh'ynryan who broke the lull.

"I've known of your people for some time, Drolanjan, but never have you shared the history of your people's descent."

The Drolanjan smiled indulgently. "History, legend, who can say?"

"I'm confused," Vergal added. "I have come among you to find the Stone at your behest. Yet your people's reason for being is to conceal the thing I seek. How can this be?"

"Again, you fail to understand. Our patriarch entered the Great Below millennia ago to conceal the Stone. Since that time, his descendants became very unlike their progenitors. The generations grew successively paler, slighter, the energies of this place seeping from the earth to bathe their bodies and transform them as you see us now: Beings of stark skin and gleaming eyes. Our vision adapted to penetrate the gloom of these caverns as easily as we once beheld the surface lands. We became the Nay'fein, a race of guardians long since separated from the thing they were meant to protect.

"No," he said, straightening. "We must find it. An epoch has passed; our people deserve to look again upon that which required such sacrifice."

The Drolanjan shook his head ruefully. "I scoff, Vergal, but like all my people, I believe in my heart the story of our descent. How else to explain our race—like you, yet fundamentally different?"

He fixed Vergal with a penetrating glance before continuing.

"How else to account that one such as you exists and has arrived to join us? The elder's prophecy that Nay'fein ignored has come to pass. The Stone called to the One, and he has come to claim it. To hinder the completion of that which is inevitable is futile. Instead, we seek to hasten it, that our people might find favor with the Stone and witness its awakening."

Vergal recalled the incident on the Drolanjan's plaza when they arrived in the Nay'fein's city. The king's neckband had blazed to life, and he had glimpsed behind that burnished spark the enormity of the power that fuelled it. There had been voices, certainly, voices that had cried out. But had they called to him? Vergal frowned, trying to sort the jumble of thoughts that had followed when he had lost consciousness and fallen to strike his head. He afterward related what he had heard, and all had been delighted. But now, as he tried to unravel the tangled threads of his thoughts, Vergal wondered if he had accurately reported what he had experienced that day on the plaza of the king's palace.

"That is why you ferry me through these tunnels," Vergal said, more to himself than his companions. "You believe the Stone will speak again, as when we arrived." He frowned and shook his head. "I have heard something in these caverns; that is a certainty. But now I wonder exactly what it was."

"Do not wonder, Vergal," Sh'ynryan said reassuringly. "For one so young to wield such power in the Words is unprecedented. To hear the Stone ... there can be no doubt you are chosen.

"Thousands of years of history and expectation hurtle toward their conclusion. They will meet in you."

The Drolanjan, his face and eyes animated, nodded eagerly in agreement but offered nothing.

Vergal made no reply. He rose from the table and moved away, absorbed in his thoughts.

"Don't concern yourself with him," the Drolanjan told Sh'ynryan. "We've prepared for our lives what will come to pass. He's had little time. The boy has much to reconcile."

Sh'ynryan nodded. "He's proven himself a remarkable boy." The Mage sighed. "I went about this all wrong," he lamented. "The manner in which I delivered him to you, I mean. I ripped him from everything he held dear, without pause nor explanation and in cruel fashion, and I know he despises me for it." The Mage laughed drily. "I cannot very well blame him for that, can I?"

The Nay'fein king shook his head. "You did what you must," he countered. "An endless line of seekers—Mages such as yourself—have seen their lives consumed in the search. But you found him. In all of history, you were the seeker who realized his quest! You brought him swiftly because it was needful, so do not dwell on how he arrived. When Vergal lays hands upon the Stone, all mortal concerns will be replaced. When he comes into his birthright, he will see the necessity of your course and bless you for remaining faithful to it."

"I understand this in my heart. And I think in the latter days of our journey, I tried to make amends. But his devotion to his sister is absolute, and I robbed her of him and him of her." Sh'ynryan sighed deeply. "I have caused such misery to this family over the years."

The grip the Drolanjan laid on Sh'ynryan's was biting, and the Mage looked with surprise at the fingers fastened to his wrist.

"You will not allow sentiment to interfere," the Drolanjan growled. "That this thief, this Teraud, was dispatched to further your ends is a small matter. Men die every day. And if they die unwittingly or otherwise in the cause of a greater good, then their death stands above the crush of humanity, for at least it was not in vain."

The Drolanjan leaned away from the ruins of his supper. He looked at Sh'ynryan archly.

"I gather, then, Vergal knows not of your involvement in his father's death," the Drolanjan said.

"Of course not."

"This sister. Does she know?"

"How can she?"

"Then all is well. The One is among us. You and I will share in his glory. He will share the secrets with us, do not doubt." The Drolanjan laughed harshly. "It's ironic, no? He will possess the greatest power in all the world, yet he will naturally seek wisdom and guidance in how best to wield it. We will rule in his name!"

Sh'ynryan lifted his eyebrows at the Drolanjan's words but allowed them to pass. The Mage had his own ideas of what might happen when Vergal took up the Stone. Conquest and domination were not among them. Instead, he envisioned a world government, where the petty squabbling and prejudices of nations were moot in the light of the prosperity the One would bring to all men. And the Mages, the faithful seekers throughout history, would be the lieutenants who executed his will.

The men sat companionably together, lost in their thoughts for the future. Distracted, it took them both time to register the tumult arising in the tunnels beyond.

Light stuttered brightly in the cavern's mouth. Horrified screams and the acrid smell of charred flesh trailed the erupting brilliance.

More flashing light in the corridor threw stark shadows of the Kastneths as the huge monsters reared to meet the unseen enemy beyond. By the next burst, the long shadows had crumpled. Musical, taunting laughter rose above the sounds of carnage—a woman's laugh, gleeful.

The servants tending the royal entourage screeched and fled to the rear of the cavern, where they hid among the strewn boulders and rocky outcroppings. The company of bodyguards charged into the corridor beyond.

Panicked, Sh'ynryan and the Drolanjan pushed back from the table. Each stabbed a worried glance at Vergal, who stood frozen near a far wall, his mouth open in a perfect circle of surprise as he surveyed something out of Sh'ynryan's sight in the glowing red corridor beyond.

"Vergal, come away!" Sh'ynryan bellowed.

Vergal did not respond. Nor did he move. He stood staring out of the cavern entrance. Sh'ynryan raced to his side. "What is it?" the Mage demanded, skidding to a stop beside the boy. "What creature attacks?"

A fierce corona filled the cave's throat. Sh'ynryan shaded his eyes from its brilliance. He could make out nothing except a baffling swirl of scurrying contours.

The Drolanjan rushed to join them but screamed in pain when the full force of the light struck his squinting eyes.

"What is it?" the king demanded, shielding his face.

"Vergal?" Sh'ynryan said, drawing the boy close to him. "What is out there?"

Vergal began to laugh, a sound pregnant with disbelief and tears.

"Yes," Vergal said quietly, his voice nearly drowned beneath the piercing screams of death and pain erupting in the vault beyond.

He dragged the sleeve of his wrap across his weeping eyes.

He laughed again. "Why, it's my sister!"

CHAPTER FORTY

Jalwyn watched even the rock of the cavern burn. Alonna's destruction of the place was complete.

Ablaze with radiance, her eyes incandescent, Alonna unleashed the shimmering force surrounding her in waves. Everything that lashing tongue of power touched ignited. The wondrous stone constructs of the Nay'fein city melted beneath her onslaught. The soaring stalagmite palaces slumped in upon themselves, their walls sagging and flowing like wax sliding the length of a candle. Few dwellings avoided the fury; nothing her wrathful glare encountered survived or remained standing.

Jalwyn—still helpless in the wash of her blazing path—witnessed the destruction first-hand. Alonna had become something more than human, he knew, but her merciless rage caused the Mage to fear she had also become much less.

The Nay'fein had long since ceased any pretense of a defense. The weapons they brandished and hurled failed to penetrate the glowing nimbus surrounding her. The conjurations of their most powerful Mages availed nothing.

Nay'fein fled, screaming into the dark tunnels honeycombing their cavern's walls. Her brilliant aura turned their blackest holes into brightest day, and the Nay'fein's sensitive eyes could not endure. Fires guttered in the city; a pall of black smoke clouded the high ceiling, where it tattered and sought fissures and vents through which to escape. The roar of the flames overwhelmed; Alonna's dark mass of hair writhed in the furnace-blast of rising air.

Jalwyn, aloft and captive in her revolving wake, witnessed but felt nothing of these things. Sustained, protected from the bedlam all around, he could only marvel at the shining form of the woman he loved, transformed into a marauding angel of death.

Alonna's eyes probed the ruins below. An unnatural hush fell over the city, unbroken save the crackling flames. Silently, Alonna descended, Jalwyn plunging helplessly behind her. She stood surveying the carnage through the nimbus encircling them.

The globe surrounding them flickered and died. Alonna's hair fell forward in a tangle to veil her face.

Jalwyn stayed silent, thinking her overcome by the grief of her destruction. When Alonna raised her head again, her teeth glittered behind a hard smile.

"He's not here," she said softly. "But one approaches who knows where he is."

Jalwyn saw nothing but tattered ribbons of rising smoke. He turned to tell Alonna as much when his head erupted in blazing pain. The Mage only faintly registered the length of cord wound tightly around his neck and the attached polished stones that struck his temples. The bola cast from the darkness had done its work. Wearier than he had ever been, sickened by all he had experienced, Jalwyn embraced the oblivion that awaited him.

Alonna watched the Mage slump to the ground. The blazing lights replacing her eyes flared brightly in the gloom.

"I could have killed you as easily," a voice called out of the smoky veil. Alonna did not recognize the language but understood it completely.

"I doubt it," Alonna replied in the perfect inflection of the alien dialect. "He is not dead. Otherwise, you would already be destroyed."

"Having seen what you wrought here, lady, I believe the truth of your words," the voice called respectfully. The speaker was still unseen, but an image of him rose clearly in Alonna's mind: One of the residents of this city, a slender, well-muscled specimen beneath a shock of unruly white hair.

A host of figures materialized, led by the tall warrior she had glimpsed in her mind. The company of armed warriors held glowing ornate maces hewn from stone.

Alonna watched their approach, unmoved.

"We request a parlay," the leader called. Alonna caught a flash of the speaker's name in his voice: Ker'alstil.

The chorus of voices ringing through her mind quieted, and, at once, she heard every word this man ever uttered, beheld every image his eyes had ever seen. She knew him completely, instantly, in a flitting, fast-moving kaleidoscope of blurred sight and sound. Those images included a certain dusky-haired boy she had pursued across a continent and the betrayal and murder of that boy's lone comfort on his long journey to the Great Below. She acknowledged Guile's demise sadly. She mourned the death of Vergal's companion and friend.

Ker'alstil bowed his head deferentially to the woman standing above him. The warriors in formation behind him followed suit.

He knelt and scooped a fistful of the cooling ashes and allowed them to pour between his clenched fingers. "You are powerful indeed to reduce my city to this," he said. Alonna plainly heard the anger in his voice, though Ker'alstil strove to conceal it. "Tell me, why have you come? Why have you done this thing to a peace-loving people?"

"You have something precious to me," she answered.

"What is it? Surely it will be given if you stay your hand."

"My brother. I see him in your mind, but not in this place. Where have they taken him?'

Ker'alstil, confused, turned questioningly to his companions, who mirrored his befuddlement. Then recognition dawned. He noted Alonna's pale skin behind the thin aura that still shimmered faintly around her. The lustrous dark hair, the blue eyes—a surface dweller, and one who bore a remarkable resemblance to one of few others he had met.

"Of course!" he exclaimed. "You have come seeking the One."

The words were spoken in a different language, but they rang familiar in her ears. How many lips had spoken those same words—the One—since she had embarked on her quest to find Vergal? The words wearied and angered her at the same time.

Alonna's unrelenting glare unnerved him, and Ker'alstil jumped swiftly to his feet.

"I can take you to them," Ker'alstil said hurriedly. "Of course, you want your brother, I understand. You shall see him. I only ask your indulgence as they have moved far into the tunnels, many days' travel away. You above all women are honored, for you are his blood. I know not how, but you share the power into which your brother will enter."

The Nay'fein bowed again. "I will take you to him, lady. And all Nay'fein will rejoice in your reunion."

"Despite the destruction of your city?" Alonna asked teasingly.

"Palaces can be rebuilt, new streets laid, for our domain is immense," the Nay'fein said excitedly. "Under the leadership of the One and the Drolanjan, he will glorify in the day he comes into his legacy; the loss we have endured will be counted a small thing by comparison."

"Yes, a small thing," Alonna replied distractedly. The voices were singing again, this time urgently. *Daughter... come... see.*

She shook her head to clear her thoughts. First, there remained business to complete.

"Step forward, Ker'alstil," Alonna demanded. "I wish to discuss 'a small thing' with you."

Ker'alstil, suddenly wary, stepped hesitantly forward.

"You injured my companion," she said, gesturing to where Jalwyn lay prone on the rocky cavern floor. "I forgive this, for you acted in defense and in ignorance. You need not fear retribution for this."

Ker'alstil smiled gratefully.

"But," she said, and the Nay'fein's smile melted, "there is another you wronged, neither in defense nor in ignorance. This I cannot forgive."

"Lady, who?" the Nay'fein pleaded, dropping to his knees. "Tell me who it is, that I might right this wrong and gain your favor."

"I need not say. Look, he approaches even now."

Alonna pointed behind the Nay'fein.

Ker'alstil turned his head. Already on his knees, he slumped, nevertheless. Only his outstretched hands prevented his head-long pitch into the ashes.

Out of the swirling embers strode Guile, his sword and dagger reflecting the firelight, his expression grim.

His gaze fixed on Ker'alstil.

"No," Ker'alstil gasped. He turned to Alonna. "This is impossible! He died; I know!"

"Yes, you killed him. And in so doing, you robbed Vergal of his friend, his comfort!" she replied.

The aura cocooning her flared to life.

"But I have invited him back," Alonna laughed. "He and I both are curious to see how you fare in equal battle."

Alonna stabbed her hand at the astonished Nay'fein standing in ranks behind Ker'alstil. The warriors burst apart, pillars of dust whirling where once they stood.

Ker'alstil screamed.

"No, lady!" he pleaded. He prostrated. "Please! I am your servant! Spare me."

"Take up your weapon, Ker'alstil," Alonna replied. "It is your only hope. Look, he waits for you to defend yourself. See in him the honor you lack, doomed Nay'fein."

Guile stood over him, his blades gripped tightly but held low to his sides. The mercenary appeared in all respects as he did in life except for the unnatural stillness shrouding him. The cruel wounds Ker'alstil's mace had inflicted and the bloody puncture of Calvith's carved blade remained. Otherwise, Guile stood whole, restored, deadly silent, cold eyes filled with imperturbable resolve.

Guile raised his sword in a salute to Alonna. Tears stung her eyes in response.

"Does he know?" she asked softly.

Grimly, Guile shook his head. Tendons creaked. The movement looked stiff and painful, though the dead face betrayed no hint of discomfort.

"You were his friend," she said, weeping now. "Did you love him as he loved you?"

The lips formed the words clumsily and delivered them on a blast of charnel-house air.

"I...do," the thing that had been Guile croaked.

Ker'alstil, trembling at its feet, now noted the unnatural sheen of Guile's skin, the flat gloss of his lifeless eyes. It was Guile, yet not him. It was a shell, with a whiff of its former wearer still lingering.

"The border between life and death is inviolate," Alonna whispered. "I cannot restore you, Guile."

She pointed at Ker'alstil. "But I can offer this," she said. "And in this, I pray you find your peace."

The Guile-thing nodded and turned inhuman eyes on the cowering Nay'fein.

Guile's stiff lips spread slowly in a rictus grin. The sepulchre stench baking off the thing filled Ker'alstil's nostrils.

Alonna dipped and lifted Jalwyn in her arms. Cradling the Mage tenderly, she took again to the air, riding the harsh currents of her catastrophe.

She smiled briefly when the screaming rose behind her.

CHAPTER FORTY-ONE

Alonna moved swiftly, her passage bathing the weird stone walls in radiance and illuminating her path ahead. Not that she needed light. Alonna suspected she now had few mortal needs.

Jalwyn stirred in her arms. Alonna hushed him, closing her shining mouth over his in a delicate kiss.

The thrill that simple act sent through her made her reconsider. Perhaps not all things human were to be dispensed, she mused. Alonna was tempted to rouse him—an easy enough thing—but decided against it. She wanted no distraction when she found her brother.

Alonna followed a convoluted course she had plucked from the mind of Ker'alstil. The Nay'fein had been an expert explorer in life (Alonna perceived he lay dead beneath the now inert corpse that vanquished him), and though he had not known Vergal's precise route into the labyrinth, Alonna easily filled the gaps in Ker'alstil's understanding with a far-reaching comprehension of her own.

The voices raised burbling, incoherent paeans in her mind, and Alonna knew she drew near. Swinging sharply around a jutting shelf of rock, she came upon them.

Alonna barely restrained her joy; her mind's eye penetrated the steaming mouth of a cavern yawning on the far wall. Vergal sat beyond, his abductor near to him.

Between them, a retinue of Nay'fein and their armored beasts were overcoming their initial shock at her sudden appearance and sallying into battle formations.

Annoyed, Alonna dispatched her opponents. Warriors charred and burst into ash. Sizzling bolts surged from her outstretched hands to obliterate rows of armored Kastneths. The rock walls sagged and shed molten tears as Alonna blasted them with unearthly heat.

Rallying, the Nay'fein Mages took to the air to escape the flowing river of hot rock beneath their feet. They hurled radiant globes of force that burst and dissipated as harmlessly as summer rain against Alonna's shining shield. Roaring columns of fire bathed her in searing flame. Alonna laughed inside the maelstrom, dismissing it with a negligent flick of her hand.

Aghast, the Mages redoubled their efforts, crying out in the strange language of magic that was suddenly as legible and beautiful to Alonna as an open book of poetry. Their gesticulations opened shimmering rifts in the fabric of the screaming air, through which emerged great and ponderous beasts.

The creatures wore frames shaped by the imaginations of those who had summoned them, for no mortal had ever beheld their true forms. Fire wept scalding tears from between cracks and fissures in their scaly hides. Alonna turned the Mages' conjurations back upon them. The beasts, creatures of flame and stone, reached to pluck the hovering Mages from their lofty perches, snaring them with claw and mandible.

Alonna nodded approvingly, quietly admiring the imaginations of the Mages who had formed their summoning into bodily shells. Her appreciation of the creatures so distracted her that she only faintly registered something else had captured their attention. With rumbling growls, the creatures began to wade ponderously through the lava...

...toward a slim figure standing quietly in the cavern mouth beyond.

"Stop!" Alonna cried, stretching out her hand. The advancing beasts responded to Alonna's call by dissolving, released by her voice to their unseen plane.

There was silence.

Vergal stood below, watching her in open-eyed astonishment.

"Alonna?"

With a cry, she flew to him. Alonna's feet no sooner touched the cavern floor than her brother filled her arms. She pressed flurries of kisses to his brow, to the unruly hair of his head.

Alonna drank in his scent, his feel, his sounds. She experienced him utterly. With new ears, she heard the healthy thud of his heart and the steady rush of blood through his veins.

Through new eyes, she glimpsed the handsome youth into which he had grown over the year and more of their separation and beheld the promise of the man he would soon become. The voices singing in her ears trilled a psalm: *Vergal! Vergal! Vergal!*

Vergal—returned to her, healthy and whole! She scarce believed it. Alonna feared to release him lest it also rouse her from a dream and dispel a beautiful illusion.

No, it was no dream, no illusion. She held Vergal in her arms. Vergal, the one stolen, now returned!

At length, it was Vergal who held her away. He searched her face with eyes wide though not fearful, astonished but not disbelieving.

"Alonna!" His face reflected her radiance. His voice trembled, but the hands clasping her shoulders remained steady. "What happened to you?"

Alonna's mouth opened, then closed. She could have in that moment satisfied his curiosity on any number of mysteries: Secrets buried under the earth and beneath the sea; their childhood speculations of worlds like their own, populated by people like them, circling distant stars across the void. These things and more she had glimpsed and apprehended since the power had seized her. Leave it to her little brother to ask the one question she could not answer.

"I don't know," she said. She brushed stray strands of hair from his forehead, an automatic gesture. "Something amazing has happened, something that will change the world."

Vergal grinned and fell back into his sister's arms. "Amazing things have been happening a lot lately," he agreed.

They crouched together on the cold stone for what seemed a long time, locked in each other's embrace.

"I'm sorry, Alonna," Vergal said at length, breathing the words through the mass of her dark hair.

"For what, darling?"

"For leaving you."

Alonna frowned. She pulled away and fixed him with stern eyes. "You didn't leave," she said crisply. "You were taken; a wrong I will soon rectify." She fixed a steely glare over his shoulder to where she sensed the two men beyond. One of those men had abducted Vergal, and that man she vowed to kill. The other was the murderer of her brother's protector, the king who had ordered his execution. He too would die.

Alonna fully intended to complete the quest that drove her across the wilds of Arasynia.

For the moment, however, she was content to revel in the prize at the end of her long road. She embraced her brother again. She felt as if she might never let go.

Against her shoulder, Vergal sighed. It was a doleful sigh; one a man might make. It startled Alonna to hear it. Then the fact she was startled jolted her more deeply. What could surprise her now, in this transcended state where the secrets of existence lay bare to her probing eyes?

"No, not for leaving you then, Alonna," Vergal said in that same unnerving tone. "I am sorry I must leave you now."

CHAPTER FORTY-TWO

Alonna held her brother at arm's length and studied his eyes. The radiance there grew sharper until Alonna realized it was no longer a reflection but an emanation.

Her hands on his shoulders dimmed in contrast to the brilliance of Vergal's face. The light surrounding her stuttered and blinked, flowing from her to suffuse Vergal in a shining aura.

She drew back.

The voices rang a final peal in her ears:

Teraud, forebearer, steward.

Alonna, sister, sustainer.

Vergal, son, our One!

A wrenching sensation wracked Alonna.

With a cry of loss, she was delivered of the power. She felt it depart her bodily. Understanding filled the void. The force that suffused her in the goblins' cavern had wielded her; not she it. It filled her, but only as fluid fills an empty vessel. She had merely been the riverbed over which it flowed on its way to a deeper sea, its true destination.

On its way to Vergal.

Across from her, Vergal's countenance shone like the suns she glimpsed in the vastness of the void. She had seen so keenly, so completely then, but now the truths she beheld with all-seeing eyes faded fast, like a memory of a dream, something that never existed even though it had been truly experienced.

Alonna pressed her fingers to her forehead. She had not noticed the silence behind them until now.

"The voices no longer sing for you, but they have not departed, Alonna. I hear them!" Vergal said.

His aura intensified; Alonna raised her arm against the glare. Eyes that once plumbed the depths of stars now beheld only the material world. The universe contracted around her, restoring Alonna to an existence dull and grey, by comparison, seen only in simple patterns of light and darkness.

"Now do you understand?" a voice asked.

"You!" Alonna screamed, leaping to her feet.

A dark shape loomed behind Vergal. Alonna could not discern its features until it stepped within the pool of Vergal's radiance. A smooth, long-fingered hand fell lightly across Vergal's shoulder. A face appeared bathed in his light.

"Do you understand?" Sh'ynryan asked again. Alonna thought the Mage spoke to her, but it was Vergal who nodded.

"Of course," he said gently, in his new patient, knowing tone.

Snarling, Alonna started for the Mage; her fingers hooked into claws. She meant to rend the Mage with bare hands. Vergal's fingers closed on her wrist, freezing her utterly in mid-stride. His hold did not harm her, but she was powerless to resist it.

"Let go, Vergal," she screamed. "He took you from me! He killed father and mother! I know; his own written word convicts him. We must avenge them!"

Vergal—the being who had been Vergal and who with every passing breath became something more—merely smiled.

"Alonna, sister, treasured one, be calm and quiet your heart," Vergal said. His gentle voice carried the weight of a command. She obeyed it instantly, and her tense body went slack.

A coal of warmth kindled within her, filling every limb with languid tranquillity. She nearly laughed at the notion she intended violence to the man now watching her over Vergal's shoulder.

She smiled at Sh'ynryan. He smiled back.

"Alonna, thank you," Sh'ynryan said, his voice serene. "I know it matters little now on this side of revelation, but I truly regret the pain you suffered."

The peace stealing over her made the memory of her former rancor seem ludicrous. Had she ever truly experienced such anger? Studying Sh'ynryan now, she mustered only a ghost of the emotion that had sent her across a continent in pursuit of him. Even that soon disappeared, dissolving like smoke beneath the placidity washing off Vergal in gentle waves.

"What is happening here?" Alonna breathed.

"Destiny," Sh'ynryan said simply.

He turned adoring eyes on Vergal, who stood in silent contemplation of visions only he beheld.

"You witness the culmination of eons of prophecy," Sh'ynryan said hoarsely, "the manifestation of Creation in the One. The powers abide engraved in cold stone and in the hearts and minds of Magi, but they long to walk the world bodily, in the person of your brother, chosen and foreknown from the age of Chaos!"

Tears stood in Alonna's eyes. "Why Vergal? Why us, our family?" Alonna asked. "Why greatness from those so low?"

"You answer your question," the Mage whispered, his eyes fixed on Vergal. "As Creation withdrew and sacrificed for the sake of man, so it chooses to emerge in one who suffered and lost. Why this boy? You might ask why death claims the young and spares the elder? Is one man more deserving, or his fellow merely less so? Why the mountains, the sky, the stars, and oceans in our world? Why Vergal? This is simply the reality of our existence, not a question to be answered.

"I've spent most of my life searching for your brother," he went on. "I knew he was coming, but I did not know the manner of person he would be. Even after all I've seen and done, it still seems as random and capricious a selection as I can imagine, but now, having beheld him, I can imagine no other donning this mantle."

They looked at Vergal, who remained preternaturally still, his eyes distant, the hint of a smile curving his flushed lips.

The Mage shook his head ruefully and barked a single, gruff laugh.

"Though in hindsight, perhaps I should have realized from the beginning. Events pointed to your family. A veil has been ripped from my eyes, and I stand blinking in the harsh light of day on a path I imagined I had only been traveling by night!"

"Tell me," Alonna begged.

"What should I tell you?" Sh'ynryan answered. "Would you hear the speculations of an evil old man?"

"Evil?" Alonna said, "Yes, your acts have been evil because they are borne of your imperfect humanity. Yet, they served the righteous end. How can any stand in this searing light and not believe it? But I would know how this thing has happened, or at least your speculation on it." Alonna frowned, straining for a memory that would not surface. "It seems I knew such things for a time," she said slowly, "but that time has passed."

"I profess no great insight into what has happened, certainly nothing like you have experienced," Sh'ynryan said.

"Allow me." Vergal's interjection—resonant, regal, unearthly—startled them.

"Sister," he told Alonna, taking her hand. He turned bright eyes on Sh'ynryan. "My father," he said, "for that is what you have become, Sh'ynryan, in all ways that matter."

He stepped forward, clasping them both, enveloping them in his warmth. Sh'ynryan sobbed gratefully. Within the circle of their arms, Alonna floated on the breaking swells of Vergal's projected harmony. To be loved by such greatness, to lay claim to it, thrilled Alonna to the core of her being.

A tremulous voice sounded behind them. "Alonna?"

Jalwyn stood shakily, supporting himself against a wall, watching them with wondering eyes. "What are you doing, Alonna? This is Sh'ynryan, the man against whom you swore revenge! Why are you in his arms? And who is this? What has happened here?"

Alonna's responding laugh wavered between tears and joy. "Jalwyn!" she cried, running to him. He collapsed in her arms, the last of his energy expended in rising to his feet. He turned incredulous and slightly injured eyes upon her. Alonna knew he suffered a betrayal in waking to find her in the embrace of an avowed enemy. She laughed again, helpless to contain herself when she considered the lunacy of the situation from Jalwyn's uncomprehending view.

"Much has happened, Jalwyn," she whispered between warm kisses. Jalwyn sighed and clung to her tightly. Alonna supported him easily, astonished by how frail the man seemed in her arms.

"Welcome, Jalwyn," Vergal greeted the Mage when he and Alonna joined the group. His smile was friendly; the glowing hand that closed over Jalwyn's was warm. The trepidation enervating Jalwyn melted at his touch.

"You are Vergal," Jalwyn said, basking in the tranquil aura.

Vergal leaned close so that Jalwyn alone heard his words, "And you are the man who owns my sister's heart."

"And she mine," Jalwyn said seriously.

Vergal drew back, smiling at his gravity, but said nothing.

"Come," Vergal said. His companions' legs moved instantly, responding to the power of his voice. "Much has been revealed, and I am pleased to share it with you. But someone waits beyond."

Veils of steam parted before them as they entered the pool cavern. An eddy of mist opened to reveal a half-clad Nay'fein man huddled on the floor. His long hair pooled over his shoulders. His fingers were laced over his face, concealing it. The man's slender frame shook convulsively with his sobbing.

"Drolanjan," Vergal said, taking pity on him. "Why do you weep on this, the day of your most ancient prophecies' fulfilment?"

The Drolanjan raised wet eyes. "Blessed One, your coming is as ash, for those who awaited your arrival for millennia are no more!" he sobbed. "I have peered into the city of my fathers. My eyes sting from the glare of its burning! The smoke of its devastation pollutes this realm. How can I rejoice when I am left alone to witness what the Nay'fein together were created to behold?"

The Drolanjan gathered his feet beneath him. He crouched, beast-like, on the rocky floor. His face twisted in a fierce snarl; his hand emerged from his filmy robe brandishing a wicked, stone-crafted knife.

The blade pointed at Alonna. "The witch did it!" the Drolanjan screamed. He sprung from his haunches and dashed toward Alonna, knife upraised.

Caught off guard, Alonna stepped back from the Drolanjan's charge. Jalwyn moved protectively in front of her. Neither need have worried. At a gesture from Vergal, the Drolanjan's charge was arrested mid-flight, and he stumbled. The knife flew from his hand to plunk in a nearby pool.

The Nay'fein king slumped to his knees, sobbing. "You deny me my vengeance?" he protested.

"I do," Vergal said simply. "You have been both guide and tutor, Drolanjan, preparing my heart and mind for that which has come. But I will not suffer my sister to be harmed."

"She destroyed my people!"

Vergal shook his head. "Not so," he said. "Many fled into the tunnels—more than you can imagine. Those who perished were warriors, and they died warriors' deaths. The city is destroyed but of necessity. So long as it remained, it presented a temptation to you, a reason not to go."

"Go?" the Drolanjan whispered pitiably. "Where will we go?"

Vergal smiled. Peace again, sweet and salving, flowing tangibly from his beaming face. They all felt it; even the Drolanjan, whose inconsolable weeping faltered, then ceased.

"Follow me," Vergal advised happily. He turned slowly to encompass them with mirthful eyes. "I have a short time to show you many things."

Water roiled in the cavern's central pool, the same hot spring basin in which a short time ago Vergal had bathed. They turned as one to face it. Steam billowed in copious clouds; the scalding water boiled away. The water in the pool evaporated, its boiling steam funneling wraith-like past them, siphoned into the tunnels.

Vergal strode confidently to the basin. Though he had made no gesture nor spoke a word, none doubted his handiwork. They joined him tentatively at the ledge, the drama of the Drolanjan's aborted attack now forgotten, even by him.

A jagged fissure appeared on the dry basin floor, glowing green like corroded brass as it widened.

Jalwyn flinched from the sickly brilliance. "What is it?" he asked.

Vergal answered him readily. "It is a portal to a place only once beheld by mortal eyes before it was sealed forever. Or so it was thought."

"The Temple," Sh'ynryan breathed, recalling the legends of Nay'fein's flight underground with the Stone.

The Drolanjan swept reflexively into a bow at the mention of the place.

The fissure gaped, crumbling around its ragged edge. The emerald light beyond bathed them.

"All of this time..." the Drolanjan muttered in awe. "It was always here, beneath the very place I have bathed since I was a child!"

"The portal is where it chooses to open," Vergal said sternly, "and the temple is where it wishes to be found. Do not presume the Stone always existed where a child diving for coppers might find it! Such imaginings cheapen the power of the place you seek."

The Drolanjan stepped back a pace. "Forgive me!" he said hurriedly. "I intended no offense."

"I take no offense. I tell you these things for your own well-being. We visit hallowed ground, where all shall be tested."

Vergal sighed and lowered his eyes. "Perhaps me, most of all," he said sadly.

The fissure widened, the brilliance bloomed, blotting out their vision. Then all was darkness, except for the limned figure of Vergal, a small and solitary shape wreathed in power, watching them from across a black gulf of space.

CHAPTER FORTY-THREE

They fanned out cautiously over the floor of an enormous cavern. Vergal's momentous instructions resounded in their ears.

The cavern far surpassed any yet seen in Undermarch. The leering stalactites so familiar in the tunnels were gone. The ceiling simply disappeared above, lost in impenetrable blackness. If there existed walls to form a rocky vault somewhere high above, Jalwyn did not see those either. The vastness of the space overwhelmed his senses, the enormity broken only by innumerable rows of squared basalt columns, emerging like silent sentinels from the gloom. They stretched ahead with every tentative step forward.

Jalwyn might have thought he trod a massive lava field on the top of the earth, not far beneath it. The stone floor rippled away unevenly in all directions, giving a sense that it flowed on without boundaries. It took only a glance skyward to dispel the illusion. No stars pierced the blackness; no sliver of moons rode the velvet of the void. The oppressiveness of the place settled like a shroud, wrapping them tightly.

Yet, they walked without stumbling, their eyes endowed with vision to penetrate the blackness.

They beheld their surroundings as if bathed in a twilight blush.

In this new world of darkness, Vergal cast the only light; his words had been the only sounds in silence.

The boy smiled, and the gesture filled Jalwyn with both warmth and dread. Vergal appeared much as Jalwyn imagined him from Alonna's descriptions: Jet-black hair framed a pale, fine-boned face, dominated by wide blue eyes, not unlike his sister's. Before their meeting, Jalwyn felt strangely protective of the youth. Vergal was the object of Alonna's undying love, and, by extension, that made Vergal's happiness of paramount importance to the Mage.

However, the authoritative tone and his distraction with all things temporal were not the hallmarks of youth: a king or a priest perhaps, but not a boy. The vibrant aura surrounding Vergal added to his strangeness, but Jalwyn felt something indescribable though fundamentally wrong with the shining figure.

"You among all who dwell in the world are favored," Vergal boomed. "Look with reverence and speak only with care, for you stand near Creation in the form which it has reposed since near the dawn of time."

The Drolanjan, who among them had stood confidently in the darkness, fell to one knee.

Vergal laughed. The sound was deep, not a sound a boy would make.

"You do well to show obeisance, Drolanjan," Vergal announced.

His voice reached them as if he had spoken in their ears rather than from across a dark gulf.

"Those of not so versed in the history of the Nay'fein, hear me well.

"In a past age, Creation wearied of man's striving. It lamented it had become a weapon in his hands. Chaos reigned, and the earth lay in ruin as men fought great battles, each wielding the power of the names inscribed on the Stone to strive against his enemy."

Vergal's head bowed slightly. His narrative plainly saddened him as if he was reliving a personal tragedy.

"Nay'fein, a Mage of renown and a leader of his people, took the burden upon himself to carry away the Stone. Nay'fein led his people out of the realms of sunlight, his only purpose to fulfil his vow—to hide the Stone deep in the earth, where man would not again abuse the power of the names of Creation.

"In time, he came here," Vergal said.

The glowing figure sighed and glanced about him.

"Behold the prison of countless years, the static vessel of eons. Creation yet governs the world. It is an unfolding force, blossoming toward a fruition unknown even to itself. But its essence elected to reside in darkness, in order to save man—its greatest achievement—from power he could not be trusted nor hope to control.

"Until now."

"Although it is everywhere at all times, Creation most truly resides here. It longs to be free of this place. Who among us, seeing this darkness, can argue with its intent?"

None could. None did. Vergal nodded knowingly.

"Then I challenge you: you who consent that the darkness is evil, find the Stone! Bring it into the light; bring it to me!"

"In return, I offer a reward," Vergal proclaimed. "The Stone awaits the first hand in eons to fall upon it. Bring it to me, and the bearer shall be rewarded above measure!"

Vergal's gaze fell meaningfully on the Drolanjan, still bent on one knee.

"It could mean the restoration of a kingdom and a nation," he said softly.

His eyes moved slowly, fastening next on Sh'ynryan.

"Or power and kingship among those who tread the world above."

He turned to Alonna, who stood holding Jalwyn's hand in the darkness.

"It could mean the granting of the dearest wish of any heart," Vergal finished, his eyes intent on his sister's face.

Tears coursed down Alonna's face.

"I've found you, Vergal," Alonna whispered. "And I've found the man I love," she squeezed Jalwyn's hand tightly. "I have all I ever want or need."

"You limit your desires to your reason, Alonna," Vergal answered. "You say your heart is full and lacks nothing. Yet I read your heart, sister. Grief, anger, and loss dwell in you still."

Alonna frowned. When she spoke again, her voice was raw, fearful. "I know of what you speak, Vergal, but to ask the impossible is to ask nothing at all. I don't remember much of my experience with that power that possesses you now; I only know it found common cause in my search for you and made me the vessel of its deliverance. It is all a muddle in my mind, and I think perhaps that is for the best."

Alonna's chin lifted; her voice grew firm. The frown deepened into a veritable slash across her brow.

"But I do remember in that brief time how I considered the very thing you suggest. I reached out for them, Vergal; I called to them. And their trail led to a wall of pure oblivion, as high and wide as the gulf of eternity. My hand could not cross it; my voice could not penetrate it."

Alonna shuddered. "Outside the wall stood multitudes of the dead. They wailed and strained against the wall and, slowly, some passed into it. It was like watching someone enter the ocean, struggling against the waves until the waters, at last, closed over him. It was chilling. For every soul that passed the barrier, a new one stepped into its place, renewing the struggle its fellow had only just quit. Some could not pass, and they will throw themselves against that wall forever. I assailed it also, but it rebuffed me. Those inside remained beyond my grasp."

Alonna's chin slumped; her head twitched with silent, strangled sobs. Jalwyn, pitying her, reached for her hand. She gently disengaged it from his grasp and crossed her arms across her breast, soothing herself against the memories.

"There was one who answered your call, Alonna," Vergal chided softly. "For love of me, in gratitude to him, you restored him."

"It was no victory, Vergal. He stood outside the wall when I discovered him, straining alongside the others. The restoration I granted him was not life at all. He wore his skin as an ill-fitting garment. He shrank within it because it no longer belonged to him."

"Yet Guile came," Vergal pressed. "One who had passed from this world held an interest in it still. A task remained undone, and one who had moved beyond mortal concerns consented to a purely human hunger for revenge. The dead are not so unlike us, Alonna. Like us, they wish to address matters left unresolved."

"Those beyond it cannot cross the barrier," Alonna said firmly. "They are lost to us, Vergal, perhaps only until our own deaths, but perhaps for all time."

"Not so, sister. I heard their voices. I glimpsed their faces in the realm beyond. In eternity, they concern themselves still with temporal things. I can reunite you. The wall will surrender to me, and they can walk beside you again. They can be reformed from dust, their souls wedded again to flesh. Your parents were taken from you, but they can be restored. They can dance at your wedding; they can know their grandchildren. They can grow old and die in proper course, their souls sated and at peace, content after a life well lived to pass the great wall in bliss."

Alonna leaned heavily against Jalwyn, trembling.

"But surely you would want this, too," she cried. "They are also your parents!. If you can do this thing that I could not, why do they not stand here now? Why do you offer them only by way of a reward?"

"Because Creation has a plan, sister," Vergal replied. The aura limning him had dimmed, Jalwyn thought, though perhaps that was only a trick of his eyes. "I am myself still, but also something so much more. My concerns are no longer purely my own."

"Then why don't you retrieve the Stone?" a voice demanded harshly. Jalwyn was mildly shocked to realize it was his own.

Stunned faces turned to him in astonishment. No one had dared ask the question they all wanted answered.

Vergal frowned.

"I cannot," he admitted at length. "Something restrains me still. Creation first demands this test, and I confess I do not know why."

Vergal laughed harshly. "I behold worlds spinning in the void; I hear stars singing in the heavens. But I cannot answer your question, Jalwyn. A tremendous power flows through me, as though I were a narrow channel connecting two great oceans, but I can no more set foot upon the Temple floor than you could comprehend the mysteries I now see. For good or for ill, these are its terms. The Stone demands to be removed by hands like those who placed it here so many ages ago.

He shrugged. "Perhaps it is a needful thing; perhaps it is only a penchant for the dramatic or a quest for a sense of closure. One guess is as good as any. For now, a weight is held in the balance. The Stone demands you retrieve it. And now I abjure you do the same."

Vergal's sudden cry thundered to fill the emptiness. "You will be called upon to pass the guardians! The way to the sanctum will be fraught with danger. Go! Your prize lies ahead. Bring forth the Stone. But beware. No reward is earned without effort."

Vergal opened his mouth as if to say more but quickly closed it again. His eyes were grave as they swept the group standing below. He said nothing more.

They went, spreading out and disappearing into the darkness. Only Jalwyn and Alonna left together. The Mage thought this fitting since they had become as one.

CHAPTER FORTY-FOUR

Sh'ynryan was the first to meet a guardian. Despite Vergal's warning to be wary, the Mage walked distractedly over the rippling stone floor. His thoughts whirled. While Vergal had been specific about the reward awaiting his sister Alonna, he had made only passing reference to what Sh'ynryan could expect.

"Power and kingship among those who tread the world above," Vergal had stated simply, yet Sh'ynryan marveled at how completely the words encapsulated the fondest desires of his heart.

He was an old man now, or at least nearly so. His life had been an itinerant one. A suite of rooms was maintained for him at the Order House in Zistah, but that was more a nod to his station than a home. He had last visited the place years ago, and that had been little more than a pause between endless roving in search of the One. Now his roaming neared its end. Sh'ynryan sighed resignedly, reflecting on a life spent in single-minded pursuit. He wondered what distractions he might find in the world now to replace the quest that had driven him across the world and back in the span of decades.

Undermarch

Sh'ynryan thought the leadership of the Order and its Mages might be a worthy substitute.

The great Throne of Magi likely sat vacant in its alcove these days, Sh'ynryan thought. The elder of the Order, Harbesh Neomonitis, would have traveled from Zistah to the Order House at Speakwater to be within range of Sh'ynryan's last known location. Though he hadn't a chance to speak in-depth with Jalwyn, the surprise presence of another red-robe in the Undermarch indicated his Brethren had sent a representative to track him.

Sh'ynryan smiled, imagining himself seated in Neomonitis's carved obsidian throne, his rambling complete, his hand steering the Magi into a new era of power, with the full and true Words of Creation restored to the Brotherhood. Neomonitis must first be deposed, Sh'ynryan considered, but surely that is what Vergal intended.

Absorbed in such thoughts, Sh'ynryan failed to note the footsteps that had fallen in beside him, taking up precise time with his own. An indistinct blur of red and white in his peripheral vision startled him out of his reverie. He looked up into the wizened, smiling face of Harbesh Neomonitis. The eyesight Vergal had bestowed to penetrate the darkness viewed the elder Mage in gradations of black and white, the hoary whiskers of his beard seeming to shine, and the long folds of his red robe deepening to bloody maroon.

He should not be here, a panicked corner of Sh'ynryan's mind shrilled. However, a louder, dominant voice rose above his alarm, assuring him the elder's sudden presence in Undermarch made complete sense. Sh'ynryan smiled weakly at his new travel companion, buying time to sort out the confusion mushrooming in his mind.

"Of course, I am willing to abdicate for you, honored Brother," Harbesh Neomonitis said easily. The pair trod companionably together over the uneven floor. "It is you, surely, who deserves leadership of the council. You, not I, dedicated a lifetime in faithfulness to the ancient prophecies. Our Brethren, who should have believed, having tasted the power of the Words, did not hunger as you did for the full repast. Many scoffed instead. In word only, we honored that faction within the Brotherhood that worked to usher in the day of Vergal's coming.

"Even our blessing to your quest was only to quell what might otherwise become an uprising! We thought your quest harmless, trivial, and, I admit to my shame, a fool's errand. But you, honored Brother, prevailed. Not only did you find the One, but you also brought him to his inheritance and earned his love."

Neomonitis smiled, though his stooped head shook sadly with the gesture. "Have no fear, Brother," he said. "I offer you the Throne of Magi, with both my blessing and a plea that you forgive an old man his obstinance."

Sh'ynryan gratefully laid a hand upon the rune-covered robe covering the old man's arm. He snatched it away, surprised by the unnatural heat baking from the skin beneath. He frowned, considering this. Something extremely amiss was transpiring, not the least of which concerned the old man at his side should be hundreds of miles above and east of the cavern through which they walked.

A worm of fear stitched through Sh'ynryan's consciousness, but only for half a heartbeat. No sooner had alarm rose than a state of bewilderment flooded in to submerge it beneath a soothing layer of musings.

Vivid imaginings of mounting the throne in a council room ablaze with ceremonial banners and candles assailed him. The cheers of the assenting Mages reverberated in his ears when the medallion and the staff—tokens of his rule—were laid in his hands.

How long he walked in the grip of his vision, Sh'ynryan was never to know. Intermittently, the Mage was aware of a gentle but uncomfortably warm hand upon his arm, guiding him as he walked, turning him gently this way or that at times, but otherwise, leaving him to his contemplations.

Neomonitis's soft voice was murmuring some explanation for his presence in Undermarch, some great feat of sleuthing and magic that uncovered the adventurers' trail underground. He had followed to show his fealty and to bear witness to Sh'ynryan's triumph when he uncovered the Stone.

Footfall followed footfall, with the gentle cadence of Neomonitis' voice to drown the faint echoes of their passage. The cavern blurred past the bemused Sh'ynryan, lightening gradually from barren rock to a half-glimpsed background of stunning color and true light. Subtle radiance of purple, yellow, green, and red thrown from alien formations of stone and fractured crystal smeared past, glimpsed through the corners of eyes fixated on an inviolate vision all their own.

In time, Harbesh muttered, "This way, Mage, you are not far now." Sh'ynryan frowned. The voice had changed subtly. He thought he detected a sibilant hiss beneath the elder's cultured tone.

The strange sound jolted him from his reverie, even as he stepped over the precipice of a steaming rift in earth.

Sh'ynryan plummeted. The Mage's lungs burned, and a searing mist stung the flesh of his lips, eyes and sizzled in the hairs of his beard. Tumbling bonelessly, Sh'ynryan spotted below a seething pool of acid rushing to greet him. Above him, a taunting, unearthly laughter followed him down into the pit.

Sh'ynryan never heard the splash of his impact in the acid. The caustic mist swirling far above the pool had already melted his ears, eyes, and face before he ever broke the surface.

CHAPTER FORTY-FIVE

The Drolanjan's true name was Abel'trey, though only his birth mother had ever called him that before the royal wet nurses arrived to assume his upbringing. He dwelled on the power in a name as he picked a cautious route between the crumbling basalt pillars. A babe born like any other in the world became himself fully only after the parents bestowed upon him his name. The name became him and defined him—essential to him!—just as the words etched on the Stone framed the powers they represented.

How he longed to read from the Stone, to gently glide his fingers over the ancient etchings and whisper the names of Creation in the true inflection and cadence that had been diluted and dulled in the eons of oral tradition that preserved the Words in the world.

A lifetime spent waiting, planning, and searching, and, at last, the day had arrived. He nevertheless increased his pace, mindful of the broken terrain, driven by a mounting sense of urgency.

Abel'trey sent his magic probing into the darkness but glimpsed nothing dangerous or even of significance. Still, he resolved to keep his guard. Vergal's warning had not found deaf ears.

However, one can only endure the same unchanging scenery so long before impatience settles in. Abel'trey cursed the chamber of pillars, and he cursed the monotony of the path ahead, and, despite Vergal's admonition, he cursed the One's raven-haired witch of a sister, Alonna.

While muttering his imprecations, the Nay'fein permitted a fatal distraction.

The king had simultaneously grieved the magical visions of his city's destruction and seethed at its assailant. The devastation of the Nay'fein's ancestral home cavern had been complete. Only steaming slag remained, and Abel'trey's heart rent at the loss. Despite Vergal's assurances, Abel'trey found it difficult to comprehend how too many of his people would have escaped the carnage.

If only I had spared Guile! the Drolanjan lamented. Surely, the presence of one Vergal trusted and loved in the Nay'fein city would have stayed Alonna's hand. At the time, it made sense to dispatch him. The mercenary's ceaseless yearning to return to the surface, his constant black brooding and dissatisfaction, had initially only insulted the Drolanjan's gracious hospitality, but, in time, he had come to regard it as dangerous. He needed to prevent the man from infecting Vergal with the same unreasonable longing.

He first planned only to keep the two separated. He effectively imprisoned Vergal under the guise of educating him. The mercenary he ordered into the outer reaches alongside the patrols, ostensibly to acclimatize the human to his surroundings, but in the secret hope that a marauding denizen of the labyrinth might solve the Drolanjan's problem.

However, Guile's skills foiled the plot. Even his Nay'fein companions had begun to show admiration for the man beyond the veneer of civility and praise their king had ordered them to affect.

In time, the problem rose to a head. Guile became demanding, and Vergal grew restless. It proved a recipe for disaster, should the two cross paths. The Drolanjan, his heart heavy but knowing the wisdom of his edict, sentenced the human to death.

But had it been wise? The Drolanjan was not used to second-guessing himself. Removing one problem created a much larger one in infuriating Alonna, but he could not have possibly foreseen the witch's attack. He had failed to consider Vergal's reaction. Surely, Vergal discerned the Drolanjan's treachery even now. The One had said nothing about the matter. Abel'trey silently blessed the boy. Indeed, such a mundane matter no longer concerned Vergal's transcended sensibilities.

Abel'trey hoped that was the case. In the meantime, he walked dejectedly, sunk in his misery and grief and longing for his people.

"Father! Is it you?"

The sound of his dialect being spoken was balm to his ears after long exposure to the guttural language of the surface people. He who spoke offered greater succor, however, as he immediately recognized his son's voice.

"Ker'alstil!" Abel'trey cried. The king's caution had flown; relief galvanized him with a longing to gaze on the face that called to him out of the strange gloom—the surface folk said it resembled 'twilight'—of the Temple cavern.

"Father!" came Ker'alstil's voice again, urgently. "Father, remove yourself from the corridor. Find cover! Something stalks between the pillars, but we have found a place of safety."

Abel'trey stumbled in the direction of the voice. He was confused—one stretch of pillars seemed as unremarkable as the next—but he took heed of his son's warning and moved swiftly.

"Ker'alstil! I cannot see you!"

"We are here, father, in the pillars! Hurry! We hear the beast's movements."

Shivers coursed Abel'trey's spine, and the coppery taste of fear flooded his mouth. His heart thudded in his chest. "Where are you?" the Drolanjan cried, all pretense of stealth gone, desperate now to reach his son.

"You are close, father," Ker'alstil called, though his voice rose fainter now. "Many of our people are wounded, as am I. I cannot retrieve you; come to us. Hasten, my king!"

The Drolanjan began to run. The pillars filed swiftly past as he fled down the narrow, endless corridors formed by their arrow-straight rows. Above the slap of his feet upon the rippled stone floor, Abel'trey thought he detected heavy footfalls keeping steady time with his.

"Ker'alstil!" he cried desperately.

The footfalls pursuing him fell out of time, and Abel'trey heard them distinctly now—a heavy counter thud to each of his own bounding strides. Whatever chased him seemed to be gaining, though he dared not spare a glance behind to confirm his suspicions. Nor did he need to when a rumbling, sodden growl lifted every stark white hair of his head in terror.

"Son!" Abel'trey screeched, chasing his own rolling echo down the endless corridor of pillars. "By the Stone, Ker'alstil, where are you?"

Ker'alstil's voice was close, eager when next it called.

"Oh, my king, you are close now! Run, run!"

Gibbering in terror, the Drolanjan laid down his footfalls in blazing succession. His lungs burned, his legs throbbed, but pure adrenalin drove his flight. The thing pursuing pounded tirelessly behind, closer still.

Ker'alstil's voice again, light, merry, rising directly ahead, "At the next pillar, father," he cried happily. "Turn sharply. It can't pursue you here. Now! Turn!"

Abel'trey's arm jabbed out; his fingers hooked the rock pillar, and he skidded sharply around the corner of the column...

...and into the outstretched talons and craggy mouth of something most definitely not his beloved son.

CHAPTER FORTY-SIX

Jalwyn hooked Alonna's elbow and spun her to face him. Her eyebrows lifted inquiringly.

"What's the point?" he asked her.

Alonna laughed, relieved. "For an instant, I thought you meant to strike me!"

Jalwyn frowned. "Surely you know I'd sooner knife my own heart than that."

Her gauntleted hand caressed his cheek. That oddly gentle touch beneath her rough leather glove recalled memories of their first dangerous meeting. He folded his hand over hers, pressing his cheek more firmly into her palm.

"I know that," she repeated softly, watching him nuzzle her hand.

Jalwyn smiled. "A guilty conscience, then?" he jested.

She sighed, "In the past year, I've received everything my life lacked: Money, adventure, love..." here she smiled sweetly at him "...and, now, my brother is restored to me. I wonder if the request I made of Vergal was more to keep a streak alive than a true desire of my heart."

They were the words Jalwyn wanted to hear. The Mage released her hand and gripped her shoulders. His eyes sparkled in the unnatural twilight.

"I ask again, what is the point? Your parents have passed. Despite Vergal's talk of unquiet 'corners of the heart,' I believe you've accepted their deaths. In fact, I believe your acceptance of your tragedy empowered your quest to find your brother. You knew he was truly all remaining to you, the only member of your family still in your power to restore to yourself."

Alonna's grin was rueful. "I've re-thought my position on what is within my power these past few hours," she told him. "Haven't you?"

Jalwyn shook his head. "Don't do this to yourself," he begged. "Honor your parents, rejoice in your brother's liberation and the destiny that awaits him. But do not anchor yourself to the past. Join me in a new future we can make together." He drew her tight to him.

Alonna stepped out of his embrace. She looked around herself, almost fearfully.

"Don't you feel it, Jalwyn?" she whispered. "Even if I wanted to, I could no more turn aside from the task laid upon me than will myself to die. His will is my will now. If you're honest, you will see the same is true of you."

Jalwyn shook his head. "He has laid no geas upon me."

"Perhaps not directly, but I know you too well. You have made my quest your own through all of this. Vergal knows you will not stop now."

Jalwyn opened his mouth to counter but closed it again. He had no defense against the truth.

"You must continue on?" he asked.

She nodded. "I must. It is not only a desire but a compulsion, a needful thing." She slapped his arm playfully. "Do not fear the pall surrounding us, Jalwyn. My brother would permit no harm to come to me."

Jalwyn nodded, though not entirely convinced.

They continued walking, hands clasped, content in their quiet appreciation of the other. The lines of basalt pillars marching ahead of them appeared endless when they set out, but regular space between them soon expanded, the columns dwindled and then disappeared. Some few steps more, and the ceiling which had been lost to them suddenly appeared, sloping out of the darkness to level off at a comfortable slope over their heads. Its appearance left an impression of walking inside from out of doors.

A riot of subdued colors greeted them. Pale light of every hue limned every feature of the place, from the rocky outcroppings twisting into vaguely humanoid shapes to the dazzling facets of huge crystals protruding from the walls.

A stone tablet rested in a hollowed alcove ahead. Two shadowy figures knelt there as if in adoration of the object before them.

Jalwyn and Alonna turned wary expressions on each other.

"It cannot be this easy," Alonna whispered, and Jalwyn nodded his agreement.

The prostrate figures in the distance straightened, though they remained on their knees. Alonna jumped reflexively, startled by their sudden movement. They kept their backs to them, but Alonna discerned the figures of a man and a woman.

Jalwyn shook his hands free of his voluminous sleeves in preparation to cast if necessary. Alonna drew her scimitars in a steely hiss.

The sound startled the figures. They flinched and, reaching to embrace each other, turned to face Alonna.

Her scimitars slid from boneless fingers at the sight of them. They clattered on the polished stone floor, and Alonna followed them to her knees.

Jalwyn, alarmed, knelt beside her, supporting her lest she pitch on her face.

The dark-haired man at the altar—for surely that is what it was—appeared vaguely familiar to Jalwyn. He wore plain leather britches and a gauzy white silk shirt, open at the neck to reveal an arc of smooth tan skin beneath. The woman was a dusky beauty, her features framed by dark hair drawn back and knotted behind her head. Her simple linen gown clung to a lithe figure that again struck Jalwyn with an unsettling sense of recognition.

The man and woman looked at each other in astonishment. Trembling, they stepped into the circle of each other's arms and turned in wonder to Alonna.

When Alonna began to weep, Jalwyn had his answer.

Beneath the features of the man and woman, the Mage was glimpsing the imprint of the woman he loved. And for the first time since she was a child, Alonna was looking into her parent's eyes.

"This cannot be," the man said in a choked voice.

The woman in his arms began to cry.

"Alonna, my child, is it really you?" the man asked hopefully.

"Father." The word gurgled out of Alonna faintly, but the man at the altar seemed to hear it. Teraud smiled warmly. Steadying his wife, he planted a kiss on the woman's cheek and released her. She sunk against the altar for support, weeping violently. Teraud outstretched his arms and took a hesitant step forward.

"Alonna!" Teraud called.

"Father! Mother!" Alonna howled.

Teraud threw back his head and whooped joyously. He held clenched fists high above his head, screaming triumphantly. The woman—Marillee, Jalwyn recalled Alonna telling him— stepped forward shakily, gripping Teraud's waist for support.

"Daughter," Teraud choked, holding out his hand. "Come here to us. I dare not step forward lest, like a dream, the image of you tatters and drifts away, and I wake again in the darkness."

Alonna, her chest hitching, nodded obediently. She rose shakily to her feet, her arms nerveless at her side. Marillee released her husband and stepped forward, her arms flung wide to receive her daughter.

"How we've longed to hold you, dear one," Marillee wept. "All this time, in the darkness, we remembered," she said. "We remembered how we left you, without explanation, without hope, and how we grieved! How beautiful a woman you have become, and how powerful, that you found this place."

The skin of Marilee's face bulged and rippled as if something had flitted briefly beneath its surface. Jalwyn, who watched the reunion wordlessly, gasped and drew back. Teraud noted the motion and snarled, revealing sharp white teeth.

"Say nothing, Mage!" he hissed. His handsome features contorted in the same fierce manner as the woman's. The flesh of his exposed neck undulated. "Breathe a word, and I shall carve your throat!"

Silky lips closed smoothly over the bared fangs. The bulge in his throat abated. When Teraud turned to Alonna, his smile was beatific, welcoming, his face handsome and exuberant once more.

Jalwyn, dumbfounded, looked to Alonna, who took her first unsteady step toward her parents. If she had noticed anything amiss or heard Teraud's admonition, she gave no indication. Jalwyn's mouth worked furiously to cry a warning, but fear paralyzed him. Only strangled, wet sounds ensued.

Now, Marillee snarled and threatened Jalwyn with her fangs. The teeth curled wickedly over her lips. Marillee's eyes grew hard and cunning; the thing in her face writhed riotously beneath the skin. Whatever moved there seemed near to bursting forth.

Alonna took no notice. She staggered forward another two steps briskly, dazed. The lurching movements carried her within mere feet of the outstretched arms awaiting her. Her proximity to the unholy things beckoning her roused Jalwyn to action.

With a cry, he stepped forward heavily on one foot, thrusting his splayed hands in front of him. A globe of sizzling white force burst from his open palms and careened across the cavern to strike Teraud's chest squarely. The crackling ball burst and the impact threw Teraud heavily against the altar. Bolts like lightning danced across his body in the aftermath.

Alonna screamed. She rounded on Jalwyn. "Stop!" she screeched. "Jalwyn, what are you doing?"

"Alonna, beware!" Jalwyn cried.

Alonna turned in time to get buried under Marillee's charge. With an inhuman shriek of rage, the woman took Alonna heavily to the ground.

Jalwyn leaped into their midst, winding his hands in Marillee's long hair and pulling hard. That action saved Alonna's life. Marillee's great fangs snapped a whisker from Alonna's exposed throat.

Marillee's hair fell loose from its roll, and Jalwyn gathered new handfuls and heaved. The woman strained forward, desperate to fasten her teeth. Her jaw snapped loudly; spittle sprayed in long gobs. Alonna screamed in abject terror, beating her clenched fists on the grotesquely bulging face of the thing disguised as her mother.

The thing's hair ripped at the roots, but it did not relent. Desperate, the Mage summoned a fan of flame. It leaped down his fingers and into the thick mat of Marillee's tangled hair. The hair flared like a torch dipped in pitch. Jalwyn yelped, jumping aside and shaking his scalded hands. Alonna shrieked curses and kicked herself free.

Jalwyn pulled Alonna to her feet. They backpedaled, pausing only to allow Alonna to retrieve her fallen blades.

Marillee writhed on the cavern floor, slapping open palms on a head that had become the heart of a blazing crucible. Beneath the flames, the skin of her face charred and split, revealing the roiling musculature restrained beneath.

A lizard-like snout jutted free of the bursting skin. Screeching, the beast shook its head vigorously, and the last flaming vestiges of its human face flew free in smoldering patches of skin. The simple linen dress covering its body was shredded, revealing the scaly skin of a powerful body. The creature began to pulse and expand to enormous proportions.

Another beast stepped out of the glare to face them. It stood nearly half the height of the alcove and glared balefully down on them. It stood on taloned feet that closely resembled the clawed hands it held balled into fists. A ponderous tail twitched behind it. Smoke rolled from a scorched wound in the creature's scaled chest where Jalwyn struck it.

The lizard-man cast a cold-eyed glance at its fellow, who was rapidly swelling to match his own towering height, then turned soulless eyes on Jalwyn.

"You harmed us in our mortal shells, Mage," the thing croaked. A whip-like tongue played over its pointed teeth when it spoke. "You will find our true forms not so accommodating."

Alonna brandished her scimitars. It was a useless gesture against the monolithic beasts lurching toward them.

"What are you?" Jalwyn demanded. His fear was terrible, but his anger hot. A battle-lust had overcome him. The weariness that normally claimed Jalwyn when he performed his art was nowhere in evidence. He entertained a momentary notion to take Alonna's scimitars and rush forward to meet them with bare steel.

The thing impersonating Teraud threw back its serpentine head and laughed.

"We are the guardians," it said. "We protect that power which has been denied to man. We are the fierceness of anger and the emptiness of eons. We are your death!"

The creature fixed them with a baleful stare.

"You are the first of your kind we have seen in millennia," he said, "We hungered to destroy your kind even then. We foretold your race would grow; that its power in the Words would be diluted as the ages passed. We, who are eternal, stayed our hand, preferring the greater prize of patience. Now a world of teeming masses awaits our domination, a richer hunting ground than the tribes of scattered barbarians who first visited here."

The lizard-like things laughed, their tails flailing.

Alonna's gentle touch upon Jalwyn's arm startled him. He was surprised to see her smiling.

"Don't listen to them," she whispered. "They are lying."

Jalwyn looked at the lizard-things, who froze and looked back.

"What do you mean?" Jalwyn demanded.

She didn't answer. With that same sweet smile upon her face, she gripped his arm once more, then released it and turned toward the guardians. Three swift steps carried her directly in front of them.

"Alonna, no!" Jalwyn cried.

Snarling, one of the beasts raised a taloned hand above his head, poised to crush her. Alonna stood gazing calmly up at her approaching death. Before he could recover from his shock, before he could call a Word of Power to mind in a final attempt to save her, the terrible claws descended.

Alonna did not flinch.

The arm slammed into the crown of Alonna's head—and disappeared in a puff of mist.

The Marilee impersonator remained, screamed, and bared her fangs, leaping forward.

"Begone," Alonna said softly.

The attacking beast unraveled in mid-flight, dissolving in the same ethereal cloud as its mate.

Jalwyn's head swam. He sat down heavily on the floor. He was overcome, whether by things he now knew or thought he once knew, he could not say. He only looked up when Alonna firmly lifted his chin to meet her eyes.

His confusion melted like the illusionary monsters at the sight of her. He pulled her close, burying his face in the soft cradle of her flesh between neck and shoulder. The scent of her coal-black hair, the clean fragrance of her skin, transported Jalwyn to an empty inn room in Caliss, where this woman had accosted him and set in motion events neither could have foreseen.

He kissed her, softly, deeply, savoring her taste, thrilled by the mystery that was Alonna, the sister, the daughter, the warrior, the lover, the solver of ancient secrets.

He savored the closeness of the woman he desired to make his wife.

When at last they parted, she was smiling. He smiled in return and asked the single question that had occurred to him when his lips were pressed to hers.

"How did you know?"

Her lips twitched to kiss him again, but Alonna denied herself. She supposed there would be plenty of time for that going forward. For now, she enjoyed his amazed expression and giggled at his wide, astonished eyes.

"Alonna," he said ominously.

Alonna relented to her temptation for another kiss before she answered. "I remembered something I read in Speakwater, in Sh'ynryan's journal. It was a quote he copied from the Codex of the Legends."

"And what was that?"

"This is not a direct quote, mind you, but it went something like this…" Alonna paused to organize her thoughts. "'Nothing in Creation suffers the destruction of its own name, lest it also ceases to exist.'"

Jalwyn considered that for a moment. He didn't see the connection. "So?" he asked.

"So, look."

The tablet from the alcove lay toppled on the floor, broken in pieces.

"Impossible," Jalwyn said, rising. "The Stone defied all attempts at its destruction in antiquity. Every text agrees that the Stone is indestructible."

"I saw it fall in the skirmish; I saw it break," Alonna said.

Jalwyn steepled his hands over his mouth, staring at the fragments. "How can this be?" he demanded.

Jalwyn went to retrieve them. He swore.

The fragments were blank.

He sunk to his knees. "An illusion, all of it," Jalwyn said.

"Come, Jalwyn," Alonna urged. "I wager that a Mage and a Nay'fein king lay somewhere nearby under the mistaken misapprehension they are dead."

He looked over his shoulder at her.

"To what end all this then?" Jalwyn said, bewildered. "Vergal called this a test; he demanded we retrieve the Stone."

Alonna remembered Vergal's words at their reunion in the caverns above. *No, not for leaving you then, Alonna...that I must leave you now.*

"A test, perhaps, but also a distraction," Alonna deduced, "that Vergal might take his leave of us, of me."

"Then where is the Stone, the names of Creation?" Jalwyn demanded.

Alonna smiled sadly.

"I believe they exist elsewhere now, etched on a boy's heart."

EPILOGUE

They built a castle on green, rolling land near the March.

It took years to construct. They spent that time joyfully, watching their home take shape but also traveling.

They often answered Sh'ynryan's invitation to join him in far-flung realms, to help collect the Words of Power that, over the years, had begun to appear, miraculously, singularly, and always etched in stone, in the deep wild places of the world.

Sh'ynryan never knew what Words to expect or when they would appear, but their arrival invariably addressed a need in the world at the time. As head of the Magi, he initiated the worthy and the upright into the Brotherhood's secrets and entrusted to them governance and oversight in his absence. And when at last returned, Sh'ynryan basked in the feats of the Order, in its good works, and in its accomplishments for the benefit of all people.

Thus, the Names of Creation continued to be revealed by degrees to man, as he proved his faithfulness and wisdom to use virtuously that which had already been granted.

These sojourns always put Alonna in mind of her brother's last words, in this world at least: *Your prize lies ahead...But beware. No reward is earned without effort.* It amused her still, the needless trial at the Temple, a test only of their hearts and their efforts in pursuit of their fondest dreams. Alonna in light of developments since revealed would forever have reason to be astonished, incredulous and humbled by the gifts rendered as a result, then and now.

They made infrequent trips underground, too, to the realm the elder Sh'ynryan still insisted upon calling Undermarch. However, the term was surely a misnomer since passages to the land beneath the world now dotted Alasia. Trade posts rising at each end of these corridors between the surface and deep were surely destined to become great cities—above and under the earth—inhabited harmoniously by surface dwellers who delved below and those Nay'fein who emerged, wide-eyed with wonder, to survey the realms of the sun.

The Drolanjan Abel'trey presided as Emperor over the scattered cities of his people and was given honor in statue and song, above and below, for his dedication to peace and understanding between the two people.

Jalwyn and Alonna never worried about embarking on these journeys with Sh'ynryan, which the Mage's growing craft completed in the blink of an eye. In these absences, they knew their growing brood of children would always be loved and well cared for by devoted maternal grandparents, who had met their return and every new day they had been given as if in a beautiful waking dream.

ABOUT THE AUTHOR

Derek Gordanier was born in Kingston, Ontario, and raised in the nearby town of Gananoque. A graduate of Durham College's Print Journalism program, Derek is a former newspaper reporter and editor who worked for weekly and daily publications in Eastern Ontario. He has also worked in the Parliament of Canada.

Undermarch is his first novel.

He is married and the father of four children. He lives in the village of Spencerville, south of the city of Ottawa.